The

Book Reapers

BR

Mark C. King

Other Books by Mark C. King:

Sigmund Shaw: A Steampunk Adventure
Whispers of Bedlam Asylum
Tomb of Hannu

Carousel of Faults
The Moss Maiden of Kinderhook

Short Stories:

The Pitiless Prisoner of Hamlin

This book is dedicated to the quiet ones. The ones who pretend to find interest in inanimate objects in order to avoid conversations. The ones who know that they are better than their lack of words. *For the silent hopefuls.*

"Harry, promise me that you will never lend that book to anyone. It does harm."

- The Picture of Dorian Gray

One

BR

I understand – I hurt because of – the horrific potential of the written word. Knowing what I do, it is with hesitancy that I put pen to paper to record the events of my life. My inexperience as a writer does not preclude me from creating a Dark Book and, with every pen stroke, I fear that I will cause harm to others. It would not be purposeful, mind you, but neither could it be considered guiltless. For any reader of my account, I beg that you proceed with caution.

My name is Naomi Gladwyn and, to tell my story correctly, I must start with a mysterious event that happened two years prior to my birth – the ghost ship, *Mary Celeste.*

As you are likely aware, in November of 1872, the sailing vessel, *Mary Celeste,* left New York harbor on its way to Europe. However, about one month later, the vessel was found drifting, completely abandoned, several hundred miles off the coast of Portugal. One would naturally assume that to abandon a ship in the middle of the ocean, it must have been under heavy threat of sinking, but this is where the story becomes bizarre. The *Mary Celeste* was in very capable sailing shape. There was some water in the hold, but nowhere near enough to harm the ship. Adding to the strangeness, there were no overt signs of violence, such as you might find with a pirate attack. The cargo, personal items – even valuables – were still onboard. The only thing missing was the sole lifeboat. For some unknown reason, the crew felt compelled to leave the ship, and none of them were ever heard from again. Close to twenty years later now, it's still considered the greatest of maritime mysteries.

Why do I bring up this strange account? Because my uncle was on that ship and was never found. The ripple effect of that chilling event has haunted my life, starting with my poor father. For you see, when it became known that the *Mary Celeste* had been abandoned and that the crew –

particularly his brother – was missing, it drove my father to the brink of insanity. It is a special kind of torment not knowing. Perhaps if my father could be sure that his younger brother was dead, he could have rested his mind and conscience. Perhaps he could have grieved to completion instead of lingering in pain. But he did not know, and his solution to the insidious and relentless torture was to drink.

That solution may have helped *his* pain, but it caused agony for my mother. They had only been married a little over a year when he turned to alcohol, and the man she loved was now hidden under the influence of mind-altering drink. It must have been terrible to watch that once good man – her true love – turn into a wicked stranger. Never wealthy, the income became even scarcer as my father had a difficult time working, and much of the money that was earned went to his habitual escape.

When I was born, about three years into their marriage, I may have been the most unwanted child in history. Not for lack of love, at least not on my mother's part, but because she was terrified of the life she would be able to provide for me with her husband in the state that he was.

When I was a few months old, my father's drinking finally stopped – along with his life. Being so young, I have no memory of him, no recollection at all. In a drunken stupor, he had walked in front of a carriage and was trampled to death. Whatever little had remained of the man my mother loved, was now gone. Whatever income that survived his drinking was also gone and my mum and I were in a bad way. We moved to a shack, near the Thames, with two other women and one other child. I vaguely remember playing on the muddy water's edge with that child, a young boy name Charlie.

My mother worked whatever jobs she could, cleaning, sewing, baking, anything. I fear the thoughts of what dark places she may have delved into to create our meager living. A poor widow has few options to earn money and very few of them are pleasant.

When I was six years old, my mother fell ill with pneumonia. We didn't have the funds for doctors or medicine, and she died within a few months. Having no relatives, I was taken to Bromley Female Orphan Asylum in the south of London.

Now, you may wonder how I know of all these things if I was only six years old at that time. The answer is in a letter my mother wrote before her death. That precious letter contains my father's history, my mother's sorrow at the life she gave me, her proclamations of unwavering love, and the sincere hope that a better life would somehow find me. It's the only item I have of my family and, through the years, I often hold it to my chest and breathe in its comforting aroma – which minimally captured the smell of home.

I will spare you the minute and sorrowful details of my years in the orphanage, but it doesn't take much imagination to picture the situation. It should be easy to see that a six-year-old girl cried inconsolable tears for weeks upon weeks at being taken from her mother, her world being destroyed. There should be no problem in understanding the agony I felt at longing for my broken-down, but familiar, home by the river. It should take no stretch of the mind to comprehend the spirit-crushing loneliness, despite being surrounded by other children, that threatened and shaped the very person I was becoming. Most of all, it should be a simple matter to know that I missed my mother so much that the pain inside of me was worse than any physical ailment; that, although young and unable to comprehend such an enormous concept as life and death, I would wish to fall into a dreamless sleep and never wake to the reality of my hurtful and pathetic life.

Despite not delving into the dreadful details of those times, I will, however, comment on one aspect of an orphan's life. It takes the form of the most common pastime that we children would partake in. It was somehow both wonderful and painful; simultaneously comforting and cruel. That pastime didn't have any official name, but we generally thought of it as the 'if only' game. Never a day went by when the game was not played among the lot of us – and likely even more so in private. It could be summed up with the phrase, 'If only I was not an orphan…' From that simple start, dreams would be built of the life we wanted.

For me, it was either, 'If only my mother had not died' or 'If only the Mary Celeste made it safely to port." From those beginning statements, I would create false and impossible happiness.

Oh, the cruelty of that game! Although building the fantasies felt amazing, it made the realities we faced seem harsher by comparison. And yet, the game would not, could not, stop. Perhaps this means that our human desire for happiness, for something better, is stronger than despair.

Perhaps it means that we are creatures that find ways to amplify our misery.

Even now, I still don't know what to make of the game, but I still play. I still weave make-believe worlds of happiness with my mother and father; and I still get viciously slapped by reality.

There is, however, another type of make-believe that is far kinder and helped to make my wretched existence tolerable. I speak, of course, of the sublime brilliance of books. However, I cannot talk of books without talking of another person that has influenced my life with great happiness and great sadness – Daphne.

Two

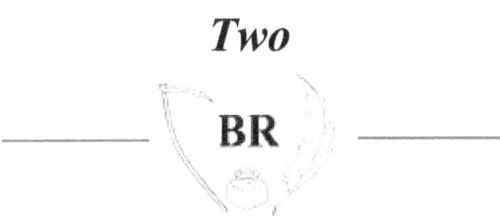

BR

Within a short carriage ride from us, in Croydon, was the Durant Orphanage. No one is certain as to the cause of the fire on that winter's night in 1883, but it evidently started in the foyer of the building after all the children had gone to bed. Fourteen girls died along with one caretaker.

The surviving children were split up and sent to different homes. Five were assigned to us in Bromley. I remember that night, being woken up by the head mistress, Mrs. Sherwood, oil lamp in hand with a group of children standing behind her. Even now, I can see clearly those new girls, hair mussed up, dressed only in nightgowns, soot on their faces and clothes. Most haunting was the strange mixture of terror and blankness in their eyes – strange, in that it's not common, not strange as in unfamiliar, for I know that feeling well. I know the war between painful grief and the guilty escape of numbness.

They didn't have many possessions with them, which was no surprise, for even if they had time to collect all their things instead of rushing out and escaping the burning building with their lives, it would not have added much. For me, there was only one possession that I would have cared about, and while looking at these poor girls joining us, I slid my hand under my pillow and felt the comforting texture of my mum's letter.

Being that the hour was very late, there was no time to setup spaces for the new arrivals, so the headmistress told us that we would have to share our beds with them for the night. Maybe because I was particularly small – even for an orphan – or because I was somewhat near to the door, one of the girls, with red hair and pale skin, was assigned to my bed. As she walked over, I saw that she was carrying something, a book, which caught my attention as it was a surprising possession in an orphanage. When she climbed into my bed, I noticed two more things; first, she smelled like smoke. I don't know why it took that smell to make the horror of the event standout, but it was at that moment that it felt real, tangible, and terrible. The second thing I noticed was that she held the book to her chest while she lay on her back. That was a gesture that I knew. The book was special; perhaps it was a gift from her mum, like my letter.

Despite the unusual events, talking was still strictly prohibited as it was after dark. So, shoulder to shoulder we lay there, two complete strangers, silently coming to terms with what the night had thrown at us. After a little while, my eyes had just started to grow heavy, but were suddenly focused when I heard subtle noises and felt the bed shake. In an orphanage, the quiet crying of one of us was as familiar as the sound of the cold wind that seeped through the imperfect window frames. My bedmate was in tears. Was she simply recovering from a terrifying night? Had she lost a friend, perhaps even a sibling, in the fire? I did not know. In the darkness, I still dared not talk, but I reached for her hand and squeezed it. She squeezed back and would not let go. I don't know how long it was until I fell asleep, but when I awoke in the morning, our hands were still together.

It's funny, the things that standout in your memory when you look back, but just the thought of that grey morning still gives me a feeling of warmth. During the winter months, the orphanage was always cold, especially in the mornings since the heating fires were not kept up overnight. But that day, I woke up without the accustomed shivers – obviously because of sharing the bed. I felt a warmness that was so contrasting with the cold air of the room, so incredibly soothing, that I wanted to close my eyes and revel in that comfort until the spring.

Eventually, I turned to face my bedmate, but I only could see the back of her head – a red tangle of hair. Compared to my ordinary brown locks, it seemed exotic. The book still rested on her chest with her arm around it, much like I have seen mothers holding their babies. The curiosity I had for that girl was matched by the mystery of the book and what it could mean. Could she actually read it? What book was it?

And most importantly, *could she read my letter?* Up to that point in my life, the letter remained a mystery. None of my fellow orphans, nor myself, could read, and the workers at the asylum were unwilling. But now, there was new hope!

That last thought was so exciting that it took all my patience to not reach over and nudge the girl awake. I had to remind myself that she had

had an extremely difficult night and that the peace of sleep was one of the only escapes for an orphan. So, I lay there, still holding her hand, and wishing as loud as I could that she would wake up.

During the excruciating wait, I made it even worse by worrying. What if the girl could not read? Or perhaps she could, but would not help me. Orphans were an interesting group – we generally supported each other, but there were always a few that were difficult and even mean. What if the new girl was like one of them? There were so many reasons that I came up with, for how my letter would remain unknown, that I had worked myself into a near panic when the red-haired girl finally moved and released my hand. I looked over as she turned her head to me. She blinked her eyes a few times while I smiled at her.

In a quiet voice, for many were still asleep, the girl said, "I'm sorry that you had to share your bed with me. Thank you."

She had an Irish accent, which fit well with her skin and hair color. I responded, "I'm not sorry. This is the warmest I have been since summer ended. My name is Naomi Gladwyn. What is yours?"

"Daphne. Daphne Crimmins."

Looking at the book that was still resting on her chest, I asked, "Daphne, where did you get such a marvelous book?"

"It's one of three," she said sadly.

"One of three? I don't understand."

Her face took on a look of sudden sadness and her eyes started shimmering. "I had three books," she said through ragged breath, "but only one survived. They were from my family, but the fire..." she could not finish before the tears came.

I put my hand on her cheek as she quietly cried. "I'm sorry," was all I could think to say. Before long, I started to cry as well. There we lay, face to face, crying in a shared grief.

When Daphne spotted my tears, she asked, "What's the matter?"

At nine years of age, I could not understand or sort through my feelings well enough to answer her question accurately – not that I'm an expert on feelings now. But, looking back, I know it was due to heartfelt sympathy for that girl as well as the terrifying thought of losing my mum's letter in a fire. But at that time, all I could say was, "I'm not sure. Your sadness made me sad too."

Daphne smile through her tears and said, "That's very sweet. May I ask how old are you?"

"I'm nine. And you?"

"I'm twelve."

In the grand scheme of things, three years is not very much, but to a nine year old, I thought Daphne was practically grown up. It was very common for many of the older orphans to not associate with us young ones, and I was afraid that Daphne would soon reject me because of the different of our age. But I was very much mistaken.

Mustering up a little courage, especially since I knew how much older she was, I asked the question that had been consuming my thoughts, "Can you read?"

Daphne's eyes lit up a little and she said, "Oh yes! I can read very well."

It was the answer I was hoping for. Still, despite my keen desire to have my mother's letter read, I hardly knew that girl and had reservations as to sharing something so personal with her. What if she took it and hid it – sometimes the older girls were very mean. What if she refused? What if she laughed at it? I had been so close before to having the letter read, or so I thought, only to have my hopes dashed. I could not help but be pessimistic and guarded.

My concerns, however, were balanced by a burning need to know the contents of that note. It had been in my possession for three years and its words remained as unattainable as the day I received it. For her part, Daphne did not seem like one of the mean girls; something about her made me trust her to be kind. I took in a breath and asked, "Would you be able to read something for me?"

"From my book?"

I shook my head and said, "No. I have a letter from before…" Every orphan knows what 'before' means. It means before they were orphans; before when they had a family; before when they were happy. Some do not have a before, since they were orphans since the beginning, but all understood. I continued, "Before my mother died and I was brought here, she wrote me a letter. I cannot read, so have not been able to know what she recorded for me."

Daphne's face took on a surprised look and she said, "Could not one of the caretakers have read it to you?"

"I have asked, but they always would say I am too young. Whether that is true or not, I believe I deserve to know what my mum has written me." I came across a bit more forceful than intended, but I could not hear that excuse anymore. If Daphne was not going to read it for me, fine, but I would not tolerate that angering reason even one more time.

After a moment of thought, Daphne nodded and said, "I will read it to you."

Immediately, I threw my arm over her and exclaimed, "Oh, thank you!"

"Shhhh!" someone in the room hissed – it was, after all, still quite early in the morning.

While still hugging her, I whispered into Daphne's ear, "Please don't disappoint me. There is nothing in my letter that can be worse than not knowing."

When I released the embrace, Daphne said, "I promise, I will read you the letter."

Reaching under my pillow, I carefully pulled out the paper. The feel of it on my fingertips was as familiar as breathing. I passed it near my nose, trying to pull in the faint aroma of home. As I stared at it in the grey morning, I felt a touch of disappointment as it was too dark in our room to possibly read. Squinting, I could barely make out the writing on the page.

Daphne must have understood my thoughts as she commented, "It will not be too long before there is enough light to see properly."

I nodded and thought bitterly, *of course there would be a delay*. My letter would not give up its secrets without that one last wait.

Putting the precious note to my chest, I lay there with a mix of excitement, nervousness, and frustration. Through the years, I had often speculated as to what the content of my mum's letter was. On good days, I envisioned it being an outpouring of love and a message of hope about the future. On bad days, I feared a message of pain and hatred. Occasionally, I would think that the note contained nothing important at all, perhaps something as mundane as a recipe for soup. My speculations ran the gamut. But now I was on the very threshold of finally knowing – for better or worse.

To try and stop the strong emotions, I literally counted the time away as I waited for the light to grow. I could not read, but numbers and I understood each other. I started at one – naturally – and counted up

One hundred.
Three hundred.
Seven hundred.

At one thousand two hundred and thirty-four, Daphne spoke, "I think it's light enough if you would like me to try and read it now."

I could hardly believe that it was going to happen. After all those years, I would finally know the contents of my most precious possession. My stomach felt ill from anticipation. Some of the other girls were starting to wake and make some noise, but I paid them no attention. How could anything distract me from my greatest desire?

Daphne pushed the book from her chest farther down to her legs and sat up against the wall. After pushing myself up, I handed the letter to her and was pleased that she handled it very carefully, almost as if it would break in her hands. She looked at me – in the morning light I could see that she had green eyes – and asked, "Are you ready?"

As impossible as it may seem, in that moment I was not sure. I became frightened at the potential content of my mother's words. Without consciously knowing it, I had put tremendous hope into that piece of paper. But I would not let that moment pass! "Yes," I answered with hesitant determination.

Daphne read:

My Darling Naomi,

I am sick and I am afraid that I will not be with you much longer. I need you to know that I am sorry for the life that I provided for you. I wanted so much better. I promise you that I did my best, but it fell far short of my expectations; far short of what a precious girl deserves. Perhaps, with my death, somehow you will find a better life.

You never knew your father and I feel it is my duty to tell you a little about him. While we were courting, and for a year after our marriage, he was a fine man. I loved him and he loved me. We did not have much money, but we had enough. After that first year is when things became difficult. You see, his brother went missing on the Mary Celeste. No one was ever found from that cursed ship, and the unknown nature of his brother's whereabouts weighed heavily on your father's mind. To escape his pain, he turned to mind altering drink. His employment decreased; our money decreased, and things became very hard. If only they could have found your uncle's body, perhaps your father could have rested his mind.

Then I became pregnant with you. We barely had enough to subsist on and I was terrified of bringing a child into this world. But know that I loved you. I think your father did too, but his drunkenness left little of the real man that I had once knew.

One night, heavily under the influence of alcohol, your father walked into the street and in front of a carriage. The driver could not possibly stop in time and your father was killed.

I miss the man I married, I cry for him, but hardly shed a tear for the shell he became.

I do not fear death; I only fear leaving you alone in this world, my precious girl. But I seem to have no say in the matter. Know that you were loved and that I am sorry.

Forever your mother

My mother loved me. I always knew that, but to hear those words removed the tarnish of doubt that time can inflict. Much was there to consider, but I focused on that one joy. My eyes started to tear as the pent-up emotions of years of waiting, of desperate desire, were suddenly released. I pulled my legs to my chest and hid my face in my knees and sobbed.

I felt Daphne put an arm around me which caused me to look at her – she was crying too. Later, when I asked why she was crying, she said the simplest, but most beautiful thing – that she felt *my* pain in *her* heart.

Three

BR

I am not going to detail the remainder of my time in the orphanage, the countless mundane memories, but there are two noteworthy events that must be shared for my complete narrative to be meaningful. Both revolve around my dear friend, Daphne.

You might think, as I did at the time, that Daphne reading my letter was the greatest of gifts she could have given me, but you would be wrong. It was, without any doubt, a significant moment in my life, but Daphne would provide even better.

She taught me to read and to love books.

The ability for an orphan to read is rare, as the time it took to teach that skill was simply not worth the effort. For what purpose was reading when your life course would lead you to menial labor tasks? Our training generally consisted of cleaning and keeping quiet.

Daphne's reading ability somewhat segregated her from the other children. Most were in awe of her, but a few were intimidated – that leading to an occasional snide comment. I was certainly one that was in awe and counted it a great privilege that I could call her my friend. In fact, after that first night and morning, we became nearly inseparable. She didn't care that I was younger than her and we soon grew as close as sisters – at least, as close as I imagine sisters to be.

Of course, her kind demeanor made her liked by most all the children, but never more so than when she read to them from her book.

I realize that I have not told you what her book was, other than that it was something very precious to Daphne. The book was a story by Jules Verne called *Twenty Thousand Leagues Under the Sea*. As she had mentioned, it was one of three that she had owned after having become an orphan, and was the only one that survived the fire at her previous home. They had belonged to her father, a school teacher, and were all she had of her family. I'm thankful that she was able to save one of them, but I was sad for her at the loss of the other two.

Now children, and especially orphans, for whatever you may think of them, are exceptional storytellers. So much time is spent in the fantasy worlds that their young minds create, that their imaginations are exquisitely vast. Without much to occupy ourselves, telling stories to one another was a favored pastime. However, an orphan's story is generally tainted by the sadness of the 'if only' game. I guess we had farther to fall from the height of our dreams. But when Daphne would read aloud from her book, it was quite unlike anything any of us had experienced before. Perhaps because it was not one of *our* stories, that it made for a gentler return to reality.

I will admit that the book often disturbed me, as it talked about shipwrecks which inevitably led me to think about my uncle and the *Mary Celeste*. Still, much of the story was about the three companions, the enigmatic Captain Nemo, and the amazing undersea world that they all experienced – that *we* experienced through the reading of Daphne. That was the beginning of my love of books.

Within a month or so of Daphne's arrival, I cannot count how many times I had her read to me my mum's letter. Perhaps it was the constant request, or perhaps it was simply because she wanted to share the great pleasure of reading with me, that she took it upon herself to teach me.

The patience of Daphne was great. Time and again, I would get frustrated and nearly be in tears over my limited progress. I would even ask her to give up on me. She never did and would say, "Don't worry. It will come with a little more time." And she was right.

I remember very clearly the first time that I read my mother's letter for myself. I stumbled over several of the words, but still managed to actually understand it. The message was the same, but it felt different; the letter was finally mine. Until that moment, it had never been under my complete control, as I was always reliant on someone else to read it to me, but now it was a possession solely my own. There were no more mediators between my mother and me.

After reading my letter, my appetite for words became ravenous. I soon took on reading *Twenty Thousand Leagues Under the Sea*. It was daunting; tremendously bigger than my simple one-page letter. But the more I read, the easier it became. Soon, I was not focusing on how to sound out words but was able to appreciate the story. It was exhilarating! At times I would forget everything and feel like I was sitting in the lounge of the *Nautilus* while staring out of its panels at the illuminated ocean life that floated by. It was an escape of a most welcomed sort. Hours were spent reading – hours where I forgot that I was an orphan.

The problem we had now was that there were two readers and only one book. Daphne often lamented the loss of her other two books – both for the sentimental value and for the destruction of such precious items. Still, she was able to put them to some good use. From her memory she would tell their stories to us all. *Around the World in Eighty Days*, also by Jules Verne, was one of the most enjoyable adventures I could ever imagine, and I wished I could read those pages for myself – for I was learning of the power of the written word.

As enjoyable as Jules Verne was, the most popular story that she told to us orphans was that of Frankenstein's monster – the other book that was lost. How we would all huddle together around her and listen in gleeful fright at the macabre tale. That was a book that I was not so sure, at least at that time, I would have wanted to experience for myself.

But what to do about the problem of only having one book between the two of us? Daphne considered removing pages so that the book could be read simultaneously in separate sections, but I would not allow her to do any harm to that family heirloom. The answer came from a surprising source – Mrs. Sherwood, the headmistress. Although generally cold, she performed the warmest of surprises – she was able to arrange for two book donations. I can never forget the smile on her face when she presented them to us. The one that she handed to me was, *The Count of Monte Cristo*, by Alexandre Dumas. The book handed to Daphne was *Little Women*, by Louisa May Alcott. I knew nothing of those stories, and even thought the titles were a bit plain, but I was overjoyed to have them.

As you could probably imagine, all of our free time was spent reading the pages of those new stories. When completed – it took me much longer as I was less experienced, and my book was quite a bit thicker – we switched and read the other story.

Naturally, we read the new stories to the other children. *The Count of Monte Cristo*, with its tragic but superb coincidences, deep intrigue, and, of course, the wonderment of a hidden treasure, served to fascinate us all.

However, the most beloved book among the orphans was *Little Women*. How could a story about four happy sisters in a loving family not resonate among us poor wretches? Such a family was what we all wanted – whether it was looking forward to a potential future or looking back to what we had. I found it particularly interesting how all of us identified with a different sister. The older orphans wanted to be Meg, the wisest of the sisters. A few of the precious girls loved Beth, the kindest and most gentle of them all. Although no one spoke up as wanting to imitate Amy, the youngest, we had several girls that captured her spirit. Naturally, most wanted to be Jo, the protagonist tomboy who wanted to be independent – orphans are naturally independent – and would not easily accept society's thoughts on how women should act.

It is hard to judge one's self, so I don't know which of the four sisters I'm most like, but I truly loved Jo. She was creative, strong, and brave; everything I hoped I could be.

Those years spent reading and discussing were some of the happiest of my life. Unfortunately, it was not to last.

Looking back to my thirteenth year, I find myself cringing at the thoughts that get stirred up. That was the time of the second event that needs to be explained before truly starting my story.

In January of 1888, Daphne fell ill. She acquired a fever that was soon followed by a persistent cough. They were the tell-tale signs of consumption – that deadly malady that had killed countless people across all of Europe. Immediately the caretakers moved Daphne to a small room and would not allow anyone inside to try and prevent spreading the affliction.

Daphne was not the first orphan that I knew to be segregated because of that illness, but I desperately hoped she would be the first to come out of that dreaded room alive. I was terrified at losing my friend.

Although I was not allowed in the room with her, the caretakers provided a chair and allowed me to sit outside of her door to talk with her. I was even allowed to skip my chores in order to spend time with Daphne. My companionship was the only treatment they had to offer.

At first, Daphne would speak some and we would have conversations – broken up often by periods of coughing. But as the weeks went by, the conversations became more one sided, and her need to rest became greater.

Each time she slept I would feel a panic start to grow in me – *what if she didn't wake up?* Another side of me was happy for the bit of peace she had when she was asleep, for her waking hours were filled with coughing and unpleasantness.

Eventually, I could expect no talking from Daphne and I would read to her. All day long I would read aloud from our books. However, I only read certain sections of *Little Women*, for I could possibly bear to articulate the illness and eventual death of poor Beth. To this day, although I still have that very book, I cannot open it for the memories it generates and the pain it causes. Just the sight of its cover causes my breath to catch.

In late February, a Monday, Daphne died. I was in my usual spot, reading outside her door, when one of the caretakers had come to check on her. When the caretaker walked out, the look on her face caused me to know that my dear friend was dead. My eyes teared even before I was told, "I'm so sorry. Daphne has left us."

The pain and sadness that came took away all my strength. I could not even hold myself up in the chair and fell to the floor sobbing. I rolled into a ball, crushed, not wanting her to be gone.

I spent the next week in my bed – barely eating or drinking, and missing my friend more than I thought possible. Dear reader, if you have lost a friend, you know of the pain I write of, if you have not, then I would not want to make you feel this misery. For all of our sakes, we shall skip the details of that deepest and most painful of melancholies.

Although it seemed impossible for a time, eventually I adjusted to life without Daphne. I went back to my chores, went back to taking meals with the other orphans, and went through the daily living in the orphanage, but feeling completely empty and ambivalent. The only time where I could feel something, other than numbness, was while reading. The escape provided in my books was the sole remedy for my troubled spirit. My only friends, now, were found in the written word – friends that could not permanently die. For the power to revive those who the author chooses to fall, is as simple as turning to the beginning of the book.

At this point, there is nothing more I need to explain before introducing you to the heart of my account. If you have stuck with me through the telling of my pitiful childhood, I hope to make it up to you with boldness, mystery, and adventure.

Four

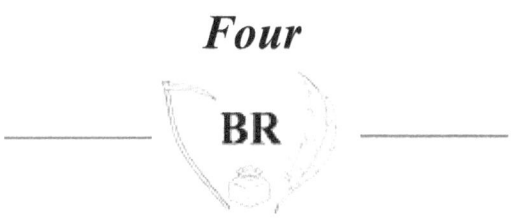

BR

Little by little, as the days colorlessly went by, I sank deeper into the mire of despair. I often found myself spending many hours absently gazing out of the second-floor dormitory room window, head against the cold glass, where one can see the outskirts of Bromley, a peaceful countryside village, with undulating hills, woodlands, and dirt roads. The pleasantness of the view was incongruent with everything in my life.

On one of the small hills was a house of extraordinary size and beauty. Being the largest structure, by far, that we could see, it became the focal point of many of our 'if only' stories. Oh, the extravagant tales that were weaved around that place! Daphne, in particular, adored that house and would create beautifully imaginative dreams about parties and princesses. Even I was not immune to such thoughts – creating my own 'if only' worlds in that beautiful home.

It was those dreams that kindled my most bold decision and changed my life.

At Bromley Female Orphan Asylum, the age of seventeen was significant as that was the age when a girl was old enough to be placed into society. Although that may sound like a new and great freedom for an orphan, it was usually not so. The job prospects for such an underprivileged person are quite miserable. Some were assigned posts in the worst of homes, paid poorly, and treated abysmally – for no respected family would have an orphan as a servant. Most girls were placed in workhouses doing menial tasks for long stretches, under awful conditions, and provided little income.

I will speak plainly, so that the danger and terror is clear: prostitution is not uncommon. That, in itself, is horrifying, but made all the worse by Jack the Ripper – for it had only been a few years since those frightening string of murders had taken place. As you can see, an orphan's future had little to look forward to and much to fear.

When I was nearing my seventeenth birthday, in the early winter of 1891, I was terrified of being sent away from the orphanage. My life prospects were, as mentioned, horrifying and I felt scared and quite unprepared to handle them. In the weeks I had remaining, before my taking some wretched position, I spent much of the time fretting. *Couldn't there be some other solution?* When I examined my needs, I determined that I really did not require much; a bit of food, a warm bed, and, of course, time to read. That was all. There must be a way to accomplish such a meager life.

In late November, a few days before my scheduled departure, I found myself staring out at the large home on the hill. I had a blanket wrapped around me as it was evening and quite cold, especially when sitting near the glass. Soft light could be seen escaping through a couple of the estate's numerous windows, and smoke emanated from only two of its many chimneys. It struck me that the place never looked fully occupied, certainly all of its windows were never lit. Such a waste! So much room and with only a fraction of it actually being used.

Why not give me a corner? That was the very thought that started my daring plan.

Perhaps I could *take* a corner?

Clearly, I dreaded the employment being offered to me, so maybe I could postpone that life while taking hidden refuge in the large home on the hill. It was an audacious thought; complete lunacy; but I could not escape the fact that they had so much, and I so little. Surely justice demanded a bit of equity between the two.

Even if my plan was to fail, I could still return to the orphanage and present myself for whatever assignment had been found for me. As far as I could tell, I had nothing to lose. Perhaps, in time, as I learned about its occupants and needs, I could even figure out a way to procure employment at the home – fulfill one of my more subdued 'if only' dreams. So sudden and intense was that new desire that I wanted to leave that very moment. However, there was no way I could leave unnoticed until after bedtime. I worried that the few hours I had to wait would be enough to overcome my impetuous idea.

At dinner, I ate every drop of the weak soup provided – who knew when my next meal would be. After dinner, I volunteered to clean the dishes. That served two purposes; first, it helped keep my mind somewhat occupied. Second, it gave me access to the kitchen and allowed me to sneak two apples for my plan. It wasn't much, but the cupboards were generally bare.

As bedtime neared, I waited until no one was paying me any attention and quickly climbed under my covers with all my clothes on. I made sure the blanket was pulled completely to my neck so as not to give anything away. I wish I could tell you how excited I was, but the truth is, I was terrified. Not only was my plan weak and full of unknowns, but I would also be leaving one of the only places I had ever considered my home. It took my imminent departure to truly understand the safety that I had come to feel at the orphanage.

When all the lights were extinguished, the room became quite dark – the overcast skies not even allowing starlight to filter through the window. In the darkness, I listened to the noises around me, to the breathing of the other children, and wondered when I should make my start. I'm not sure how long I laid there, but eventually the time seemed right. I climbed out of bed, slowly and quietly, listening for any sounds of alarm. On the cold floor, under my bed, I felt around until I found my belongings and laid them on top of the bed – which consisted of the three books, my mum's letter, and my other dress. Folding the blanket around them and tying the ends together, I created a type of satchel that I could sling over my shoulder. My shoes I held in my hand.

In stockinged feet, I tiptoed through the room and out the dormitory door. The hallway beyond was nearly pitch black and I was only able to navigate from memory. The slight creaks sounded incredibly loud in the nighttime silence, but they didn't seem to garner any attention.

As I snuck down the stairs, hugging the wall, I continued listening for any sounds of movement. One of the caretakers, grumpy Miss Gulch, slept in a room on the first floor and the last thing I wanted to do was to get caught and have to try and explain myself to her. An old clock ticked the seconds away and, as I passed close by it, I saw that it was after midnight.

The front entrance was always locked, and I did not know where they kept the key, so I proceeded towards the back door. Unfortunately, that meant that I would have to sneak right by Miss Gulch's room. My ears strained to hear anything as I slowly crept down the hallway, being as quiet as I possibly could. I hardly dared to breathe while my heart beat quickly and loudly. The caretaker's door was open a crack, and I stared into the pitch-black slit waiting for Miss Gulch's sour face to suddenly appear. A few steps beyond the caretaker's room, I gave a small sigh of relief.

As I approached the back door, I was relieved to see that its key was, as usual, hanging on the wall just to the side. That could have been an insurmountable obstacle if it had proven to be missing. As I picked it up, the metal felt ice cold on my fingers. I inserted the key and turned it ever so slowly. The metal lock mechanism made clicking and pinging noises that I thought were surely loud enough to wake Miss Gulch. Either the sounds were not as loud as I imagined, or Miss Gulch was a heavy sleeper, because no one appeared and tried to stop me.

I stepped outside and closed the door softly. While putting my shoes on, it took a moment for the shock of what I was doing to hit me, and only a moment more for the cold air to further challenge my resolve. Being outside, on my own, late at night, was the most daring thing I had ever done – it was far from the proper behavior of a young woman. Although quite nervous, I cannot deny also feeling excited. I thought of Ned Land, the impetuous and brave harpooner from *Twenty Thousand Leagues Under the Sea* and figured I would likely need more of his influence before the night was through.

The back of the orphanage was a small fenced in area where the children could spend time when the weather was good. Withered leaves piled against the right fence as the cold wind vainly tried to push them through. I walked across the brown grass to the small gate and gingerly opened it. Stepping into the lane beyond, I was now truly outside of the orphanage and its grounds. I hugged myself and felt very small.

The first test of my resolve came rather quickly. I was only a dozen steps down the dirt lane when I heard a noise from my left. Now, a young woman walking about after midnight would be quite a difficult situation to explain, so I had to be very cautious not to be seen. The instant that I heard the sound, I quickly hid behind the nearest item, a tree just off the road. I knelt down and peeked to the side of the trunk to try and locate the source of the disturbance. I hoped it was just a bird, an owl perhaps, but then I saw a light. It was a constable!

Bromley was not a large area, nor prone to unrest, and, as such, had one constable that only visited occasionally. The chances of him being in Bromley that night, and right near the orphanage, were quite poor. Yet, there he was. Any confidence I had gained, which was little since leaving, was completely swept away. My fears grew stronger, the air felt even colder, and part of me wanted to jump out and plead mercy to that officer of the law. However, either because of courage or cowardice, I didn't move.

The street he was walking down met with my lane and he would reach the intersection soon. I continued to watch, the lantern light gently swinging, as he approached.

It was so cold, and I was so nervous. *What am I doing?*

When he reached the crossroad, I knelt lower and wondered which way he would go. I started to shiver. He paused for a moment and, to my great relief, turned around and started walking back up the street he had just come down. Not only had he not spotted me, he was heading away from the direction that I intended to go.

I waited behind the tree for several more minutes, shivering and rubbing my arms miserably, to allow the constable time to put plenty of distance between us. When I finally stood, my knees were stiff, and it took many steps for the life to come back into them.

About a half-mile down the dark lane – having not come across anyone else but frightened a few times by the noises of unseen animals – I reached a crossroad that, depending on which way you turned, led into the heart of Bromley or to the countryside. I turned right and headed away from town. I had seen that country lane countless times from the window, and, in the daytime, it looked very pleasant with its carts full of vegetables traveling from the farm to the market. But there, on the road at night, it was not pleasant; it was cold, lonely, and scary. However, twenty dark and very bitter minutes later, I reached the edge of the estate, my goal, without incident. From the road, I looked up the hill, beyond a few trees, to the great silhouette of the building. It appeared so much larger than from the orphanage window. The size, along with the dark night surrounding it, made it look quite intimidating.

I could still turn back. I could return to the orphanage and no one would be the wiser that I had ever left. However, as scared as I was to proceed with my insane plan, I was more scared to return and face the wicked life being offered me. Going back might have been easy for that moment, but it meant I was allowing my future life to be dictated for me. I concluded that following the path of least resistance was tantamount to giving up. Despite lowly thoughts of my worth, I was not ready to give up.

With what little determination I could muster, I took a step forward towards what I hoped was the lesser of my evils

Although dark, I clearly saw the main path that led from the road up the hill and to the front of the building. Although I was not entirely sure of my plan, going up the front path to the main entrance would certainly not do. Instead, I climbed over a small wooden fence and walked through a field of soggy grass up towards the side of the large structure. Although the climb was a bit tiring, it at least helped to fight against the cold – except for the moisture that I could now feel seeping into my old battered shoes.

At the top of the hill, I stopped behind a tree a mere twenty yards from the side of one of the building's wings. I could make out large, dark windows in that part of the immense stone structure, but no entrances. Although the front of the building was perfectly dark, there was a faint light that came from partway down the back of the home. Having no other ideas, I ran across the open space between the tree and the house and followed the light like a moth to a flame.

As I stole along the side of the home, I could not help but to reach out my hand and let my fingers drag along the smooth stone of the house – a silly experience of turning that longtime fantasy into something more tangible. As I got nearer to the light, I could see that it originated from a window that was next to a door. Slowing my pace, I moved cautiously and quietly towards the illumination.

Screech!

My heart nearly stopped from fright at the sudden noise at my feet. I fell backwards to the ground and put my hands in front of my face to blindly guard against whatever was happening. After a moment of nothing, my wits returned, and I realized that I had disturbed a cat that had been sleeping in the shadows. I laughed to relieve some of the fright, and, after several seconds, my heart slowly returned to its normal cadence. Standing up, I brushed myself off, let out a shaky breath, and continued forward.

When next to the lit window, I paused and listened. I thought I heard a bump from inside, but it could just as well have been my heartbeat. Somewhat satisfied that no one was alert to my presence, I slowly moved

22

my head so that I could peer through the glass. There was a lit candle on a table and, as I looked around the dimly illuminated room, I could make out a stove, large cupboards, a wash basin, and another doorway. More importantly, no one was around that I could see – but somebody must have been awake, for why else would there be a lit candle.

With more courage than I thought I had in me, I went to the door and tried the handle. It hardly moved before I could tell that it was locked. A gust of wind blew and the nervous excitement that had caused me to temporarily forget the cold retreated to that reminder. I rubbed my arms and wondered what I would do then.

As my eyes dipped down, I noticed that the door had many scratches on it, about knee-high. That was something that I had seen before, as the back door of the orphanage had similar markings from the stray cats that wanted in either for warmth or for the food that we orphans could not help but provide. Occasionally, a poor creature would come around after dark and make such a noise at the door that mean old Miss Gulch would come out and throw a pail of water at it. That thought made me wonder what they might do here.

With the hint of a plan, I decided to act. I was getting so cold that the prospect of being found out was becoming less and less scary as it probably meant getting out of the freezing night air. With my numb fingers, I scratched at the door, making a sound – if I do say so myself – very similar to that of a cat. After a few seconds of vigorous scratching, I stopped and listened. At first, there was nothing, and I was about to start again when I heard a noise. I listened close and…yes! Someone was definitely coming. I hurried away from the entrance and hid in shadows behind the nearest shrub.

After a few more seconds, I heard the door unlock and saw a person, an older man, bald with just a bit of grey hair over his ear, candle in hand, step outside. His first look was at the ground, evidently expecting a cat, and then he looked around. I didn't move and was relieved when his gaze passed by me without any notice. *What now?* I really had not planned it too well. The door was open, but with a person there, it was not of much use.

"Dantés!" the man hissed. "Dantés, you dumb cat!"

Kneeling behind the bush, the cold ground could hardly be felt through my already numb limbs. However, my finger brushed across a small stone. A silly thought came to me and, figuring that I had nothing to lose – that line of logic is really quite powerful – I proceeded. Taking the stone, I slowly brought my arm back and then, when the man's gaze was away from me, I flung it very hard over the person's head and along the side of the house. It landed with some noise about twenty paces beyond the door.

"Is that you, Dantés?" the man hissed again, while looking at the disturbance. "I have half a mind to let you freeze out here." Then, to my great excitement, the man left the door and started heading towards where my stone had landed.

Moving as fast as I dared, I quietly made my way to the entrance and slipped inside the kitchen area while the man continued calling for the cat. At first, I was surprised to find the room in darkness. Quickly, but not quick enough to not feel a little embarrassed, I realized that, of course, the man had taken the lit candle with him. No matter, I knew there was a doorway on the far side of the room. Taking off my shoes – partly from habit, partly to reduce the sound of my steps – I walked swiftly towards where I recalled the doorway was and proceeded to run into the corner of the table. I clenched my jaw so as not to yelp at the sharp pain in my hip. At least the table was heavy and didn't move or make any sound at my blunder – but it sure did hurt.

Pushing the pain aside as best I could, I used the edge of the table as a guide and proceeded across the room, limping a little now. I soon came to the open door, which led to a dark hallway beyond. My eyes were adjusting to the lack of light, which turned the absolute blackness into a mix of dark grey with black shapes – thankfully it was enough to navigate without walking into any more furniture.

Although terribly frightened at what I was doing, as I tiptoed along the hallway, I still managed to relish the warmth of being inside – my limbs tingled from the welcomed change. *But where was I to go?* Of the many hours spent watching the house from the orphanage windows, one thing always stood out – the rooms on the second floor of the east wing were never illuminated. I did not know what was in those areas, but I figured that it could be a place to hide.

Slowly creeping down the dark hallway, I froze when I heard a noise from behind me – the kitchen door. There was a scrambling sound and, out of the darkness, a small object – the cat – ran by me as if being chased by the devil himself. Still frozen in place, heart thumping, I heard the kitchen door close and saw a faint light coming from the hallway entrance. The man had evidently found the cat and returned.

Moving quickly down the hallway – my stocking feet slipping a little on the tile floor – I came to a large space. It was hard to tell for sure, but it looked like, or at least felt like, I was in the foyer of the house. Another noise came from behind me. *Had I raised suspicion?* Straining my eyes in the darkness around me, I made out the outline of a staircase and hurried up its steps to the second floor. I paused at the top to try and orient myself, for, being in a strange building – at night, no less – it's easy to get turned around. So, mentally, I retraced my path and figured what direction I needed to go to reach the east wing rooms.

I crept quickly down the second-floor hallway, listening for signs that I was being followed, and passed many doors on either side of me. At the end of the corridor, a large window stood before me on the far wall – there was nowhere else to go now except for one of the rooms. I turned to the door on the right and found it locked. My heart raced as I had not expected such an event. A noise sounded from the foyer below and I quickly went to the door on the left and – finding it unlocked – quietly opened it. Peeking inside, I stifled a scream as I saw several ghostlike objects; some thin and tall; some short and wide. Through my terror, I heard another noise from somewhere behind me. What to do? I knew that I needed to get out of the hallway, but *what* was in that room? Examining the objects once more, I took a little solace that nothing moved. With a deep breath – and forcefully reminding myself that I did not believe in ghosts – I entered the space with the strange things, hoping that they would be less harmful than being caught. Closing the door, I sealed myself in with who-knows-what, and then listened for sounds from the corridor while staring warily at the dark objects around me.

Eventually, when I was satisfied that I had not been followed or raised any alarms, I mustered my nerve and approached the mysterious beings of the room. My anxiety and fright gave way to complete embarrassment as I realized that what I was seeing was furniture, but with sheets thrown over them to keep the dust off. I let out a nervous laugh and took a moment to calm myself.

On the far side of the room were two windows. I walked to one of them and looked out at Bromley. The town was very faint in the darkness, and only a few lights cut through the night. I'm not sure why, but I really wanted to see the orphanage building, but it was too dark to make it out. In all the times I had looked at this house from the orphanage window, I never thought I would ever be trying to do the opposite.

Although alone in that strange room, nervous and afraid, I took a little solace in the thought that I thought Daphne would be proud of me.

Five

BR

Little things woke me up. The light was wrong. The bed was wrong. The smells were wrong. Even the silence…was wrong. Frightened by that collection of abnormalities, I took in a quick breath, pushed myself up, and opened my sleepy eyes to a world of white. I suddenly felt trapped, like I was stuck in some hideous cocoon, and I pushed at the casing until realization finally sunk in. I was in the large house, lying on a couch, under a sheet. With a breath of relief, I grabbed the covering and slid it off me.

The previous night, once all the excitement and nervousness had worn off, I felt extremely tired. Needing a bed of some sort, I did a quick survey of the covered furniture. There were a couple of cushioned armchairs and a couch. I removed my belongings from my blanket and placed them on one of the chairs, hidden under its cover. Taking the blanket, I crawled under the sheet for the couch and curled up. My hope was that if someone was to look in the room, they would see nothing of interest, just covered furniture.

Whether or not someone checked the room overnight, I do not know, but one thing was certain – I had not been caught. Smiling at the success, I became more excited as a very simple piece of logic struck me: if I could go unnoticed for one night, why not another? Why not several? How far would I dare take my scheme?

Of course, the daytime was when I was in the most danger of being discovered. With that concern, I stood up from the couch and I walked to the door. With my ear placed against it, I could hear the occasional voice, far too faint to make out actual words, and sometimes the footsteps of someone ascending or descending the stairway. Even after many minutes of listening, there was never a sound that came close. Unfortunately, that didn't bring me much comfort. I had no idea what the schedule of the house was; what the servants did and when; and knew that I would need to be on guard for every possibility.

So, without any other priority, I brought my blanket over to sit on, a book to read, and I started my vigil with my back against the door. I figured that I should be able to hear anyone approaching with enough time to hide.

My back aches at the memory of that excruciatingly long and uncomfortable day. Every noise caused me to tense up; to listen closely and be ready to spring into action. Passing the time by reading was out of the question as I was so concerned about being found out that I simply could not focus. Also, it didn't take long for my position on the floor, even with the blanket as a cushion, to become uncomfortable and eventually painful. I tried sitting in alternate ways, but each new option only gave relief for a few minutes before a different pang arrived.

And then there was the apple core problem. Obviously, as the day went on, I became quite hungry, and turned to my only food, the two apples that I had brought. Sometime around midmorning, I ate one of the fruits. When all I had left was the core, I became completely flummoxed as to what to do with it, since I had no waste bin. I walked to the window and contemplated throwing it out onto the lawn, but if a gardener or servant was to discover it, the core could raise questions. It was the silliest of conundrums, but for what felt like an hour I held that piece of leftover fruit by its stem and wondered what to do. The solution ended up being rather simple, maybe even obvious for some; I ate it. It provided some odd crunches, and surprising chews that I was not entirely pleased with, but the flavor was generally that of an apple. Sometime in the evening, I did the same with the second apple.

The other issue I faced that long first day was a lack of water. Although the juicy fruit helped some, I became more and more concerned at my growing thirst. Just the idea of not being able to get a glass of water whenever I wanted proved to be very disconcerting and, I think, even amplified my desire for it. But I was stuck. I refused to even consider opening the door until long after the nighttime hours.

Thus, I spent that first day scared of being caught, in constant discomfort, struggling with apple cores, and far thirstier than I had ever been.

One of the only reprieves I allowed myself was a full examination of the room and its objects. In the late afternoon, with still enough light to see well, I had become a little more confident that I was safe from discovery –

at least safe enough that I could take a short break from my post at the door. In addition to the couch and chairs that I had already mentioned, there was a small end table, a carpet rolled up against one of the side walls, and, interestingly, an artist's easel. That last piece made more sense when I looked at the objects that were leaning against the wall, also covered – paintings. As an orphan, I had very little exposure to art, but I found the pictures to be beautiful. All were of landscapes, with green hills, pleasant streams, and happy animals. It felt like a shame for those paintings to be tucked away inside of that abandoned room.

At one point, I briefly looked out the window and spotted my orphanage in the distance. From that vantage point, the building didn't look as familiar as I would have expected, but it was definitely the place. I wondered what Miss Gulch and the orphans thought when they discovered that I was missing. Would they care? Perhaps, when I was established somewhere and safe, I would let them know that I was alright.

A few hours after the winter's sun finally gave up its light and I had reached the end of my patience – my thirst making me desperate, I decided it was time to find water and food. I entered the dark hallway and listened for any noises. After a few seconds of silence, I slowly and silently made my way towards the stairs. My eyes were already accustomed to the darkness, so I was able to move without concern of bumping into anything – my hip was still quite bruised from the kitchen table.

About halfway down the east wing hallway, a sudden and intense feeling of fright welled up in me. Of all the things my mind could be contemplating, it jumped to the idea of the large house being haunted. I froze in panic, thinking that an apparition would appear at any moment. Not that I believed in ghosts, but imagination can surmount logic in uncomfortable darkness. My breathing became shallow and I could feel my heart beating faster. And then the silliest of ideas disarmed the entire situation. That night, in that house, *I* was the apparition. I was the unwelcomed ghost that haunted its hallways and disturbed its peace. For some reason that was an empowering thought, and, with renewed confidence, I continued forward.

At the bottom of the stairs, I again paused and listened closely for any noises. There was nothing but silence, so I crept down the hallway that led to the kitchen. Although it was still very quiet, I was concerned that the man would be up late again because of the cat. My thirst drove me forward.

In the dark kitchen, I went immediately to the wash basin and turned on a small stream of water from the faucet. Underneath, I cupped my hands to catch the liquid and drank deeply with the greatest of pleasure. Never had anything tasted or felt as good as the water quenching my dryness. I wanted to drink without stopping and had to force myself to pause and take breaths. After my thirst was subdued, a calmness come over me. The desperation that I had felt for much of the day was finally gone.

With my most pressing matter resolved, the next item on my list was food. I looked through the cupboards and found many items – flour, sugar, salt, and other common things that would not help me without actually heating the stove. Near one of the cupboards was a small door that led to a pantry. In there, among other items, I found a crate of carrots and another of apples. Taking three of each, and arranging the ones I left behind to look as if the crates had not been disturbed, I was about to leave the kitchen when I had another thought. I did not want to go another day without water.

Finding an old tin mug that didn't look like it would be missed, I filled it with water and then, with all my spoils, quietly made my way back to the room on the second floor.

There was one last problem that I faced – the need of a lavatory. Fortunately, that was overcome by a search of the rooms near mine. The evident wealth of the homeowner provided all of the most modern of amenities.

With that last issue resolved, I realized, with some astonishment, that I had everything I needed. I had access to food, water, shelter, and all the time in the world to read. I'm not sure how many people would have found any satisfaction in those circumstances, but as for me, I was content.

The second day was better than the first; much more relaxed. I spent far less time listening nervously at the door and was able to get comfortable on one of the armchairs and read my books. Occasionally I would get nervous at a particular sound from somewhere in the house, but, like the first day, no one came close to the room.

My confidence became so high that, during the day, I snuck to the lavatory and filled my stolen cup with water. It was amazing how bold one could grow in such a short amount of time.

At night, I made my trip to the pantry and grabbed another day's worth of meals.

Although the third day was much the same as the second, the fourth day, or, more accurately, the fourth night, provided something of extraordinary importance, which I will now share.

Six

BR

Never, do I think, had my patience been more tested than when I overheard talk about the house having a library. On a daytime trip to fill up my water cup, I overheard two of the servants talking – discussing various duties. I paid it no mind until the word *library* was spoken. At hearing that, my hand froze as it reached for my door handle and I nearly spilled the water I had just retrieved. I put the cup down and as quickly as I dared went to the end of the hallway so that I could see down to the foyer where the conversation was happening. As I carefully peered over the ledge, I saw two female servants, an older one and a younger one, talking together. Unfortunately, the remainder of their discussion didn't bring up the library again. I watched as the older servant headed towards the kitchen, while the younger one headed down the west wing hallway.

I entered my room and sat down with the exciting thought – *this house has a library*! The joy of what that revelation would mean raised my spirits to unprecedented heights. But it was only midafternoon and there were many hours until the staff would retire for the night. There is where my patience was taxed, for, despite the dangers, I struggled with my desire to leave immediately and find that precious room. In the end, I was able to restrain myself until the safety of night.

When those long hours of waiting finally ended, I left my room with as much excitement as I could ever remember having. Although hungry, as I tiptoed down the stairs, I decided to find the library first. My great anticipation to see a room full of books overcame my desire for food. But where to look for it?

When the two servants went their separate ways, one went to the familiar kitchen area, while the other went to an area I had not explored – which seemed the clear option. The first-floor hallway was much wider than the one I traversed each night in the upper east wing. The doors were also a lot farther apart, giving the impression of larger rooms. About halfway down the corridor, on the right, was a set of large double doors. *Could this be it?* I felt butterflies in my stomach at the potential of what was to come. I turned one of the handles and slowly pushed the door open. Although there were no lights inside, I could make out a large space, a high ceiling that could not be seen due to darkness, several tall windows on the far side of the room, many pieces of furniture, and walls that were lined with countless books! I had only ever dreamed of a room like that!

Stepping inside, closing the door quietly behind me, I walked to the nearest shelf and ran my hand along the spines of a row of neatly arranged books. Quite suddenly, I laughed. Not from humor, but from happiness. That was followed by unexpected tears, mostly of joy, but a little from thinking about how much Daphne would have enjoyed that moment.

I walked away from the shelves and paused in the middle of the grey room. From that spot, I slowly turned in a circle to take in all the books, all the unknown stories that surrounded me. I felt a kind of literary warmth, as if the books radiated a special heat known only to those who appreciated the written word. If there was any doubt as to my recent actions, I knew that finding that room, that library, justified everything.

In a state of impossible bliss, I perused the shelves, reading titles of books – having to put my face very close to make out the words in the low light – wondering which one I should take – borrow – to read in my room. When I came across *Frankenstein* by Mary Shelley, I knew it would be the one. I remember Daphne telling that story to us and, although frightened by it, I couldn't resist reading it for myself.

Taking the heavy volume off the shelf, I realized that it left a very noticeable gap among its neighbors; like a prominent tooth missing from a smile. I adjusted the books around a little until the missing volume was not so obvious. I hoped it would be enough.

I was all the way back up the stairs when I remembered that I had not stopped at the kitchen yet. That was how excited I was at the prospect of reading a new book.

After returning to the first level, and procuring some food, I anxiously returned to my room, wanting to dive into my newfound story. When safe behind my door, the excitement of everything turned to a touch of disappointment. I forgot the very obvious, but currently insurmountable, fact that it was too dark to read. I would have to wait until morning's first light in order to start the new book. *Oh, the all too familiar agony of waiting!*

Seven

BR

Envision, if you will, standing on a small hill that overlooks a beautiful glen. From that spot, you can see a castle with colorful banners shining in the sun, a pleasant looking village in the midst of a festival, orchards with trees that are weighed down with fruit, a soothing brook meandering through the forests, and your only obligation is to wander around and enjoy everything you see. That is the type of feeling I get when starting a new book. So many amazing possibilities awaited me; so many discoveries and surprises. To that point in my life, I have had that pleasure only three times. But then, in the house with its fantastic library, I had the potential of hundreds of new stories, perhaps thousands!

The morning after discovering the library, as soon as there was light enough to read, I got comfortable on one of the armchairs in my room and opened Frankenstein. Even the sounds of the spine creaking as I opened the pages were exhilarating and new. I was familiar with the general story from Daphne, but to read it was so much more intimate and exciting. I had been through my other three books so many times that I hardly needed to take in the words on the page in order to know what they said, but now I had fresh page after fresh page! I was like an explorer on a new continent.

In that simple, yet wonderful, way, I passed my time. Although I would take breaks to rest my eyes or stretch my legs, I knew that I would never tire of reading.

And the library! Every night I would return to that wonderful space – whether or not I needed a new book to read. If only I could live in *that* room; wake up to books, read all day in one of its luxurious chairs, perhaps near the window, or by a roaring fire, and then fall asleep surrounded by the comfort of a thousand stories. Never had one of my 'if only' dreams been more tangible.

However, even though I desired to spend all my time in the library, I restricted it to only a few precious minutes each night. Those few minutes, I reasoned, were far better than getting caught and never being allowed in the room again.

For the next several days, my life fell into a satisfying routine. During the daytime, I would read, while paying some attention to the sounds of the house – which never came close enough to alarm me – I would eat the food that I would get the night before, and then, once dark, I would sneak out to the library for a few minutes, and then make my way to the kitchen. Every few days, I would switch which dress I was wearing, and then wash the other one in the lavatory tub.

Deep down, I don't think I had really believed that my audacious plan – secretly taking a corner of the house for myself – would have lasted more than a night or two, if that. But at that point, I didn't see any end in sight.

Day after day, I read, I ate, I snuck food, I visited the library, and I slept. Despite the somewhat unsavory means of existence, everything I needed was accounted for. I often wondered how long I could live that way; how long could I be the household ghost. It was not ordinary, by any means, but barring any changes, I'm not sure I knew of another way that I could live better.

You might reason, dear reader, that I would become lonely, spending day after day by myself, but that was not the case. I found a calmness, an almost blissful peace, during that time. In the orphanage, one is never alone, and the anxiety of being around so many people would often agitate me. I remember instances where the constant noises and motions of the other kids were so overwhelming, that I would pull my blanket over my head just to feel separated from everyone else. I needed a stillness of sight and mind. It's not that I don't like people, for I loved the time I spent with Daphne, and had some good experiences with some of the other children, but in most instances, I preferred quiet and solitude. While some people garner energy from association, I need to be alone to rejuvenate mine. Perhaps given a greater amount of time in the house, my solitary existence would have been an issue, but in those first weeks I was completely satisfied with myself and the associations I had with the characters in my books.

After several days of my peaceful routine, I heard an uncommon commotion from somewhere in the house. It was afternoon, and I started to hear several voices. Putting my book down, I took my place at the door. I could hear both men and woman talking but could not make out what they were saying. Despite the daytime hour, I felt it important to have some understanding of what was going on, so I opened the door in order to try and hear better.

"Was it a successful trip, Mr. Stafford?" I heard a man ask.

"No, Patrick," answered another male voice. "I cannot call it successful. But that, in itself, is probably a good thing."

Evidently, that was the master of the house returning from a trip abroad. Would his presence affect my stay?

"You must be hungry, Mr. Stafford. Can I prepare you something to eat?" a woman inquired.

"Yes, please, Melba. That would be much appreciated."

I listened at the open door for another minute or so, but soon, everyone dispersed. In total, I had heard four voices; two male and two female. In addition, I had names to put to some of the residents. The owner of the house was Mr. Stafford. The older gentleman servant must have been Patrick. I also had the name of one of the women, Melba – perhaps a cook, since she offered to make a meal? That left one more female unaccounted for. In reality, knowing their names mattered little, if any, but I liked that small bit of knowledge. Although my existence was necessarily unknown to them, knowing their names made me feel a bit more like I belonged there.

With Mr. Stafford and the rest now out of ear shot, I closed the door and went back to reading. However, I could not help but pay a little extra attention to the sounds of the house for the rest of the day. I honestly could not think of a good reason that another person in the home would cause me any issues – my room was clearly a forgotten area – but I remained vigilant as I desperately did not want my stay to come to an end.

I cannot say that I worried for nothing, as you will see, but several more uneventful days went by with my routine not being altered or challenged in any way. Sleep, read, eat, and get food. It seemed that the return of the house's owner was a complete non-event for me. Outside of occasionally hearing his voice, in his comings and goings, nothing changed in my daily existence.

All of that, however, came to an end quite suddenly and drastically.

It was late and I was heading to the library for my nightly pleasure. I had finished my latest book, *Romeo and Juliet* by William Shakespeare, and was excited to pick out a new one. The anticipation of an unknown story became one of my greatest joys. What adventure, romance, or mystery would be in store for me next? Perhaps because I was so enamored with those thoughts, I missed any signs that I was not alone when I entered the library.

The room, as it always was at that late hour, was very dark. I headed to the shelf that I had taken *Romeo and Juliette* from and carefully put it back. I then tilted my head and started reading the titles of other books, looking for one that stood out to me.

My heart nearly stopped when a voice out of the darkness said, "Good evening, my dear. I think it is high time that we had a little chat."

Eight

BR

Very slowly, I turned towards the sound of the voice. I wished desperately that I had somehow imagined it or that I was misunderstanding a common sound. Of course, I had not. I looked around the dark room for the person behind the words but could only see the black outline of the furniture. Suddenly, there was a flash – a match strike – and rising from one of the large cushioned chairs that faced a fireplace, was a finely dressed man, complete with jacket, waistcoat, and tie. With the match, he lit a lamp on the small table next to him, which softly illuminated the room.

I was frozen in place. I didn't know what to do or say. Occasionally, throughout the daytime, I had given thought to how I might react if I was discovered. But at night, I became so confident, or at least the likelihood of discovery felt so low, that I didn't even consider the possibility. I was thoroughly unprepared.

My shock soon gave way to abject fear. *I was going to be arrested.* I would go to jail and perhaps not even qualify for whatever ghastly employment that the orphanage could find for me. Maybe I did have something to lose after all. My future suddenly looked bleaker than it ever had. *What had I done?*

While those horrific thoughts sped through my mind, the man said in a reassuring voice, "You have nothing to fear from me. I am not going to harm you."

I took a moment to examine the gentleman in front of me a little closer. He must have been close to sixty years old, his hair was mostly grey, but not without some last vestiges of its once dark color. He was not particularly tall, although not short either, and had a slim build. What I noticed most of all, in my fright, was the seemingly out of place kindness –

even amusement – of his face. His mouth was set with a small smile, while his light-colored eyes were somehow comforting.

"My name," said the man, "is Thomas Stafford. May I ask yours?"

It was the owner of the home. I wanted to run. I wanted to cry. All the badness of my potential future life came rushing in on me and I was filled with cold dread. I instantly realized just how much I did not want to leave. I didn't want to become one of those wretched women who found comfort from their miserable existence in alcohol and nowhere else. In many ways, I didn't want to become like my father.

Finally realizing that I had been asked a question, I managed to choke out an answer, "I'm Naomi Gladwyn, sir."

"Well, Miss Gladwyn, I'm excited to meet you. Please, have a seat," he indicated a matching armchair near the one he had been sitting on.

Was he being sarcastic? Was he prolonging the agony of my eventual arrest? I could think of no good outcomes to the meeting, but when I tried to read his face, I still only saw a welcoming kindness that flew against all my reasoning. I swallowed hard to try and keep my emotions under control. For some reason, I didn't want to break down and cry in front of that man.

I walked from the shelves to the offered chair and gingerly lowered myself into it, as if I was expecting a trap. I clasped my hands tightly in my lap as Mr. Stafford took the other seat, rotated it a little to better face me, and sat back comfortably, as if we were about to have as natural a conversation as there could be.

He looked me in the eyes silently for a moment, but I could not hold his stare. I shifted my gaze to the floor in shame and embarrassment. I had reasons for what I had done, for sneaking into his home, but I had no defense. I had never felt so at the mercy of another person.

"I cannot tell you," he said, "how surprised I was to learn that I had an unknown guest in my house."

Although terrified and ashamed, I forced myself to look at him while he spoke to me – he deserved any respect I could give him after what I had done. His face still carried a look of warmness which made his usage of the word 'guest' stand out a little.

"How old are you?" he asked.

I had not thought much about it, but sometime during my stay, I had turned seventeen. I know some people celebrate birthdays, but that was something that we are not accustomed to in the orphanage. "I'm seventeen years old, sir."

He nodded and asked, "Tell me, how long have you been living here?"

With a small voice, I answered as honestly as I could. "I'm not exactly sure, sir. I have lost track of the days. But I would imagine that it has been the better part of three weeks."

"Three weeks!" he exclaimed, scaring me a little by his enthusiasm. "Why, that is simply incredible! Who would have thought?" His face took on an impressed look.

At that point, a little of my fear was transitioning to confusion. I was still far from any sort of ideal emotions, but confusion was an improvement from fear in those circumstances. Mr. Stafford didn't seem upset at what I had done, but rather, he seemed interested, even excited. Was I dealing with a sane person? That thought opened all sorts of new worries that I refused to entertain.

He asked, "Where have you been sleeping all this time?"

My initial thought was that I didn't want to tell him. A small part of me impossibly hoped that maybe, if I didn't give up the location, I could hide in that room once again – after my upcoming and inevitable removal from the house. I dismissed that, of course, and answered, "In the east wing, at the end of the second-floor corridor, on the left."

Mr. Stafford thought for a moment and then asked, "Are there any paintings in that room?"

"Yes, sir."

He nodded as if agreeing with the choice. "I take it that the reports I have been hearing of missing food are due to your visit here as well?"

"Yes, sir."

"And the misplaced tin mug, also you?"

I nodded and then blurted out, "Yes. I'm sorry. Truly I am. For everything." Part of me meant the apology. The man had done nothing wrong to me and yet I invaded his home and stole his food. Another part of me knew that it was probably the most exciting three weeks of my life and if I had the opportunity, I would likely do it all over again. I will let the reader judge my ultimate sincerity.

Without acknowledging my apology, he asked, "Where are you from, Miss Gladwyn? What circumstances brought you here?" He leaned forward, practically emanating anticipation. For some reason, he appeared truly interested in what my answer would be.

Why that man would care about me was beyond my understanding. Perhaps he was stalling for time while one of the servants was fetching the police. Figuring I had nothing to hide, I explained, "I came from the Bromley Female Orphan Asylum, not far from here. Since I was of age, I was being forced to leave; to be given employment in some vile place, and I decided to run away; to try and hide from the life that was being offered me."

With his still kind voice, Mr. Stafford said, "I think you were right to fear your future prospects. I know of the places and the types of people that you would, no doubt, fall under and they are generally atrocious. I respect your decision to attempt to find something different. Everyone has the right to try and choose better for themselves."

Over the last three weeks, I had given many thoughts to what it would be like if I was found in the house. Some of the scenarios I created were harsh, but even the kinder scenarios were far from what I had experienced so far. That man was justifying, even agreeing with, what I had done.

"May I ask," he continued, "what happened to your parents? Did you know them?"

The compassionate look on his face again surprised me. I guess I was not accustomed to concern from other people. "I don't remember my father. I was very young when he died. However, my mum gave me a letter that told me about him. He was a good man at one point, but when his brother disappeared from the *Mary Celeste*, my father became a drunk and eventually died by stepping in front of a carriage."

"The *Mary Celeste*?" Mr. Stafford asked intensely, gripping the arms of his chair and leaning so far forward that I thought he might tip his seat. "Your uncle was on that terrible ship?"

"Yes, sir."

He sat back heavily and stared off at the wall with wide eyes. After a few moments, he looked at me and asked, "This is not some made-up story, is it? Your uncle was really on that ship?"

"Yes, sir, he was. I have a letter from my mum that explains it. It's in my…in the room I had been sleeping in. I can retrieve it, if you would like."

"That will not be necessary," he said, some of the intensity leaving his face. "What happened to you and your mother after your father's death?"

"We moved into a small home, a shack really, near the Thames, along with two other women. We lived there until I was six. That was when my mother fell sick, pneumonia, and died. I have no relatives, so I was taken to the orphanage."

"My dear, Miss Gladwyn, you have undergone more tragedy at a young age than most will in their entire life. I'm truly sorry."

Despite my determination not to cry, tears welled up in my eyes. It had been years since someone had shown me empathy like that. Seeing the emotions, Mr. Stafford produced a handkerchief and gave it to me to dry my eyes. "There, there," he said softly.

A minute, or so, of silence passed between us as I composed myself. What would happen next?

"May I ask, Miss Gladwyn, what brought you to my home? There are many houses in Bromley and surely there are some that are closer to the orphanage."

"There are places closer," I nodded, "but this house is quite famous among us orphans."

"Famous?" His face, which had become contemplative, was changing back to amusement. "How is my home famous?"

"Well, you see, sir, in the orphanage, from the dorm room window, this house can be seen. Being the grandest structure around, we children would often develop stories, fantasies, about what life might be like here. It's very silly, I know, but this house had become almost mythical."

"How very fascinating. I had no idea." Mr. Stafford paused in evident amusement at the thought of his house having such an effect. Changing the subject, he then said, "When you entered the library tonight, I noticed that you had a book with you. Which one was it?"

I had to think hard to remember, as my mind was far away from books. "Romeo and Juliet, sir."

"What did you think of it?"

Did he really want to discuss books? Nothing about the meeting made any sense to me, but at least it did not make sense in a non-police way. Again, I had to focus my mind to recall the story. After a few seconds, I answered, "I found William Shakespeare's wording to be difficult. It contained wonderful phrases, but the old English caused me to read at a snail's pace."

Mr. Stafford nodded and commented, "He wrote his books, well plays actually, over two-hundred years ago, so the vernacular of his day was different from ours. Wording aside, what did you think of the story?"

"It left me with a feeling of sadness – how could it not? Romeo and Juliette loved each other dearly but were opposed because of family pride. I was frustrated at the stubbornness of those around them that kept them separated. In the end, they died – eventually choosing death over being apart. I wished a better ending for them."

"It is," said Mr. Stafford, "the most tragic love story ever told. I have read it several times, and, with each reading, I wish that the families would somehow change and that the two lovers could be together. Or, at least, that Friar Laurence's messenger makes it to Romeo in time. Of course, the story never alters, but I always hold out hope – I guess orphans are not the only ones prone to silliness."

Despite the circumstances, I found the conversation to be very interesting, almost enjoyable. His admission of how he felt about the book, along with his wish that the story could change and end on a happier note – something that I did too – was comforting. It felt like a normal conversation between two people who enjoyed reading; like something Daphne and I would do. I had to remind myself that he was the owner of the house that I had broken into and it was only a matter of time before I would be handed to the police.

"So," said the man, "you have a fondness for books?"

"Yes, sir. Very much so."

"You may find it interesting that your love of books was your downfall – that is, how I discovered that someone unknown was staying in my home. You see, I spend much time in this room, and when I noticed the shelves being disturbed, I knew something was afoot. You obviously arranged the books in a way so as to hide the missing volumes, and that would likely have gone unnoticed in many places, but here, I am exceedingly familiar with all these books – as unimportant as they are."

As unimportant as they are? I felt that statement to be an insult. Although I was in no position to argue, I could not hold my impertinent tongue, and said in a stern voice, "These books are *not* unimportant. Books are some of the only joys I have ever had in my entire life. With all due respect, I cannot agree with you."

Instead of being angry at my challenge, Mr. Stafford put his hands up in front of him, smiled, and said, "I apologize, Miss Gladwyn. I meant that they were unimportant only in a relative sense. For I, too, love books. They have provided me with such wonders throughout my life, that I cannot imagine being happy without them. Rarely a day goes by without me partaking of this pleasure."

I didn't know what he meant by saying that the books were unimportant in a relative sense, but I was satisfied that he shared an appreciation much like mine.

"Well, Miss Gladwyn, I must admit that this conversation has been most interesting, and I find you to be a remarkable young woman. But it is quite late and now we must talk about what to do with you."

This was it. The end of my stay; the end of seeing that library; the end to almost any hope of future happiness. I looked intently at him and waited for his judgment.

There was a long pause while he seemed to be considering something, almost as if he was appraising me. He said, half to himself, "I wonder…" Then, a decision evidently made, he asked, "Have you ever read The Picture of Dorian Gray, by Oscar Wilde?"

I didn't know how that related to me or my predicament, other than maybe it contained some punishment that he wanted to apply. Regardless, I had not read it nor had even heard of it. In answer, I shook my head.

"Not too surprising; it was only published last year. Very well, then, I would like to propose a sort of test."

I cocked my head to the side in complete surprise – my mouth no doubt agape – and studied his face. His expression still appeared kind and gave no sign of sarcasm or jest.

He continued, "I would like to have you read that book and, in three days' time, we will discuss it. How does that sound to you?"

Never had I been more dumbfounded. The man, who largely held my future in his hands, was asking me to read a book. "I don't think that I quite understand."

With a smile, he said, "I guess it's rather off-the-beaten-path, as they say. But what I'm asking is simply what I said. I would like you to take the next few days and read the book. On the third night, we will discuss it.

There are a few conditions however, but I think you will find them acceptable."

Conditions? My head was spinning. "What conditions?"

"First, since I will now consider you a proper guest during this time, you will move into a proper room. Second, you will no longer steal food, but allow my staff to prepare your meals. Third, you will return the tin mug you have been using. Lastly, there will be no discussion about the Dorian Gray book until the third night. You may discuss with me or any of my fine staff, anything you like, except that one topic. Are these conditions agreeable to you?"

Despite the straightforward and simple instructions, I didn't trust myself to understand them correctly – they were too good to be true. "What you are saying is that I'm to be your guest for the next three days and my only obligation is to read the Dorian Gray book and not discuss it until the third night?"

"Precisely. Do you accept?"

"What happens if I fail the test? Will you turn me over to the police?"

Shaking his head, he responded, "I do not want to get into details as to what will or will not happen after that discussion, but you can rest your mind completely with regards to the police. I will not be notifying the authorities about you at any point – not now and not in three days' time. You took a little of my roof, and a bit of my food – well, I have more than enough of both. In return, you have provided me with a most enjoyable experience. I'm happy to say that we can call ourselves even. Do you agree?"

It was incredible. Not only would I not be arrested, but I was not even going to be held accountable for my actions. I don't know what he had in mind, but he was being far more generous than I would expect from anyone.

Since his terms were all to my benefit, I said, "That is very kind of you, Mr. Stafford, and yes, I agree. I agree to considering ourselves even and I agree to the test."

Standing from his chair, he exclaimed, "Wonderful!" and then turned to the shelves. "Let's see here…" he muttered to himself pursuing the different volumes. "Ah, here it is," and after sliding a book out, he turned and handed it to me.

The book had a beautiful leather cover, in pristine condition. I reverently passed my hand over its textured surface.

"Patrick!" called out Mr. Stafford. A moment later a man entered the room with a candle in hand – it was the same man from the first night. Even though it was late, he was fully dressed, evidently aware that his master had planned for our meeting.

Indicating me, Mr. Stafford continued, "This is Miss Gladwyn and she will be staying with us for a few days. Miss Gladwyn, this is Patrick Bollmann and he will show you to your room."

The servant gave a nod and said, "Yes, sir." Then, looking at me, "Please follow me, miss."

I stood from the chair, hardly able to grasp the sudden and completely unexpected outcome of the night. I looked at Mr. Stafford, and he smiled and said, "Goodnight, Miss Gladwyn."

"Goodnight, sir," I managed to say and then, with the book in hand, I turned and followed Patrick out of the library. *What exactly had I gotten myself into?*

Nine

Encompassed in softness and warmth, I woke to the most pleasant morning that I could remember. The mattress was like sleeping on air. The blankets – multiple blankets! – were so warm, and their heaviness made me feel like I was in a constant embrace.

Rain and wind sounded against the guest room windows, which made the large four-poster bed seem all the more comforting and secure, as if there was not a safer place in the entire world.

I started to reflect on the previous night's events; being caught by Mr. Stafford, the surprisingly good-natured conversation, and the strange test. I thought that, perhaps, it would all seem more reasonable in the light of a new day, but it did not.

I glanced at the bedside table, where the book, *The Picture of Dorian Gray*, rested. It seemed unassuming and ordinary. What made that specific story so important? *Was* it important – outside of the test? Perhaps it was simply a favored book of Mr. Stafford's.

At the sound of a rap at the door, I looked up. A man's voice, the servant, Patrick, announced, "Miss Gladwyn, breakfast will be ready soon. Please join us in the dining room, at your leisure."

"Thank you," I called out as I heard his footsteps heading away. I was not sure what to make of him, or more importantly, what he made of me. The previous night, Patrick had led me to the art room to collect my few belongings, and then brought me to the guest room on the second floor of the west wing. Although he was not at all unkind to me, we did not talk much. I feared that he may not think too highly of someone who, while under his watch, had secretly lived in the house for the last few weeks. I hoped he could forgive me.

Turning my thoughts away from Patrick and to the promise of food, I somewhat reluctantly climbed out of the magnificent bed and got ready in one of my plain dresses. Along the wall, opposite the bed, was a chest of drawers made from impossibly smooth wood with shiny brass handles. On top of it was a silver hairbrush that had small designs etched into its surface. Next to the chest of drawers was a large and spotless mirror. I looked at my reflection and frowned. In that house of wealth and beauty, I was the most out of place item. I smoothed my dress as best I could; I used the brush to try and tame my hair; I even pinched my cheeks to give them a little color. The end result was…well…the best me I could put together.

I walked into the hallway and realized that it was the first time that I would be able to really see the interior of the house in the daytime. Although it was a grey and rainy morning, there was still plenty of light to see the details that I had not previously been able to appreciate. The corridor outside of the guest room had a few small tables along its sides, with delicate vases, beautiful fresh flowers, and silver candle holders. On the walls were paintings spaced along both sides of the hallway. One in particular caught my eye, a lovely summer scene of a pond that had a small island not far from the shore. I found the picture inviting, as if it was calling me to participate and enjoy that warm day by the water.

At the end of the hallway, near the stairs, I reached the landing that overlooked the foyer. Demanding all of my attention was the incredible chandelier hanging from the ceiling. During all of my nighttime excursions, I had never realized that it was even there. It was the most beautiful object I had ever seen; with its many golden arms, like perfectly shaped branches, the crystal leaves that glimmered rainbow colors even in the grey light, and the flower blossoms that held the candles – currently unlit. I tried to picture how wonderful it must look when fully ablaze.

Pulling myself away from the sight of the chandelier, I walked down the stairs. At the bottom of the steps, I came across a woman, whose eyes, when catching sight of me, lit up. She walked over quickly, seemingly excited to make my acquaintance. Clothed in a servant's uniform, a modest dark dress, her sandy colored hair done tightly in a bun, she gave me a very pleasant smile as she approached. Although a little older than me, she was far younger than Mr. Stafford or Patrick.

When near, she said, "You must be Miss Gladwyn. My name is Helen Giles and I'm the housemaid. Welcome!"

"I'm pleased to meet you, Miss Giles."

"Please, call me Helen. Mr. Stafford allows us, actually he prefers us, to be a little less formal in the house. How did you sleep?"

"Very well, thank you."

"Are you heading to breakfast?"

"Yes, but I'm not entirely sure of the way to the dining room."

"Well, then," Helen said cheerfully, "follow me. We are only a few steps away."

I followed her along the hallway that led to the kitchen. Partway down she stopped at a side door and said, "This is the dining room and I believe Mr. Stafford is already inside. Now, I must be off. It was a pleasure to meet you, Miss Gladwyn."

"Please, call me Naomi," I said with a smile. Of all people who didn't deserve formalities, I was foremost. "I was pleased to meet you as well."

Helen grinned and then walked back towards the foyer while I stood alone for a moment in front of the dining room door. I was nervous, although I could not say exactly why. I guess much of what was happening didn't feel real; certainly didn't feel warranted. I half expected to walk in and have Mr. Stafford tell me to leave. But when I entered, nothing like that happened.

The dining room was a good size room, with elegant wallpaper, fine furniture that housed exquisite plates, but was dominated by a large table, capable of easily seating at least a dozen people. Three vases of beautiful fresh flowers stood as centerpieces. Sitting at the corner of the table was Mr. Stafford. At my arrival, he stood up, smiled, and said, "Ah! Good morning, Miss Gladwyn. I'm so happy that you could join me. Please take this seat here," He indicated a chair across from him.

From another door in the room, Patrick stepped in and immediately pulled the chair out for me. Who was I to receive such kindnesses? I sat and with a small voice said, "Thank you."

Once seated, Mr. Stafford took his chair and asked me, "Did you find your room acceptable?"

Acceptable? Was he kidding? "Oh, yes, sir. It was perfect in every way. Thank you."

"I'm glad to hear it. Are you hungry?"

I nodded, hoping to not seem too eager as I was famished. After all, I had only eaten a few apples, carrots, and other small scraps that I could find for the last few of weeks. Thankfully, I didn't have to wait long as a kindly looking older woman entered and brought the food. Placed in front of me was a plate full of eggs, toast, sausage, and ham. The smell was heavenly, and the amount was stunning – never in my life had I been given so much food at one time. On the table, between myself and Mr. Stafford, the woman set butter and a jar of blackberry preserves. It took all of my self-control to use the utensils, as I would have rather scooped it all up with my hands and shoved it into my mouth.

I will not bore you, dear reader, with the details of each bite, but rest assured that I was eating the greatest meal of my life, up to that moment. Know that I took full advantage of the preserves – an extreme rarity in the orphanage – spreading a thick layer on my toast. I think I would be very happy to have preserves at every meal. In fact, I think I would be happy to have preserves *for* every meal!

As breakfast came to an end, my stomach felt a little upset – I guess it was not accustomed to such fine food – but mostly I felt a great satisfaction and happiness. To some degree, I was living one of the 'if only' games. I could not help but worry as to what would happen at the end of three days, but I tried hard to not think about that.

Mr. Stafford sipped his tea and then asked me, "Did you enjoy your breakfast?"

"Very much! It was one of the greatest meals I have ever had."

"High praise! I will be sure that Melba, our cook, receives your compliment."

A voice from behind one of the doors called out, "No need, Mr. Stafford, I heard it for myself," and in walked the kindly looking older woman. She approached me and introduced herself, "I am Melba Throne, and if you need anything, dearie, do not hesitate to ask."

"That is very kind of you, Miss Throne. Thank you."

With a pleasant smile and a small nod towards Mr. Stafford, she left the room.

"How many people work for you?" I asked.

"Three people. Although they assist each other in all aspects, Melba is charge of the food and cooking, Helen, I'm not sure if you met her, she handles the cleaning, and Patrick is in charge of the stables and the grounds."

"Helen showed me where the dining room was. They have been very pleasant to me, although I'm not sure Patrick likes me very much."

"Why do you say that?"

"He seems very quiet and formal around me."

Mr. Stafford smiled and said, "Patrick is quiet and formal around everyone; a true professional. I have known him for well over thirty years and it is rare when he does not treat me as his employer."

"But you *are* his employer."

"Yes, but after all this time, I hope I'm also his friend. I certainly consider him as one of mine. Besides, I don't think you need to worry about him liking you."

"How come?"

"Did you notice the fresh flowers around the house?"

"Yes, they are quite lovely."

"Indeed. Patrick is not one that is prone to collect flowers very often, but he did so this morning – in the rain, no less. The flowers are in honor of you, Miss Gladwyn."

"Me?" I could not believe it. I thought about Patrick going out in the cold, wet, grey morning in order to gather flowers, *for me*. My eyes stared to water at the pure and unexpected kindness of the gesture. Despite our wild fantasies and 'if only' games, most don't feel they actually deserve any of the things they dream up. I certainly didn't feel I deserved any of the kindnesses that had been given to me so freely.

"It is clear," said Mr. Stafford, "that you are not accustomed to being treated in such a manner. But, rest assured, your genuine appreciation makes it all the more worthwhile."

With a small voice, I could only manage, "Thank you, sir."

Mr. Stafford was silent for a moment, allowing me time to compose myself, and then asked, "Tell me, Miss Gladwyn, I know you have a great fondness for reading, have you read many books? I ask as I don't imagine that the orphanage had a great selection to offer you."

"It did not, sir. I have three books and have read each one countless times. In that respect, I have read many books. In regard to the number of different books that I have read, that amount is small. I can add ten or so to those original three, since I have…arrived here."

"That makes me very excited for you," commented Mr. Stafford enthusiastically. "So many unexplored worlds yet to be discovered! Would you say that you have a favorite book?"

"Yes, sir. Little Women by Louisa May Alcott. There was not a girl at the orphanage who didn't dream of being part of the March family. However, that book contains the sadness of Beth, which reminds me of the loss of one of my friends, Daphne. As much as I love it, I find it difficult to read."

"A favorite book that is difficult to read due to the emotions it creates. That is an interesting conundrum. Isn't it amazing how the written word can generate such strong feelings in us?"

"Yes, sir. Although, sometimes I do not wish for them."

At that comment, Mr. Stafford took in and let out a long slow breath. He then said, with barely contained emotion, "Me too."

I'm not sure what affected him so greatly, but, clearly, he was struggling with some painful memory of his own. Shaking the emotion away, Mr. Stafford said, with renewed vigor, "Although you are free to do whatever you want, may I make a suggestion?"

"Yes, sir. Of course."

"Patrick has a fire going in the library, and there are few things, in my experience, as wonderful as reading in a comfortable chair by a cozy fire. In fact, that is how I plan to spend much of my day, and I would be very happy if you would join me."

I had not actually given much thought as to what my exact plans were, other than finding someplace to read the Dorian Gray book. Spending a day in that library, especially under the conditions that Mr. Stafford outlined, sounded amazing. "I would like that very much."

Rising from his chair, Mr. Stafford said, "Excellent! It's settled then. I will be in the library within a few minutes. Please join me whenever you so choose."

After he left the room, I sat alone at the table in a state that can only be described as disbelief. I wanted to laugh, to cry, to yell out in gladness. *How could all of this be happening to me?*

When I gained my composure once more, I hurried to my room and retrieved the book – pausing briefly along the way to once again marvel at the chandelier – and headed towards the library. When I entered, I was in the most wonderful space I had ever been in. I had talked previously of how incredible the library was at night, but in the full light of day, it was breathtaking. The different colors and textures of the books – which I could not make out previously – now exploded from the shelves like all the rich colors of a forest in the fall. With full purview of the room, from floor to ceiling, I found that there were even more books than I had imagined. The best summation I can give is to say that I loved that room. Love is not a word I use lightly. I loved my mother, I love Daphne, and I love reading. I could now add that library to that short, but most significant, list.

When I turned my attention from the shelves, I found Mr. Stafford sitting in a chair by the fire. He was reading from a large book and on his lap rested a grey cat with hints of brown. The chair next to him, the very chair I sat in on the first night we talked, was available and I took it. Mr. Stafford looked up from his book, gave me a small smile, and said, "I know you must be eager to start reading, but I think I should first introduce you to Dantés, my cat."

I smiled at the sleepy animal, looking as content as a creature possibly could, and said, "We met briefly the first night I came here. We gave each other a scare."

Mr. Stafford gave a little laugh and said, "Don't worry, Dantés has a short memory. He really is an affectionate cat."

Although I did want to start reading, I had to ask, "Dantés? Like Edmund Dantés from *The Count of Monte Cristo*?"

With raised eyebrows, Mr. Stafford gave me an impressed look. "That is precisely the origin of his name. I have always named my cats after characters from books. Before Dantés, there was Ishmael, Ophelia, and...let's see...ah yes, Victor. Do you know which stories they are all from?"

"Victor could be a reference to Victor Frankenstein."

"Precisely, very good! And the other two?"

I thought for a moment, and although I loved books, my knowledge was limited – in fact, being able to recognize two of the names was quite a fortunate coincidence. "I'm afraid that I'm not familiar with Ophelia or Ishmael."

"Well," commented Mr. Stafford, "you have plenty of time to discover those notable characters. Now, I think I have disturbed you enough," and with that, he went back to reading his book.

My chair was very soft and comfortable, which was not something I noticed that first night, since I could feel nothing beyond my nervousness. The fire gave off a wonderful heat and made joyful snapping sounds. I found that if I was not careful, I could spend lots of the day mesmerized by the dancing flames and glowing coals. I finally turned my attention to the book. I have been excited to read before, but that was the first time that I was nervous. It felt like my very future was inside.

As the day wore on, the various servants, Helen, Patrick, and Melba, made occasional appearances to make sure we were comfortable. Tea and biscuits were brought – and thoroughly enjoyed – around midmorning. We had the noon meal in the dining room, as we did supper – every meal seemingly better than the previous one.

At one point in the afternoon, the combination of the warm fire and a full stomach was so thoroughly comforting that I actually fell asleep sitting in the chair with the book on my lap. When I awoke, I felt a little embarrassed, but no one seemed to notice.

Of all the experiences presented to me on that day, the only one that I did not completely enjoy, strangely, was the book itself; *The Picture of Dorian Gray*. The story started off well enough, with an artist wanting to paint a portrait of his handsome young friend, Dorian. There were even some interesting thoughts about whether a work of art tells the viewer more about the subject or more about the artist. But that fine beginning soon gave way to the shallow, selfish, even ruthless actions of the protagonist. It seemed that all of the likable characters in the book ended up hurt or dead. And then there was the picture; the cursed object that reaped all the age and badness of its subject.

Why would Mr. Stafford want me to read that book? It must have held some meaning for him, but I could not fathom what it was. Dorian's parents had both died when he was young – could Mr. Stafford be trying to make a connection to my parents? That didn't make too much sense as Dorian was taken in by wealthy relatives and had an upbringing far from anything I had experienced. I wanted to ask if there was something in particular that I should be looking for, but I did not as that was one of the stipulations.

Regardless of how I felt about the book, I was determined to pass whatever test was in store for me. So, for each of the three days, all I did was read the account of that horrible man, Dorian Gray. The wonder of my surroundings continued to mix strangely with the bleakness of the story.

By the end of the third day, the evening of the test, I had read the book a total of four times. Although nervous for the imminent discussion, I knew that I had done all I could to understand the story.

After dinner on that third night, Mr. Stafford and I were once again in the library. The wind outside whistled past the windows while the occasional gust shook the panes. The dreary weather made the fire we sat in front of seem all the more cheerful. After adding another log to the flames, Mr. Stafford turned to me and said, "Well, Miss Gladwyn, I think the time has come for the test, and to finally discuss the book. Are you ready?"

Ten

BR

Ready? In the sense of having read the story and could discuss many of its particulars, then yes, I was ready. Ready for the potential outcome of the discussion? I didn't feel ready at all. The dread I had encountered in the orphanage at the prospect of leaving, and the life offered to me, started to return. Only then it was worse, as I had had a taste of the sublime. I had actually lived an 'if only' dream. How could I face my pathetic realities after that?

I held the book tightly in my lap and nodded. "Yes, sir, I'm ready."

"So, what did you think of it?" asked Mr. Stafford, his face showing nothing but warm interest.

Afraid of insulting my host, for it was not a book that I particularly enjoyed, I tried to choose my words carefully, and started by saying, "It was undoubtedly interesting; quite unique among the handful of stories I have read. Although, it seemed a little backwards to me."

"Backwards? Interesting. How so?"

"Well, in most of the stories I have read, you generally feel compassion for the main character. You want them to overcome the bad and be rewarded with good. Even in the case of persons that end up being questionable, such as Frankenstein's creation, the author makes you understand why they came to be that way – an acceptable explanation that merits our sympathy. But with Dorian Gray, he is a dreadful man and the only explanation given for his actions is his vanity and selfishness. He gives glimpses of being likable, but they were so thoroughly overshadowed by badness, that I did not cheer him on, nor want a happy conclusion at all. It was quite the opposite feeling as to what I expect when reading a story."

Mr. Stafford tilted his head and gave obvious thought to my comment. I dreaded some sharp retort, but after a few seconds, he said, "That is a very interesting observation. I have never heard of it described as 'backwards' – in comparison with other stories – but I think it's a rather fair conclusion."

Despite my nervousness, I gave a small smile at what I had to perceive to be a compliment.

"So, tell me," continued Mr. Stafford, "why do you think Mr. Wilde wrote a book with such reproachable characters and an ending that, although just, doesn't leave the reader with anything but a kind of lingering sense of dread?"

That was a question that I had asked myself since the completion of my first time through the book. What was of value in the story? Particularly, I had been looking for the value from the standpoint of Mr. Stafford – but I also wondered at a general level. I answered, "More than anything else, I believe it to be a warning. A warning against a life of selfishness, as well as a warning against poor associates."

"A warning? Very good! Go on."

"Well, in regard to selfishness, I think the lesson is obvious. Dorian cared about his looks, his pleasures, and hardly anything else. He only did things that made him happy, regardless of the effect on others, which led to bad ramifications to all that were around him. Despite his desire for happiness, his choices led him to be completely miserable."

"Alright," commented Mr. Stafford, "that is perfectly accurate and, as you said, obvious. Tell me more about the warning against poor associates."

"As awful as Dorian Gray was, I think the true villain of the story is Lord Henry. There were glimpses of Dorian showing a sense of humanity, but Lord Henry filled his head with such shallow philosophies, that Dorian made loathsome decisions. I wonder what his life could have been like if he had only associated with the artist, Mr. Hallward. Perhaps his inklings of kindness could have been encouraged into making him, if not a good person, a decent one.

"Related, is the fact that Dorian himself became a bad associate. It seemed that everyone who came into contact with him ended up very badly. He left a trail of broken and ruined people throughout his life. As I said, by the end, I had no sympathy for him.

"I would hope that reading this story would cause people to think about the effect their associates have on them and the effect that they have on their associates."

Mr. Stafford nodded approvingly and said, "These are very excellent observations, Miss Gladwyn. Tell me, can you think of any other warnings that the book conveyed?"

I thought for a few moments and then a new idea struck me. There was a bit of an unanswered reference presented in the story, which certainly could pass for a warning. I said, "I did not initially think of this as a warning to the reader, but it certainly could be considered as such. There was the French novel that Lord Henry gave to Dorian." I saw Mr. Stafford's eyes take on some excitement – I had evidently struck a chord of interest. "The story doesn't say the name of the novel, but it so affected Dorian that he lived out many of the parts of what he read – sordid and fleshly desires. In fact, in one of his few moments of self-awareness, he asked Lord Henry to promise to never give that book to another person for fear of it influencing others as it had him. I believe he said that, 'it does harm'. I guess the warning would be against the effect that reading certain books could have on a person."

Mr. Stafford sat back in his chair, his fingers picking his bottom lip absently, and stared in my direction, though not at me. He was clearly lost in thought. What would come next? How had I done thus far?

After a very long minute or so, Mr. Stafford's eyes regained focus and he said, "Miss Gladwyn, your observations and opinions on The Picture of Dorian Gray are quite excellent. Of course, opinions cannot be faulted, for who can judge another person's feelings. But you gleaned a most important aspect of the story. And, although you have given me no reason to be, I am still a little surprised at where we find ourselves."

I could not tell from what he said if that was good or bad. Was the test over? Did I fail? What did any of it mean? My fear started to grow.

"If you are willing, I would like to ask you a few additional questions," said Mr. Stafford.

"Yes, sir. Of course."

"As you are reading a book, any book, have you found times that the story has made you happy, or sad, or frustrated, or even scared?"

I thought for a moment and knew that answer to be in the affirmative. "Yes. I believe I have felt all those things and more."

Mr. Stafford nodded and asked, "Is it not amazing that written words about make-believe events, about people who do not exist, can cause us *real* emotions? Does that not speak to the power that a story can possess?"

I had not given such direct thought to the point he was making, but I understood completely. I said, "It's such power that makes them the escapes that they are. Without such emotions, I don't think I would have been able to lose myself in the stories, to put aside my actual surroundings, no matter how difficult they were, and be transported to another place."

"Have you," asked Mr. Stafford, "ever read a book that *forced* you to act in a certain way?"

I thought for a moment and then answered, "No, I would not go so far as to say that. I mean, I have been influenced by stories. For example, I gave consideration to, and drew strength from, the example of Ned Land the night that I first came here."

Mr. Stafford smiled. "Not to go too far off of our topic, but I will admit that I have given thought to the bravery you showed in running away and sneaking into my home. I think Ned Land would have been proud of you."

I covered my mouth as I gave a little laugh. It was strange how disarming Mr. Stafford could make a situation – even one that could mean something as utterly important as my future.

"What if I was to tell you," said Mr. Stafford, "that there are books that exist that are so influential, so emotional, that a person can hardly help themselves from acting out the story? Much like the case of the novel that Lord Henry gave to Dorian Gray."

A book that forces you to action? It was a terrifying thought. "As much as I love reading, I think I would want to stay far away from a book like that."

Nodding in agreement, Mr. Stafford said, "And you would be correct to feel that way. You see, I know Oscar Wilde, the creator of the Dorian Gray story."

I should not have interrupted, but I was so surprised and impressed I nearly shouted, "You know the author?"

"Indeed, I do. Mr. Wilde is a very interesting man, and with this book he took it upon himself to give the warning that you found. Although Dorian Gray and Lord Henry, and all the other characters are complete fiction, Mr. Wilde knows that there are books among us that can cause the horrific actions that Dorian Gray experienced."

"You don't mean…" I paused, as it could not be true.

"I mean exactly what you fear," Mr. Stafford answered, filling the silence, and then stopping to allow further implications to sink in. "There are stories that are so influential, written in such a uniquely emotional way that the reader is obliged to act them out. These *Dark Books*, as they have come to be called, are very rare, thankfully, but they exist."

I could not help but look at the numerous volumes surrounding us and felt a chill, as the once great promise of safe adventures gave way to sinister connotations. I turned back to my host and asked, "Why are you telling me all this?"

"I'm telling you this," said Mr. Stafford, "because you have passed the test."

Eleven

BR

Unlike the emotions I expected at passing the test, I didn't feel happy or excited, but instead worried and scared. If what Mr. Stafford was saying was true, then there were terribly alarming books that were dangerous.

I asked, "What does that mean? 'I passed the test.'"

"It means," answered Mr. Stafford, "several things. First, and probably foremost, it means knowledge. You are now aware of something that very few people know about."

"The Dark Books?"

"Correct. Tell me, does their existence frighten you?"

The more I thought about them, the more they scared me. I nodded and said, "Yes, very much so."

"Good. That means you already can see the harmful potential they hold."

"Why have I never heard of them before?" I asked.

"That is an excellent question," said Mr. Stafford. "There are a few reasons for that, which we will get to, but the first reason is that these kinds of books are very rare. To illustrate, look at all the books in this room." He waved his arm in a sweeping gesture.

I looked at all the shelves, at the incredible number of books.

"There are near a thousand volumes in here," continued Mr. Stafford. "They represent a varied cross section of some of the finest authors and stories in the history of the world. Of all of these, not a single one of them is a Dark Book. Which, by the way, is why I referred to them as unimportant books that first night. They are unimportant in that they are safe in comparison to Dark Books."

"Are you saying that these authors were not…what? Talented enough?"

"No, I'm not saying that at all. In fact, some of the authors in this room *have* created Dark Books. What I am saying is that the vast majority of books are safe. With regards to talent and Dark Books, talent is only a part – a small part, actually – of the equation. Have you ever done any writing, Miss Gladwyn?"

I shook my head. "No, just a small amount while learning my letters."

Mr. Stafford smiled and said, "Well, outside of when a person first learns to write, like yourself, or perhaps a letter to a friend, most people have not done much serious writing. Please don't take this as an insult to you, or anyone for that matter; for writing can be considered an art, a release of creativity, like playing music or painting pictures, and only some people find it to be a satisfying way to express themselves. Now, if you are an individual that does choose to write, you will find that the art of putting thoughts into written words can be most difficult. Why, a single paragraph that could be read in mere seconds could take hours, weeks even, to craft. This is the typical experience of authors."

Leaning closer to me, he continued, "However, I have talked to more than one author who has created a Dark Book, and I learned of quite a different experience among them; different from what is typical, but among these Dark Book creators, expressions of extraordinary similarity."

My heart raced with fear. I was still coming to terms with the existence of Dark Books, and now I was about to hear something of their very creation. For the first time, but not the last, I wondered if passing the test was a good thing after all. Although frightened, I couldn't help but ask, "What did they have in common?"

"The unnatural ease of writing. Most authors will tell you that there are times when they are more inspired, or more creative than other times. But for these individuals, as they created their Dark Books, they were in a state that was beyond mere inspiration. They were consumed by their work. Without exception, they were all undergoing extreme emotions and poured their thoughts, their feelings, their very hearts onto the paper. One commented that, although it is often a struggle to find the right words to express the proper feelings, with his Dark Book, the feelings could hardly match the magnitude of his words. If such a thing is possible, it's as if they transferred their terrible pain into the story. It relieved their own burden but made it one that could now be given to others. Interestingly, none of them knew what they had created, the strong power that their words could have.

As the author, they are immune to the influence of their story. It's not until later, when the strange and often terrible actions of others who have read their work come to light, that it becomes known that something is wrong."

I was almost afraid to ask, "What strange and terrible actions?"

Mr. Stafford looked at me for a moment, and then asked, "Are you of stout heart, Miss Gladwyn?"

I knew that the reason he asked that question is because the strange and terrible things must be truly bad and it's not customary for women to be included in rough talk. I nodded and said, "Yes, sir. I believe I am."

With a small smile, Mr. Stafford said, "I think you are too," Then, with a more serious look, "I have to imagine that you are aware of Jack the Ripper. Is that so?"

"Yes, of course," I answered.

"The atrociousness of those murders, the...*mutilations*. A very, *very* twisted mind was at work during that bleak period. Although the murderer was never captured, he was stopped. You see, through much investigation, and danger, we believe that we found where he was living. Although he escaped from our grasp, we found a book in his possession."

"A Dark Book?"

"That's right. And, in the safety of friends, I read some of it."

"What?" I exclaimed. "You read a Dark Book?"

"There, there," Mr. Stafford said calmingly. "I assure you that all precautions were taken, and I was perfectly safe. We had to be sure that it was what we were after. I only read a few chapters before it became clear what it was. I still remember the blackness of the tale; the utter contempt and the absolute hatred for women it spewed. Without a doubt in my mind, it was the reason behind – the motivating force of – Jack the Ripper. With the book no longer in his possession, its influence waned and the killings stopped."

"What happened to the book?"

"We destroyed it; burned it to fine ash."

"Who was the author?" Did I want to know?

"We never found out who wrote it. The book contained no names."

"Could there be other copies?" I asked, as scared as I had ever been in my life.

"It's very unlikely. The book was merely a handwritten journal. I'm certain that that it was never published or disseminated."

I let out a long and unsteady breath. "How do you know? What if there are more?"

"Then we will find them."

"'We'? You work for the police?"

"No, the police have very little interest in books – at least in regard to their investigations. The 'we' is the other reason why these Dark Books are not generally known. The 'we' is the order I belong to: The Book Reapers. Our mission is to find these harmful volumes and remove them from the world."

"The Book Reapers?" I repeated, struggling to take in another piece of unbelievable knowledge.

"We are simply a quiet collection of book lovers from around the world, serving a small, but important, function of finding and removing Dark Books. I know this is a lot to take in, but it is the heart of the test I gave you; knowledge of these books and of this order, and…the opportunity to join us, as my apprentice."

I sat there staring at Mr. Stafford in stunned silence. A dangerous and scary world had just been revealed to me – a difficult thing to comprehend – and now he was asking me to join it. A strong gust of wind shook the windows, but I hardly paid it any attention, as I was thoroughly overwhelmed with uncertainty.

I had many questions, but the one that escaped my lips first was, "Why me?"

With a warm smile, Mr. Stafford said, "To say we met under unusual circumstances would be a gross understatement, would you not agree?"

I nodded and felt that he was being kind in his description of my intrusion into his life.

He continued, "You had the intelligence, strength, and courage to fight against the life that you were destined for. You snuck out late at night, broke into a strange home, and lived there for weeks unnoticed. The legal aspects aside, I find all of it remarkable. There is a strength of spirit in you that is undeniable. However, such actions are not enough. To be a member of The Book Reapers, you must have an appreciation for books and the power that the written word can have. This, Miss Gladwyn, is the main reason why I offered you the test. You have proved that your mind matches your spirit."

Those were some of the kindest words ever spoken to me. Did he mean them? He certainly seemed sincere. The main problem was that *I* did not believe them. I was a worthless orphan that had done one rash thing in my life. I ran away from the orphanage, not because I was brave, but because I was scared.

I argued, "But I'm not strong or brave. I'm entirely ordinary."

In his continued kind voice, Mr. Stafford said, "You underestimate the trials of life. It takes strength and courage to face the daily pressures that this world throws at us and to still come out with a sense of hope. So many individuals resign themselves to unhappiness; but not you. You rose above the relentless pull – the gravity, if you will – of this world."

With a quiet voice, I said, "I am not so sure of myself."

"That is another item in your favor. Do you know what one of the biggest problems we find with those who love to read?"

I shook my head.

"One of the biggest problems," he answered, "is arrogance. One cannot read without learning. Knowledge should make for a better person, a more compassionate demeanor, and a wiser mind. But many miss those benefits and instead start to feel a sense of superiority. They take the wonderful knowledge and twist its purpose to selfish ends. You, my dear, do not suffer from any such delusions of grandeur. Your humility – you may view it as self-doubt – is a strength."

I looked at him with wide eyes, wanting to believe what he was saying. I certainly had not thought of myself in that way.

"Before you answer me about the apprenticeship," said Mr. Stafford, "let me tell you a little about what it entails. After all, you should have full understanding of what you are being offered.

"First, as my apprentice, you will live in my home. The room you have been staying in for the last three days will become yours."

I nearly agreed to be his apprentice right at that moment. Obviously, there was much I still didn't know, but what could possibly make me not want to continue living in that wonderful home? Although every fiber of my being wanted to fall to my knees and shout out 'yes', I held my tongue.

I'm sure Mr. Stafford saw my excitement, for he gave a small pause and a knowing smile before he continued. "I realize that this is all quite sudden, it certainly is for me, but I don't see a lot of options. Returning you to the asylum is out of the question, for I could not bear being remotely responsible for the life they would offer you. There are other solutions that I could think of, but I really do believe that you would be an excellent apprentice. Of course, you would need somewhere to live, so what could by simpler than my home – I have more than enough space."

"How long would it be for?" I asked.

"Apprenticeships generally last several years. After that, we would have to see."

Several years living in that beautiful house? How could I possibly refuse?

Mr. Stafford continued, "If you accept the apprenticeship, your tasks would include several things. First, you will be responsible for reading books – lots of them."

A responsibility? More like a dream!

"Second, you'll be responsible for reading the many newspapers that I have delivered. As you will learn, keeping up with current events is very important. Third, you will accompany me on assignments to search out suspected Dark Books. Eventually, if the time comes when I feel you are qualified, you may be sent on your own assignments."

The idea of assignments, of being in close proximity to a Dark Book, gave me pause. Even though I sat by the warm fire, the very thought of those books made my skin feel cold and clammy. I was truly frightened at their existence.

"Miss Gladwyn, I don't expect you to answer me now. Take a day to consider this and we can talk tomorrow night. This is, I imagine, all quite unexpected."

"Yes,"

"Very well, how about we retire a little early this evening? You have much to think about."

"No, sir. I meant, 'yes' as in I accept the offer of being your apprentice." I did not need more time. No amount of thought would lessen the opportunity that was presented to me. I was very scared of Dark Books, but not more scared than the miserable life I was heading towards outside the orphanage. Maybe I was still picking the perceived lesser of evils, but once the words left my mouth and I thought about life in that amazing home, I felt I picked the greatest of all goods.

"Are you certain?" asked Mr. Stafford with a serious tone, but kindness still in his eyes.

With every ounce of conviction that I possessed, I answered, "I'm completely certain."

With a small chuckle, Mr. Stafford said, "I don't know what power brought you here, Miss Gladwyn; providence, fate, divine direction, or pure coincidence, but I am very grateful that it did."

Before I could respond, the library door opened and in walked all three servants, Helen, Patrick, and Melba. They had smiles on their face and their hands were clasped in front of them in a gesture of joy.

"Congratulations," said Patrick, a touch of enthusiasm leaking through his formality.

"Oh, yes!" said Helen. "I knew you would accept; I just knew it!"

"It will be a welcome change to have someone new around here," commented Melba.

Despite the many thoughts, the strong and undulating emotions, I laughed. Between the warmness of Mr. Stafford and the happiness of the servants, I pushed any nervousness aside and settled on the joy of the moment.

The apprenticeship was not an adoption, but there was no denying a blissful feeling of acceptance unlike anything I had experienced before. Still, it felt unreal. After all, they barely knew me and now I was going to live there? Could there have been a more unlikely outcome to my escape from the asylum?

Twelve

BR

Never in my life had I felt such a sense of prolonged excitement and contentment. Those following weeks were simply amazing.

However, with regards to my apprenticeship, it turned out that, although I accepted the offer, it was not official. The leadership of The Book Reapers were the ones that made the final decision and that would happen at a semi-annual meeting in about six weeks' time. Until then, I was in a sort of preparatory phase.

One morning – in the library, of course – before either of us became engrossed in a book, I asked Mr. Stafford, "How did The Book Reapers start?"

"Ah, a little history lesson. Excellent!" he said excitedly. His enthusiasm and energy when discussing things made him very approachable with questions. He never made me feel like I was badgering him.

"Well," he continued, "we first need to talk about Dark Books for a moment. Now, we have every reason to believe that Dark Books have been created for thousands of years."

"*Thousands?*" I asked, quite surprised.

"That's right. Mankind has been recording their thoughts and experiences for ages. It's certainly possible, almost inevitable, that someone along the way recorded their emotions in such a way as to create a Dark Book – perhaps a Dark Scroll, since codices were not at all common until at least the second century AD. In whatever form it took, however, there were no easy mechanisms for copying text other than by hand. These older writings, Dark or otherwise, generally didn't get a wide circulation and most did not survive the passing of time. Thus, we cannot be sure about Dark writings until closer to the sixteenth century."

"Why then?"

"This is the time period that the printing press became an efficient way to mass produce books. It was after this time that the first published Dark Book was discovered."

"What was it?"

"The details are scarce, but we know it was a very sad book, the cause of several suicides, and was written by William Shakespeare."

"Shakespeare wrote a Dark Book?" I could hardly believe it.

"He did. Now remember, Dark Books are not created maliciously; they are the result of extreme emotions. Shakespeare must have been a man of great emotions to write the masterful plays that he did, so it's not surprising to me that he is the only author, that is known, to have created *two* Dark Books in his lifetime – one of his plays published earlier in his career, one later. Fortunately, a wealthy, and very bright, student had read the first book not long after its release and managed to resist the impulses that were created. That young man's name was Daniel Thompson, and he became the first Book Reaper. Thompson, realizing the surprising source of the powerful emotions he had to overcome, proceeded to gather some of his close associates and together they tested his theory about the book and its power. Before long, they were certain. Realizing the frightening potential of what they discovered, the group worked to remove the book from circulation and eventually succeeded in practically erasing it from history. In fact, outside of what I just told you, nothing is known of that play, not even its title."

"That is incredible!"

"I wonder," Mr. Stafford mused, "how many people have been saved by the intelligence, courage, and actions of that original group. After the first book, they started searching for the possibility of other books with similar influence – within a year, they had found one more. Obviously, books are written all over the world, so the group expanded their membership to include other languages and countries. The expansion continues to this today."

"How many members are there?"

"I don't know the exact number, but it's around five hundred full members, with another fifty, or so, apprentices, like yourself."

"Well, I'm not an official apprentice yet."

"That is true," he smiled, "but I'm confident."

"May I ask another question?"

"Of course,"

"Why are Dark Books not widely known?"

"That," explained Mr. Stafford, "is an interesting question and a continually debated topic among the order. The main factor of keeping these books secret is an event that happened in the mid-1700s. From a remote village, in Iceland, reports were starting to creep out about some strange activity. One of our order was assigned to investigate and found that a Dark Book was the source of the strange acts. He proceeded to inform the worried people of the village that a book was behind the issues and that they should be safe with it removed. However, the villagers took to viewing all books as suspect. With that mindset, whenever a bad thing happened, a book was blamed. It led to the wanton destruction of much literature. Nothing short of a great travesty!"

"That is terrible! So, it's feared that the same reaction could happen again, or on a greater scale if Dark Books were known?"

"Yes, that is the fear. Many argue that it would not be the case and that the world would be safer with the general knowledge of these books. But many are worried that the ramifications would be severe. In the end, the Book Reapers have decided to continue to fight these evil stories and to not be responsible for the public declaration of their existence. If they become known, so be it, but it will not be from our hand."

After a few seconds of thought, I concluded, "How utterly awful. I wish, more than ever, that they did not exist."

Mr. Stafford nodded his agreement and said quietly, "As do I."

Until my appointment became official, my main assignment for those six weeks, practically my only assignment, was to read. Mr. Stafford said that the best way to identify a Dark Book, and the best protection from them, is to be thoroughly familiar with safe books – their cadence; their feel. As you can probably guess, I was beyond thrilled with that assignment. I could not believe that my life was to revolve around one of my greatest joys.

So, I read; page after page, chapter after chapter, book after book. I hold many vivid and happy memories of that time, sitting by the fire with Dantés on my lap and following Alice down the rabbit hole into that strange Wonderland; or reading by lamplight in bed about the relentless intensity of Captain Ahab and his doomed pursuit of the white whale; or sitting near the window as the brilliance of Shakespeare washed over me while a light snow fell outside.

I fell asleep at night wishing I could keep my eyes open to read more. I woke up in the mornings with anticipation of the next page. Reading is such a simple pastime, but it rewards so thoroughly and generously.

Although I spent the majority of my time in books, I did manage to spend some hours outside the house with Mr. Stafford or with his wonderful staff. I will never forget the surprise that Helen and Melba gave me one day – not long after I accepted the apprenticeship – when they invited me along with them to go to town to pick up foodstuffs. At that point, I had not left the house in over three weeks, so the prospect of taking a cart ride to the center of Bromley sounded very appealing.

Patrick hooked the cart to Sally, one of the two horses, and the three of us ladies were off. Being that it was early winter, it was a bit cold, but we sat close to each other on the cart bench and were so distracted by our laughter that we hardly even noticed the weather. Our first stop was at a small bakery – really just the kitchen of a house – owned by a French couple. We purchased several delicious looking pastries, two of which we could not help but share right away between the three of us. I think I could have eaten an entire of box of them, they were so good.

After the bakery, we stopped at a general store where Melba directed the man behind the counter to load the back of our cart with many items – bags of flour, coffee, tea, sugar, salt, and other things that would keep her kitchen stocked for the duration of winter. I found Melba to be highly organized and one that would never be caught unprepared if she could possibly help it.

Next we went to a clothier. I assumed something was being repaired or created for Mr. Stafford, but I soon found out that that was not the purpose of the visit. When we walked inside, Melba went to talk to the clerk while Helen directed my attention to several dresses that were on display. They were all so lovely, especially compared to the two old threadbare garments that I owned. That was when the real reason for the trip to Bromley was revealed: Mr. Stafford had arranged for an entire wardrobe to be made for me. When Helen told me that, I screamed in excitement. I was immediately embarrassed at the uncontrolled sound that I made, but Helen laughed, and when I looked over at Melba and the clerk, they wore amused smiles. I was grateful that there were no other customers at that time.

A kind woman took many measurements and said that all the clothes would be ready in three weeks' time. I know it was selfish of me, but I hated the wait. However, one of the display dresses met my measurements, so they had me put it on right there in the clothier. Behind a partition, I quickly changed out of my old dress and put on the new one. It was a simple light blue dress made of soft cotton. When I stepped into view of everyone, I saw their smiling faces. The clerk led me to a large mirror so that I could see myself and I hardly recognized the girl looking back. Who was that nicely dressed young woman? My brown hair and pale skin were familiar, but the unbridled smile was not. To my knowledge, that was the first piece of new clothing I had ever worn.

Melba asked if my old dress had any sentimental value – it did not – so she suggested that I wear the new one out of the store and the old one could be discarded by the clerk.

As if that was not enough, they also purchased new sleeping garments, robes, slippers, undergarments, stockings, ribbons, and even a new pair of shoes to replace my worn-out ones. For the countless time in only a handful of days, I asked myself, *how could this be happening to me?* I had no reasonable answer for all of the good fortune.

On another occasion, Mr. Stafford and Patrick took me along with them on a hunt. Helen, and especially Melba, protested the very idea, saying that traipsing through the woods is no activity for a lady. However, despite their protests, I decided on going.

The first challenge was what to wear. I would not dare walk through the forest and bushes in my one new dress, so I decided on my remaining one from the orphanage. Patrick provided me with an old jacket of his to help keep me warm. The sleeves went past my hands, but I had no choice as I absolutely needed something to fight against the cold. A green scarf wrapped around my neck and over my head finished off my ensemble. I refused to look at myself in a mirror, but the barely contained laughs of Helen and Melba mixed with the amused smirks of both Patrick and Mr. Stafford told me everything I needed to know about how ridiculous I looked. Well, it was not like I was going to town dressed in that manner.

We left about midmorning, the skies were grey and the air was quite cold. Our breath fogged around us as we made our way down the far side of the hill towards the border of the nearby forest. Mr. Stafford and Patrick both carried rifles.

As we reached the woodland edge, it didn't give a welcoming appearance. Since it was winter, the branches were all bare and the ground was covered in wet, brown leaves. The only real color change in the forest was the grey sky overhead.

Even though there was a small path that we followed, the spindly bushes grabbed at my coat and dress, while low branches swiped at my arms and head. Despite the heavy jacket, I grew colder and colder. My nose was numb, and I tried to warm it by tucking it into my fist.

Whatever the physical hardships were, I was not going to complain. There was no way that I would give Mr. Stafford or Patrick any cause for regret at asking me to join them. My fortitude was tested mightily before long. Our path was largely covered in leaves, so you could not see what was beneath them. One of my steps did not find solid ground, instead, my shoe – my new shoe! – disappeared through the leaves into mud up to my ankle. I pulled it out and could not believe the mess that came up with it. A lot of emotions passed through me in that moment. My misery grew as my foot was now wet and even colder than it had been. I was also sad that my new footwear had been so blemished. Most of all, I felt like I had disrespected Mr. Stafford and the gift he gave me of those shoes.

Maybe I could clean it off. I wiped at the mud and found that it improved matters only a little – and now I had muddy hands. *What have I done?*

"Mr. Stafford," I called out as he and Patrick were continuing on, oblivious to my little problem. "I'm afraid that I stepped into a mud puddle. I think I have ruined my new shoes. I'm so sorry!" I felt like crying but did not.

"I see," said Mr. Stafford, no doubt noticing the sad look on my face. "Well, that is a common occurrence this time of year. Just be glad it was as shallow as it was. I once stepped into a puddle that went up to my knee. Are you alright to carry on?"

Once again, he took a distressing situation and disarmed it. He didn't even seem to care about what I had done to the shoes. Perhaps he didn't realize. I answered, "I'm alright to carry on, but I think I have ruined these fine shoes."

With a wave of his hand, he said, "Don't worry about that. They have simply become your forest shoes. In my opinion, everyone should have a pair of shoes that they can get as dirty as they like. You now have yours. The only thing left is to procure you a new pair of shoes for general use, and I'm sure that can be accomplished tomorrow."

I looked at my mud coated shoe for a moment and then looked up and smiled in relief. I was still cold, and my wet foot was starting to feel a little numb, but I said, "Then I guess I'm ready to continue if you are." I was more determined than ever to see that hunting trip through.

Fifteen miserable sloshy minutes later through the monochromatic landscape, Mr. Stafford gave a signal to stop. We knelt down and he whispered, "Alright, I think this will work." I noticed that his and Patrick's nose and cheeks were very red; at least I was not the only one who was cold.

I looked around our area and didn't see any animals. In front of us was a very gradual downward slope covered with many bushes. While trying to figure out what they saw that I did not, a loud *BANG* went off to my left and I fell to the ground from shock. My ears rang and I was disoriented for a moment. Another *BANG* sounded and I covered my ears from the pain. Then there was another followed by another.

When the blasts stopped, I could only hear ringing. I looked at Mr. Stafford and Patrick, smoke swirling around them, and they were both smiling at each other. What had just happened?

After a second or two, Mr. Stafford looked over at me and his face immediately took on a worried look. He asked – it sounded distant and muffled, but I understood, "Are you alright?"

"It was so loud," I said, no doubt yelling it out.

"I apologize; we should have given you warning. Patrick and I have done this so many times that we already know what the other person is going to do." He held out his hand and helped me off the ground.

"What happened? Did you get something?" I asked, still a little dazed.

"Ah, yes," said Patrick. "Three shots, three birds."

Although I was not completely sure, I said, "I thought there were four shots…"

"The first shot scares the birds into the air," explained Patrick.

I looked around for a moment and then asked, "Where are they?"

Mr. Stafford pointed at the downward slope and said, "Somewhere among all those bushes. One fell just left of center, and the other two were on the right. Patrick, you take the left, while Miss Gladwyn and I take the right."

Patrick nodded.

"Come along, Miss Gladwyn," smiled Mr. Stafford, "let's find these birds and head back. My nose is freezing."

The brush, like everything else in the forest that time of year, was brown. We walked through, pushing little branches aside, and scoured the floor to find the shot birds. Patrick found his first and held it up for us to see. The colors of the bird – a pheasant – were also brown which explained why it was so hard to locate.

After another few minutes, I found one, a little farther to the right than anyone had thought. I gingerly picked up the dead animal, like I had seen Patrick do, and held it up for the others to see. The bird was quite beautiful. I have never been that close to a pheasant and was surprised to see the multiple colors of its feathers. I felt a little sad that we had killed it. Patrick took it from me and placed it into a sack he had brought.

A couple of minutes later I spotted the third one.

"Good show," said Mr. Stafford, an enthusiastic smile on his face. "If it took too much longer, I might have needed to start a fire – I am absolutely freezing. Speaking of the cold, how is your foot?"

"I'm not sure, exactly. I can't feel it."

"Well then, let's not dawdle," he said and started back up the slope towards the way we had come. Patrick and I fell in right behind.

As we walked along the path, Mr. Stafford asked, "Do you know what is better than sitting by a warm fire while drinking a hot beverage?"

"No, sir," I answered.

"Sitting by a warm fire while drinking a hot beverage *after* being outside in the cold," he looked back and smiled. I smiled in return and was momentarily warmed by the thought of sitting in the library by the glowing embers.

When we reached the house, Melba met us at the front door and, when catching sight of me, said, "Good heavens! You are a mess!"

"I'm sorry," I said. "It was a bit more wet and muddy than I had anticipated."

"Hurry up and get changed, and then come warm yourself by the fire. I will have tea waiting." With that, she gave a disapproving glance at Mr. Stafford and Patrick. Neither said anything but had sheepish grins on their faces.

I did as I was asked, and it felt so good to put on dry clothes and stockings. When I entered the library, I was alone, so I took my usual chair next to the fireplace. I hardly remember a nicer feeling than the immense heat that washed over me. A few moments later, Melba walked in and gave me tea. The hot beverage was most welcome and added to my joy. Mr. Stafford was right: sitting by the fire with a warm beverage after being out in the cold was absolute bliss.

Although I was glad for the hunting experience and the following warmth of the library, I declined the next time they offered me a spot with them. I told them that I think I would enjoy the forest better in the summer.

It was during one of those other hunting trips that I got up the nerve to ask a question of Helen. I should mention that, during those weeks, a kind of natural hierarchy happened – Melba was very matronly and looked after me like a mum. Patrick was guarded with his emotions, but I could not help but think of him as a sort of grandfather. Mr. Stafford, well, he was the closest thing I had known to a father. Now, Helen, being the nearest one to my age by a wide margin, was like my older sister and I felt very comfortable talking with her, asking questions that I was embarrassed to ask anyone else, and even sharing some of my feelings. That particular day, while she was helping me make up my bed, I asked, "Was Mr. Stafford ever married?"

I could tell immediately that the question troubled her. A look of hesitancy mixed with a little sadness made me realize that it was a sensitive subject. She struggled inwardly for a couple seconds, clearly trying to decide how to answer me. Finally, she looked up and said, "Alright, listen. We do not bring it up, but Mr. Stafford *was* married. Her name was Emma, but she died only a few years after their wedding. This was all before my time here, but from what I have gathered from Patrick and Melba, it crushed him. Those were dark days of inconsolableness."

Mr. Stafford's comments and actions when I talked of losing my mother made more sense. He well knew the pain of a lost loved one.

Numerous other happy experiences happened over those weeks leading up to The Book Reaper's meeting that I bore you with, but it should be understood that those days were completely and utterly wonderful. I grew very fond of Mr. Stafford and all of his staff. They were so kind and generous and unlike most anything I had experienced prior. To say that I felt safe, that I felt like I was 'home' when I was with them would be accurate, if not a touch presumptuous. As difficult as it was, I allowed myself to push aside my awkwardness and feel like I actually belonged.

Besides the occasion when my new clothes arrived – an event that made me feel like a princess – there was one more significant day, prior to The Book Reaper's meeting, which I want to make known. It was the day that Mr. Stafford took me to London.

Thirteen

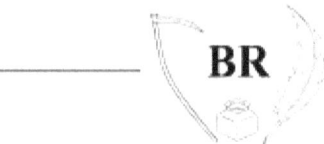

BR

During breakfast, three days prior to the semi-annual Book Reaper meeting, Mr. Stafford announced that he would be going to London for a little business and then a stop at a favorite book shop. He asked if I would like to join him. Although I was in the middle of *The Strange Case of Dr. Jekyll and Mr. Hyde* by Robert Louis Stevenson, and enjoying the bizarre tale immensely, I could not turn down the opportunity. It had been years since I had seen the city or the water of the Thames – the very river flowed past my one-time home.

It was late January at that point, and a particularly bitter cold spell was upon us. I was dressed in a heavy wool dress and a dark wool cloak. Patrick pulled Mr. Stafford's carriage near the front door, and even in the small amount of time out of doors, between the house and vehicle, the morning wind seemed to pass right through me and gave me a deep chill. The enclosed cabin was a welcome change, although still a bit cold at first. Mr. Stafford got in and sat across from me, his back to the front of the carriage. I felt bad for Patrick as he was outside on the driver's bench.

I was so preoccupied by the weather and trying to warm up that it was not until we were near the main road that I remembered the last time I had been in a proper carriage: the day I was taken to the orphanage. I can recall the confusion and utter sadness at strangers taking me away from the only home I knew and bringing me to a foreign place. Those memories lessened, a little, my excitement of the morning. Still, it didn't sting as much as it could have. The past several weeks had, to some extent, taken away part of my overall bitterness about my youth. By any standard, my childhood was difficult, but I had since found an excellent way of life.

"So," said Mr. Stafford, interrupting my thoughts as I stared out the window, "I have an unofficial assignment for you, my unofficial apprentice."

An assignment? I was quite certain that I was not ready for an assignment – unofficial or otherwise. I looked at him, immediately nervous, and asked in a small wavering voice, "A Dark Book?"

"Yes," he answered, "sort of. As you know, our main destination today is a book shop. This is a treasured place of mine that I have been to numerous times. I'm familiar with their inventory and am quite confident that there are no Dark Books for sale – outside of any new arrivals since my last visit. But I want you to think of the store as a brand new, completely unexplored shop, and to consider how you might locate a Dark Book amongst its inventory."

Being that the assignment was more about strategy and approach than actually finding a Dark Book, I felt a bit of relief. Still, it made me realize more acutely that the apprenticeship was focused around those terrifying things. The thought that those stories could *make* someone do such horrid things was terribly frightening – especially for me. Until recently, I had no real control over my life – with bitter results. But now I had taken some control – with unimaginably good results – and the thought of losing that new freedom to a Dark Book was overwhelming. Just thinking about it made my breath quicken and caused my chest to feel heavy.

"Are you alright, Miss Gladwyn?" asked Mr. Stafford. "You appear very concerned."

"It's just..." could I explain myself? I didn't want to disappoint him. "It's just that I'm deeply concerned about these Dark Books. I don't want to give control of my life to someone else's story. I don't want to do bad things."

"That is exactly how you should feel," said Mr. Stafford warmly. "Respecting the influence that these books can have is one of the most crucial defenses against them. You are correct to not underestimate their ability to harm."

Once again, the exact words that I needed to hear were given. Not only was Mr. Stafford not disappointed in my feelings, he was encouraging them. Although still frightened of those books, I felt a little better about my involvement.

"In addition," he continued, "as my apprentice, I will be here to protect you. You will face these fears alone."

"Thank you, Mr. Stafford," I said, looking him in the eyes and appreciating the kindness and friendship he had shown towards me. I'm not sure I ever had a protector – certainly not one like him.

"Now," he said, "give attention to your assignment. We will reach the bank where I have a little business to attend to, then we will have lunch, and then the book shop. Take this time and give thought as to how you might discover a Dark Book among a room full of books."

I smiled and nodded. The carriage rattled towards London, the bumpy winter roads becoming a little better the closer we got to the city, and the two of us in the enclosed cabin kept it, if not warm, than at least comfortable. Although I enjoyed the passing views, I tried to focus on my assignment. How would I locate a particular book out of many? The idea of a needle in a haystack came to mind. I tried to imagine Mr. Stafford's library as a book shop and wondered how I could possibly find a Dark Book if one existed. I figured that I could rule out the books I had already read, which help me realize the importance of reading as many books as possible – the very thing that Mr. Stafford had had me doing for the past several weeks. Beyond that, I could not think of what to do other than start to read the unknown books and hope I could realize a bad one before it influenced me. Not exactly a reassuring approach, but how else could I possibly tell? The enormity of the assignment, not just of mine, but of the Book Reapers in general, became much clearer.

As we neared the city and the buildings grew in size and frequency, I had a harder time paying attention to my own thoughts. As an orphan, I never left Bromley, so I became enthralled with the enormity of the metropolis before us. In addition, the last time I was that close to London was the day I was taken from my home. I feared the strong emotions it all could create, but found myself more interested in the city, my assignment, and my newfound life to become too melancholy. That, however, caused me to worry that I was losing the love I had for my mother. It was not true, but it still felt a bit callous to not break down at the memory of my onetime life; my onetime family.

In the city, the overcast skies were made darker by the smoke from countless chimneys. The streets became more congested with other carriages, and more and more people could be seen walking along the pavement – well bundled and moving with purpose. There was a different feel there, a type of energy that one didn't have in the quiet countryside.

Mr. Stafford, after giving me my assignment, busied himself with various papers from his leather bag. I wondered what business he was attending to, for in the past several weeks, he never talked about his employment and I felt too hesitant to ask.

We crossed the Thames over London Bridge and the onetime familiar river took all my attention. I could not help but remember the days playing along its shore, watching the boats moving to and fro, of my mother holding my hands above my head as I ventured into the water. Being near the city didn't invoke strong emotions, but the river did. Although I expected some of them, it was still surprising how sharp they were. I think Mr. Stafford noticed my misty eyes, but kindly drew no attention to them.

Once past the river, we made our way to Threadneedle Street, to the Bank of England. As we approached the massive building, with the majestic Royal Exchange just across the street from it, the traffic grew even thicker. It was amazing to me that so many vehicles and people could move through a single area.

Patrick pulled the carriage up close to the side of the road and Mr. Stafford put his papers back into his bag. Looking at me, he said, "My business should not take long. Will you be alright here by yourself?"

With all that activity around to look at, and the assignment I should have been thinking about, I had plenty to occupy myself. "Yes, sir," I said with a smile.

"Very well. I shall be back as soon as I can." Mr. Stafford left the cabin, letting in a little cold air with his departure, and then walked towards the large bank doors.

After a moment, I thought about Patrick sitting outside. I yelled towards the ceiling, in the direction where he was stationed, and said, "Patrick! Can you hear me?"

"Yes, miss," I heard in reply – a little muffled.

"It must be terribly cold. Would you like to join me in the cabin and warm up a bit?"

"That is kind of you, Miss Gladwyn, but I will decline. I have become accustomed to the temperature and think it would only be more difficult to ruin that by warming up."

"Very well," I said. "Whatever you think is best. Just know that you are welcome if you change your mind."

I don't know how long Mr. Stafford was in the bank, but it was less than an hour. The time went by quite quickly as I was enthralled by all the people around. I would see a carriage go by and wonder where they were going. I would watch a group of ladies walking down the pavement and make up entire stories of where they came from and what they had planned for the rest of the day. I was so distracted by all those activities, that I gave a little jump when Mr. Stafford opened the carriage door at his return.

He took his seat and said, "Now the boring part of the day is over. I hope I didn't make you wait too long."

"Oh no, sir. I was quite occupied by the busyness of the street."

Mr. Stafford looked out the window and said, "I sometimes wonder if we will get to a day where there will be more people than this city can handle. It occasionally feels like that already."

"I enjoy seeing all these people," I said. "I will admit, though, that I do not believe I would like to live here. Long amounts of time, in close proximity, with so many around makes me feel anxious. Even in the orphanage, with all the other girls, I could feel that way."

"I think we can agree," commented Mr. Stafford, "that life in the country is better suited for us." I smiled and he asked, "Are you hungry?"

I had not thought of food as I was so distracted, but now that he mentioned it…, "Yes, sir."

"Me too," he said and then rapped his knuckles on the wall of the cabin. That signal caused Patrick to pull out into traffic – evidently already knowing our destination.

We stayed on the north side of the Thames and wound our way through several streets – getting less congested as we moved away from the bank – until we came to the restaurant. As soon as we stopped, Mr. Stafford got out of the cabin and held the door for me. The air was still cold but my heavy clothes were up to the challenge – at least for a little while.

As we approached the entrance, I looked in the windows and saw ladies and gentlemen sitting at elegant tables with finely dressed waiters moving about. *We were going to have lunch here?* I'm not sure what I expected, but certainly not that. Once again, I could not help the feeling of being out of place in my surroundings. When we went inside, and I could better see the environment, my inadequacies felt even more magnified.

"Ah, Mr. Stafford," said a smiling man near the entrance. He approached, looked at me, and then said, "A table for two?"

"Yes, please, Harold."

"Very good. Follow me, please."

We followed Harold across the busy dining room to a table at the far wall. The smell of the food was wonderful and helped me to think of something besides my uncomfortableness. Harold held my chair for me, and Mr. Stafford took the seat opposite of mine.

After the specials of the day were announced – I'm not sure I understood a single thing he said – Mr. Stafford looked at me and asked, "Would you mind if I order for the both of us?"

He probably realized my looks of confusion, so I was more than happy at his suggestion. "Yes, thank you."

He gave the order to Harold, evidently some kind of fish, and the server hurried off to fulfill the request.

"I find," said Mr. Stafford, "that a meal of fish is as much, if not more so, about the seasoning or the sauce as the fish itself. I'm happy to say that the chef here has some of the most inventive combinations that I have ever had. I think you will enjoy it."

Before I could comment, a finely dressed older man, with a thick white mustache, approached the table. When Mr. Stafford caught sight of him, he stood and said excitedly, "James! How nice it is to see you!"

"Hello, Thomas! It has been too long." The men shook hands and seemed genuinely pleased to be seeing each other. James looked at me and said to Mr. Stafford, "And who do we have here?"

"This," said Mr. Stafford, "is Miss Naomi Gladwyn. She is…" he paused, and his face took on a look of uncertainty.

What exactly was I? I was not his child or relative. I was not a servant. I was an unofficial apprentice to a quiet organization – not exactly something that is announced. I was very much an oddity in the world.

After a second or two of silence, I blurted out, "I'm an orphan." It may not have been well mannered, but it was the truth. If I was going to be out of place, at least I would be out of place for the actual reason.

"An orphan?" asked James in a surprised tone. "That is very interesting." Then, looking at Mr. Stafford, he asked, "Philanthropy?"

"No, I would not say that, exactly. Miss Gladwyn is an enterprising young woman who will create her own destiny, provided she receives a little help."

"Well, then," said James, "I expect to hear nice things about you, Miss Gladwyn. Now, I will take my leave. It was very pleasant to meet you, Miss. It was good to see you again, Thomas."

"Nice to meet you, sir," I said in reply.

"James," said Mr. Stafford, "we must get together at some point in the near future. I will have Patrick arrange something."

"Excellent! Enjoy your lunch."

When James turned to walk away, Mr. Stafford sat back down. I felt a little embarrassed at my outburst and, although I looked at him, my head was down. He looked back with an inquisitive appearance. *Was he upset with me?*

I could not take the silence, so I finally asked, "What am I?"

"That," said Mr. Stafford, "is a very interesting question. It was not until I was introducing you that I realized that our situation is quite unique. We must think of something, as I expect you to be with me on many trips. Obviously, to call you my apprentice will not work – too many unanswerable questions."

I nodded. "I could be a servant of yours. A maid, like Helen."

"That would also raise questions, as it's not at all normal for a maid to be traveling and having lunch with their employer. No, it needs to be something different."

"Would it be too shameful to call me a relative?"

"Shameful? Absolutely not. However, that is something, for your sake and mine, that I will not do lightly. Also, having just announced yourself an orphan, that opportunity has already passed us by."

"Oh. I'm sorry."

"Not at all. But I do hope that you view yourself, not just as an orphan, but as an intelligent, independent, and brave young woman. Although we cannot do anything about our past, we have every ability to make our own future. You do realize that, don't you?"

"I think so. But what could my future be? If I was to become a member of the Book Reapers, is that my occupation? Will they pay me a wage? What happens if you were to…if you were to die? Would I be on my own, with no future, once more?" I was pouring out all of my concerns to him. Concerns that I had had all along but could only comprehend and articulate at that moment.

"I understand your questions, Miss Gladwyn, and they are valid. I apologize that I did not realize them sooner, but now that you have stated them, they are as clear as crystal. I should have addressed them long before now."

"I realize that I'm not your responsibility, Mr. Stafford. You do not owe me a future. Or anything for that matter."

A sad look crossed his face, as if I had hurt his feelings. He said, "You are very selfless, Miss Gladwyn, and I think I may have an answer to all of our questions." After taking in a breath and releasing it, he said, "I want you to be my daughter. Yes, you are, or were an orphan, but I can adopt you. It answers anyone's questions as to what you are, and it provides for your future, no matter what happens to me."

Adoption? The conversation had gone down a very different path than I had expected. We had only known each other for a little over a month, could I attach myself to him in such a permanent way? "I don't want to be adopted in order to just answer some questions."

"I would never propose that," he answered seriously. "My family has many businesses, and I could hire you as a worker for one of them, but I want more for you than that. I don't need another worker, but I do need for you to be cared for."

I looked at him and didn't know what to say. His continued kindness didn't make sense. He was, however, sincere – he was always sincere when he said nice things – but I simply could not understand why.

He continued, "You have lived in my home for some six weeks – not counting the three hidden ones – and during that time I have found you to be an absolute joy. Your enthusiasm and appreciation for all the things around you is wonderful. I find myself looking forward to sitting in the library, reading, and discussing books with you. Our meals together are perfectly enjoyable. And the staff...well, they adore you. Although I had not planned for this at all today, trust that this proposal is completely genuine and has everything to do with who you are and how I feel about you."

Tears welled in my eyes. *He really did want me in his life.* There was nothing that would have made me think otherwise, but to hear it said so plainly was as wonderful as it was shocking. Did I really think so little of myself? Did I really think that no one truly wanted my presence – that I was, at best, only tolerated? The truth was, I did think so little of myself. Despite the many compliments over the past weeks, I realized that I had not really believed any of them. I was not intelligent, brave, a joy to be around, or any of the other nice things said about me. I was just Naomi the orphan; a girl who deserved nothing more than what any other worthless orphan was given.

"Why?" I finally managed to say through my emotions. I knew that the question meant exposing that I did not believe all the reasons that were provided already, but I had to ask. To accept love with so little confidence can be a frightening prospect. I was scared to believe.

"Naomi," Mr. Stafford said kindly, addressing me with my first name for the first time. "I fear that a difficult life has made you very guarded. You have emotional scars that are invisible to the eye, but, for those that know you, are as visible as a lighthouse on a clear night. You have been hurt deeply by the loss of friends, and I don't blame you for questioning me; for protecting yourself from something that could cause a new hurt if it was taken away. But I beg that you accept this offer. Not just for your sake – for you will be taken care of for the remainder of your life – but for my sake as well." His eyes began to water. "Give me the privilege of your presence. Allow me to care for you as if you were my daughter – for I think I have already started to view you that way."

We looked at each other in silence, tears in our eyes. Although I knew the answer I wanted to give, I could not form the words. Every molecule of my being wanted to say *yes*, and yet I could not help but feel that I should not accept, that I could not agree and put this gentle and kind man through the tediousness of me. Has ever a better offer been given and one so hesitant to take it?

Interrupting everything was Harold, the server. "Lunch is served," he announced as he placed a plate of food in front of me and then another in front of Mr. Stafford. "Is there anything else you require?"

Without taking his eyes away from mine, Mr. Stafford answered, "Thank you. That'll be all."

"Very well," said the server and strode away.

After a few more moments of silence, Mr. Stafford said, "You do not need to decide right now. Take as much time as you need. After all, this is not a small decision."

Whether I was only given another second, or given a hundred years, the answer would not be any more obvious than it already was. Pushing down my self-doubt and having the rare thought that I may actually have positive attributes, I said, "Yes. Yes, I will be your daughter if you would have me."

With the food all but forgotten, Mr. Stafford quickly stood from the table and I got up and flew into his arms. I hugged him tightly and he hugged back with equal force. The two of us jumping up and embracing in the middle of a restaurant must have been shocking to the other patrons, perhaps even scandalous, but I didn't care, and, to the great credit of Mr. Stafford, he did not seem to care either.

When we released, Mr. Stafford, eyes red, looked at me and said, "Follow me."

I walked behind him as he approached his friend's table. "James," said Mr. Stafford, "I would like to *properly* introduce you to Miss Naomi Gladwyn, my daughter."

Fourteen

BR

Everything felt different. Mr. Stafford and I were back in the carriage, riding towards the bookshop, London was still crowded, the weather was still cold, and yet, it was a new world. I was part of a family again. It was not the kind of family that one typically dreamt about in an 'if only' game, with a mother, father, and brothers and sisters, but it was nonetheless special. I had Mr. Stafford, as kind and generous a man as I could ever want to be around. In addition, Patrick, Melba, and Helen had become so very dear to me.

"I have," said Mr. Stafford, "a silly question. Would you mind if I address you as Naomi in our private conversations?"

"I would not mind at all," I answered. "However, I could not possibly call you by *your* first name. Please don't be cross if I continue to refer to you as Mr. Stafford, or Sir."

With a warm smile, he said, "I think that is appropriate. After all, our age difference still requires certain acts of decorum. I am quite old enough to be your grandfather."

"Yes, sir."

After a small shake of his head, he said, "I'm going to be very straightforward with you. As I mentioned, I had no intention of having a conversation about adoption today. Yes, I had considered the notion over the past couple of weeks, but I figured it would be a bridge to cross after the passing of more time, in, perhaps, a more expected way. A small part of me – a *very* small part of me – worries that we are being hasty. I tell you this not to cause you worry, or to insult you, but to share with you a bit of me and my thoughts. However, despite the fact that there are these small, nagging doubts, I only have to think of all the joy you have brought to my home to thoroughly defeat them."

Was there any end to his kind words? "I will admit, too, to some nervousness on my part. Although, I have far less to lose than you do."

"Oh, I disagree," he said to my surprise. "You have every bit as much to lose as anyone else. This…adoption – I still have to get used to the idea – is largely about trust. I trust you to continue to be a good person, to grow and learn, and be someone I am proud of. In turn, you trust me to support you, to be there when needed, and to give guidance. If I was to fail you, there would be great pain; the same pain that I would feel if you failed me. I think that what we both have at stake in this arrangement is quite equal."

I understood what he was telling me, and he was right. Trust in another person can be a wonderful thing but can also be the source of our greatest pain. I trusted in my mum, but, through no fault of her own, she broke my trust when she died. The same with Daphne. The darkest periods of my life were due to the trust I had in another and the eventual loss of that trust. It was sobering to think that I could cause that kind of pain in someone else; possibly to Mr. Stafford. The fear of it all was chilling.

"I don't want to disappoint you," I said quietly.

"Nor I, you," he responded. "But please don't take my thoughts as doubts. If I was truly worried at all, you would know. Now, on to different matters. We are nearing the bookshop and we have not talked about what you have come up with in regard to your assignment."

Assignment? I had forgotten all about it – I think, dear reader, that you can understand how that might have happened. I needed to remind myself what it even was and then what conclusions I had reached. After a few seconds of contemplation, I said, "I'm not sure I have much of an approach other than to start reading the books that I'm not familiar with and then hope to discover any Dark Books before I get too influenced by them."

"Very good! Now, you hit on a very important point when you said, 'books I'm not familiar with.' As I mentioned, and as you no doubt are beginning to understand, familiarity with many stories is a key to our literary endeavor. Your approach is sound, although difficult when you think of all the books that a shop or library might hold."

"Yes, sir. It is daunting."

"Well, I'm sorry to say that I will make it a little more daunting still. You see, getting a Dark Book published is not an easy thing to do. In most cases, books go through multiple readers and editors before it makes it to the press. That process will generally root out such a story before it makes it very far – for even people who are not aware of Dark Books know, when they read such a story, that it could not possibly be mass produced."

"So, how do they get published?"

"There are a few ways. First, as was the case with Shakespeare, an author can be so well regarded that the usual processes are skipped prior to publishing. On other occasions, a person may be powerful enough, or wealthy enough, to have something published regardless of what it is – generally circumventing any editing process. The third way is the most insidious. It's not common, but some people have gotten ahold of a Dark Book, realized the power of what they had, and then incorporate it into someone else's story."

"How so?"

"I have only heard of this once, but a Book Reaper had come across a copy of Oliver Twist that had a Dark Book imbedded into the beginning of the story. Now, a publisher thinks that they are just printing a copy of a very well-known book, when in reality, they were publishing something quite different."

"That is awful! Who would do such a thing?"

"Unfortunately, there are some that enjoy the chaos that a Dark Book can cause. A warped mind as ever was."

The idea of purposely promoting such pain was repulsive.

"So, tell me," said Mr. Stafford, "how would you detect such a book?"

"Well, once again I would need to be familiar with the story. I guess I would have to look through the first chapter or so and make sure that it matches up to my memory."

"Excellent! I would also recommend that you look at the middle of the book and the last chapters in order to rule out any hiding spot that may be different than the book's opening. We take no chances."

"Yes, sir." I replied, happy to be having guidance. The carriage soon stopped, and we exited outside of 'Miller and Sons Book Shop.' It took up the first floor of a multistory building on the corner of two streets. The glare on the windows made it impossible to see inside, but once through the door, we were in a somewhat dark, but soothing, space filled with shelves and tables full of books. The smell was of leather, paper, and wood – a not unpleasant combination.

Walking straight from the door, Mr. Stafford headed towards a small desk with a spectacled man sitting behind it. When near, the man, with a neatly trimmed white mustached and mostly grey hair, looked up from the paper he was reading and said, "Ah, Mr. Stafford! Welcome back!"

"Hello, Michael Paul, it's good to see you. How have you been?"

Michael Paul – evidently the shop owner – rose from his chair with a pleasant smile and shook Mr. Stafford's hand while answering, "I have been very well. Business is good in the wintertime as people spend less time out of doors and more time reading."

"And how is Ann?"

"Oh, she is around here somewhere. She is well. And who is this young lady?" asked Michael Paul, turning his attention to me.

"This," said Mr. Stafford, "is Miss Naomi Gladwyn and, you will probably be surprised to hear, she is soon to by my adopted daughter. This is Mr. Michael Paul Miller."

"Good heavens!" the shop owner exclaimed while his eyes became large with excitement. "Ann!" he called out. "Ann! Come here!"

I was a little taken aback by the sudden excitement.

From somewhere among the shelves we could hear movement and then a woman's voice called out, "What is all the fuss?" When Ann came into view – a happy looking woman whose hair seemed whiter than her age – she immediately smiled and approached Mr. Stafford. The two shopkeepers certainly seemed very pleased to have him around. "Mr. Stafford, how nice it is to see you."

Before he could respond, Michael Paul said excitedly, "He is adopting this young woman as his daughter!"

Ann, turning her now astonished face towards me, took a moment to come to terms with the news, and then opened her arms wide and hugged me. While still in the embrace, she exclaimed, "My dear, I'm so happy for you both!"

I hugged her back and was quite humbled by the enthusiasm and joy that those two showed at the announcement.

"What is your name?" Ann asked me after releasing the hug.

"Naomi Gladwyn, ma'am."

"Such a pretty name. I'm very pleased to meet you.

"I'm pleased to meet you, too."

"Well," said Mr. Stafford, "as far as introductions go, I think this was quite extraordinary. Michael Paul and Ann," he said to me, "run this fine bookshop – the best in London! – and are some of the kindest people you will ever meet."

"We *are* very wonderful," said Ann, nodding with a huge smile, who then gave into laughing at her mock arrogance.

Michael Paul, with knitted eyebrows said, "You know, it might have been a mistake bringing her here."

I grew concerned at the comment and wondered what he meant.

"After meeting us," he continued, "she might realize that she could have done better than you, Mr. Stafford."

It was not until everyone started laughing that I realized that it was all in jest. I know I had just met them, but I liked Michael Paul and Ann immensely.

When the laughter subsided, Ann said, "Well, I need to get back to work. We had a man in here a bit ago who sneezed so violently that his body knocked over a shelf. I will be reorganizing for the next hour." Before she turned to leave, Ann smiled warmly and said, "Again, I am so happy for you both."

As she walked away, Mr. Stafford looked at me and said, "So, are you ready to start your assignment?"

I looked around the shop at all the books and felt intimidated. Still, if that is what he wanted me to do, then I would do it. "Yes, sir. I'm ready."

"Very well, go ahead and get started – but just with the books you know. I will busy myself with Michael Paul and any new arrivals he may have."

I nodded and walked over to one of the shelves. As I approached the first set of books, I felt a great uneasiness. I know that Mr. Stafford had said that he already had examined those books, but what if he missed one? What if among all those volumes there was a Dark Book? The safety of Mr. Stafford's library did not extend to the shop. I passed my hand along the spines, feeling the textures while I read the titles. I crossed many unknown works and feared what they had to offer.

Before too long, I found *Twenty Thousand Leagues Under the Sea*. I smiled at it, almost as if it was a friend. Taking it off the shelf, I opened it to an early chapter to verify that someone had not replaced the story with something that didn't belong. I was happy to find that the *Abraham Lincoln* was chasing the *Nautilus* across the ocean. I then turned to the middle of the book and read a little about Captain Nemo and the three companions wearing underwater suits and looking at oysters. At the end of the book, I read the escape attempt and the maelstrom. Everything was familiar and right where it should have been. That particular book was safe. I put it back on the shelf with a small sigh of relief.

I continued the exercise around the bookshop, every so often taking a familiar book from the shelves and reading various parts to verify its contents. For the better part of an hour I went from shelf to shelf and book to book. It must have taken Mr. Stafford weeks to verify every book in the store!

When I completed my assignment – no hidden Dark Books – I went back to Mr. Stafford, who was talking with Michael Paul, and told him my findings.

"Excellent!" he said. "A bit tedious, would you not say?"

"A little," I confessed.

"It is, but it helps to remember why it's being done. Still, it's tiring all the same. Well, now that you are finished, I have something for you."

"What is it?" I asked – an admittedly silly question in a store full of books.

From the desk that Michael Paul was sitting behind, Mr. Stafford took up a thick brown book and handed it to me. I read the title out loud, "The Odyssey of Homer, by Bryant."

"Are you familiar with it?" asked Mr. Stafford.

I shook my head while continuing to examine the fine book.

"It's a story that is around, what would you say Michael Paul, three thousand years old?"

"That sounds about right."

I looked up in disbelief and exclaimed, "Three *thousand* years?"

"Amazing, isn't it? Homer, the author, was a Greek poet and he wrote this wonderful tale of adventure. I'm a little ashamed that it's not already in my library. But this version, translated from Greek by William Cullen Bryant, will make for an excellent addition. I do hope you enjoy it."

"Thank you, Mr. Stafford. Thank you!"

We said our goodbyes to Michael Paul and Ann – who again said how happy they were for us – and started the ride back to Bromley. The winter sun was getting low on the horizon as Patrick took us across the Thames and southwards toward home.

As we neared the house, I felt some nervous excitement – for none of the staff, including Patrick, knew of the events of the day. I was mostly sure of a positive response, but a small part of me could not help wondering if any would be upset. *Why do I torment myself with so much doubt?*

The carriage was brought close to the front door and we entered the foyer. Melba and Helen greeted us there and before either of them could turn back to their duties, Mr. Stafford asked them to stay for a moment as he had something to announce. A couple of minutes later, Patrick, nose and cheeks red from the cold, joined us.

"I have some significant news," started Mr. Stafford. "Miss Gladwyn and I have come to an agreement. She is going to be my adoptive daughter."

There was second of silence as everyone processed the announcement; then celebration. Helen, Melba, and even Patrick, all hugged me as they kept on with sayings of how wonderful it was and how happy it made them.

As we talked excitedly in the foyer, I knew that I would never forget the joy of that moment. How very special it is to feel wanted!

Fifteen

BR

Reliving the day of The Book Reaper's meeting causes me pause. I woke that chilly morning to great nervousness of my apprenticeship proposal, but had I known exactly how the day would progress, I should have been terrified.

I chose a green dress – one of my new ones, of course – and felt that it looked equal parts beautiful and respectful. It had occurred to me that I would be representing Mr. Stafford and I did not want to embarrass him in any way.

We ate breakfast together, as usual, although the conversation was more about if I was nervous than our usual subject of the books we were reading. I admitted that I was. While we were eating, a sudden question came to my mind and I asked Mr. Stafford, "Are *you* nervous?"

I was a bit concerned about the answer, as I felt it expressed his direct thoughts on me. He said, "Truth be told, yes, I'm a little nervous." He must have noticed my downcast expression at his response, for he continued quickly, "I'm not nervous about *you*. Not at all. Your love of books, your attitude, your spirit, amongst many other qualities makes you a perfect candidate."

"Then why are you nervous?"

"I'm nervous about The Council."

"What is 'The Council'?"

"They are the leaders of The Book Reapers; well respected, longtime members. My fear is that they will not see past your background – which is, admittedly, a bit unusual for an apprentice – and miss the clear qualifications that you have."

His words stung a little. I know that Mr. Stafford didn't think poorly of me whatsoever, but to have my childhood – which I had no control over

– held against me didn't feel entirely fair – even though I did it all the time. "What is a *usual* background of an apprentice?"

"Most are students. Avid learners that have loved and read books since their youth. They are different than you in that they have read many more books and their sponsors usually have known them for a much greater amount of time – generally for years."

"Perhaps you should wait then," I suggested. "Not try to make me an apprentice until some future date."

"I had thought about that. But, in the end, there is no real reason you should not be made my apprentice. Besides, The Council has been encouraging me to take on an apprentice for many years. Now that I have finally chosen one, I think it would be poor form to deny my selection."

"What happens if I am not selected?"

"Then we will try again at a subsequent meeting. This I know for a fact: if you continue to be willing, at some point you *will* be my apprentice."

"So, what happens if I *am* selected?"

"In many ways, not much will change at all. You will continue to expand your knowledge of books by reading. We will continue to visit bookshops, including new ones eventually, in an effort to locate any Dark Books. I will involve you even more in the reading of newspapers, as that is where we look to see the potential results of a Dark Book. The only significant change will be that your counter will start."

"My counter? What is that?"

"Once a person becomes an apprentice their 'counter of books read' begins. Although you have read many dozens of books, your counter will be at zero – like every other apprentice. This counter will be a number that is with you throughout your involvement with society. My number is currently at seven thousand and eight. At each meeting, every member submits their new number. It's a way for The Council to see that the love and appreciation of books is continuing among us all. It's also a very influential part of determining promotions."

"What kinds of promotions?"

"Well, you, for example, will start as an Apprentice, Third Class. After you read one hundred and fifty books, you qualify for Apprentice, Second Class. Three hundred books and you will qualify for Apprentice, First Class – which is the highest level for an apprentice."

"What other titles are there?"

"Each title has the three classes, like Apprentice, and they go like this: after one is fully initiated into the order, they become a Bibliomessor – which is Latin for Book Reaper – this would take a person's counter up to a thousand books before they could be considered for the next promotion. Then we have Bibliophiles – Book Lovers – this would take a person to twenty-five hundred books. Bibliophagists – Book Devourers – this level goes to four thousand. Next is Deditus Libris – Dedicated to Books – which goes to six thousand, if I remember right. Bibliognosts – A Knower of Books – which would go to ten thousand. And our highest title is a Bibliodominus – A Master of Books – which someone could qualify for once their counter eclipses the ten thousand mark."

"Ten thousand books?" I asked, as if I had misheard.

"That is correct. It's a daunting number, to be sure. In fact, if you were to read one book every day, it would take you more than twenty-seven years to reach that level. There are only a few Bibliodominus' among us."

"So, if I continue to read a lot, then I would move up the ranks because of my counter?"

"Not exactly. Although the counter is important, it only allows a person to *qualify* for a promotion. You see, a person's qualities and traits cannot be ignored. As I mentioned to you before, some become arrogant with the reading of many books and that is not an individual that belongs in any sort of leadership role."

"If you are over seven thousand books, where does that put you?"

"I'm currently a Bibliognost, Third Class, but I expect to be promoted to Second Class at today's meeting. However, these higher titles make little difference. I view it as not much more than a way to congratulate a long-standing member."

Although I could not remember all the titles, it was clear that Mr. Stafford was a member of note among The Book Reapers. Despite my already great affection and respect for him, I could not help but see Mr. Stafford in a little different light. Among other things, I felt a sense of pride. Yes, I was proud of him, but also humbled by how that influential man had taken me in. Of course, my self-doubt also made an appearance, and I could not help but wonder how an unfortunate orphan like me could possibly be acceptable to such a person as him.

With breakfast finished, I put on my heavy cloak and prepared to leave. We were fortunate as The Book Reaper meeting was held in nearby London. We had only a carriage ride ahead of us, but many members had to travel great distances to reach it.

While Mr. Stafford put on a heavy wool coat over his black suit, Melba and Helen stood in the foyer with us and looked positively anxious. It didn't help my nerves any, but their many wishes of good fortune, assurances of apprenticeship, and fond farewells were very appreciated. Patrick waited on the driver's bench of the carriage and simply gave a small nod and a smile to me as we went outside and loaded into the vehicle's cabin.

With a knock on the side wall, the carriage started moving and we were on our way. Once again, as we approached the city, the traffic became thick with people and carriages. We crossed the Thames and were very close to Big Ben. It was about the tallest structure I had ever seen, and I always found it to be completely glorious.

At some point, I noticed Mr. Stafford wearing a gold ring that I had not seen him wear before. When I enquired about it, he took it off, handed it to me and said, "That serves as identification among the order. It is our crest."

The top of the ring was large and round, about the size of a coat button, and had engravings on it. Although backwards, I could make out 'BR' in the middle of the ring, with what looked like an inkwell beneath the letters, and then on one side, a feather quill, and on the other side, a scythe. Although difficult to make out, there were two numbers, also backwards, inside the inkwell; a five and a three.

"Why are the letters and numbers backwards?"

"Because the ring can be used as a seal. When pressed into melted wax, it gives an imprint with the orientation of the letters as one would expect."

It seemed obvious after he told me. "What does 'five' 'three' mean?" I asked.

"That is my rank. I'm in the fifth group and I'm class three."

I nodded in understanding and, after a few more moments of examination, I handed it back to Mr. Stafford. The already mysterious group took on even more intrigue.

We continued north for a ways and the buildings became slightly less prevalent. We eventually stopped in front of a beautiful stone structure, three stories tall and very wide. Carriages were entering the circle drive while others, after releasing their passengers, were exiting. Patrick pulled us into the queue and within a few minutes, we were getting out of the cabin and walking into the building.

Inside, we found ourselves in a large and elaborately decorated lobby. The floors were a checkered combination of rich brown marble mixed with white. There were several crystal chandeliers that gave off a brilliant glow. The walls were covered with fine floral wallpaper and there were paintings of different people hanging throughout the room.

Many nicely dressed men and women were in the space, conversing and moving about. "There are so many people here," I commented.

"The winter meeting," said Mr. Stafford, "is always an unknown when it comes to attendance – what with difficult travel conditions – but it looks like we will have an excellent number this year."

He led me towards the left and to a large doorway. Beyond was another room, even bigger than the lobby. That space must take have taken up that entire half of the building. It was no smaller than fifty yards long, and at least as wide. The ceiling was very high and also had multiple chandeliers to provide light. The space itself was taken up mostly by rows and rows of cushioned seats. Occupying the far wall was a large wooden structure – like one might see in a court room.

Mr. Stafford guided me to a seat towards the back, and said, "Unfortunately, I have some responsibilities that I must take care of right now and I have to leave you here alone. But don't worry, this is a friendly group. When it comes time to present you as my apprentice, I will be right next to you. Alright?"

I definitely didn't want to be alone, but what could I say? I gave a smile that I didn't feel and nodded.

Mr. Stafford smiled back and repeated, "Don't worry. Everything is going to be fine." He then turned and walked out of the room.

Sitting there alone, I looked around at the many different people. *Were there any others being presented as apprentices today?* I saw a few younger members and thought that they could qualify. While looking around the room, I was careful to not make any eye contact with anyone as I did not wish to have a conversation with a stranger. With all of my nervousness, along with being in an unfamiliar place, I simply didn't want the added anxiety of meeting new people.

Fortunately, no one approached too close. When men around the room and in the lobby-area started announcing that the meeting was about to begin, I felt a little relief that the time for potentially meeting strangers was over – at least for the moment. Unfortunately, as the room began to fill, there was no sign of Mr. Stafford. I saved the aisle seat, for when, or if, he showed up. On the other side of me was a middle-aged man who gave me a polite nod when he sat.

When everyone was arranged, a man at the front of the room stood before the group and said, "Welcome, ladies and gentlemen. We ask that you rise in respect for our council members. With that, everyone stood – I followed suit – and in walked seven people from a side entrance. The wooden structure, opposite the lobby, was a kind of raised desk, quite large, and the council members sat behind it.

To my surprise, the second person from the left was Mr. Stafford! *He was on The Council?*

The man in the middle, who had snow white hair and a thick goatee, announced that all may be seated. Then, after taking a look around the room, he said, "This gathering of The Book Reapers may now begin."

Sixteen

BR

Everyone gave respectful attention as the lead councilman extended greetings to all and gave special recognition to those who traveled long distances to be there. Although I was still a little shocked at seeing Mr. Stafford among the leadership, I did pick out destinations such as the United States, Asia, South America, India, and Australia.

Next, he introduced himself and the other six with him. "As most of you know, I am James Turner, head of The Council. My fellow councilmen and councilwomen are as follows: to my right are Mr. William Baker, Mr. George Cooper, and Mr. Abbot Green. To my left are Mrs. Sophia Dockery, Mr. Thomas Stafford, and Mr. Bernard Murray." Each individual nodded their head at their name being called.

Mr. Stafford caught my eye and smiled. I shook my head slowly and smiled back. If it was his plan to surprise me, then he was completely successful.

"The first item on our agenda," said the lead councilman, "and the entire purpose for our order is the discovery of Dark Books. Since our last meeting, three have been found."

According to Mr. Stafford, the meetings happened every six months, which meant that the rate of discovery was far higher than I thought, certainly far higher than I had hoped. I wanted the Dark Books to be exceedingly rare.

"First," continued the councilman, "is Miss Vargas."

A middle-aged woman in the audience stood. I was too far in the back to see her face very well, but she had brown skin and black hair. "Thank you, Mr. Turner," the standing woman said in accented English. "I became aware of disturbing reports out of Valparaiso, Chile. At first, I thought it was a standard affair of a person with lesser means assaulting one with great means – for there is always animosity between classes. But when these attacks were duplicated, it became necessary to investigate. I, along with two others of our order, Mr. Silva, and Mr. Carrasco, traveled to Valparaiso and talked to those who were aware of the assaults. We soon became convinced that a Dark Book was behind the issues. Eventually, we tracked down a journal that held hatred for the upper-class. We, of course, took it, and then waited to see if the problems continued. They did not."

"Very good, Miss Vargas," said the lead councilman. "And where is the book now?"

"Destroyed, sir."

"Excellent work! Were you able to find the author?

"Yes, sir. A family man, who just had his home taken away from him, wrote his thoughts and feeling down in the journal. He had no idea that his work affected people in such a way. There were no copies."

"Thank you, Miss Vargas, you may be seated. Next we have Harold Rumsfeld."

A man, in his late twenties I would guess, stood from the group and said, "Thank you, Mr. Turner. I was on holiday in Sunderland, England, and was visiting a small curio shop. Naturally, I looked at any books that they had available and was stunned to see a copy of *An Elaborate Goodbye* – a known published Dark Book."

At the title, a few whispers could be heard from around the room.

"How many copies did they have?" asked the lead councilman.

"Just the one, sir."

"Did you destroy it?"

"No, sir. I gave it to Mr. Stafford."

Everyone turned to look at Mr. Stafford, who stood up and said, "I received the book from Mr. Rumsfeld and have destroyed it."

The lead councilman looked at Mr. Stafford for a moment, and then turned his attention back to Mr. Rumsfeld and said, "A bit out of the ordinary, but not wrong. I would recommend, Mr. Rumsfeld, that in the future you destroy such books quickly and not pass them along."

"Yes, sir."

I wondered why he brought it to Mr. Stafford. Perhaps Mr. Rumsfeld was not entirely sure how to handle the discovery and wanted guidance from a council member?

"Our third find," continued Mr. Turner, "is by Mr. Steinhauser."

Another man, tall and broad shouldered, stood up and said in a German accent, "Thank you, Mr. Turner. I became aware of some alarming and rather strange occurrences in the outskirts of Hamburg. Animals were being butchered in the night. Obviously, I figured that a wild animal was in the area, as did most of the locals, but then, one night while on watch for the predator, some farmers caught a man attacking their livestock. He appeared crazed and was, sadly, shot dead. However, the attacks on the animals continued. Perhaps one person can go mad and could act in that odd manner, but I found it hard to believe that it would happen to multiple people without influence."

Listening to the account made me feel sick. A Dark Book had caused someone to go out at night and viciously attack livestock. It was appalling and terrifying. Those books create monsters!

Mr. Steinhauser continued, "I, along with my apprentice, investigated the issue and eventually came across a handwritten book. I read a small portion and was thoroughly disgusted and convinced that it was what caused the horrific episodes. I destroyed it on the spot. Since that time, no more attacks have been reported."

"Were you able to locate the author?" asked Mr. Turner.

"No, sir. Despite our best efforts, no one knew where the journal came from. However, we felt confident that there were no other copies of it."

"Excellent work, Mr. Steinhauser. That book sounded particularly disturbing."

Mr. Steinhauser nodded and sat down.

The next part of the presentation gave attention to the advancements of various members. For the next hour or so, they announced many names and then the rank that the person had been promoted to. I was pleased to see several women announced during that time period.

Of course, I paid most attention when the lead councilman announced Mr. Stafford. "Because of your excellent service to this order and for your continued appreciation of the written word, shown by your counter reaching over seven thousand, you are hereby promoted to Bibliognost, Second Class."

There was enthusiastic applause at the statement. Of the others that received promotions, none were anywhere near the counter of Mr. Stafford. That, and I had to believe his general likability, made his announcement seem particularly well received among the gathered group.

After a few more announcements, the lead councilman said, "Let us now take thirty minutes for an intermission before we continue the meeting. We are all adjourned."

People started to stand up and conversations immediately began around the room. I looked at Mr. Stafford and saw him head out of the side doorway. I hoped he was coming to see me as I was once more alone and, again, a bit overwhelmed in the crowd of people.

Thankfully, Mr. Stafford entered the room from the main entrance and came right over to me. With a playful smile, he asked, "So, what do you think?"

"Why did you not tell me you were on The Council?" I demanded.

"I'm sorry," he said. "However, although it's an important position that I take seriously, it's not an important part of who I am. Besides, I wanted to see the look on your face when you saw me up there. Let me say that you did not disappoint."

Even though I wanted to be indignant, I could not stay angry at him. My scowl turned into a smile and then into a little laugh.

Mr. Stafford shared my laugh and then asked, "What are your thoughts so far?"

"If I understand the timelines correctly, then three Dark Books have been found in the last six months."

Mr. Stafford nodded and said, "That is correct."

"To be perfectly honest, it alarmed me. Not just the stories that went along with the findings – particularly the one in Hamburg – but that they are more common than I had expected. I would have thought that one every year would have been a lot."

"There was a time when one a year *would* have been a lot. But with easier access to writing materials, and the commonness of modern printing presses, more people are turning to recording their thoughts and ideas, which means more possibility for Dark Books."

"Promise me that you will be there when I come across my first one."

"I promise. Now, come along, we can get some tea."

For the duration of the intermission, I stayed right next to Mr. Stafford's side. He talked with a few people and kindly introduced me as Miss Naomi Gladwyn. He left off the part about being his adoptive daughter – I was not sure what to make of that.

When an announcement was made that the meeting would be restarting, Mr. Stafford turned to me, "I have to go again. This next part is the presentation of apprentices."

With a bit of concern, I said, "You told me that you would be by my side."

"Don't worry, I will be," he then turned and walked off.

I made my way back to my chair and watched as the leadership council took their seats on the raised platform. I looked at Mr. Stafford and found him looking back at me. He gave a small smile, but I was certain that I saw nervousness on his face as well.

"It is time," said the lead councilman, "for the Presentation of Apprentices. First on the agenda is Mr. Jonathan Hudson. Mr. Hudson, please step forward with your apprentice and tell us about him."

A middle-aged man in the crowd stood up and next to him stood a younger man, probably about my age, and they walked to the area in front of the council members. Mr. Hudson said, "I present to The Council, Edward Hudson. As you know, Edward is my son and is currently a student at Cambridge University. He has shown a superb appreciation for books, and I believe that, with my continued guidance, he will make an excellent Book Reaper."

"Young Mr. Hudson," said the lead councilman, "we have received information on your background prior to this meeting and everything is in order. Do you have any reservations at joining this order?"

"I do not, sir," he answered in a loud but obviously nervous voice.

"Very well. Are there any questions among The Council?" The lead looked to his right and left, but no one made any indication. "All in favor?"

Each on The Council gave an 'aye' to indicate their approval.

When completed, Mr. Turner announced, "Mr. Hudson, you have our approval to take Edward as your apprentice."

"Thank you, sir," the two men responded before retaking their seats among the audience. A polite applause followed the announcement.

My first thought was that it was not so bad. In fact, it was far easier than anything I had anticipated. Although I was still nervous, it was not as severe as it had been.

"Next," announced the lead, "we have Mr. Thomas Stafford. Mr. Stafford, please step forward with your apprentice and tell us about her."

Mr. Stafford stood up and signaled that I should approach. I walked down the center aisle of the seating – aware of many people watching me – and met Mr. Stafford in front of the platform. I looked at the remaining council members and felt very small and exposed. Every eye in the room was upon us and I did not like that feeling at all.

"I present to The Council," said Mr. Stafford in a loud voice, "Naomi Gladwyn. Miss Gladwyn is in the process of becoming my adopted daughter." The Council did not react to that – no doubt they had my background information already, but many in the audience made varying sounds of surprise. After a moment's pause, Mr. Stafford continued, "Miss Gladwyn has a special love of books, a healthy fear of the potential of Dark Books, and the qualities of intelligence and bravery that are required to be a Book Reaper. I endorse her with all my being."

Although nervous, I felt a warm tingling at the kind words – mainly because I knew that he believed them. More than ever I didn't want to disappoint him.

"Young Miss Gladwyn," said the lead councilman, "we have received information on your background prior to this meeting and it is quite…shall we say…unique. It states that you had almost no access to books until quite recently, is that correct?"

"Yes, sir," I responded. "My library was limited to three books until only a few months ago."

I felt the stares of The Council beating down on me, examining my person and my spirit.

Mr. Turner asked, "Do you have any reservations at joining this order?"

I thought for a moment and then answered, "I am frightened of Dark Books. The thought of being out of control because of someone else's writing scares me deeply. However, I do not want others to have to experience that danger and I will use my fear as motivation to help these unsuspecting ones."

"Very well. Are there any questions among The Council?" The lead looked to his right and left, but, unlike with the previous apprentice, a man on his right indicated that he wanted to ask something.

Mr. Turner nodded and the man addressed me, asking, "How many books would you say you have read, Miss Gladwyn?"

"I'm not exactly sure, sir. I have not kept track. I think a fair guess would be around fifty."

A few nervous looks were given among The Council and whispers could be heard in the crowd behind me.

"Are there any other questions?" asked the lead.

Another of the council members indicated a question and asked me, "Is it true that your uncle was one of the men that went missing on the *Mary Celeste*?"

More murmurs danced across the crowd. I'm not sure why my uncle mattered to the group, but I nodded and said, "Yes, sir. It's true."

Again, I stood there feeling more exposed than at any time prior in my life.

Mr. Turner asked once more if there were any more questions, and that time there were none. After a moment's pause, he said, "All in favor?"

"Aye,"

"Nay,"

"Nay,"

"Aye,"

"Nay,"

"Aye,"

It was a tie! The audience whispered and talked excitedly while The Council took on a contemplative look. I glanced at Mr. Stafford – he had not voted – and he gave a minute shake of his head. I'm sure he was addressing my conclusion that since I was to be his apprentice, he did not get to vote.

Amidst all the sounds and confusion at the situation, Mr. Stafford said loudly, "May I approach The Council?"

Everyone quieted down and Mr. Turner said, "You may."

"Wait here," Mr. Stafford whispered to me and then walked to the very edge of the platform.

I tried to make out what was being said, but the volume of their voices was quite low. Obviously, they were talking about me and what they should do. At least once during the private conversation, each member looked in my direction.

After a couple excruciating minutes, Mr. Stafford walked back to my side. I glanced at him, but he just stared at The Council, jaw tightly clenched.

"We have come to an agreement on how to address this deadlock," said the lead to the gathered members. "We have concluded to conduct the Hargreaves Test." Gasps and murmurs fluttered through the crowd. I didn't know what the test was, but it had the clear attention of everyone that did.

I whispered nervously to Mr. Stafford, "What is the Hargreaves Test?"

"You are going to have to read a Dark Book."

Seventeen

BR

Sounds continued all around me, but I hardly heard them. *There must have been a mistake!* They could not possibly want me to read a Dark Book! I looked up at Mr. Stafford's face and saw him looking back at me with hurt in his eyes. "What do they mean?" I asked, starting to feel panicked. "I don't understand!"

"I'm sorry, Naomi. It's the only way."

"Why?" I pleaded.

Before Mr. Stafford could answer me, the lead councilman said, "Everyone, please remain calm. I know this is unusual, but we feel that it's the best course under these unique circumstances. Mr. Stafford?"

"Yes, sir?"

"We have two more apprentice presentations. If you would like to prepare Miss Gladwyn during this time, I suggest that we carry on without you."

"Thank you, Mr. Turner. I think that would be best." Turning to me, he said, "Follow me."

I followed Mr. Stafford out of the room, through the side door that the council members had used. We were now in a small sitting room, with plush chairs, several lamps on side tables, and a few shelves with books. Under different circumstances, I would have found it cozy, but at that moment, I was in a state of shock. I was being told that I had to read the one thing that this group was dedicated to stop.

"Naomi,"

I didn't want to do it.

"Naomi,"

I was so scared.

"Naomi,"

What have I done?

"Naomi,"

I finally looked at Mr. Stafford and realized that he had been trying to get my attention. "Naomi, I'm sorry. I know how you feel about Dark Books, but I would not have suggested this if I didn't think you could handle it."

"*You* suggested it?" How could he do that to me?

"I did. All decisions must be unanimous. A tie is as good as a refusal. I needed a way to prove to them that you are exceptional."

"But I'm not exceptional. I'm just a worthless orphan who broke into your house, stole your food, and has somehow made you feel sorry for me." I started to cry. Clearly, I did not understand the kindness that had been shown to me; I didn't actually believe that I was cared for other than by a sense of pity. I certainly didn't think myself exceptional! I put my hands over my face as the warm tears flooded my cheeks.

Mr. Stafford put his arms around me and pulled me into his chest. "There, there," he said soothingly. "I know you are scared. I know that this is a heavy burden to put on you. But I need you to know that you are not a worthless orphan and that the care and concern that I have for you is not because of feeling sorry for you, nor from pity, but because you have completely won me over with who you are. However, I think I have misjudged the depth of your pain. For that, I am truly sorry."

I took a small step back from his embrace and wiped at my eyes. As always, his words were kind and sincere. Why was it so difficult to believe that someone could actually like me? I looked at Mr. Stafford's face and saw what I always saw: warmth and empathy.

"We will call this off," he said. "You don't have to do this. Perhaps at the next meeting, or the one after that. You don't need to do this now."

I was surprised at the conflicting emotions that warred in me at those most wanted words. There was a sense of relief, a light in a dark place, but there was also a sense of anger. I was becoming angry with myself for not trusting in Mr. Stafford and for possibly letting him down. I wanted to tell him that I would like to leave – part of me wanted to run and never look back for the shame I would feel at failing that most excellent man. But a growing part of me felt like I would do anything to make him proud.

"I will do it." The words were out of my mouth before I could hardly consider them. I could hardly believe that it was me who uttered them.

"Are you absolutely sure?" he asked me.

"I am," I answered, not feeling absolutely sure at all.

Mr. Stafford shook his head, as if in disbelief, and said, "I know you struggle with these kinds of thoughts, but I hope someday that you will see how remarkable you are."

I gave a little smile and threw my arms around him in a strong embrace. "Thank you, Mr. Stafford. I...I love you."

"I love you too, Naomi."

The door to the room opened and the council members walked in. Mr. Turner asked, "Is everything alright?"

"Yes, sir," I answered in as firm and convincing a voice as I could muster – I'm fairly sure that it was neither.

"Mr. Stafford?"

"She is ready," he answered simply.

Mr. Turner let out a long breath, as if he did not entirely agree with the events that were about to happen. Finally, he said, "Mr. Cooper, please take Miss Gladwyn to the room. Mr. Green and Mr. Baker, please collect the book."

A man, Mr. Cooper, approached me and said, "Please come with me."

I followed him out of the room and was comforted to have Mr. Stafford walk at my side. We walked down a long hallway that opened back into the main lobby. Many of the members were in that space conversing, but all quieted down and looked at us as we made our way across the area to a hallway on the far side. It was amazing that, as scared as I was, I still managed to feel even *more* uncomfortable at all the attention.

Now in the far hallway, we passed several rooms and finally came to a closed door near the very end of the corridor.

"What now?" I asked Mr. Stafford.

"The Bibliotaphs will bring the Dark Book and..."

"Wait, what is a Bibliotaph?"

"Sorry. A Bibliotaph is one who conceals books under lock and key. The order keeps one Dark Book and it is the responsibility of the Bibliotaphs to protect it. That is what Mr. Baker and Mr. Green are. When they arrive, we will put you in this room and provide you with the book. We will then lock you in until you are done reading."

As I considered what I was being told, I stopped caring about Bibliotaphs, or even about being locked in the room, I cared about one thing. I pleaded, "What if it makes me a monster? I don't want to hurt anyone!"

"Don't worry. I will be here, along with the entire council, to make sure nothing bad happens to you or anyone else."

I trusted him. Somehow, I would be alright. Nothing felt right or good, but I knew that Mr. Stafford would never let harm come to me. Those thoughts gave me a slight warmth of feeling that departed quickly when I saw the two men approaching with a small chest being carried between them. The Dark Book was inside.

When they were near, Mr. Cooper pulled out a key and unlocked the door. I followed him inside, half expecting a room of horror, but found a small space with no furniture except for a comfortable looking chair, a desk with a drawer, and a lamp. Mr. Cooper entered first and lit the lamp.

I stood to the side as the two Bibliotaphs placed the chest on the desk. Each one produced a key and unlocked a separate heavy lock that kept the container secured. They opened the lid and took out a rather plain looking burgundy book. Although it appeared innocent, it seemed like the most evil thing I have ever laid my eyes on. After placing the book on the desk, they silently carried the chest out of the room.

At that point, Mr. Turner entered and said, "Everything is now in place. Miss Gladwyn, the test is simple. You will read the entirety of that book. At the conclusion of your reading, we will determine if you have passed the test. You may have a minute with Mr. Stafford before we begin."

I nodded in understanding and he left the room with Mr. Cooper. I looked at Mr. Stafford but didn't know what to say. I was afraid, but I wanted to make him proud. He stepped closer and said, "Remember, the feelings of the book are not your feelings. It will not be easy, but you can overcome them. I believe in you."

I still didn't know what to say. How could I express my emotions in the waning seconds that were left? So, I closed my eyes and took a deep breath. When I opened them, I saw the warmth of Mr. Stafford's smile that had not failed me yet.

"It is time," announced Mr. Turner solemnly from the doorway.

I nodded at him and then gave a small smile to Mr. Stafford. He looked at me for a second, his eyes full of kindness, and then turned and left the room. I watched as Mr. Turner closed the door and then flinched as I heard the lock engaged.

With nothing left to do, I sat in the cushioned chair in front of the desk and looked at the Dark Book before me. The cover was worn leather and had no title. I reached to slide it closer but hesitated before touching it. My hands hovered over its surface as if the mere act of physical contact could infect me with malevolence. I knew that was not the case, for it was the words that were dangerous. I finally dragged it closer, fear growing stronger, and opened the cover. I was surprised to find that it was not a published book, but a handwritten journal.

With cold shaking hands, I turned to the first page, looking at the looping script – half expecting to see it written in blood as opposed to the black ink that was actually used – and wondered what motivated the author to write that particular story. My pulse raced as I considered the few, but thoroughly disturbing, outcomes I had learned about for those who had read Dark Books.

I closed my eyes again and took another deep breath. I needed to start reading, I needed to get through the book and prove that Mr. Stafford's faith in me was not misplaced. I was not entirely sure how I felt about myself, but I was certain of my feelings for him.

With thoughts of making Mr. Stafford proud, I began.

For obvious reasons, dear reader, I will be guarded in what I tell you about the book, but I hope to express the thoughts and feelings that it generated if not the story's details. I cannot forget the opening lines or the initial confusion I felt at them – for they were not of any particular violence or evil as I had feared:

Am I destined to fail? It would be a relief to think that my shortcomings were part of a bigger plan that I had no say in. But no, I do not believe in fate or in being destined to a certain outcome. I am completely and utterly culpable for my mistakes and for my downfall.

As I continued reading, I found a story about a man, a commendable person, who wanted to improve the world around him. He saw, very clearly, the troubles that men and women suffer through, and the needless situations that cause such hardships.

Were it not for the greed; greed for money, for power, for prestige, life could find a sublime balance.

To my great surprise, as I finished the first chapter, I found myself empathizing with the main character. I was actually interested in starting the next chapter – something that made me wonder if it actually was a Dark Book after all – and interested in what triumphs and misfortunes awaited the protagonist. At that point, it did not seem like anything more than an interesting story.

After the second chapter, I was becoming thoroughly engrossed. I related to the characters, deeply felt the misery and unfairness around them, and, so too, grew in my desire to want to help. At that point, my main feeling was a sense of justice.

As I continued reading, the world around me became smaller and smaller. The Book Reapers, the meeting, my apprenticeship, even Mr. Stafford, became almost nonexistent. My focus, my life, were in the pages of the story. I read how that good man tried to improve the conditions he saw, tried to lighten the load of a twisted society. However, his attempts failed. Over and over again, he met defeat. Regardless of what he tried, nothing changed.

At some point I became aware of the tears rolling down my cheeks at the pain I felt for that good man. His great desire, a desperation of sorts, to help was completely thwarted in every way. The problems were vast and had such a foothold on society that they were insurmountable. What could one man possibly do?

My enemies overpower me. Even my allies turn to betrayal. Of what worth is a conscience if it is to be ignored? What purpose is justice other than a reprimand of the good? The momentum of badness is a force beyond reckoning; a force that crushes and shatters any who oppose.

The great sadness I felt for the man soon turned even deeper and darker. For the latter half of the book delved into his complete despair at his lack of ability to create change. Page after page he wrote about the meaninglessness of existence, the shortcomings of every person, the utterly bleak view of one's own worth.

I envy the never were. My very breathing mocks me. I hate every breath. Why must this worthless man continue to exist? Could not the earth itself swallow me up and deliver me to the peacefulness of hell?

At some point, the emotions garnered by the book transitioned from the good man and became about my own worthlessness. I felt the inability to improve anything I saw around me – especially myself. My tears increased, now motivated by personal pain in addition to my empathy.

Looking back, I can write with some objectivity, but at the time of reading, I was all consumed by despair. I hated life. I hated myself. I saw only inadequacies, failure, and pain. My anger grew and I found myself hating my father, hating the *Mary Celeste*, even hating my mother and Daphne for dying. It was as if every piece of light in my life now added to the darkness that they had once fought against.

When I read the last words of the story – *No more. I cannot continue.* – I was beyond any concept of time. Although I found out later that the book took about three hours to read, there was no answer that would have surprised me. Time mattered for nothing in the state I was in. I cried. I sobbed. I was beyond any emotional control. Severe sadness oppressed me to the point that I thought I would shrivel and die – *and be content to do so.*

Although the story was over, I found a piece of paper attached to the last page. It was written in different handwriting and it read:

There is help in the back of the desk drawer.

I didn't know why it was there or what it meant. Did it refer to the desk I was sitting at or some random desk once owned by the author? In the state I was in, I didn't care much, but I still looked at the desk and found that it had a single drawer. Was there help inside? I wanted to know, not for the help, but to laugh at the very idea of something overcoming, helping against, those powerful emotions.

I slid opened the drawer and saw nothing at first. The note said the back of the drawer, so I kept pulling – it was quite deep – and then something started to come into view. It took a moment to realize what it was and how it could help.

Resting in the back was a gun.

To my great surprise, it was the terrible help I desired at that moment. The next thing I remember, the gun was in my hand – I don't recall picking it up. It was heavy and cold.

No more.

My hand started to shake as I raised it towards my head.

I cannot continue.

The barrel felt cold as it touched the skin on my temple.

No more. I cannot continue.

I felt the trigger; felt the resistance it gave to my finger as I applied pressure.

The feelings of the book are not your feelings. Somewhere in the back of my mind, I heard Mr. Stafford's words. I gasped, struggling with emotions of misery and despair, but mixed with the tiny inkling of a larger issue.

You can overcome them. It felt impossible, and yet, the thought of Mr. Stafford, with his warm smile and his generous kindness, kept my finger still. The blackness of my mind warred with pinpoints of light. I felt completely out of control. I pressed the barrel harder against my head to try and keep it from shaking. What should I do?

I believe in you.

"Why?" I screamed out through my tears and pain. "Why? I'm nothing!"

Still, his encouraging words echoed through my mind keeping the darkness at bay. My hand shook even more. The gun pressed harder against my head. I felt like I was going crazy – completely broken.

Finally, I screamed with all my might, trying to release the emotional pressure, and threw the gun across the room. I then swept my arm across the desk, sending the book to the floor – nearly upsetting the lamp – covered my head with my arms upon its surface, and sobbed violently.

Eighteen

BR

The fringe of my pretty green dress, along with my nice shoes, were getting muddy and wet as I walked along the banks of the Thames. It was dark out; it felt late although I was not sure of the actual time. The squishing of my steps and the sound of the rivers flow were relaxing, but soon were overshadowed by the startling sounds of screaming and wailing.

I quickened my pace, frightened, wondering where the cries were coming from and why. Ahead of me, up the embankment, was a long, beaten up, old wood building with candlelight emanating from its windows and gaps in its walls. Another wail pierced the night and I was certain it came from the dilapidated structure. I turned to go up the rise, towards the building, but slipped in the mud. I raised myself upright and saw dirt down the front of the dress. Before I could even feel bad, more cries sounded out and I again turned my attention to moving forward. I started walking up the hill and found that it was far steeper than it had originally appeared. I grew tired but continued onward. Step after difficult step slowly brought me closer.

When I was finally near the old building, I heard not one wail but several. Whatever was happening was not isolated to a single person. I cautiously approached the closest window and peered inside. In the dim light of the room, I could see multiple people, some lying in beds, others on the floor writhing in agony and crying out for help. For a moment, I stood there, frozen, unable to move or even articulate a word for my shock and fright. When I could finally break my fixation, I moved away from the window, my limbs reacting slowly, feeling like lead, and I looked for a door. I wanted to enter the building; I knew that I could help if I could just get inside.

As I moved along the wall of the old structure, I came across many more windows – I peeked in as I moved past and saw the same scene as the in the first one – but I could not find an entrance. The pitiful screams continued, growing in intensity and number. My heart pounded in my chest as more time went by without being able to help.

I made it all the way to the corner of the building without finding any doors. I turned the corner and went down the side wall. Again, no way in. I reached the next corner and turned down the front of the building and felt confident on finding an entrance there. As I hurried along, however, I only found more windows. My frustration spiked as my desperation grew. Not knowing what to do, I ran to a window and started to yell, "Let me in! Please! Let me in!" But no one paid me any attention.

Another horrific scream pierced the night – that one from behind me – and I looked away from the old building towards the new terrifying sound. Across the street were several large stone buildings and soon I could hear the same kinds of wails and cries coming from them. I started to cross the road when the sounds of the entire city – everyone screaming in agony – fell upon me with a crushing weight. Everyone was sick. Everyone was dying. And I could not get to them. I could not comfort them. I could do nothing.

I fell to my knees and covered my ears as inconsolable sobbing wracked my body. The sounds grew louder, more pitiful, and I thought they would tear me apart. As they reached a point where my sanity was nearly ripped from my body, I awoke in my bed.

The complete darkness of my room and the quietness of the house shocked me in comparison to my nightmare. My ears buzzed from silence. An instant later, I was crying. The feelings of terror, of utter helplessness, loneliness, and failure lingered into my waking world; chasing me from my dreams and capturing my fragile spirit. I had no defense.

I buried my face in my pillow as I sobbed desperately. Somewhere, deep inside of my mind, I knew that the feelings were because of the Dark Book, but that knowledge did little to provide solace. In the middle of such an emotional attack, rational thought holds little sway. I cursed myself in the darkness and prayed for any relief.

My prayer was answered as I eventually cried myself into dreamless unconsciousness. Not that anyone is aware of the moment of falling asleep, but I was completely surprised to find myself waking up to the morning light, and the sound of a tap at my door.

I felt exhausted, as if I had not slept at all. It took an immense amount of effort for me to simply turn my head towards the door and the sound. I tried to call out but found my throat dry and unable to utter a noise. My dream still weighed on my spirit. The tap came again, and I swallowed to try and moisten my vocal cords. It only helped marginally, and I croaked out, "Yes?"

"Naomi," came the familiar voice of Mr. Stafford. "I was just checking up on you. How are you doing this morning?"

In my state of exhaustion, any question would be difficult to answer, and that one was particularly troublesome. How was I? There were many answers I could have given: miserable, exhausted, devastated, profoundly sad, but I settled on a generic, "I'm not feeling very well."

"I understand," was the response through the door. Did he? Could he? Had he ever read an entire Dark Book? Mr. Stafford continued, "Naomi, I'm going to do something this morning that is very rare for me. I'm going to insist that you join me for breakfast."

I was not hungry. In fact, my stomach felt a bit sore and agitated. Beyond my lack of appetite, I didn't want to move. Anything more than lying in my bed all day sounded perfectly abhorrent. I had hardly any energy and even less ambition. I asked, "Mr. Stafford, could I skip breakfast? Just for today?"

There was a pause before he answered. When he did, it was with a very kind voice, "Naomi, I know you must truly feel awful. The ordeal of a Dark Book is significant, to say the least. But we have things we must talk about. As difficult as it may sound, I have to insist that you join me. Will you do that for me, please?"

Mr. Stafford was never demanding. His insistence was very much out of character and surprised me some – a surprise that helped me to think a little about something other than my misery. Despite my hatred at the thought of getting up, I could not deny him. "Alright," I answered wearily. "I will join you shortly."

"Very good. Thank you. I will be in the dining room."

His footsteps disappeared down the hallway and I lay motionless for another minute. I stared absently at the ceiling and wished for some excuse, anything, to stay in bed. None came and I managed to force myself to move. My limbs felt heavy and would only obey slowly. My mind felt weak and practically useless, like a kettle with just enough water to whistle, but not enough for tea.

Thoughts of the events after the test clouded my mind. At some point, after throwing the gun and collapsing on the desk, I remember Mr. Stafford kneeling next to me, while I repeated, "I'm sorry. I'm so sorry."

"There, there," he had responded in a soft voice. "There is nothing to be sorry for. *I* am sorry that I put you through that."

I remember hiding my face in my hands and exclaiming sorrowfully, "I didn't want to disappoint you."

"Disappoint me? My dear, precious, Naomi, you have not disappointed me."

I looked at him, wondering how he could possibly say such a thing. He looked back, smiled and said, "You have passed the test!"

The rest of the night's events I could only recall in hazy memories - more like wicked flashes of lighting. I remember being ushered from the building to Mr. Stafford's carriage. I vaguely recall the numbness I felt during the ride home. Then I was in bed. A whole night's activity remembered in three cloudy thoughts.

Going a little deeper into yesterday memories caused me to start rubbing my temple where I had the gun pressed against it. Somewhere along the way home, it was mentioned to me that the gun would not fire; that it was the culmination of the test – if you pulled the trigger, you failed. No physical harm would be caused. But are there not things that could be harmed that are worse than physical?

I took my hand away from my head and closed my eyes. I tried to push down the memories, if only for a moment's peace. After opening my eyes again, I focused on getting dressed. My wardrobe – full of beautiful clothes and usually a source of great excitement for me – completely failed to alter my mood. I pulled out the first dress that my hand came across and I smiled grimly when I saw that it was quite dark. It seemed fitting.

Once dressed, I made my way down the stairs to the dining room, giving no attention to anything – even the chandelier – or anyone. It was a state of uncaring numbness to the world around me. I had read of people being put into trances and wondered if this was what it was like.

When I entered the dining room, Mr. Stafford stood up until I took my seat across from him. With my hands in my lap, I sat quietly, eyes focused on the table in front of me. Melba came in, putting down a cup of hot tea, and asked if there was anything in particular I would like that morning. Without looking up, I thanked her and told her that there was not. Instead of walking out of the room, Melba stayed where she was, and I could feel her gaze upon me. *Please, go*, I thought, not wanting to interact more than I already had. Eventually, I looked up and saw her concerned face looking back at me.

I was not so callous as to disregard her feelings. In fact, I was a bit surprised at the level of worry she showed. I still didn't feel worthy of such attention – especially that morning – and my eyes began to fill with tears. Melba kneeled down next to my seat and held me. I cried into her shoulder without limit, while she kept repeating that everything would be alright. Looking back, I'm not sure what I was crying about more: my wrecked emotions, or the seemingly unbelievable kindness of my found family.

I don't know how long we were like that, but eventually my tears subsided, and Melba released me. When she stood up, I saw her wipe away her own tears. I was unable to frame words, but I hope she saw the gratefulness that I felt.

"If you change your mind about wanting to eat something," she said, "do not hesitate to ask."

I gave a small smile and nodded. When she left the room I slowly turned towards Mr. Stafford. When I looked at him, he reached across the table, handed me a handkerchief, and I could see that his eyes were red. Although I could not understand, it was clear that I was not suffering alone.

He gave me a minute to compose myself – and was kind enough to not stare at me the entire time – and eventually said, "I'm not going to harp on the difficult emotions that you are feeling. That could even be counterproductive. You see, the effect of reading a Dark Book is much like a person walking through a field; they both leave behind an impression. However, with a little time, the impression – if the act is not repeated – will fade and disappear. For those poor individuals who have read a Dark Book repeatedly – worn a well-trodden path, as it were – it can take a long time to overcome the effects."

"How long?"

"Well, every situation is unique, but I remember one individual who did not show signs of improvement for close to three months. That is, however, quite an exceptional case. For those who have read a book only once, like yourself, it can take only a matter of days to overcome the negative effects. Even faster with some help."

"What kind of help?"

"To put it simply, distractions."

"What do you mean?"

"I imagine that when you went to bed last night that you could not help but think about the book and all the emotions it stirred up. When you awoke this morning, no doubt you had the same challenges. Am I correct?"

I nodded.

"That is perfectly normal; expected behavior for such a traumatic experience. In a short period of time, your mind has adapted to entertaining those thoughts, almost as if they were normal. Those feelings, however, are not normal at all – they are not even yours. We need to help your mind to consider other thoughts, less painful thoughts, and to create a new and happier path through the field."

"Alright," I said hesitantly, at least understanding the logic behind what he was saying. "What kinds of distractions?"

"First and foremost is the Ring Presentation Ceremony, tonight."

"What is that?"

"It's when all those who received promotions, or have been accepted as apprentices – like yourself – receive their new ring to indicate their position. After the ceremony, there is food, music, and dancing."

I couldn't imagine a worse torment than the thought of going to some kind of celebration while in the condition I was. Despite feeling a touch better for having gotten out of bed and releasing some emotions into the arms of Melba, I was still a far cry from wanting to participate in anything beyond, perhaps, sitting quietly next to a fire – even reading felt too taxing. Happy music, laughing guests, the attention of receiving a ring, all felt beyond my power to handle. A sense of panic started to well up in me.

"I know," said Mr. Stafford, "that this may sound like the very last thing you would like to do. But I'm confident that as the day goes on, you will continue to feel better. By the time of the event, I don't pretend that you will be feeling quite yourself, but you will at least be in a position to tolerate the ceremony."

It seemed unlikely; no, impossible. My feelings of panic increased. I didn't want to go; I was terrified of going. People should not be inflicted with my presence. Immediately my mind started looking for a way out.

Desperate, I eventually said, "I'm afraid that I don't have a gown that would be fitting for such an event."

"Hmm, that *would* pose a problem," said Mr. Stafford as I felt a tiny bit of hope. He went on, "Well, as I mentioned, distractions – plural – are the order of the day and I have taken the liberty of having three gowns made for you. I think spending a little time trying them on and deciding which one you like best may be a suitable distraction."

Gowns? I wanted to think he was joking with me, but I could tell by the look on his face that he was completely serious. "Mr. Stafford," I started to protest, "I appreciate your generosity, but I fear that this may be a wasted occasion for it."

"Perhaps. But I have not given up hope. You see, I know that these emotions you are suffering through are not your own. If they were, then the notion that distractions or purchases could truly help would be ridiculous – perhaps even belittling to your feelings. However, being that you are merely under the influence of the book, we can fight it." He leaned back in his chair and said, "I will make an agreement with you. If, by the time we need to leave, you still cannot tolerate the idea of going to the ceremony, you don't have to go. All I ask is that you try and fight these feelings. Agreed?"

It was a ray of hope! I was just given a way out of the ceremony. After only a moment's thought, I nodded and said, "Agreed," I wondered, however, if there was a loophole I was missing.

"Now, about the gowns, will you try them on? If not for yourself, or for me, then for Helen's sake? She is the one who picked them out – for, I'm told, my taste in modern women's clothing is quite abysmal."

Despite my melancholy and my distress over the ceremony, I couldn't help but give a small laugh at his comment. That tiny piece of happiness made me think that, perhaps, there was hope for me after all...

When I left the dining room, I found Helen waiting in the hallway outside. Despite the obvious concern she had for me, I could also see excitement in her face. Taking both my hands in hers, she said, "Mr. Stafford explained to us all what you have been through. He said that you will not be yourself today, but that we could help. I know that the gathering tonight is probably unappealing, but I can promise you this: if you go, you will look amazing!"

I appreciated Helen's kindness. I actually felt a little bad, in that, she might have loved the idea of going to a fancy ceremony, while I was reluctant. "Thank you, Helen. Mr. Stafford said that you were the one who picked out the gowns for me."

"That's right," she smiled, "and you should be thankful that I did. Mr. Stafford dresses fine for a gentlemen, is a warm and generous person, but he does not know the first thing about women's clothes."

I smiled and commented, "I believe he used the word 'abysmal.'"

Helen covered her mouth with her hand and said, "Oh, he heard that, did he? Yes, I may have made a statement to that effect…"

I gave a small laugh – the second of the morning – and could feel the subtlest of cracks in my fortress of melancholy.

"Come along," said Helen, leading me by the hand down the hallway. "I have waited long enough to show you these."

"How long have you had them?" I asked, just realizing that, of course, they would have to have been created previously.

"A little over a week. Mr. Stafford commissioned them about a month ago."

"But why?"

"For tonight's ceremony. He wanted you to have everything you needed."

"But why did he not tell me?"

"I think he didn't want you to know about them in case something happened and you were not accepted as his apprentice. It might have added undue pressure."

There were multiple ways to regard that statement. Unfortunately, in my influenced state, I could not help but think that Mr. Stafford doubted me; that he did not really believe that I would be accepted. I struggled with those thoughts as Helen led me through the foyer and down the corridor towards the library. When we stopped outside of its doors, I was a little surprised, and asked, "Why are we here?"

"I needed to set the gowns out earlier," answered Helen. "But I obviously could not place them in your room while you were there, it would have ruined the surprise. So, they are here." She then opened the door for me.

I didn't have to search for the dresses as they immediately grabbed my attention. Lying on the couch – looking a little like invisible people – were the three gowns. I paused after only a step in the room taken aback by their beauty.

"What do you think?" asked Helen excitedly.

I took a few more steps closer, looked back at Helen, then back at the dresses and said, "They are absolutely beautiful."

If I had been in better spirits that morning, I could imagine myself screaming and dancing around them with Helen in pure ecstasy. As it was, the astonishment and appreciation I felt in the face of my sadness is a testimony to how wonderful I thought them to be. However, my cruel conscience would not let me enjoy them completely as it pricked me with the thought, *you don't deserve them.* With that fear, I turned and looked at Helen.

She stepped closer and asked, "What is the matter? Is there something wrong with them?"

"No, not them. Me."

"There is nothing wrong with you," said Helen kindly. "I can't say that I know all the feelings that you are going through, but I know *you.* Have we not become like sisters over the last many weeks? Have we not shared our thoughts and feelings so that you know me better than anyone, and I you?"

It was true. Helen and I were very close and was the one I most confided in. I nodded my head.

"Then trust me," Helen pleaded. "You are a wonderful woman. This house has always been a pleasant place, but since your arrival, it has become…special. You are loved and appreciated. Please don't think so poorly of yourself."

I knew what Helen was doing, but there was a vicious circle of self-loathing at play. The nice things she said made me feel even worse for my severe melancholy; as if the very emotions of sadness were an affront to all that had been done for me. Those were wicked feelings – feelings that could turn the kindest of compliments and twist it into a reproach.

"I know that book really affected you," continued Helen, "and I know that it will take some time to overcome it. So, for now, let us focus on the gowns. Don't think about anything else except which one you like best. How does that sound?"

At that moment, it was good advice. Allowing myself to dwell on all the sadness was reinforcing the 'path' that Mr. Stafford had talked about.

And, after all, I promised I would fight. After a deep breath, I nodded at Helen.

"Good," she said and then led me by the arm closer to the couch.

I looked at the gowns objectively – not as one who was to wear them, but more like a person looking at a piece of artwork. Each one was absolutely beautiful. The first was of a peach color that was so light that it almost looked white. The skirt had three layers of lace that made it look both innocent and elegant.

The second dress was cream colored, but had an exciting, yet tasteful, purple corset accented by a light purple ruffle that went around the middle of the skirt.

The third dress was the one I immediately liked best. It was made of a beautiful deep blue material with grey patterns accenting the skirt, like vines and leaves. The neckline was also blue but overlaid with grey lace. All three dresses were wonderful, but the blue one stood out.

"Which one do you fancy the most?" asked Helen.

"The blue one."

Helen smiled and said, "That is my favorite as well! I thought you would choose that one. However, you will need to try on all three, for the fit of the dress is nearly as important as the style or color."

Trying on three dresses felt like a lot of work. However, I had no excuse not to do so – besides, it would make others happy and they deserved anything I could do to that end.

"Help me to carry them up to your room," said Helen, carefully laying one dress on the other.

I picked up the blue one, lifting it high so as to not drag it upon the floor. When we reached my room, we laid them all on my bed.

"Which one first?" Helen asked.

I thought for a moment and then decided, "Let me try the purple one."

"Saving the best for last?"

I smiled as that was exactly what I was doing.

Helen assisted me in putting on the dress with the purple corset. When adorned, I stood in front of the mirror and examined how I looked. In my influenced state, it was almost like I was a third person watching it all happening. My mind and spirit were so far away from wanting to get ready for a party, that it was hard to believe that it was me that was actually doing those things.

The dress looked nice, although I think the waist was a bit off. Still, if I had to wear it, I would have had no reservations about it.

Next, I tried on the light peach dress. When I looked in the mirror, I saw a vision of a sad angel. The light color, mixed with my pale skin, made me think of pure and fragile innocence; a marble statue that could fracture at the slightest disturbance. The image in the mirror was haunting and I had to look away.

"What is wrong?" asked Helen.

"It..." how could I explain? "It's too personal. It's like I'm wearing my doubts and concerns as a garment for all to see. It's beautiful, but I'm not strong enough to bear it."

"Well, then let us try the blue one and hope for a good fit."

The blue dress was a bit heavier than the other two and I immediately felt more protected – especially in comparison to the peach dress. I stood in front of the mirror and saw what I had hoped; a girl in a pretty dress. The dark colors hid my emotions while the heavy fabric felt like welcomed armor. Besides adoring the look of the gown, I loved the defense it provided. It was definitely the one.

I turned to Helen and asked, "What do you think?"

"You look every bit as beautiful as I knew you would. But do *you* like it?"

I looked down at the floor between us. I did like the dress, but I didn't like what it was ultimately representing – attendance at the gathering. Although Mr. Stafford said I could decide not to go, I knew that it was unlikely that I would actually decline. Even my great melancholy would not allow me to completely disregard the clear desires of those around me. Perhaps Mr. Stafford knew that all along.

I finally answered, resigned, "I like it too. It is the one I will wear tonight."

Nineteen

BR

It had been a difficult, tiring morning and afternoon. My emotions felt like a boat in a storm, being buffeted about violently and without mercy. Now, as the clock struck four, it was time to leave for the Ring Presentation Ceremony. All I wanted to do was to crawl into bed.

Earlier, after having tried on the gowns, Helen had me model the blue one – the one I had chosen for the ceremony – to Melba. I will never forget Melba's face as I walked into her kitchen and she caught sight of me. The stoic and composed woman actually let her mouth hang open for a second as she looked at me in stunned silence. After the moment passed, she exclaimed, "Oh, my dear, you look absolutely beautiful." And she ran to me and hugged me.

"I had my reservations," Melba continued, "in allowing Helen such an important responsibility, but she has done superb. Let me look at you again," and she released the embrace and took a few steps back.

"If only," said Melba with a hint of sadness, "we could get your demeanor to match your dress. But I know you have been through an ordeal. At least, or so I have heard, you have decided on attending the ceremony – I'm very proud of you for that. Doing something for someone else, especially when we do not want to, is a demonstration of caring, of friendship, and love. It's a kind of sacrifice."

"*Sacrifice?*" I exclaimed, not feeling I deserved any praise. "How could going to a party be considered a sacrifice? I feel as if I'm the most unappreciative and spoiled child that has ever existed!"

"Miss Gladwyn!" Melba said sternly. "That is enough of that talk." She paused to let the words sink in. She continued, "Tell me, do you really *want* to go tonight?"

I wasn't sure what to say. I stared at the floor as if an answer would suddenly appear. If it made no difference to anyone else, then, no, I did not want to go. I gave a little shake of my head and, in a very small voice, said, "No."

"Alright then. And, tell me, are you going to go tonight?"

In barely above a whisper, I answered, "Yes."

"And *that* is why it's a sacrifice. It makes no difference on what the event is – just that you are going to do something that you don't want to for the sake of others." Then, in a very kind voice, Melba asked, "Do you understand?"

I did. In no way did I want to attribute such noble thoughts to myself, but I understood what she was saying and how my actions applied. With my eyes still on the floor, I answered, "I understand." Then, looking up at Melba, I managed a smile and said, "Thank you."

"We all need reminders from time to time."

The rest of that afternoon was spent cleaning, dressing, brushing, primping, pinching, smoothing – basically, more time on my appearance than I had ever spent. Helen took the preparation very seriously and, as I was in no condition to fight, I gave in to all of her directions. Fortunately, she made room for lunch – my appetite had returned – but I don't think she was at all happy about taking time away from getting me ready. As it was, she finally gave her approval with only a little time to spare.

As the hour to leave arrived, I will admit that, although still suffering from the effects of the book, I felt a fair bit better than I had that morning. Whether it was from all the distractions or the passing of time – likely both – I was not absolutely dreading the ceremony anymore. Although I still would have been happy to stay home, I cannot deny that I had a tinge of excitement as I got into the carriage.

Mr. Stafford sat diagonally across from me, as my gown seemed to take up most of the cabin. The dress was clearly designed for large open spaces and not cramped vehicles. Mr. Stafford smiled pleasantly, and I worried that he would ask, again, how I was feeling. Although I was feeling a bit better, I really didn't want to discuss it.

In an effort to head off the topic, I asked, "What will the ceremony be like?"

Over the pleasant clip-clop sound of the horse and the crunching of the wheels on the road, he answered, "It's generally very pleasant. Yesterday's meeting is far more solemn – out of respect for the seriousness of our assignments – but tonight is usually less reserved; more of a celebration. I look forward to it."

"How long will it last?"

"That's a good question as it has been many years since I have stayed until the end. The ceremony is generally over within an hour, but the music and dancing can go on for as long as people are interested."

Looking back, it strikes me as funny at how our mind contemplates things. All day long I had been fighting my dark mood and worrying about the anxieties of being in a large crowd again, but there was another issue that was in front of me the entire time and only as we rode towards London did it dawn on me. The gathering was, among other things, a *dance*; and I didn't know how to dance. In the orphanage, occasionally the girls would make up little routines, but nothing official or proper. My already tenuous battle with anxiety just took a massive blow.

"Once the ceremony is over," said Mr. Stafford, probably unable to read my distress in the fading evening sun, "we can leave whenever you like. I'm afraid that I pushed a bit hard to get you to come, but I will not make you stay long. I'm very proud of you for attending. It shows that my faith in you is – as I always knew – completely justified."

His words gave me some comfort. Feelings of unworthiness and inadequacy are difficult but are somewhat soothed by reassurances. Also, the ability to leave when I wanted gave me some comfort as it was the first real bit of control I had over that entire day – for, although I was given the opportunity to not attend, the reality was that my conscience didn't give me that option.

Deciding to address my newest concern head on, I said, "Mr. Stafford, I need to confess something to you."

He tilted his head slightly and asked, "What is it?"

"I never learned how to dance. I should have said something sooner, but I didn't think about it until just this moment. I'm sorry."

"Oh Naomi, it's I who should apologize. I knew of this gathering from the beginning and yet I said nothing to you until this morning. I have barely given you enough time to get dressed, let alone to receive dance lessons. But trust me, you have nothing to worry about."

"Why not?"

"First, you are not required to dance. Second, after watching a few dances, you will pick up enough steps to participate – if you so choose.

Third, if you would like to dance, but don't feel comfortable to do so with a stranger, I would be honored to dance with you."

I smiled at his offer, warmed at the thought of dancing with that kind man. However, the thought of dancing with a stranger passed through my mind and sent a nervous – but not entirely unpleasant – chill down my spine. For the hundredth time that day, I didn't think I was ready for the night.

When we reached our destination, the building looked and felt different than it had the previous day. Through the darkness, its windows and doors were lit up brightly while happy music could be heard emanating from within. Even on that cold night, and despite my experience the day before, it managed to feel welcoming.

As we waited in the queue of carriages, I stared out the window at the other guests entering the building. I caught glimpses of their fine dress as their silhouettes disappeared into the lighted doorway. Despite all of my apprehensions, I could not deny my growing excitement. To think that I was dressed up and going to a kind of ball was hard to comprehend – even at that moment. I thought back to the 'if only' games and how we occasionally would create just such a dream. But even the more optimistic of us didn't think that such a fantasy could actually come true.

When we stopped, Patrick climbed down and opened the door. Although it was bitterly cold, I hardly noticed as the full sound of all the conversations, of laughing, and of music reached my ears. I took Mr. Stafford's elbow as he escorted me up the steps to the entrance and felt insignificant in the face of all that wonder. My eyes moved constantly, and I hardly blinked for fear of missing even a moment of that amazing vision. Inside the massive lobby, it was a cacophony of beauty. Men, some in military uniforms, most in finely tailored suits, and women in gorgeous dresses of every color and style, were all around.

Mr. Stafford guided me through the lobby, but I hardly noticed my steps as I was thoroughly enchanted by my surroundings. As we approached the door to the meeting room – which was now a ballroom, complete with tables, a space for dancing, and musicians – we were stopped by an older woman.

"Miss Gladwyn," the woman said, "I am Mrs. Sophia Dockery."

She looked familiar, although I was not sure why. She wore a grey dress with rich purple accents, and her mostly grey hair was arranged tightly on her head. After another moment, I remembered why she looked familiar: she was one of the seven council members. I curtsied and said, "I am very pleased to meet you, Mrs. Dockery."

"I wanted to tell you," said the councilwoman, "how sorry I am that you had to endure that test yesterday. It is not something we administer often and is almost unheard of for someone being presented as an apprentice."

I didn't know what to say, so I simply nodded my head.

"I feel that it is my duty," the older woman continued, "to tell you that we went to such extreme steps because of the position of Mr. Stafford. Now, you had my vote from the beginning, but some felt that an apprentice to a council member needed to be absolutely beyond reproach. I'm sorry – to both of you – that not all the members have the same faith in Mr. Stafford's judgment."

"Why is that?" I asked, unable to hold back the question.

"I have given up on trying to figure out how everyone's mind works but rest assured that any lack of faith has nothing to do with Mr. Stafford himself. It's probably just an old-fashioned sense of misguided propriety."

I nodded in a show of understanding but wished things had gone differently. A thought occurred to me and I said, "Mrs. Dockery, may I ask you a question?"

"Of course."

"During the test, has anyone pulled the trigger?"

She took in a breath and let it out before answering, "Yes. Over my decades of membership, I know of a few that pulled the trigger."

"What happened to them?"

A look of alarm crossed Mrs. Dockery's face and she said excitedly, "You *were* told that the gun would not fire?"

"Yes, someone told me that last night."

"Good. I did not want you to think that we were a bunch of murderers killing innocent book lovers." A smile tugged at her lips indicating the ridiculousness of the very thought. She continued, "However, to answer your question: the majority of those that pulled the trigger have decided not to join our society – and we hold no ill will towards them. What we do here is not for everyone."

"But some have joined, even after failing the test?" I asked.

"Yes, a few. You see, the test is not an absolute. It shows the condition of the person at that time. It also clearly demonstrates to the initiate the reality of what we are up against. Those that fail are clearly not ready and most see the challenge as too daunting. Some, however, fail, but they carry on in their desire to help. I commend those that fail and yet continue. Overcoming one's faults, real or perceived, is a measure of a person that demands respect. Would you not agree, Mr. Stafford?"

I looked at Mr. Stafford as his eyes focused momentarily in the distance and then he said, "I do."

"May I ask why it's called the Hargreaves Test?"

"Alexander Hargreaves," answered Mr. Stafford, "is the name of the author of the Dark Book that you read. Around of the time of his journal being discovered, well over a hundred years ago, The Council developed the test. It's used infrequently, but still holds some value."

"Perhaps," sighed Mrs. Dockery, clearly not convinced of the value. She continued, "There is one other thing that I want you to be aware of, Miss Gladwyn. During the duration of your test, Mr. Stafford never took his eyes off of you."

I could not think how that was possible. I knew for a certainty that I was alone in that room.

Seeing the confusion on my face, Mr. Stafford said, "You were not told this, but the room in which you did the reading is set up with cleverly hidden watch points so that individuals in the adjacent room can observe. There were never less than two council members watching you the entire time."

"And one of them," said Mrs. Dockery, "was Mr. Stafford. Hour after hour he refused to move. During every moment of your reading, his sight never left you."

I looked up at Mr. Stafford and he said softly, "I told you that you would not be alone."

My emotions were already overwhelmed – anxiety, sadness, excitement – but I still managed to make room for appreciation. "Thank you," I said to Mr. Stafford and then turned to the councilwoman and said, "And thank you, Mrs. Dockery, for explaining these things to me. I do appreciate it."

"Of course, my dear. Now, with these unpleasantries behind us, let me tell you how happy I am that you are one of us. Do try and enjoy the evening." With that she turned and started waving down another guest that she wanted to talk to.

"Mrs. Dockery," said Mr. Stafford, "will likely be the head of The Council one of these days. She is as intelligent as anyone I have ever met but is also able to navigate the difficult world of people and personalities."

"It was," I agreed, "very kind of her to approach me like she did."

"It was. But don't worry about the other council members, they are good individuals. Now, let us find a table to sit at for the ceremony."

We chose a spot that was about halfway down the room and on the left side. The tablecloth was silk, the glasses were crystal, and the centerpieces were of beautiful ceramic. I was almost afraid to move for fear of breaking something.

Mr. Stafford went to get us something to drink and I returned to examining the people in the room. My initial excitement and wonder were starting to wane and the anxiety of being around so many people was starting to return. The book's influence still weighed upon me and seemed to accentuate my thoughts of being inadequate or unworthy of such an experience.

A few of the guests looked my way, but I would turn my head and pretend to be busy with something on the table in an effort to keep them from approaching. It apparently worked, as no one had tried to converse with me by the time Mr. Stafford returned with two cups.

I took a sip of the warm beverage and was not at all prepared for what it was. It had a deep fruit flavor mixed with many spices and had a pleasant sweetness to it. "What is this?" I asked.

"That is mulled wine," Mr. Stafford responded and then took a sip of his own.

At his answer, I immediately put the cup on the table, almost dropping it as if it was too hot to touch and drew my hands back. Seeing my reaction, Mr. Stafford asked, "What is wrong? Don't you like it?"

"It has alcohol," I said, thinking of my father and his drinking. For some reason, in that moment, I saw a parallel between my views of a Dark Book and strong drink – both altered the mind and could cause a person to do bad things.

"It does have some alcohol in it," said Mr. Stafford. "I didn't know that that was an issue, but now I see that I'm mistaken. Your father?"

I nodded, appreciative of his insight so as to not have to explain myself.

"Well," said Mr. Stafford, "the choice is entirely yours. But know that, in moderation, alcohol is perfectly safe and can be enjoyable."

"I don't think that tonight is a good night for me to find out," I explained, already feeling overwhelmed for many reasons.

"I understand. Allow me to get you a different beverage."

He was about to stand, but I didn't want to be left alone again. I quickly said, "No, that's alright. I'm fine for now. Perhaps later."

We soon fell into talking about the different people in attendance that Mr. Stafford knew. He also pointed out several of the ones who had travelled quite far and I found it exciting to be in room with people from all over the world. Before long, our conversation was interrupted by the announcement:

"The Ring Presentation Ceremony is about to begin!"

Twenty

BR

$\mathbf{M}$y attention turned to the front of the room as Mr. Turner, head of The Council, along with one other gentleman, stood, waiting for all to be seated. It took a couple of minutes before the conversations died down and everyone found their place. Once quiet, Mr. Turner said in a strong voice, "Welcome, ladies and gentlemen, to our Ring Presentation Ceremony."

Polite applause followed the statement. He continued, "Let us waste no time in getting to the latest accomplishments for our members. First, we have a high-level promotion. With his counter eclipsing seven thousand, and for his continued excellent service, it is an honor to announce that Mr. Thomas Stafford has been promoted to Bibliognost, Second Class."

Enthusiastic applause sounded through the room as Mr. Stafford stood up and approached the council head. When before him, they shook hands and then Mr. Turner looked at the man at his side. That man held a thin wooden box, a little bigger than a dinner plate, and when he opened it, glints of metal could be seen. The man removed one of them – a gold ring – and handed it to Mr. Turner. Mr. Stafford then removed his own ring, handed it to the councilman and took the new one. Applause sounded once more at the finish of the exchange.

Mr. Stafford turned to face the gathered members and said, "It is with great appreciation that I accept this honor. When I first joined the order, this position, reaching these numbers were not even a thought; and yet in a twinkle of an eye, here I am. Our paths may go in unexpected, and even unsure, ways, but with a little focus, our goals can be reached."

More applause. Mr. Stafford looked like he was about to walk back to his seat, but he hesitated and then said, "I would like to take this opportunity to say one more thing. This rank, along with being on The Council, puts me in a position of maintaining the highest standards for our order. I am looked to as an example. I understand and accept this. This also means that my apprentice will also be held to a higher standard. This, too, I accept. I have the utmost faith in Miss Gladwyn and her capabilities, but I ask one thing from you all: please judge her on her merits and not on her past. One can only control who they are now and who they will be; to examine a person on any other basis is unfair. That said, I'm certain you will appreciate her as I do."

Mr. Stafford then started walking to his seat. There was silence for a moment, as what was said was apparently an unusual statement, but before he reached his seat, the audience broke into energetic applause once more.

I looked at Mr. Stafford as he approached his chair, ignoring the applause around me, and once again was struck by the kindness and sincerity of him. When he met my stare, he gave a smile that seemed to say, 'I hope that was alright.' It was and I gave the most appreciative smile I could manage in return.

When he sat down, I leaned over and said, "Thank you,"

With his eyes on the front of the room, he tilted his head towards me and answered, "You are very welcome. We are grateful...I'm grateful...to have you here."

The ceremony continued with several men and women being promoted. Each one approached the lead councilman and exchanged their ring for a new one. All said a few words of appreciation.

Mr. Turner then announced, "Now we have come to the apprentices. With four approvals, this is a standout year. First, we have Mr. Edward Hudson, sponsored by his father, Mr. Jonathan Hudson."

The young man stood and approached Mr. Turner amidst polite applause. The audience watched as they shook hands and a ring was presented. In addition to the ring, he was also given a slip of paper. After putting the ring on, Edward turned to the audience – looking very nervous – and said in a broken voice, "Uhh...Thank you. Thank you." He then hurried back to his seat.

"Our second apprentice," announced Mr. Turner, "is Miss Natasha Petran, sponsored by her father, Mr. Grigore Petran."

A young woman, no older than me, stood and approached. I didn't recognize her from yesterday's meeting but realized that I was in the side room with Mr. Stafford for two of the apprentice proposals.

Natasha was tall and thin, had long dark hair and bright eyes. Her turquoise dress shimmered as she walked past our table. After accepting her ring and the piece of paper, she said to the audience in a heavy eastern European accent, "I will do everything I can to make you proud of me."

Fortunately, the speeches from the apprentices were very short. Even so, my anxiety grew at the thought of standing in front of all those people and then having to address them. I hoped I could manage a simple 'thank you.'

"Next," said Mr. Turner, "we have Mr. Ruggieri Palladino, sponsored by Mr. Stefano Valenti."

The man that stood was no younger than thirty years of age. Besides being the oldest of the four apprentices, I also noticed that, unlike the other ones, his sponsor was not a relative. His complexion was dark – clearly someone from the south. With a name like Palladino, he must have been Italian.

After receiving his ring, he addressed the crowd somberly, "I have seen the effects of a Dark Book firsthand. I count it, not so much a privilege, but a duty to fight these devastating tomes."

The applause was subdued as he made his way back to his seat.

"Our final apprentice for the evening," continued Mr. Turner, "is Miss Naomi Gladwyn, sponsored by Mr. Thomas Stafford."

I stood up, paused, looked at Mr. Stafford – who gave me a nod of encouragement – and walked towards the head of The Council. Although I didn't notice at the time, I was told that the applause was quite lively; that people understood and acknowledged my passing of the test.

When I reached Mr. Turner, I gave a respectful curtsy. In return, he smiled and said, "Congratulations, Miss Gladwyn. You have truly earned this."

He then looked over at the holder of the rings and I took a step to my left to stand in front of him. From the box, he brought out a silver ring and handed it to me. My hands were shaking from nerves and it was all I could do to take it from him and hold it tightly in my fist; I would try it on later. I was then handed a slip of paper.

It was now my turn to address the audience. Without knowing what I would say, I turned and faced everyone – that was probably a mistake as the multitude of faces looking at me made me feel quite small. However, a small part of me knew that I was now one of them. The ring I was holding in my hand was a physical symbol of belonging to the society. And then I knew what I wanted to say. I wanted to tell everyone that a sense of belonging is an amazing thing. That the comfort of knowing you are not alone is, perhaps, taken for granted; that I had not had a sense of belonging since I was very young. And now, within the space of a couple months, I had a family and now a society of like-minded associates. I wanted to thank them for including me; to thank Mr. Stafford for his kindness and generosity.

I also wanted to say that they all had made a mistake and that I did not deserve to be there.

But I said nothing. All of the expressions were trapped inside of me. It was as if a battalion of armed soldiers were staring down my thoughts and feelings, daring them to try and pass – there were no brave ones. So, in a kind of internal surrender, I simply said, "Thank you," and hurried back to my seat.

"That concludes," said Mr. Turner, "The Ring Presentation Ceremony. We will have a brief intermission before the dancing begins."

While he was announcing those things, I opened my hand and examined the ring. Although it was silver, not gold like Mr. Stafford's, it was very similar. It had a large round design that had the seal of the Book Reapers – the letters 'BR' with an inkwell below it, a quill along one side, a scythe on the other, and the numbers zero and three in the inkwell. I tried it on and found that it fit my index finger perfectly. Then I at the slip of paper given to me. It turned out to be a bookmark that listed all of the levels of The Book Reapers and the book counts that correspond to them.

Interrupting my examination, Mr. Stafford said, "I'm very proud of you for being here tonight. I know that it was difficult. Our agreement was that we could leave whenever you liked once the presentation ceremony was completed. But I must request one last favor. I know I have asked a lot today, but this favor is not for me. You see, Mrs. Dockery's husband died a few years ago, and we have a kind of tradition of sharing a dance together. She loves to dance, and I cannot bear her sitting alone and missing her partner. Will you allow us to stay for at least the first song?"

"Yes, of course," I answered. "That is very sweet."

Mr. Stafford smiled and said, "She is a very capable and self-sufficient woman, but there is no getting around the fact that dancing requires two."

I already knew that Mr. Stafford was a caring individual, so I cannot say I was surprised at his request, but it certainly expanded my concept of his kindness. I also thought about what Helen had told me, that Mr. Stafford had also lost a spouse, although much farther back than a few years. I never thought of him as lonely but had to admit that I could not rule it out. Perhaps the dance was just as important to him as it was to Mrs. Dockery.

After a couple minutes, the announcement was made for the musicians to start up. As the music filled the room, couples headed to the open space in the middle and began to dance. I watched as Mr. Stafford walked over to Mrs. Dockery, took her hand, and lead her to the dance floor to join the rest.

The atmosphere felt surreal. I was exhausted – a very poor night's sleep mixed with a day full of extreme emotions – but was carrying on through excitement from the event. It was almost dreamlike to see those finely dressed ladies and gentlemen dance around the room, flashes of dark suits and colorful dresses moving in time with the music.

Regardless of Mr. Stafford's request, I think I would have wanted to stay for at least one dance, just to experience that view. Although it was never really one of my 'if only' dreams, many of the girls often thought up elaborate balls with beautiful music and fancy dresses. And here I was, not daydreaming, experiencing it firsthand. *Why me?*

Among those dancing, I saw Natasha Petran, the other female apprentice. She danced effortlessly with some young man and I'm ashamed to admit that I had a tinge of jealously. It was completely unfair – I didn't know her at all – but I wanted her skill of dance and confidence.

I continued to watch, examining the movements, mimicking them with my feet under the table. Some of the dancers were advanced, and although beautiful to watch, I paid most attention to the simpler – possibly repeatable – steps of others. When the music stopped, a polite applause was given – I clapped loudly for Mr. Stafford and Mrs. Dockery – and then the musicians started another melody. I watched as Mr. Stafford headed back to his seat and I was thinking of the nice things I wanted to say about his dancing when a voice from behind me took my attention.

"Pardon me," the voice said.

It took a moment to realize that I was being addressed and when I turned around, I saw a young man, one of the other recently appointed apprentices, Edward Hudson, standing there – looking about as nervous as he did when received his ring. He said again, "Pardon me. Miss Gladwyn?"

"Yes,"

"I…I wanted to ask if you would like to dance."

I blinked a few times trying to understand what was happening. It was the simplest thing in the world: a young man was asking a young woman to dance. And yet, I was without a single clue as to what to do.

To make matters worse, another young man, standing a little behind Edward, announced, "I would like a dance, too. Perhaps the next one?"

In shock, I looked at their faces and was completely at a loss for words. I tried to answer, to say something, as opposed to just staring blankly at them. "I…" but I still didn't know what to say.

"I'm sorry, gentlemen," said Mr. Stafford, who had made his way from the dance floor to the table, "But Miss Gladwyn will be dancing with me before any of you."

I looked up at him and realized that he had just saved me from the situation – or at least postponed it. Mr. Stafford held out his hand to me and said, "If you are ready…"

I turned to the two young men and gave a bashful smile, and then took Mr. Stafford's hand. He led me, not to the middle of the dance floor, but to the least crowded corner of it. I tried to remember the simple steps I had saw during the first dance as Mr. Stafford took my right hand and placed his other hand on my back. I put my left hand on his shoulder, and we began to dance.

With whispered reminders of, "Left, right, left, right," Mr. Stafford guided us through a simple dance. I made mistakes – several – but only received smiles as chastisement. Despite everything that the day had brought, I was enjoying my first real dance.

When the melody ended, Mr. Stafford released me and said, "You did wonderfully."

"Thank you. But I don't think I'm quite ready to dance with one of those boys. I can tolerate my mistakes with you, but I could not face them with others. Certainly not today."

As we walked slowly back to our table, Mr. Stafford said, "I probably should have foreseen this. Although we have several women as members, there are far more men. The number of young men is especially large in comparison to young women. That makes you someone who will be in high demand for gatherings like this."

Part of me felt a little excited at the attention that I would evidently garner. Part of me felt sick for the same reason. Most of me, however, despised the thought that I might receive attention because of the number of women available as opposed to receiving attention because of who I was. In a day that was already beyond the boundaries of my emotions, it was another item that I could not come to terms with.

"I think I would like to leave now," I finally said as we neared the table.

"If that is what you would like, then that it what we will do," responded Mr. Stafford. "However, please know that there is no requirement to dance and that if you would like to stay, you may simply tell these suitors that you would prefer to observe the dancers this evening."

What he said was, of course, true, but just the act of facing those young men and telling them 'no' felt like too much. My anxiety had endured all it could, and I didn't want to face another challenge.

"I know," I responded, "but the truth is, I don't think I can handle much more of this day. In fact, just the thought of my bed makes me long for sleep as much as I ever have."

With a warm smile, Mr. Stafford said, "I understand. This has been a long couple of days, even more so for you than me, but I will admit to being quite worn out myself."

Turning away from our table, we walked towards the exit. The lobby was mostly empty, everyone being in the ballroom, and our steps echoed in time with the music. Partway to the door, I heard a voice calling from behind us, "Miss Gladwyn! Wait, please."

We stopped and turned around to find Edward Hudson, one of the other new apprentices, hurrying after us.

When he came close, he said, "I am sorry to disturb you, Miss Gladwyn. But I was hoping to ask you a question – for I don't know when I will see you again."

My pulse raced. What would he ask? A dance? That seemed unlikely. I looked up at Mr. Stafford and he gave me a look that seemed to say, 'It's up to you.'

"What is your question, Mr. Hudson?" I asked.

143

"I know that you completed the test yesterday; that you read a Dark Book. You mentioned how much they scared you and, well, I feel the same, if not more so. Please, what was it like? How did you overcome it?"

For much of the afternoon and night, the plan of Mr. Stafford's to distract me had worked. I had been so busy with different things that I hardly had thought about the book. But there, with the question so plainly asked, I could feel a cold darkness creep across my mind; like a shadow stretching over a sunlit meadow, drawing away its warmth.

Before I could respond, Mr. Stafford spoke up, saying, "Mr. Hudson, I can empathize with your desire to know these things, but I'm afraid that now is not the time. The effects of such a book are short-lived, but quite intense. Being that Miss Gladwyn is only a day removed from the experience, I think it would be best to take this topic up at a future date."

A small look of defeat crossed Edward's face, but the understanding of what was said was there too. "Yes, sir," he responded a bit dejectedly.

"Tell me," said Mr. Stafford, "do you come to London often?"

"At least a couple of times a month, sir. More if my father's business demands it."

"Very well, then let us arrange to have dinner together soon. I think this is a perfectly interesting and useful conversation to have…just not for tonight."

With the defeat mostly removed from his face, Edward responded, "Yes, sir. I will send a telegram with our upcoming schedule, if that is alright with you."

"Perfectly so. Well, goodnight then, Mr. Hudson."

"Goodnight, sir. Goodnight, Miss Gladwyn."

"Goodnight," I said, wondering how I felt about what had just been arranged.

Twenty-One

BR

As the days went by from the weekend of the Book Reaper's meeting, I felt more and more normal. Normal, however, is a relative term. Normal, for most of my life, was alone and sad in an orphanage. The new version of normal – being included in Mr. Stafford's family – still felt too good to be true. Every day I wondered how I had been so fortunate to end up there while so many others had to face what I ran away from.

Still, it's safe to say that, at this point of my account, the effects of the dark book had passed. I remembered – and still do – what it did to me and the feelings it generated, but it had no real hold on my emotions any longer.

With my apprenticeship now assured, my life, as Mr. Stafford had indicated, did not change very much. I spent most of my time reading; expanding my knowledge of 'safe' books, causing my counter to increase rapidly as I devoured story after story.

Even when the document was signed that made me the legal daughter of Thomas Stafford, my life did not feel different. The blissful feelings of belonging were already upon me and there was nothing that a piece of paper could have done to make them better. The document made it official, but Mr. Stafford had already made it real.

Where my life did alter was partly by my own doing. The first of those changes was the assistance I would give to Helen and Melba. It was too difficult to see them, my friends, working and not offer to pitch in. I spent at least an hour a day helping Helen to tidy up or assisting Melba in the kitchen – preparing food or washing dishes. Besides the easing of my conscience, for I would feel guilty not helping, I really enjoyed spending time with them.

The other change to my life had to do with the many newspapers that Mr. Stafford had delivered to his home. Previously, I would look through them on occasion, but usually found the articles to be dry and boring. Now, though, Mr. Stafford had me look through each paper every day. My assignment was a little macabre, but I understood the premise: I was to look for articles about tragedy. Those articles, especially if the same type of tragedies repeated themselves over the course of time, were a possible sign of a Dark Book.

When I finished going over them, I would report anything that I thought could fit into the parameters that were set. Usually, there was nothing of interest. Occasionally, there would be an assault reported, but those seemed more of the typical kind, no book compelling it. Even the occasional death that made the newspapers was of the sort that didn't raise suspicion.

However, about three weeks after becoming an official apprentice, Mr. Stafford and I were in the library and I reported a story to him that had caught my attention. There was an article about a man in the town of Ipswich that had committed suicide. He had procured a length of rope, tied it to a rafter, put on his best suit – including a flower in his lapel – and then proceeded to hang himself. It was very sad, as he left behind a wife and two children. What was particularly strange to me was that, according to friends, the man had seemed perfectly content.

After telling Mr. Stafford of the account, he immediately asked for the newspaper and read the article himself with a frightful intensity. When he finished, he looked off in the distance, lost in thought for several seconds, and then said me, "You did very well in bringing this to my attention. Tell me, what do you think of the mindset of a person that is willing to take their own life?"

It was a terrible question. Not only had I been presented with such thoughts due to the reading of a Dark Book, but the desire to not be alive had been present with me on multiple occasions throughout my young life. However, the desire to not be alive and the actual action of trying to make that happen is an enormous leap. At my truly lowest times – the death of my mum, losing Daphne, or the terror of what my life would be like outside the orphanage – I knew that death did not frighten me. If I could have somehow judged my death after it happened, I would not have been bitter. However, the fortitude needed to harm oneself was still far from my abilities or desires – outside of the reading of the Dark Book.

I answered, "That is a mindset that is of utter despair. It would take an enormous amount of pain to bring someone to that state."

Mr. Stafford nodded his agreement and commented, "Enormous pain, or a Dark Book."

Obviously, that was what he was concerned about. "Do you really think that a Dark Book is behind this?"

"I do," he answered simply.

"Will we travel to Ipswich to investigate, then?"

"Yes and no. I will travel to Ipswich alone. I cannot bring you on this particular assignment."

I was surprised at his answer and, although disrespectful, I questioned his decision. "Why not?"

"It's too soon," he told me without adding further explanation.

I stared at him, trying to read his face, trying to see some reason for what I was being told. I could not find a satisfying answer. I could not overcome the feeling that something was being held back. Had I not proven myself with the test? Had Mr. Stafford himself not heaped praise on me as to my readiness? It didn't make any sense. Had I somehow lost his confidence already?

Not being in a position to challenge him further, I finally asked, "When will you leave?"

"Tomorrow. The sooner I get there, the better chance I have of locating the book – if one is to be found."

There was much I wanted to say, but I held my tongue. I was disappointed; hurt. I stood up silently to take my leave and turned towards the door. To my back, Mr. Stafford said, "Naomi, I'm sorry."

I turned to face him and said, "You have nothing to be sorry about. I'm sorry that I have failed you. I'm sorry that I have not made myself ready for this assignment." I then walked out of the library ignoring the call of my name.

I proceeded to my room and felt equal parts frustrated and sad. My frustration stemmed from not understanding his decision. I had, to the best of my knowledge, done everything that was asked of me. To not be trusted – especially after having passed that miserable test – was difficult to take. The sadness I felt came from my thoughts of inadequacy. The only explanation that I could think of for why I was not going was that I was not good enough; that I could not be trusted. It made me question all of the nice things that Mr. Stafford had ever said about me.

For the rest of the day, I didn't leave my room. I tried to read on a couple of occasions, but I was far too distracted to make any progress. So I spent the afternoon and evening lying in bed, bathed in melancholy. Not being at all hungry, I even skipped supper.

When I awoke in the morning, I could hear the preparations for Mr. Stafford's departure. My anger and my shame persisted, and I didn't leave my room.

My only goodbye was standing at my frost touched window and watching as Patrick drove Mr. Stafford down the drive.

Twenty-Two

BR

The next few days, after Mr. Stafford had left for Ipswich, were spent largely in a state of solitude. I still would help Helen and Melba, but not quite as much and with little or no conversation. Really, the only companion I tolerated was Dantés the cat, as he seemed to realize my hurt feelings and tried extra hard to comfort me.

Regardless, I simply could not shake the feeling of disappointment. A little of it was directed towards Mr. Stafford – evidently not trusting me enough to help him – but most of it was directed at myself. Whereas I had once felt like I was part of something, now I felt like a charity case. I could not help but feel that Mr. Stafford was just tolerating me. His words never indicated that, but his latest action was overwhelming his past kind statements.

I still spent a good amount of time reading, during those lonely days, but the experience was a poor one. My general melancholy made it difficult to enjoy a story. It is hard to read about happy endings when one is miserable. The motivation of reading, so that I could be better able to find or combat a dark book, was nearly lost as well – if I really was not to be trusted, why did my knowledge matter?

Part of me knew that my reaction was too strong, but unhappy feelings are difficult to fight – largely because I didn't *want* to fight. I gave in to the feelings; using them to justify my anger and self-loathing. Often times, I find it is easier for me to be sad than happy. Perhaps the expectations of an unhappy person are simpler to meet – for even falling short would be a kind of expectation for sadness. Why I have a propensity for such self-torture, I don't know, but it's real and a constant battle that is still present with me.

On the evening of the fourth day, from his departure, Mr. Stafford returned. By then, my emotional state was closer to numbness than to sadness; even self-loathing gets tiring. I was in the library, reading Shakespeare's *Hamlet* – commiserating with the madness of Ophelia, both for the loss of her father and the misconceptions about Hamlet's love for her – when I heard the approach of a carriage. I marked my spot in the book, closed it, but didn't get up from the chair.

When the front door opened, I could hear Melba welcoming Mr. Stafford home. I still didn't move. I was nervous. I knew that there was a conversation that Mr. Stafford and I needed to have and was not looking forward to it. Part of my concern was that I was not even sure what the conversation needed to be about – trust? Love? Apologies?

If I was not ready to accompany him on an assignment, then the fault is mine, not his. In that respect, I owed an apology for the way I acted. However, if I was not ready, then why did Mr. Stafford insist on saying things to the contrary? It was those thoughts that fueled my nervousness at Mr. Stafford's return.

After Melba's greeting, I could hear the muffled sound of a conversation and, before long, I heard steps – growing louder – as someone was approaching the library. I looked into the fire, scared of seeing the emotion in Mr. Stafford's face. Would he be angry at me? I could not blame him for I acted rather rudely – to say the least. Would it be sadness? Could I have let him down so severely that he might actually regret the apprenticeship, perhaps even the adoption? Worse than either of those would be a look of aloofness; of indifference. Anger or sadness come about because you truly care about someone or something, but if I have caused him to be indifferent to me, then that would mean my actions didn't matter to him. If I had lost his affection, I don't know what I would do.

When the library door opened, I reluctantly looked that way, fearful of what I would see looking back. Of all the emotions I was trying to prepare myself for, the one I saw was not at all anticipated. Mr. Stafford, when he caught sight of me, was *concerned*. The only question was if the concern was for something that had happened on his trip or for me.

He walked quickly to where I was sitting and kneeled down next to my chair. "Naomi," he said, "I owe you an apology."

There was no situation that I had imagined, that I had tried to prepare for, that was even close to that. My thoughts were generally around defending myself or begging for forgiveness. Seeing him, looking at me imploringly, love and concern in his eyes melted away my bitterness. How could I have been so wrong about, misjudged so greatly, Mr. Stafford? Had he not shown me, time and again, his care and affection?

Any anger I had was completely gone. My nervousness for the imagined argument changed to nervousness of being accepted by that kind man. Although he was in front of me offering an apology, I became terribly frightened of losing him. How far would I mistakenly push him before he decided to abandon me? My mother left because of sickness – something out of her and my control. Daphne was the same. But, if Mr. Stafford left, if would be because of me; because of who I am. I couldn't bear the idea as, without a doubt, it would completely ruin me.

With those terrifying thoughts, I leapt out of the chair, threw my arms around Mr. Stafford – nearly knocking him over – and cried, "No, sir, I'm sorry. I'm sorry."

He held me close while I cried and begged for forgiveness. His only words during that outpouring of emotion were the only words I wanted to hear, "Everything is going to be alright."

I desperately wanted everything to be alright.

After a couple minutes, we ended the embrace and Mr. Stafford suggested we sit and talk. I took my usual seat while he took his.

A few moments of silence fell between us and then Mr. Stafford said, "The conversation where I told you that you would not be going on the assignment, you said something that I must clarify."

I shook my head. "I acted horrendously. I'm so sorry."

"Under the circumstances, it's easy to see why you became disappointed. But you made the statement that you had failed me because you were not ready for an assignment."

"I will admit that I was confused and hurt when you told me that it was too soon for me to go. I felt that I had let you down."

"And this is why I owe you an apology. When I said that it was too soon, I did not mean too soon for *you*."

It took a moment to realize what he was saying. If it was not too soon for me, then he meant it was too soon for *him*. "I don't understand. Too soon for you?"

He nodded and said, "When you told me of the article, I knew that it would have to be investigated. I started to think about all the things that would happen and realized that I had not spent enough time preparing *myself* for having you come along. I will admit that I was scared. Taking you into an uncontrolled environment is something that I hadn't given enough thought to. So, you see, you didn't fail me. I failed you."

Nothing of what he had explained had ever crossed my mind. My natural state of self-loathing would not allow the failure to belong to anyone else. Of course, hearing the true explanation of his words made my reaction all the more beastly. I acted so poorly, and it was all just a misunderstanding.

Mr. Stafford then asked, "Can you forgive me?"

It was impossible to think that he needed my forgiveness. My debt to him was far greater than anything he could ask from me. I answered, "If you need my forgiveness, then you have it. But it's I that needs your forgiveness. I misinterpreted your words and made a complete fool of myself."

"Well, that does bring us to another topic that we must discuss."

"Another topic?"

"As my apprentice, you will receive guidance and direction from me. I hope that most of the time it will make sense and be easy to follow. However, there are times that I may ask you to do something that you do not understand or like. I need you to respect these decisions, even if it's hard to do."

I thought for a moment, visualizing the scenarios that he was talking about, and came to an alarming conclusion. "I'm not sure I can promise that."

Mr. Stafford cocked his head and asked, "Why not?"

"Well, let us say that I find another article that needs investigation. If you were to tell me to stay behind, I know that it would upset me. I don't think I could stop such a feeling."

A look of comprehension passed Mr. Stafford's face and he said, "Ah! I understand what you are saying. Let me rephrase my request. I'm not asking you to *like* everything I say. To tell you that you could not be upset at something would be like telling you to not get wet while standing in the rain – impossible. What I'm asking is that you don't linger in the rain and get drenched, so to speak. If I ask you to do something that you don't like, human nature will make you upset at it – that's alright and out of your control. But you do have the option to either fight those feelings or give in to them. I want you to fight. I want you to realize that whatever I ask of you is because I care for you and I think it's the very best decision. You may not always like it, but I need you to support it."

I thought about his words. I tried to apply them to the situation that we just went through and realized that what he was asking made sense but was not necessarily easy. "I promise to try. I don't think it will be easy for me."

"It's not easy for anyone. But it helps if you really understand and believe that what I'm asking is because of my care and love for you."

"Thank you, Mr. Stafford. And I'm sorry for the way I acted these past several days. I will do better. Also, I believe I owe an apology to Melba and Helen, too."

"Oh, were you rough on them?"

"Just melancholy and quiet."

"Well, whatever you feel you need to do."

After a moment's silence, I realized that there was something important that I had not asked about – had hardly given thought to for the last several days. "Did you find a Dark Book in Ipswich?"

"I did," he answered, his face taking on a sad and serious expression. "That poor man evidently picked it up from a street seller to read and it killed him. Now his wife and children are without a father."

"Oh, no!" I exclaimed, filling with sadness. I could not help but think of what the loss of my father did to my mum and me.

"What did you do with it?"

Without taking his eyes off of the flames, he reached inside his jacked and removed a book. The cover was worn brown and had embossed writing on it. It didn't look like a journal, but a published book. The sight of it made me sink back in my chair from fear. I hated the book, whatever it was, I hated it. "Please, Mr. Stafford, get rid of it."

After a few quiet seconds, he nodded and then gently tossed the book into the fire.

I watched intently as the book's edges curled in the flames and the vile, murderous story started to be reduced to crumbly ash. Suddenly, a new and thoroughly unexpected feeling came over me – *doubt*. I had never seen a book destroyed before and to witness it was...disturbing. I said nothing to Mr. Stafford, but could not shake that small, but real, feeling that destroying literature – even something as awful as a Dark Book – seemed, somehow, impossibly, wrong.

Twenty-Three

BR

Eventually, our lives went back to normal. I say eventually since Mr. Stafford was not quite himself for several days after returning from his trip. He seemed very tired and unusually distant. We habitually took all our meals together, but he missed several of them, and spent less time with me in the library, preferring to remain alone in his room, than I had ever seen before. I was concerned that he might have read the Dark Book he had found and that the effect was lingering on him. However, when I asked, he said that he did not read it; he didn't need to as it was a known published work. I concluded that being close to death and its aftermath was very taxing – especially to a person as empathetic as Mr. Stafford. I believe him incapable of witnessing pain and not be deeply affected by it.

After several days, however, his enthusiasm started to grow, and his generally happy demeanor showed signs of returning. After another few days, he was back to normal. Still, the effects of the assignment were not lost on me. I needed to prepare myself, not just for the things I might experience, but for trying to help Mr. Stafford; to take some of the burden from him. I didn't know how much I could bear, but I would not shrink back from trying.

After a few weeks of routineness – reading books, reading the newspapers, assisting Melba and Helen, and even another trip to London – Mr. Stafford announced that arrangements had been made to have Mr. Hudson and his son, Edward, over for dinner. I recalled the brief conversation that was had with Edward the night of the Ring Presentation Ceremony, and how it was agreed that we would get together in the near future. The near future, as it turned out, was the next night.

I gave thought to the purpose of the visit, which was to talk about my experience with the Dark Book and wondered if I could give any meaningful or useful advice. Helen, however, thought that the purpose of the visit was a start to something else entirely – that it was a step towards possible courtship.

Any chance of my remaining calm and collected about the visit of Edward was completely ruined at Helen's inference. I was a *little* nervous at the thought of discussing the Dark Book, but enough time had passed to make me feel that it would be alright; but a romantic occasion? I was *very* nervous at that thought. Deep down I knew that Helen was making it a bigger deal than it probably was, but the fact that there was *any* possibility of it being romantic in nature was enough to make me anxious.

"Fortunately," I reminded Helen, "the dinner is here, and you will be around the entire evening. I have no experience with such matters and will rely on you to make sure that I don't make a fool of myself."

Helen laughed and said, "So, there is some reciprocation of feelings, then?"

"What?" I exclaimed. "The thought had not even crossed my mind. As far as I'm concerned, this is a simple dinner."

"Oh, definitely," she responded sarcastically while giving a knowing nod. "Then you'll not need me around, will you?"

If things were headed in the way that Helen was indicating, I desperately wanted her help. I had no experience with boys – outside of the romances that I had read about in books, but those, of course, were not real. "Well," I said, "on the off chance that you are right, I really would rather not come across as a complete idiot."

Helen stepped close, rubbed my shoulder, and said, "Don't worry, you will be fine. Tell me, is he handsome?"

Handsome? I had only seen Edward three times, and each time was not under ideal circumstances. I first saw him while he was being presented to The Council by his father to be an apprentice. He was not close to me and I could not make much of a judgment from that distance – besides, I was distracted by my own impending presentation. The next time I saw him was when he asked me to dance – I was in such a state of shock, and in an emotional jumble, that his appearance didn't register as good or bad. The third time was as we were leaving the Ring Presentation Ceremony – my emotions were still frayed at that point, but that was the picture that I brought into my mind. *Handsome?* I guess I could not really say. To me, he was just a young man I had met while trying to end a particularly difficult day – frankly, he was an obstacle. *But perhaps…*

Seeing Helen anxiously awaiting my answer, I finally said, "Maybe..."

"*Maybe?*" Helen rolled her eyes. "Oh, dearie, you are further behind than I had thought. Well, as always, count yourself fortunate that I'm around."

She had, I knew, courted a couple of gentlemen over the last few years. Helen said that neither one worked out because they were too boring. I had to agree that Helen and dullness would not mix.

There was another man in Bromley who had shown some interest in her, but they were not to the point of anything official. "Just circling each other," Helen would say. I feared that, in time, she would meet the right person and be taken away – that is selfish of me, of course, but I would miss her terribly.

The morning of the Hudsons' visit passed in normal fashion. I ate breakfast, read through the newspapers, and started a new book. However, a little before noon, Helen took over the day. Not only did we spend much time poring over which dress to wear – just one of my normal ones – she tried to give me lessons on talking with boys.

I don't know how much good they were, for most of it came down to laughing at every joke and treating each statement made as the most remarkable thing ever heard. I told her that I wasn't sure I wanted to do that. Why would I want to *pretend* to find someone interesting?

"It's only temporary," Helen answered, "just until he is 'hooked'. At that point, you can do whatever you want."

I hoped Helen was joking, but I don't think she was. At seventeen, I was definitely on the younger side for courtship, and talking with Helen made me realize just how young and inexperienced with such things I was.

At half-past five, Helen and I were in the library, making final preparations before the Hudsons' arrival. I continued to fake laugh and give insincere words of interest at whatever inane topic that Helen would bring up.

"I think," she would say, "that dirt would be far more interesting if it was a lighter brown."

"Oh, yes!" I would respond enthusiastically, trying not to laugh. I was certainly capable of doing what she was directing, but I was growing more certain that I didn't want to. I may have been inexperienced, but I knew that deception or flattery was not why I wanted someone to be interested in me.

Our preparation came to a sudden end when a carriage could be heard outside of the library windows. The Hudsons had arrived.

Helen looked at me, her eyes bright with excitement, and said, "Here we go! Now don't be nervous, you will be just fine."

I grimaced in reply. Has telling someone not to be nervous *ever* worked?

Twenty-Four

BR

The sound of the Hudsons' arrival made my stomach immediately upset. Despite Helen's advice to not be nervous, that simply wasn't going to happen. I looked at the library door and took a deep breath – as if preparing for a momentous task. I then stood up with Helen and walked to the foyer to greet the guests. Mr. Stafford was already there. Helen stood near the entrance, awaiting the knock, and when it came, she allowed two seconds to pass before opening the door and welcoming the Hudsons.

"Ah, Jonathan," said Mr. Stafford with a smile as he shook the man's hand, "welcome to our home." He turned to Edward and shook his hand as well. "It is good to see you, Edward. I don't think I congratulated you on your apprenticeship. Very well done. We are happy to have you in the order."

"Thank you, sir," Edward said politely.

Helen took their heavy coats while Mr. Hudson said to me, "Miss Gladwyn, allow me to also extend my congratulation to you for your appointment. Passing that test, at any age, but especially for one so young, is quite admirable."

"Thank you, Mr. Hudson," I responded. I turned my eyes towards Edward, and he looked like he wanted to say something, but swallowed it in obvious nervousness.

Mr. Hudson was dressed in a simple, but nice, black suit, charcoal grey waistcoat, and a black tie. His dark hair was neatly parted down the middle and held close to his head. Edward's attire was a touch less formal but still very neat. His suit was of a light grey, with a matching waistcoat, and he wore a cream-colored tie against his white collared shirt. His hair, although dark like his fathers, was quite different in style. His part was on the side, and the hair was thick and wavy.

I asked myself the question of if I found him attractive, and I was not sure. I certainly didn't find him unattractive. I glanced and Helen and she gave me a look as if to say, 'acceptable'. I would have laughed if I wasn't so nervous.

"How about we all step into the library," suggested Mr. Stafford and then led the way. Mr. Hudson followed behind him, then Edward, and finally me. In the library, Mr. Stafford took his normal cushioned chair by the fire. Mr. Hudson took the chair that I normally sat in, and the two of them quickly fell into a conversation. I frowned as I looked at the other options in the room. The only place – without moving some furniture – for Edward and I to sit and talk would be to share the couch. I looked for any alternative, but nothing was to be found. Edward stood nervously, waiting for me to be seated. If I let any more time pass, things would have become even more uncomfortable, so I walked over to the couch and sat on one end of it.

When I looked up at Edward, his eyes scanned the area frantically as he had just realized that the only practical seat was on the couch beside me. I saw him swallow and felt glad that I was not alone in my anxiety. Being that there were no other options, he finally sat on the opposite end of the couch. We must have looked quite comical, him on one side, practically pushing against the arm, while I was pressed firmly against the other. If there was a photograph taken at that moment, one would conclude that we hated each other – or at least that we were afraid of each other, which was probably close to the truth. I don't know why it was that sitting on the same couch, with at least two feet of distance between us, felt so intimate, but it did. My pulse quickened.

I looked off to the side for a moment to compose myself and when I turned back, we fell into an awkward routine of almost talking, then smiling, and generally being nervous wrecks, vainly wishing that one of us would end the torture. When I heard a noise from the hallway, I turned to see what it might be. The library door was ajar and, although I'm not completely certain, I firmly believe that the noise I heard was Helen trying to stifle her laughter.

Looking back on the situation, I cannot blame her. In fact, just the thought of Edward and I on that couch makes me smile. But at that moment, trying to endure the complete awkwardness, it made me mad. That probably was not Helen's intention, but it snapped some of the nervousness out of me. I narrowed my eyes in anger at the door and then asked, "Your mother could not join us tonight?"

"Um, no. She…she passed away when I was born."

I could not believe that I had just opened our conversation in such a ghastly way. "I'm so sorry," I exclaimed, embarrassed and saddened. "I did not know."

"It's alright," he said with a shake of his head.

Desperate to get to a different topic, I practically blurted out, "How was your trip here?"

I was so thankful that I said something, and still a little flustered, I completely missed his answer.

"I'm sorry," I admitted sheepishly, "could you repeat that?"

"Oh, I just said that the ride here was fine."

I smiled and nodded, realizing that I had not missed much. I wished he would elaborate, but he seemed satisfied with his answer. I again tried to think of something to say or ask, but my mind was against me. Thoughts came slowly and unsurely. I grasped onto one of the ideas that I managed to generate and asked, "What is it that you father does that brings you to London?"

"He is an importer," Edward answered, a touch of animation coming into his voice. "He works with contacts in many countries to bring in interesting items. Many shipments come through London and that is where he examines them before bringing them to sale."

"Foreign wares? That does sound interesting. What kinds of items?"

"All kinds," he answered, clearly growing more comfortable at talking. "Perfumes from France, beautiful handmade leather items from Italy, figurines from Germany, coffee and spices from India. And that is just a small list."

"It must be exciting to work with such exotic things."

"Sometimes. I'm afraid that even these things become routine after a while. But on occasion we have things shipped to us that I have not seen before. Or, even more exciting, unexpected things."

I smiled and asked, "Unexpected things? Like what?"

Edward leaned forward a little, as if the next words were secretive, and said, "One time, in a shipment of fabric from Egypt, we found a snake."

I was not expecting that and put my hand over my mouth to stifle a yelp of surprise. "A *snake*?" I asked, completely stunned.

He nodded and said, "Yes. It was an actual snake – a cobra."

"Was anyone hurt?"

"Oh no, the poor creature was quite dead by the time we opened the crate. It gave us a good scare, though."

"How…how big was it?"

"It was a little less than two feet in length, which I guess made it a juvenile. It's amazing that something so small can be so deadly!"

"What did you do with it?"

"We were going to throw it in the incinerator but one of the warehouse men had a relative that did taxidermy, so he took it to be stuffed or something."

"Well," I said, after a moment to regain my composure, "your father's business is certainly not dull."

"It's not," he responded. And then, with a sigh, said, "I guess it would not be a completely horrid thing if I was to take it over some day."

"Forgive me if I'm being too prying, but you don't sound like you really want that?"

Edward glanced at his father – who was wholly engaged in a conversation with Mr. Stafford and not paying us any attention – and then said to me in a hushed voice, "I want to be writer."

From the way he said it, and the way he glanced at his father, I could tell that it was a point of contention between the two of them. I commented, "But your father would rather you run his business."

He nodded.

"Have you told him this, or is this still a future conversation between the two of you?"

"I have told him. He is not opposed to my writing, but he thinks of it only as a hobby, not an occupation. I told him that it's a hobby only as long as it's treated that way."

"I take it that you have not come to an understanding with him yet."

"Not yet. Perhaps if I can prove to him that my work is good, he would not oppose me so much. I mean, we are part of an order that loves books. How can one be surrounded by such wonder and creativity and not be inspired by it?"

I had given much thought and appreciation to what books had provided me, but I had not given any consideration to trying to create my own. It was a new idea and, I must admit, one that held some appeal.

Before I could comment further, Melba announced from the door that dinner was ready.

We all stood and walked towards the dining room. At that point, I was feeling much better. Despite our nervous beginnings, Edward and I had just had a proper conversation. I would not go so far as to say that I was completely comfortable, but I felt much more like myself and hopeful for a less stressful evening.

Dinner was especially good – baked ham, vegetables, bread, and custard for dessert. Melba really was an excellent cook. The conversation throughout the meal revolved around nominal things, like the weather and the poor road condition at that time of year. But when we finished, coffee having been served, our topic turned more serious.

"I think," said Mr. Stafford, "that it is time to discuss the original purpose of this visit." He looked at me and said, "Young Mr. Hudson had asked about the effects of reading a Dark Book. Enough time has passed that I believe this could make for an interesting, likely beneficial, topic. Naomi, are you prepared to talk about your experience?"

I was. I had given thought to what I would say, although I was still not so sure how helpful it would be. I nodded in answer to Mr. Stafford.

"Very well," he said. "With the exception of the actual culmination of the test – for that should remain secret – please take us through the ordeal."

Although having given consideration to the topic, the words were still hard to come by with an audience. I finally started by saying, "I need you all to understand that my experience probably doesn't amount to very much. What I mean by that is, all of my conclusions are based off of reading the one book – I have nothing to compare it to in order to find patterns. I also believe, as I imagine you will glean when I continue, that the specific effects are somewhat personal. In other words, it will be a different effect for each person."

I paused to allow my words to sink in and to allow for any question. I received nods from both Edward and his father, and a compassionate smile from Mr. Stafford, who said, "I think that is already some useful information."

I took in a breath and then began my account by saying, "Although I knew it was a Dark Book, my first reaction, as I started reading it, was surprise. I expected to read nothing but dreadful sentences full of hate or despair. But, in the first few chapters, I found a story about a person whom I would deem a good man. It was not filled with hateful messages; on the contrary, it was filled with a clear desire to help fix problems. Early on, I even wondered if it actually was a Dark Book. In retrospect, one of the more frightening aspects is that I very much *wanted* to keep reading. I was empathizing with the character and his story.

"As I continued to read, the good man's attempts at helping the issues he saw were foiled repeatedly. This is when the first strong emotions of frustration and sadness started to be felt. I cared about that individual, and I cared about the things he was trying to do."

My audience was paying close attention to everything I was saying. I felt a little undeserving of such respect but could not deny their interest in my account.

"The latter half of the book was where the damage – if that is the right word – was done. The good man became hopeless and completely lost to despair. He spoke of the absolute uselessness of his life, his desire to have never been born, and eventually, his desire to no longer continue living.

"That is where one's reaction to the words written becomes personal. I was completely distraught at what the man was going through, but I could not help but take his painful emotions and apply them to each and every shortcoming I could think of for myself. Every bitter memory, no matter how small, was magnified into unbelievable pain. Sort of like finding a small blemish on a garment and then pouring ink over it to make it worse. I have wondered how a person with a very happy life would have reacted to the book. Would the account of the good man be enough, on its own, to cause a drastic reaction? Is there anyone who has had such a good life that there is no blemish to find?"

I could see contemplation in their eyes. My words were causing them to think. Again, I was humbled by the respect shown.

Mr. Stafford then asked, "After the conclusion of the test, how did you feel?"

"In a word, horrible. I felt complete and utter despair. I wanted to not be alive rather than deal with the crushing weight of the pain. It was very difficult."

"How did you overcome those feelings?" asked Edward.

"With help," I answered, looking at Mr. Stafford. "First, I tried to focus on the reminder that the feelings generated were not actually my own. Although that didn't feel entirely true, it was enough to help; enough to not give up. Beyond that, Mr. Stafford, along with the staff here, helped to remind me of my worth and to distract me from those loathsome thoughts. Within a few days, I was feeling back to normal."

I concluded my thoughts by saying, "Although I have learned some lessons from going through that experience, I still would not wish it upon anyone."

"My dear," said Mr. Hudson kindly, "that was a most enlightening account. More than worth the effort to travel here. Thank you for your openness on such a trying subject."

"Yes, thank you, Miss Gladwyn!" chimed in Edward.

I smiled sheepishly. *Will I ever grow accustomed to compliments?* "I hope it was helpful. As I said, I think the reaction will be somewhat different for each person."

"It was helpful," said Mr. Stafford in answer to my statement.

We sat around the dining room table for a little while longer, talking about Dark Books and various theories of their creation and impact. It was interesting and I found Edward to have many strong opinions on the subject. He certainly seemed to be an excellent candidate for the Book Reapers. He even made the surprising comment to me that he *desired* to read a Dark Book in order to see his own reaction. I tried to tell him that it was not as enlightening as he may think it was, and that if I could choose to do things over, I would choose to not have read one. But he was not deterred from his interest.

As the hour struck nine, Mr. Hudson and his son started to prepare to leave. They were not going all the way home to Cambridge, but still wanted to reach London City before it became too late.

While Mr. Stafford and Mr. Hudson exchanged farewells, Edward stood close to me and said, "I enjoyed this visit very much. I hope that we could see each other again."

I read his face and found that it was much less nervous than when he first arrived. I could also tell that he was expecting, hoping, for a response in kind. I also had an enjoyable time, even with the reliving of the Dark Book, and I found that I liked Edward's company – not that we had a lot of time together in one evening. I finally said, "I hope we can see each other again, too."

A passing thought frightened me: *Is this how courtship begins?* I was only seventeen, a bit on the young side for that sort of thing – for it's common for most women to wait until they were closer to twenty. Had I just agreed to anything improper? Helen would need to help me assess the evening.

After the Hudsons had left, I bid goodnight to Mr. Stafford and then met Helen in my room.

"I must say," said Helen, sitting next to me on my bed, "things didn't start so well."

The anger I felt from earlier, from when I thought I heard Helen laughing at me, was completely gone. I answered, "You are being kind. We were terribly awkward."

Helen smiled and then said, "But you recovered very well. In fact, it looked like you two were having a very nice conversation. What were you talking about?"

I explained the conversation, about his father's work, the snake, and Edward's desire to be a writer.

"Well, at least he is not some mindless socialite. And, I might add, not at all that bad to look at."

Although I hated it, I couldn't help the blush that reddened my cheeks. "You stop," I said weakly. "It's too early to discuss things like that."

"Alright, we will go with that logic for now," Helen said with a little laugh and a wicked smile. "But what did he say when he left?"

"He said that he enjoyed the visit and he hoped that we could see each other again."

"That is good. And what did you say?" Her eager eyes gleamed in the lantern light.

"I said that I also hoped we could spend time together again."

"Not exactly Shakespeare, you two, but passable."

"Helen," I said, worried about her next answer, "I'm still young – perhaps younger than many at my age – did I say or agree to anything inappropriate?"

She gave me a very kind, matronly look, "Naomi, you were just fine. Expressing interest in seeing him again is nothing more than just that. You two are not courting, and nothing that happened tonight changed that. Your mutual interest in each other could lead to such an outcome, but trust me, it will not happen without your knowledge and explicit approval. I will see to that!"

I gave Helen a hug and thanked her for being such a wonderful friend. I hoped that I would never lose the appreciation that I felt towards her – along with Melba, Patrick, and, of course, Mr. Stafford.

As I lay in bed, waiting for sleep to overtake me, I found an unfamiliar giddiness inside of me. Even though I wanted to deny it, I knew it was because I had just spent a pleasant evening conversing with a potential suitor. Despite the 'if only' games that many of the orphan girls played, the books about handsome princes, and the stories about brave heroes, I was always too practical to think about such romantic nonsense.

Nonsense, that is, until it could become reality.

Twenty-Five

BR

How could my life, after such a miserable beginning, have turned out any better? I wondered. A worthless orphan, headed towards some ghastly employment, and, somehow, I had ended up under Mr. Stafford's care and protection. It was nothing short of astonishing. I had everything I required and more; even a useful purpose in my life – the hunting of Dark Books. No one, least of all me, would have believed any of it was possible a mere six months prior. Of course, nothing is perfect and even my amazing new life was not without its troubles, as you shall see.

Winter started to give way to spring and the outside world became a little more inviting. Hints of green gave hope amid the mud that seemed to be everywhere; really, hardly a step could be taken that time of year without fear of losing a shoe. It was enjoyable to see the months of cold and darkness give way to warmer temperatures and longer days which could only bolster one's spirit. That gradual buildup of excitement, however, came to a sudden halt on Wednesday, April thirteenth.

I awoke that morning with a smile as I saw the early sun casting warm rays across my blankets. Dantés was curled up next to me and I ran my fingers down his grey back while he stretched his legs contentedly. It was not until I was dressed and went to the dining room that I first noticed a change in the household. Not only was Mr. Stafford absent, which was not common, Melba was very quiet as she brought my breakfast. I tried not to jump to any conclusions, as it was only two small things that could be caused by a great number of normal circumstances.

After my quiet and solitary breakfast, I went to the library to read through the newspapers. It struck me as a little odd that Mr. Stafford did not join me. It was rare for us to not breakfast together, and even rarer for him to not join me at some point in the morning to read. When I finished with the papers – nothing stood out as potential for an assignment – I went

167

off to find Helen to help with some of the cleaning. I generally looked forward to that as we enjoyed our time together very much. After the uniquely quiet morning, I was looking forward to conversing with Helen even more than usual.

As we dusted and cleaned the foyer, it took only a moment to realize that Helen was also stricken by the unknown pall that had fallen over the household. My silly attempts at levity barely received a smile. Any questions I had were answered, but generally with only a word or two. Probably most alarming was that Helen did little to initiate any conversation at all – extremely out of character for her. With the way my mind works, with my propensity for self-doubt, I started to wonder what I had done to anger everyone so. Mr. Stafford did not wish to be around me, Melba would hardly talk with me, and even Helen was acting quiet and peculiar.

I racked my brain, trying to figure out the offense, but could not think of anything that I had done. Finding fault with myself was usually an easy thing to do, which made my lack of results all the more frustrating. I simply could not understand what was going on.

Finally, after exhausting everything I could imagine, I asked Helen plainly, "Helen, what have I done to offend you all?"

Helen looked at me strangely for a moment, clearly not knowing why I asked the question, and then a look of comprehension crossed her face. She asked, "You don't know, do you?"

"Know what? Please, tell me how to make amends." I still figured it had to do with me.

She shook her head and said, "It's nothing like that. I thought you were already aware, but clearly you are not. Today is April thirteenth. This is the anniversary of the death of Mr. Stafford's wife, Emma."

The satisfaction of receiving an answer was completely overwhelmed by the sadness of what the answer turned out to be. I was momentarily glad that the mood was not my fault, but I then half-wished it was. If I could lessen the sting of death, even at the price of my own culpability, I would; especially for Mr. Stafford.

"If I had known," I said, feeling the need to explain myself, "I would not have been so cheery this morning. I would not have made jests." I looked down and said, "Please forgive my callousness."

"It's only callousness if you were aware, which you were not. But now that you know, I think you will find that this will be a long and difficult day. I wish it was not this way, but the sadness of Mr. Stafford is great, and it permeates the entire house like an invisible fog until there is no escaping it."

The description scared me but was clearly born from experience. Once that I knew the circumstances of the day, I could almost feel the radiating sadness start to chill my bones.

When I finished helping Helen, I went back to the library – unsure if I hoped Mr. Stafford was there or not. He was nowhere to be found. I sat in my chair near the fire – even the usually happy embers looked sullen – and spent the first part of the morning struggling to read. Although I could make out the words on the pages, they felt like just a collection of randomness. I had no ability to focus. My mind was on the pain of Mr. Stafford which inevitably led me to my own pain for the ones that I had lost. I hoped to rise above those sorrowful emotions but was quite powerless against their massive force. I cried alone in the library for a long time. My emotional defenses were weak, and I could not help but give in to the sadness of that day.

After my tears ran dry, I sat quietly – my book completely abandoned – staring off into space in numbness. It was better than the pain but was still a lesser and difficult form of existence.

Around noon, I made my way to the dining room, not because I was particularly hungry, but because I wanted to be there in case Mr. Stafford showed up. He did not. Melba had prepared soup and I sipped at it absently, hardly caring that it was too hot at first, and then, eventually, stone cold. I was at the table for quite a bit of time, partly hoping for Mr. Stafford to arrive, partly having no motivation to do anything else.

The afternoon was no better. In an effort to be available for Mr. Stafford, I fought off the temptation to crawl into bed and try to prematurely end the day. I took my spot in the library and cycled through trying to read, trying not to cry, and trying not to feel.

Occasionally, I would see Helen, Melba, or Patrick, as they were doing their various chores, but there was no conversation, nor hardly even an acknowledgement of one another's presence. We were simply the quiet ghosts of April thirteenth.

Dinner came and went in the same manner as breakfast and lunch: quiet, sad, and without Mr. Stafford. After the meal, I, again, forced myself to spend time in the library on the increasingly remote chance that Mr. Stafford would join me. *How I wanted to tell him how sorry I was for his loss.* So, I spent more conflicted hours alone and melancholy, waiting for the interminable day to release its tortuous hold on us all.

As bad as the day had been, it became even worse. When the hour approached that I would normally retire for the night, and, having had given up any hope of seeing Mr. Stafford, I was about to head off to bed. Truly, at that point, I wanted nothing more than to crawl under my blankets and terminate that miserable day. As I was about to rise from the chair, the library door flew open and there stood a haggard and frightening looking Mr. Stafford.

From top to bottom, he was a complete mess. His hair was unkempt and his face unshaven. His waistcoat was completely open, while the shirt underneath looked to have buttons in the wrong holes – and only a small part of it was tucked into his pants.

As strange and disturbing as all of that was, the look on his face was by far the most terrible aspect – he looked like a man possessed. His breaths came heavy while he stood in the doorway and searched the room intently with his eyes. *Was he looking for me?*

I stayed in my chair, not moving, afraid even to breathe. The sorrow that I had felt for Mr. Stafford was still present but now mixed heavily with fear, for I felt like I was looking at a madman.

I continued to watch in silence until he took a few steps into the library. From his gait, I could tell that there was more wrong with him than just his appearance, for he stumbled and nearly fell over. Out of instinct, I stood up and said, "Mr. Stafford, are you alright?" My fear expanded as I had just made my presence known.

He froze in place for a moment and then slowly looked at me. From the expression he gave, I could tell that he didn't realize that I had been in the room. For several seconds, he stared at me, his face stuck between surprise and concern.

I grew uncomfortable at the silence and finally said what I had wanted to tell him all day, "Mr. Stafford, please accept my condolences for the loss of your wife. I am so sorry. I wish I could have met her."

He continued to stare at me for several seconds, then, finally, turned his head and looked off to the distant corner of the room. Another awkward moment of silence fell over the library and I was about to try and excuse myself when Mr. Stafford said quietly, "I loved her. I truly loved her."

His voice sounded strange, as if speaking was hard to do and I finally realized what was happening. Mr. Stafford was not just in the throes of despair; he was also drunk.

My fear changed but didn't shrink. I was frightened by alcohol; frightened by what it could do to people; what it had done to my father. To see Mr. Stafford, my greatest pillar of support and my greatest example, in that drunken state was terrifying. My respect for him dwindled, while my concern for the consequences of his actions grew.

"It has been many years," he continued, "and I still miss her. 'Time heals all wounds' they say. Ha! My wounds are timeless. My pain is infinite."

Although scared by his drunken state, I still felt pity for the hurt he was going through. The alcohol might be lessening his pain, but it clearly was still present. I took a step towards him but was still several paces away. I struggled with wanting to be close and wanting to stay back. I wanted to try and comfort him, but I also wanted to protect myself.

Suddenly, without warning, Mr. Stafford turned towards me, rushed over, grabbed my shoulders, and said in a panic, "Can you forgive me?" His eyes were large and intense, while his breath reeked of alcohol.

I was fairly certain that he was not asking for my forgiveness for his drunkenness – he could not have been that cognizant of the situation. He had to be asking forgiveness for something much deeper; more constant.

I shook my head and said, "Forgiveness for what? I don't understand."

He leaned in close – I could no longer see anything beyond his face, his beseeching eyes – and said grimly, "For the *deaths*…"

I stared into his agitation and tried to comprehend what he was saying. All I could think of was that the alcohol had caused him to dream up wild and untrue memories; unfair guilt at his wife's death. I was not sure what to say. I finally decided to give my forgiveness – for whatever it was worth – and try and break free from the situation.

Before I could say anything, however, a voice from the doorway sounded out, saying, "Mr. Stafford, please let me show you back to your room." It was Patrick. The servant looked at Mr. Stafford and then at me. I gave a small nod to indicate that I was alright.

Patrick walked into the room and took Mr. Stafford's arm. "Come with me, sir," he said kindly, but firmly, and started to pull Mr. Stafford away from me.

I stood still, watching as Patrick led him to the exit. Before they were into the hallway, Mr. Stafford stopped, turned, and looked at me. I steeled myself for whatever he might try and do. "Forgive me!" he cried out. "Forgive me! The deaths are mine!"

"Do come along, sir," Patrick said, while giving a strong pull on Mr. Stafford's arm. I stared while Mr. Stafford stared back. Another tug from Patrick and they reached the corridor, Mr. Stafford's imploring eyes still meeting mine. Then, they were out of view.

I stood there, blinking, hands fidgeting and shaking in front of me, overwrought with mixed feelings; sadness, disappointment, anger, and confusion. After an indeterminate amount of time, my bodily senses started to return to me, and I felt weak. I took a step back, towards my chair, and nearly collapsed from the sudden exhaustion that was flowing through me. I managed to fall into the cushioned seat, which relieved my fatigue but allowed me to now feel my tumultuous stomach. I took deep, steady breaths to try and not vomit. For the next minute, I focused on nothing but breathing and keeping the contents of my stomach place.

When the nausea passed and I could relax without concern of being sick, my focus became lost in the dying embers of the fire. I battled with thoughts of Mr. Stafford and the possible justification of his actions. Surely the death of a loved one is a reason to want to get lost in the mind-altering effects of alcohol. Would not any relief be tempting beyond measure?

Despite those somewhat rational thoughts, I still could not get over how nervous and scared I was at the sight of him in that state. Naturally I thought of my mother's letter and how my father was ruined, my family was ruined, by what I perceived to be a sinister drink. I knew I was jaded and biased, but I didn't care – I felt that I *deserved* to feel as I did; in a dark way, I had *earned* it.

As my mind chased itself with thoughts of pity and fright, I heard a sound in the doorway. I looked up quickly, worried that Mr. Stafford had returned. Thankfully, it was only Patrick.

He stepped in and addressed me, saying, "Mr. Stafford is now in bed and, hopefully, will stay there until the morning. Are you alright, Miss Gladwyn?"

I gave a very weak smile and said, "Yes," and then after a moment, said, "No," I got up and ran into Patrick's arms. "I was so scared," I cried, trying to explain my feelings that probably needed no explanation.

Patrick held me, though not firmly – he was probably uncomfortable with all of those emotions – and told me that I was safe.

I wanted to believe him, but in that moment, it was hard to do so. My secure future felt like its foundation had just suffered a mighty crack. Everything I looked forward to was built upon Mr. Stafford.

"This is a difficult day," Patrick said while releasing the embrace. "And today was worse than most."

I nodded with at least a little understanding, and then asked, "Why was it worse today?" Again, I thought that I had somehow exacerbated things.

The old servant looked at me, struggling with how to answer.

"What is it?" I persisted. "And what did he mean when he said that 'the deaths were his'?"

Patrick shifted his eyes to the floor, still battling some thought process. Finally, he said, eyes still down, "He should be the one to tell you."

"Tell me what?" I begged. *What had I done?*

Patrick, a determination made, looked from the floor and into my eyes. He said, "The death of Mrs. Stafford was a devastating loss for him. This date is one of mourning. However, it was made all the more difficult due to the nearness of Mr. Stafford's last assignment to Ipswich, the suicide."

I nodded in recognition of the reference, but not completely in understanding.

Continuing, Patrick said, "You, no doubt, saw the harsh effect that the assignment had on him?"

"Yes. He was not quite himself for several days."

"Well, the death of Mrs. Stafford, and the death of that man are related – along with others. You see, that book that he tracked down is basically Mr. Stafford's own suicide note after the loss of his wife."

Twenty-Six

BR

Early in the morning, well before sunrise, I awoke suddenly, covered in perspiration. Fleeting memories of the nightmare kept my senses heightened. With my eyes open and staring at the ceiling, I took deep breaths to calm myself while my mind tried to understand that the visuals it had just experienced were not real. It was a tough battle; the sights may not have been real, but the events they portrayed were.

I dreamt that I was outside a little tavern in the city of London. It was a foggy night, cold, and I had my arms wrapped around myself to keep warm. My purpose for being there was to watch my father as he ordered drink after drink. The tavern was dimly lit by a few candles which made my view difficult as the window I was looking through was quite dirty. The inside of the space was small, just a few old tables and a bar. During my vigil, an occasional person walked by me along the pavement, but none gave me a second glance.

It was a very strange sensation, that dream, as I knew it was my father that I was watching – even though I had no memory of him. I also knew that it was the night of his death. I wondered if that was actually what he looked like, built from memories too old and hidden to consciously bring up, or if it was just some random amalgam of features from people I had seen throughout my life. In any event, I watched as he downed a small glass of brown liquid, and then ordered another to replace it.

That is when I started to pound on the windows and scream. "No!" I yelled. "Stop! Please!" But no attention was paid to me – as is the way of dreams. I hit the glass so hard that it should have shattered, but it held firm. I tried to raise my voice even louder, but the harder I tried the quieter it seemed to get. It was an infuriating struggle against my own impotence.

When he stood up and headed for the door, my heart began to race. All the notions of him meeting his grown daughter, not knowing who I was, and what I might say in introduction, flew through my mind. However, my true concern, my real focus, was to stop him from dying.

I stepped away from the window and walked towards the entrance. I was halfway there when he staggered outside. His steps were unsure, his head weaving around as if attached to a spring, and his eyes were completely unfocused. I continued towards him, but I couldn't catch up. I cried out but received no notice.

I tried to quicken my pace, to run, but I never could get closer. He was always ahead of me, and, if anything, getting farther away. He approached an intersection and I knew that it was the location of the accident. I tried harder to move faster while I screamed with all my might; to no avail. I watched in frustrated horror as my father stepped off the pavement into the roadway just as a horse drawn carriage was passing by. I closed my eyes; I simply could not watch the death of my father. After hearing the whinny of horses and the screams of a few people, I finally looked. There in the road, unmoving, lay my dead father.

Despite my previous lack of motion, it was only an instant until I was kneeling next to him. He was facedown and I cried out, "I couldn't stop it! I'm so sorry!" I looked around for help, for anything, and found that I was completely alone in the street. The carriage, the few people that were around had all disappeared.

I grabbed my father's shoulder and tried to roll him on his back. *Perhaps I was mistaken, and he was not dead. Perhaps there was some way to save him.* I pulled with all my might and was able to get him to his side, and then finally to his back.

I looked at his face, and, although it was bloodied and torn, I clearly saw the face of Mr. Stafford. I leapt back away from him and out of my nightmare.

Combining Mr. Stafford with my father seemed a natural thing; the connection was easy to make. But what I also took away was the connection I made with alcohol and death.

There were many things that disturbed me about Mr. Stafford's drunken appearance in the library, but deep down, I was most alarmed by my concern for *him*. I didn't want him to die. I didn't want to lose the closest person in my life – *again*.

At that thought, my breath quickened while my eyes began to tear. I steadied my breath and fought against the notion. I did not want to cry. I did not want the *possibility* of something bad to completely take away my peace. Mr. Stafford was not dead. And, although he had most certainly been drunk, which deeply frightened me, it was only one time.

As I slowly navigated through the emotions stirred by the dream, my mind suddenly latched on to another memory to increase my concern. I recalled what Patrick had told me. Mr. Stafford had written a Dark Book. I had pressed Patrick for details, but he said that he had reached the limits of his presumptuousness and that Mr. Stafford himself would have to answer any further queries.

I tried to contemplate what it would be like to create something that, inadvertently, caused the death of others. It was too horrible to dwell on. I was self-aware enough to know that such a revelation would absolutely destroy me – after all, I could barely stand myself without such a horrifying burden. I wondered how Mr. Stafford had managed to carry such a weight. He was either one of the strongest people I had known, or one of the most heartless.

Those were the troubled thoughts that played through my mind while I lay in bed and waited for the morning light. *Who was Mr. Stafford?*

When I was ready for breakfast, I made my way to the dining room. I practically tiptoed down the hallway – I guess I didn't want to announce my presence in case I changed my mind at the last moment. I was nervous to see Mr. Stafford. What would he be like? Would there be another drunken episode? What would I be like?

When I entered the dining room, it was empty. I admit to some relief but could not help but wonder if there would be some kind of repeat of the previous day. Melba brought me a nice breakfast of eggs, crisp bacon, toast, and extra preserves. After setting the plate on the table, she gave a quick embrace. No doubt she was aware of last night's happenings.

About halfway through my meal, Mr. Stafford arrived. He gave a small cough to announce his presence from the doorway. When I looked up and saw who it was, I froze. I was happy to see that his clothes were well-arranged, his hair combed, and face shaven. His eyes, however, had the look of fatigue, sadness, and pain.

In a quiet and ragged voice, he said, "No need to worry, it is only Dr. Jekyll this morning. Would it be alright if I joined you?"

Mr. Stafford had never asked for my permission to dine with me before. There was guilt behind the question. It took a moment to realize that he was actually expecting an answer and I nodded my head.

"Thank you," he said as he crossed the room and took his chair across from me.

Melba came in and asked, "What would you like this morning, sir?"

"Water, strong tea, and a bit of toast, please."

"Right away, sir."

I absently picked at the eggs with my fork, waiting for whatever was going to happen next.

"Naomi," Mr. Stafford said. I looked up at him nervously. "Naomi, I need you to know that my actions last night were…" his voice caught, a tear fell down his cheek. "Were inexcusable." He wiped the tear away while desperately trying to control his emotions.

His pain broke my heart. Despite the bad events, I recalled the many good things he had done since I had met him. He was still the kindest man I had ever known. But I was unsure as to what to say. So, instead of saying anything, I stretched my hand out across the table for him to take it.

Mr. Stafford saw the gesture and put his hand over his eyes and began to weep. I watched in utter sadness as his body jerked along with his sobs. I could not help my own tears from escaping.

I left my hand open on the table, a small symbol that I was not giving up on him. After a minute or so, Mr. Stafford regained some control of his emotions. He took his hand away from his tear streaked face and actually gave a small smile when he saw that my gesture was still being offered. This time, he reached out his own hand across the table to hold mine.

His eyes met my own and he said, "May I ask you a favor?"

"Yes, of course."

"I know that I need to explain a lot of things to you. Will you give me an hour to gather myself and have a little food before we take on that conversation?"

I wanted to tell him that he didn't need to explain anything, but I didn't feel that that was true. Instead, I said, "Please, take as much time as you need."

"Thank you. One hour will be sufficient." Mr. Stafford then stood up and said, "Could you tell Melba that I will be taking my breakfast in my room?"

I nodded and he exited the dining room.

After finishing my food, I spent the next hour waiting in my room. I did not want to risk running into Mr. Stafford and have him think I was trying to rush him. That hour was interminable as I sat nervously on my bed unable to do anything but fret. As the time neared, I made my way to the library. We had not actually mentioned where the conversation was to take place, but it was safe to assume it would happen in the same place that the majority of our significant discussions had happened. When I entered, I found that I was alone. I took my chair in front of the fire, not bothering to choose a book, and waited for Mr. Stafford to arrive.

I didn't have to wait long. He entered the library without a word and sat down in his chair besides mine. He took a few seconds to get comfortable, and finally raised his eyes to me. I didn't try to hide my anticipation nor my expectation of his starting the conversation.

After taking in a deep breath, Mr. Stafford began, "This is a discussion that I should have had with you long before now. I have spent much of the morning asking myself why I had not talked with you sooner. The answer was not hard to find. For you see, I was afraid."

That was hard for me to hear. If someone like Mr. Stafford could be afraid, what hope was there for anyone? I did not say anything and let him continue.

"The noteworthy events of my life are generally tainted with badness. I guess I wanted you to see some good in me before I introduced you to the bad. I think you know that I care a great deal about what you think of me."

I nodded my head in understanding and agreement.

Mr. Stafford took another deep breath and said, "In the spring of 1851, my parents changed my life. They had arranged for me to meet Emma, my eventual wife. I had just finished my schooling and was learning the work of running father's businesses. When it came to what girl I should consider courting, my parents – having wealth – thought it would be best for me to marry someone who also had wealth. My mother had a circle of friends and one of them had a daughter about my age. A meeting was set up. Now, the idea of marrying for money or convenience of lifestyle did not appeal to me at all. I was not a hopeless romantic, but I knew that love would have to be the greatest part of any relationship that I was going to enter into. I made that clear to my parents and they were at least kind enough to agree to not give undue pressure if I truly was not attracted to the girl. All my self-righteous talk about love was for nothing the moment I saw her. She was beautiful. But more than that, after an afternoon with her, I was so captivated by her personality, humor, and kindness that I was almost certain that I would marry her. Soon after, we officially began courting. In the spring of 1852, a little over a year from meeting her, we married."

Mr. Stafford spoke so warmly of that woman, Emma, that it was easy to see the depth of his love for her – even then, all those years later.

He continued, "Once married, we were as happy as two people could be. I was growing more accustomed to the business world; Emma was busy with her artwork – some of which you saw in that abandoned room you had first stayed in – and we were just happily in love. Simple and wonderful.

"After two years of marriage, Emma gave birth to our son, Christopher."

A son? Although the words were perfectly clear, I repeated them in my head to make sure I understood what he had just said. I had never heard any mention about Mr. Stafford having any children.

"I'm not sure," said Mr. Stafford, "if anyone had spoken of Christopher to you. From your look, I think it's safe to assume that they had not."

I was so surprised that I all I could do was shake my head. The disconcerting thought came to me: What *other* secrets does Mr. Stafford have? I also could not help but wonder what happened to Christopher. Did he die, too?

"I guess it's a bit surprising to learn that you have a brother. In fact, that tin cup you had used when you first arrived had belonged to him. I'm sorry that I didn't tell you sooner. But, as I said, there is badness surrounding all of this – but we will talk about that in a little bit. Let me stick to the timeline of events.

"When Christopher was a little over five years old is when Emma became sick. She had cancerous tumors. Her health degraded quickly. I cannot imagine anything worse, any torture more horrific than watching the person you love wither away. I had a doctor or a nurse here around the clock to provide any help that they could. It the end, the help took the form of morphine or ether to reduce her pain. In the later stages, the doctor told me that the amount of pain medicine they were administering was far more than enough to kill a healthy man.

"On April thirteenth, she died. Even witnessing her decreasing health, I still found it hard to believe. I guess I'm a foolish optimist, as I had always imagined that Emma would somehow recover. I still wonder if my hope made her death all the more difficult. Probably…"

My surprise at the news that Mr. Stafford had a son was completely replaced by sadness at the story of his wife's death. For I understood the pain, at least to a large degree, that Mr. Stafford had gone through and was still suffering with.

"I do not think," he continued slowly, his breathing noticeably shallower, "that the right word has been invented yet to accurately explain the pain…the torture, of losing a loved one. It was a hurt that I simply could not bear – and, unfortunately, I don't say that in hyperbole."

It took a second for me to understand what he meant. The heaviness and intensity of his words spoke clearly of something horrific, but the meaning took another moment to follow – for it was not something readily contemplated. When the realization came, I was mortified. He was talking about ending his own life.

If Mr. Stafford noticed my shock, he didn't comment on it. Instead, he continued, "Seeing my inconsolableness, my parents took Christopher to live with them for a time, feeling that I was in no condition to properly care for him. The fact that they were right is one of my largest regrets." In obvious disgust, he shook his head slowly and said, "My son had lost his mother and I failed to help him. I was too selfish to see beyond my own suffering. In many ways, he lost both his parents that day."

At hearing the confessions, I trembled. I was nervous, sad, and a little scared. I was being told the darkest parts of Mr. Stafford's life and I knew that it would change us. My hope was that it would draw us closer; that I would have a better understanding of him. But I could not help but worry that the revelations would somehow segregate us – which, I knew, was exactly why Mr. Stafford had not told me those things prior.

"Four days after Emma's death, I was in such a state of pain that it seemed impossible to ever stop hurting. Every second of the day was agony. So, around midmorning, I dressed myself in my finest suit, including a flower in my buttonhole – yes, that small feature is why I was certain that the article you brought to me was about a Dark Book. After dressing, I went out to the horse barn, took a length of rope, attached it to one of the beams, and then fashioned a noose."

Even though I knew the direction of the conversation, to hear it so plainly was shocking. It was an event that happened over thirty years prior, and obviously was not carried out, but it was still painful and disturbing to imagine. "What stopped you?" I asked.

"A trade, of sorts. A trade that I have wished I could undo every day since."

"A trade?" I asked in confusion. "I don't understand."

"As I was preparing for that final step, something was holding me back. I was not afraid, but I felt a need to explain things. I needed to explain to my parents and Christopher why I was about to take my own life. I needed to explain how wonderful Emma was, how sorry I was, and how impossible it was for me to make any other decision. So, I left the barn and went to the desk in my room to write a letter containing that information. However, one page turned into two, then ten, then dozens and dozens. I was obsessed with the writing. I did not move from my desk for over twenty-four hours. I poured my feelings and regrets into that letter. And then, an amazing thing happened, after writing my emotions down, I felt that I could tolerate life. I was still incredibly sad, but that once insurmountable despair now seemed conquerable. In other words, I transferred the most powerful – and *dangerous* – emotions onto those pages. I created a Dark Book."

"You didn't know that you might have created something dangerous?"

"No. At that time, I had never heard of Dark Books. I was completely ignorant. All I knew was that I felt better and that I had created a deeply emotional account. Believe me when I tell you that I had no idea what I had done."

Dark Books were very frightening to me, but it was impossible to blame Mr. Stafford for creating one. He was a man going through enormous pain and found relief in writing down his thoughts and emotions. There was no malicious intent. "What happened next?"

"I spent the next couple of weeks alone and reading my book – over and over. It made me feel closer to Emma, as if reading allowed me to keep her memory alive and fresh. When I emerged from that solitude, I was a different person. I had somehow replaced much of my sadness with energy

– energy towards making my book known to everyone. I saw it, at that time, as a way to honor Emma's memory. Unfortunately, this was an easy task to accomplish. One of the companies that my family owns is a small publishing business. I took that new-found energy and worked with them to publish my writing. It didn't go through any editing; it was simply put to press because of who I was and the insistence I had that it was perfect."

Mr. Stafford paused for a moment and gazed into the fire. He continued, "Three hundred books were printed of my work, 'An Elaborate Goodbye', and sent out to various distributors. I was so excited. I saw this as the greatest way I could keep Emma alive. If I only knew…"

The pain and regret he felt was obvious in his words, his mannerisms, and his face. I understood it but could not ignore the unfairness. I stated, "But you could not have known."

"That may be true, but even the unintended consequences of our actions have their gravity."

What argument could I have given that he had not already overcome in the pursuit of his guilt? I was certain that there were none.

"A little over a month later," said Mr. Stafford, "I received a knock at my door. In walked two strangers, Mr. Franklin Dockery and his wife Sophia."

It took only an instant to make the connection. "Sophia Dockery? From The Council?"

"That's right. We all sat down together, and they proceeded to tell me about Dark Books, The Book Reapers, and then, how my book was affecting people."

I already knew the impact his writing had had on people but still could hardly bear to hear it.

Mr. Stafford continued, "They told me about several suicides that they had looked into over the last month. They told me that they found my book at the scene of them and determined that my writing was driving people to despair. My book was causing those people to kill themselves."

"What did you say?"

"Honestly, I didn't believe them. I thought they were complete lunatics. I also thought that they were ignorant barbarians – for the thought of hunting down books to destroy them was offensive to me. In the dark ages, there were times when books were banned and those that had them were harmed, but that was our embarrassing past. The perceived narrow-mindedness of those two visitors, and the claim they were making against me, caused me to heatedly ask them to leave."

From a general view, I agreed with him. The thought of destroying books – safe books – is criminal. However, I also could not dispel my confusion about watching a Dark Book burn.

"Before they left," continued Mr. Stafford, "they gave me one of my books with a newspaper article inside. Later that night, when I was a bit calmer, I read the article. I will never forget it. It talked about a man who dressed himself well, *including a flower*, and proceeded to hang himself. I made the connection easily but could not actually believe it. A coincidence, I thought."

I could not blame Mr. Stafford for being skeptical. Books that kill people is not an easy conclusion to accept. I asked, "What made you believe?"

"I started my own investigation. I still did not actually believe their claims, but if there was any proof to the contrary, I had to know. A few weeks later, I read an article in a newspaper about another suicide, this one in Crawley. As I read the telltale circumstances, I felt a cold dread creep over me. I was not convinced, but I then knew that the seemingly impossible and atrocious claim *could* be true. So, I traveled to Crawley to see if I could find any proof that my book was involved.

"The first thing I did was talk to the man's neighbors. I found out that he was young, less than twenty-five years of age, and was married the previous year. They had no children other than his students – he was a schoolteacher. It took all the courage I had to approach the small home of the man. His wife answered the door, eyes red from the constant tears, and I began to talk with her. I could not explain my real reason for being there so I made up a story about offering comfort to those who have lost a spouse. We talked for a while, me sharing my grief about the loss of Emma, and I eventually came around to the topic of books. She told me that her husband loved to read. I asked if I could see his book collection. When she showed it to me, I was at first relieved, for my book was not among them. But then, she brought out his most current read – which was on his nightstand – and I recognized it as soon as she came into view. I had to put my hand against the wall to keep from falling over. Despite all of my beliefs and doubts, I then knew that my book had killed that women's husband. Beyond that, my book, according to Mr. and Mrs. Dockery, had killed several people. The shock of such a revelation was tremendous. All I wanted to do was leave the house; to run outside, to take deep breaths, and to make all the pain go away. However, I stopped myself for just long enough to purchase the book from the wife. I gave her an enormous sum of fifty pounds for it, hoping that a bit of money could ease her pain a little and perhaps calm my conscience. I don't know if the money provided any help to her, but it did nothing to help me."

As hard as I tried, I knew that I could not truly comprehend what it was like to hear that something you created was causing people to die. But I know guilt, and I know that it would be an absolutely crushing burden to bear.

"I realized then," said Mr. Stafford, "that I had preserved my life by trading it for others. Writing that book saved me, but at a cost that I am not worthy of. I'm not unappreciative for my life, but rarely does a day pass by that I do not wish that I had finished what I had started and never wrote that book."

To hear Mr. Stafford say that he daily wished for his death, all those years ago, made my heart groan. However, my emotions conflicted with my logic. If Mr. Stafford had taken his own life, then several people would not have died. One life for many is a trade that any good person should make. But I could not help but think of the good he had done. His work as a Book Reaper must have saved many people. Despite the incredible hardship of his unintended consequences, he had made the best use of his life in service to others.

And, he loved me. He had become my family; had given me a life, and a future which I did not deserve. I had to ask, "Do you still wish that you had killed yourself?"

I was afraid to hear the answer. Despite the generalness of the question, I really meant it about me. Did he wish death over how he had helped me?

Mr. Stafford looked at me for several long seconds with his sad, but still kind, eyes. He eventually said, "You probably don't realize this, probably cannot truly understand what I mean, but, Naomi, you saved me."

It made no sense. I objected, "No! If anything, you saved *me*!"

"I hope that that is true," he said. "I hope that I have helped you. But as one gets older, they examine their life all the more; and I'm not immune to such retrospective thoughts. Unfortunately, I see large failures all along the way. I'm not so obtuse as to ignore some of the good I have done, but the bad overshadows it. My son, Christopher, he lived with my mother and father until he was twelve. My sadness at Emma's death, then my sudden energy at needing to publish my book, then the guilt of realizing what my book was doing, and finally my aggressiveness in hunting down all the copies made me unfit to raise my own child. It was only when my mother died that Christopher came back. The damage I had caused to our relationship was deep. We were practically strangers. I tried to get him interested in The Book Reapers, and for a time, we worked together in tracking down Dark Books, but eventually, our issues forced us apart. It has been several years since I have last heard from him."

The sadness of Mr. Stafford's life was beyond anything I would have ever guessed. How could such a kind person have so many trials, so much guilt?

"So, you see," he continued, "when I look back, I see many failures. But then you showed up, completely and utterly unexpected. You gave me a chance for a measure of redemption. It has been many, many years since I have felt as good about myself since your arrival. I will be eternally grateful to you."

Grateful to me? It felt so backwards. I had done nothing. *He* was the one who had provided everything. "Mr. Stafford," I pleaded, "I'm the one who is grateful. You have opened your home, your caring, and your friendship to me – a miserable orphan who snuck into your house and stole your food. You are not, and never will be, in any debt to me."

"You are wrong," he responded kindly. "You don't have to agree, but you are wrong."

It was difficult to think that I was that important to him – or anyone.

Mr. Stafford picked up a log and added it to the fire. He then turned to me and said, "There is another thing I wish to discuss with you, to apologize for."

I was not sure I could take another apology, but I also could not think what he would need forgiveness for, so I simply looked at him quizzically.

"I was incredibly callous last night towards your feelings. I know you have strong emotions about drunkenness – how could you not – and yet I still allowed myself to fall into that pit. It must have been frightening and probably made you angry. I'm sorry for what I did. What is more, I will never make that mistake again."

With all the revelations of our conversations, I had nearly forgotten about his actions the previous night. But he was right; thinking of him in that state did anger me and frighten me. I looked down at the floor between us, contemplating on how I should respond. Scolding him seemed beyond redundant. Telling him that it was not an issue would have been a lie. Finally, I looked up and simply said, "Thank you, I appreciate that."

At that point, we both settled back into our chairs while staring into the fire. It was only late morning, but I was exhausted. I would occasionally look at Mr. Stafford and saw that he looked equally as tired, if not more so, than I felt.

It had been, unquestionably, a difficult two days. I had a more complete picture of Mr. Stafford and not all of it was as good as I had hoped. But, as I sat there, part of me felt that I was closer to him than I had ever been. I also held out hope; hope that, now that I knew his struggles, I could prove to be the help, maybe even the savior, that he saw in me.

Twenty-Seven

BR

Perhaps the passing of time can be every bit the healer as the saying would have one believe. For as awful as April thirteenth was, and how shocking the revelations of the fourteenth were, within two weeks the household started to feel normal again. However, just like a physical injury can leave a scar, the emotional toll of those days left lingering effects.

Mr. Stafford slowly regained his enthusiasm. He always was completely interested, engrossed even, with whatever he was doing – reading, researching, or having a conversation. It was a contagious trait that made being around him exceptionally enjoyable. Since then, however, the scars of mid-April seemed to cause his enthusiasm to be limited, like a kite that is soaring and then suddenly tugs against the limits of its string. It's possible, even likely, that that limitation was always there, but only after learning about the hardships of his life, could I actually perceive it; his wounds being far older than just a few weeks.

For me, I had a very subtle nervousness around Mr. Stafford, as if he would suddenly become drunk again or reveal some other large and terrible secret. As I thought about that, I reluctantly concluded that my trust in him had taken a blow. To combat those thoughts, I reminded myself of all the good he had done towards me and I knew that I still loved him more than anyone alive.

I also respected how he chose to live his life – in pursuit of helping others. Of the three hundred books that were printed, he had tracked down two-hundred and seventy-eight. Besides those, he had pursued and destroyed a great many other Dark Books.

I will admit, however, that learning that Mr. Stafford had a son was a bit harder to come to terms with. To some degree, I could understand him not wanting to talk about his late wife or the fact that he wrote a book that had caused innocent people to take their own lives. But his son was alive, and I found it difficult to contemplate the two of them being at odds to the point of near non-existence. The completeness of their separation was emphasized to me in a conversation with Helen. Although she had worked for Mr. Stafford for a few years, she was completely unaware that he had a son. Christopher was gone by the time she was hired, and no one talked about him, ever.

The entire situation left me very conflicted. On one hand, I would give anything to spend time with my mother again. In that light, it was hard to understand such a break between parent and child. However, when I thought about my father, I had no great desire to meet him. By the time I was born, he was not a good man. From that viewpoint, I guess I felt a hint of understanding. But, I reasoned, Mr. Stafford was not a bad man. Perhaps Christopher was not a good son? Perhaps some significant event caused them to go their separate ways? Those thoughts and questions ran through my mind, but I knew it would be some time before I could broach that subject with Mr. Stafford. It would likely be a painful conversation and I felt we needed to recover some more before having another emotional discussion.

So, while waiting for an adequate amount of time to pass, in order to lay to rest those vexing questions about his son, I went about my normal routine: reading, chores, and pouring through newspapers. In late May, more than five weeks since the anniversary of Emma Stafford's death, the activity of examining newspapers started to reveal a possible situation. There were some attacks happening in Liverpool. Now, the attacks could possibly have no connection to each other, could easily have nothing to do with a Dark Book, but the most current report gave a clue that I needed to understand better. With newspaper in hand, I turned to Mr. Stafford and asked, "Excuse me, Mr. Stafford, what is 'The Siege of Delhi'?"

We were sitting in our usual chairs in the library, after breakfast, and he looked at me with a bit of a puzzled expression. "May I ask," he said, "why you are interested in that event?"

"I'm trying to piece something together," I answered, not wanting to give away too much – partly because if I was wrong, I would rather him not know, and partly because if I was right, then I wanted to surprise him with a complete scenario.

"Ah, a bit of a mystery; how exciting!"

I adored his enthusiasm at my questions. He put his book down and continued, "Very well, a little history this morning. The Siege of Delhi was an event, culminating in a bloody battle, during the Indian Rebellion – which took place several years before you were born."

I was not at all well-schooled in history and had to ask, "The Indian Rebellion? What was that?"

"Hmm… well, in order to explain that, I probably need to explain about the British East India Company. Have you heard of it?"

I had, but mostly in passing. At times like that I wondered how he could put up with my shallow knowledge of the world. "I have heard of it," I answered weakly. "It's a large trading company, I think."

"It was, but no longer exists. And to call it a large trading company would be like calling the Atlantic Ocean a large lake. The British East India company was enormous; practically a government unto itself. It controlled vast territories in India and even had its own army."

"A business with its own army? Why would a company need an army?"

"To expand its holdings; for profit."

I thought about that for a few moments. It sounded strange for a British company to take rule over territories in another country and have an army there. I made the observation, "I imagine that people in India were not happy with that arrangement."

"Some were actually very happy with it. A lot of wealth was produced, and not just for the British. However, many, as you suggested, did not like the influence of, or the treatment by, the company in their lands. This was at the heart of the Indian Rebellion of 1857."

"What happened?"

"The rebellion itself was finally subdued – after many thousands died – but it caused the ruling authorities in Britain to evaluate the causes behind the rebellion and eventually take steps to dissolve the British East India Company."

"And the Siege of Delhi?" I asked, coming back to the origin of the conversation.

"That was a significant battle and very costly. The city of Delhi was taken over by the natives, and the East India Company army, along with the actual British army, fought to take control back. Thousands died on both sides of the battle, including many civilians. In the end, the British won. Although only one battle, it was demoralizing for the rebellion and went a long way towards ending the whole thing."

I had read in books about battles. The valiant armies for good always proving victorious over their evil enemies. But those were stories; words written to stir the imagination. But what Mr. Stafford was talking about was a real battle with both sides feeling that *they* were the valiant armies for good. And thousands of people – families, fathers, brothers, sons, daughters, wives, sisters – dead. In only an instant of honest examination did I began to see through the *glory* of the storybook battles.

It took a question from Mr. Stafford to put my mind back on the track it had originally been on. He asked, "Now will you tell me why you are interested in this?"

I was not ready to explain. I needed a little more time to try and fit in what I had just learned. It might have been for nothing, but I could not help but think there was an oddity that needed to be pursued. "Please allow me a few minutes. I would like to puzzle on this a little more."

"Alright, then," he said with a smile. He then picked up his book and went back to reading.

I turned my attention to the newspaper article and tried to see how that new information applied – if it did at all. I read and reread the details looking for the reason that it was causing me alarm. After several minutes, I got up and gathered some of the previous newspapers that had articles that could be related. I read those over and started to see a pattern. There was definitely not enough information to be certain, but I had enough to raise my thoughts to Mr. Stafford.

I arranged the newspapers on my lap in the order I wanted to present them and gave one last mental run-through of my reasoning. When comfortable with my thoughts, I turned and said, "Excuse me, Mr. Stafford, but I believe I have something of interest to bring to your attention."

"I must admit," he commented, "since your question about the battle, I have been quite curious as to what you were up to." He once again put his book down to give me his full attention and said, "Please, proceed."

"About four weeks ago, I read about a murder in Liverpool; a man stabbed to death. By itself, I did not bring it up as there were simply too few details to draw any conclusion – especially about a Dark Book. Ten days after that, there was another murder – this I did bring to your attention as two murders in a short period of time is something noteworthy. Both victims were sailors; one a captain and one a first mate, from separate ships. You will no doubt remember that we concluded that it was something to keep attention on but that we still didn't have enough information to draw any firm conclusions."

"I remember that well. Has there been another murder?"

"No, actually, but not for lack of effort. You see, there was another attack, but this time the victim lived. It was another sailor from yet another ship. His attacker stabbed him, like the others, but the man survived."

"Well now," said Mr. Stafford, "this is quite interesting. But how does it tie into the Siege of Delhi?"

"According to Mr. Robert Havill, that is the name of the sailor, a first mate, who was attacked and lived, his attacker made statements to the effect that the stabbing was retribution for the Siege of Delhi."

Mr. Stafford sat back in his chair to contemplate that piece of information. He asked, "Does the article say how old Mr. Havill is?"

"Twenty-seven years old."

"Well that is very odd, then. Mr. Havill was not even born when that battle happened as it was over thirty years ago."

"What is more," I said, "Mr. Havill described the attacker as someone who was European and looked to be in his thirties. If that is true, then the attacker could not have been involved in the siege either; at most, he would have been a small child at that time."

"If nothing else," commented Mr. Stafford, "this certainly is very peculiar. Tell me, what conclusion have you drawn?"

"I cannot be positive, of course, but certain things are standing out to me. First, two of the ships that the sailors belonged to were about to depart for India. The third ship had recently arrived from India before the attack. The fact that all the victims had dealings with India seem to fit in with the words of the attacker."

"Tremendous observation! Go on," said Mr. Stafford.

"Let us assume that all three attacks are related. I looked at the ages of the victims and only the captain could have been old enough to possibly have participated in the siege. However, before working for a shipping company, it says that he was in the navy – so it's unlikely he would be part of a siege that took place away from the ocean. Even if he was there, the other two men were definitely not."

Mr. Stafford was no longer looking at me, but was gazing into the fire, thinking on all that I was telling him. I paused for a moment to allow time for his thoughts. After a few seconds I continued, "The third point has to do with the nationality and the age of the attacker. Perhaps an Indian man would want to seek revenge for a historical wrong, but the man was not Indian. So why would a European take revenge on fellow Europeans? Also, if he is too young to have participated in the siege, then why is he trying to exact revenge on it at all? Why would someone, who had nothing to do with something, suddenly take it upon himself to act in behalf of it?"

"And here," said Mr. Stafford, "is where it all comes together. You think that this attacker had read a Dark Book and it's influencing his actions."

"As I said, I cannot be certain. However, the possibility is there."

"Can you think," asked Mr. Stafford, "of any other reasons for these actions?"

As much as I would have like to have had an unassailable argument, I did not. I nodded and answered, "It could be that he is acting in behalf of a friend or relative. Perhaps his father was part of the siege and he is trying to right some perceived wrong against him. Beyond that, I'm not sure."

Mr. Stafford rubbed his chin as he continued to think over all I had presented. He finally said, "Let us assume for a moment that a Dark Book is indeed behind these attacks. What would be your plan of action?"

I was so busy trying to figure out the different aspects of the story that I had not even considered how to actually address it. Being so unprepared for the question, I quickly and quietly answered, "I'm not sure."

"Take a minute," he responded kindly.

I turned my head and absently gazed at some of the books on the wall while my mind tried to come up with an approach to the situation. The harder I tried, the more the ideas seemed to slip away. I wanted to come up with a plan that would absolutely end with an answer to the problem, but nothing remotely close to that presented itself. I finally gave him the only idea I could muster up. "Outside of hoping the police capture the perpetrator, I think we would need to know what ships are leaving for, or arriving from, India and keep an eye on their crew. Perhaps we would witness an attack and be able to pursue the culprit."

"That is," said Mr. Stafford, "one of my thoughts as well. Not exactly the easiest method, wouldn't you say?"

I nodded. Even if there was only one ship, it could easily have a dozen crew members. If there was more than one ship, then the number would go up quickly. If my plan was to work, we would have to be very fortunate in the person we chose.

"Well," said Mr. Stafford, "it's a good thing that we are not on our own. I would like to read over these articles myself first, but I think you have made an excellent case for a trip to Liverpool. However, we are dealing with a murderer and not a lot of clues, so I think that I will enlist some help to join us."

A couple of things struck me and made me excited. First, he was agreeing with my conclusion of the articles. Second, he was talking about an assignment and using the word 'us' – I would not be left behind this time. Third, I had never been to Liverpool – or, for that matter, practically anywhere.

"Who would you enlist?" I asked.

"I'm not sure yet. I think that the Hudsons would be good company. But I would also like more. Liverpool is a large city with a lot of people coming and going; we will need as many eyes as we can get."

Despite all the excitement at the proposed trip, a small amount of excitement was reserved for the possibility of seeing Edward again. We had not spoken since the night he and his father were our guests for dinner, but I thought of him often.

"I don't imagine that you have ever been to Liverpool?" asked Mr. Stafford.

"No, sir. I have been to London and Bromley, that is all."

"Well then," he said brightly, "I think this should make for a very interesting trip."

Neither of us had any idea of just *how* interesting it would end up being.

Twenty-Eight

BR

Once it was decided that we would be going to Liverpool, a lot happened in a short period of time. Mr. Stafford sent several telegrams to other Book Reapers – including the Hudsons – purchased train tickets for us and had me pack for multiple weeks' worth of travel. It felt a bit like I was going on a holiday – except for the facts that we were trying to track down a murderer, and I hadn't ever been on a holiday.

Helen, of course, helped me pack and shared her concerns. "Why can't your first assignment be something a little less horrible?"

I had had a similar thought. I said, "From what I know of Dark Books, they are all horrible."

Helen stopped putting items of clothing into a medium sized steamer trunk and paused to think. After a couple of seconds, she resumed her task and commented, "I know they are all horrible. I guess what I'm thinking is that a book that causes someone to harm themselves is very different from one that causes a person to harm others. You could be putting yourself in danger."

"To be fair," I said weakly, not really believing in the argument I was about to make, "we are not actually looking for a murderer, but for a book that could be motivating him. The assignment is about a thing, not a person."

Helen saw through my poor attempt to soothe her, gave me a frown, and said, "Nice try, but we both know that you will not find that book without finding the person."

She was right. I then gave her my only remaining argument, the same argument I used when my own nerves for the assignment became overly troubled. "Well, I will not be alone. Mr. Stafford will be with me the entire time. If I am certain of anything, I am certain that he will not let anything bad happen."

"I know," Helen said sadly. "But I cannot help but worry. I'm sure everything will be fine." After she closed the trunk, she stood upright, looked at me and said, "Please promise me that you will be careful and that you will do everything that Mr. Stafford says."

"I promise."

It was a Saturday morning – just two days since bringing up the newspaper articles – when we left home to head to Liverpool. Both Melba and Helen looked quite sad at seeing us go. I hoped that, after we returned safely, the next assignment would be easier for them – and me. Outside of the front doors, we shared long embraces, fighting back tears, as if I would not be coming back for some great amount of time – if ever.

"I feel a little bad at having to break this up," said Mr. Stafford, smiling. "Actually, come to think of it, I don't recall such emotion when I have gone on any previous assignments…"

"You listen to me," said Melba, sternly. "If she is harmed in any way, it will not go well for you." I noticed Helen nodding her head in agreement.

"Ladies," said Mr. Stafford imploringly, "I will not let anything happen to Naomi. Nor to me…if anyone is concerned about that."

I found Melba and Helen's concern touching and Mr. Stafford's reaction of mock insult to be humorous.

"You know very well that we care about you, sir," said Melba. "But this is Naomi's first assignment and it sounds like a particularly bad one."

"Understood," said Mr. Stafford. "I promise you that Naomi and I shall be very cautious. But we really do need to be going." With that, he opened the carriage door for me. After a last glance at Melba and Helen, I climbed into the cabin.

I was relieved, to a degree, when Mr. Stafford also climbed in and Patrick started us on our way. The emotional goodbye made we wonder, for a moment, how safe I would be. But soon, with the rhythmic sounds of the horse's clip-clop, and the kind Mr. Stafford sitting across from me, I felt the security that my guardian had always provided return. The worry melted away and, in its place, I felt enthusiasm at what the days ahead would bring.

It was a beautiful spring morning, the sun shining brightly, and the world fully enveloped in its happy green coat for the season. The fine weather bolstered my excitement. As we softly rattled down the road, I thought over the upcoming events: Euston station and my first train ride. Seeing Edward again – he and his father would be meeting us at the station. Travel to Liverpool. Seeing a new city and staying in my first hotel. Finally, the purpose behind all of it: trying to track down a murderer and locating a potential Dark Book. It was one exciting and new event after another! I should have been more nervous at the last item, but so many seemingly wonderful things would happen first, that any concerns about our dangerous purpose were pushed to the back of my mind.

As we neared the city, the skies darkened a little, not from clouds, but from the smoke of seemingly infinite chimneys. Still, the anticipatory atmosphere of spring could not be dampened and the happy look on the faces of people we passed gave evidence to that. Men walked about with chests out and heads held high – unlike the huddled and hunched look that cold weather molded them into. Women wore light coats and lingered in their steps towards whatever destination they had for the morning.

As we crossed over Blackfriars Bridge, I could see that the river was alive with activity. Many long and low barges could be seen moving up and down the Thames, carrying their cargo. Along the shore, people scurried about, lashing boats to pylons, carrying parcels to and from the ships, and a hundred other little activities that made the waterfront so unique. Even though my life along its edge was brief and I was quite young, it still serves as some of my earliest memories – and of course, time with my mother. *What would she think of me now if she could see me? If only...*

We continued northward through the city, somehow conversing on anything but the tasks ahead of us. Mr. Stafford kept our topics light, choosing to discuss the latest book he was reading, *The Prince and the Pauper* by Mark Twain. I enjoyed his musings on how odd it would be to come across a stranger that looked exactly like him. And then the entire notion of trading places and living someone else's life allowed for many interesting possibilities. I cannot be sure, but I think Mr. Stafford chose to keep our topic pleasant in order to calm any nerves I may be having. That was another reassuring sign that he was looking after me.

As we neared our destination, the amount of people and carriages increased dramatically. Most of our ride was calm and unhindered, but now it was getting harder to proceed. Patrick deftly handled the vehicle, keeping us out of harm's way while always moving us forward.

When Euston Station came into view, my attention was instantly drawn to the massive four column arch at its entrance. Even from a distance, it was impressive and seemed, to me, out of place for something as mundane as a train station.

Patrick stopped the carriage a little distance from the station and called down, "Mr. Stafford, I think it would be best to get out here and walk the rest of the way. It certainly will be faster."

I looked out the window and saw a sea of vehicles and people ahead of us and figured that Patrick was correct. Mr. Stafford hardly hesitated before opening the door to depart. Once outside, the full sound of the crowd met us – a constant barrage of unintelligible conversations. Despite all my excitement, I felt nervousness and discomfort at the thought of joining the mass of people. I half-wanted to get back in the carriage and wait for everyone to go away. That was a silly notion, but the anxiety I was feeling caused me to be a little irrational.

"Can we help with your luggage, guv?" said a voice from the crowd.

I looked over and found two young men, dressed in threadbare clothes, addressing Mr. Stafford. After a quick, but careful examination of the two, Mr. Stafford said, "That would be excellent. We have two trunks. Please offload them. You two will take one of them while my driver and I will take the other."

Without a word the two young men climbed the side of the carriage and carefully brought down our luggage. Mr. Stafford then gave them direction to take up his trunk. Patrick, with a constant suspicious glare towards the helpers, took the handle on one side of the remaining trunk and Mr. Stafford took the other.

"Stay close," Mr. Stafford said to me with a smile. It was advice I was absolutely going to follow.

Patrick commanded the two men, "We are going to the station. Lead the way." Then men lifted their burden and headed into the crowd. I was fairly certain that he asked them to go first so that he could keep a cautious eye on them.

Mr. Stafford and Patrick followed with the next trunk and I was at the tail end of the procession. I remained so close that I accidently stepped on Mr. Stafford's heals more than once.

Within a few moments, all I could see were people. The masses parted slightly to let us by and closed quickly behind us – like dragging a stick through a puddle. I had thought that the Book Reaper's meeting was quite crowded, but, by comparison, I considered it sparse. I could hardly move without bumping into someone. The cramped space, along with the cacophony of sounds and the varied smells, increased my anxiety. Breathing felt harder, the air thicker, and I was growing desperate to be out of the chaos.

I remained close to Mr. Stafford, focusing on the plaid pattern of his jacket – anything to distract me from my increasing discomfort. Every step was a victory, while every moment was becoming more and more difficult. Part of my concern was that if I reached a point of being overwhelmed, it was not like I could just end the experience. There was no quick path to get away from the crowd.

Fortunately, I was able to bear the pressure and took a little comfort as we approached the entrance. We continued inside, through the massive archway.

My anxiety was still high as the long loading platform also held a crowd of people. As we continued to push onwards, I looked at the faces we passed – nothing but strangers impatiently waiting for their train. The warm and happy feelings that the spring day had generated didn't seem to apply here. Finally, we came to the end of the platform which allowed a small reprieve. Standing on the edge, overlooking the tracks, I had the crowd behind me. The open space before me helped soothe the feelings of being boxed in. The constant sounds, however, didn't let me forget the situation.

Mr. Stafford paid the two men who helped with one of the trunks and, by the look of glee on their faces, the sum must have been generous. Patrick bid us farewell and left us to wait.

After a few minutes, a voice started to stand out from the general crowd noise. I looked around for the source and saw Mr. Hudson and Edward pushing towards us. They carried a single large trunk between them. I felt a small sense of relief as that meant two less strangers to be surrounded by – not a big comfort, but anything was appreciated at that point.

"Busy today," boomed out Mr. Hudson as they got close.

"Quite," answered Mr. Stafford. "It must be the nice weather."

After setting the trunk down, Edward walked up close to me and said, "Hello, Miss Gladwyn. It's good to see you again."

"It's good to see you too, Edward." I was not feeling overly formal. "I'm not very fond of being in this crowd."

Edward looked around, as if seeing the mass of people for the first time, and said, "This place is always like this. I guess I'm just accustomed to it."

The thought of becoming accustomed to the madness around me seemed impossible. However, in a general sense, I was becoming accustomed to being the adopted daughter of a wealthy and kind man – that was certainly more outlandish than a busy railway station.

I said, "Well, I will be happy to be getting onto the train and away from all these people."

Edward pulled out his pocket watch and checked the time. He then looked up and commented, "Should be any minute now."

As if on cue, a whistle sounded out from the distance. It was an unmistakable sign that our train was approaching, and it gave me another small degree of relief. I looked down the track, out of the archway, eagerly watching for my escape from the crowd. Before long, a powerful black machine came into view, dark smoke pouring from its stack, a deep rumble shaking me from the inside out. I had been near steam-powered boats before, some quite large, but none gave the impression of absolute power that the train engine did – water vessels seemed calm next to the barely bridled fury of that locomotive.

It moved slowly by, mere feet away, and I wondered if a herd of elephants could rival the effect that the engine had on me for its size and its strength. When it finally came to a stop, a passenger cabin was before us. It was then that I realized that the spot along the platform that Mr. Stafford had led us to was not random. As a few passengers departed, he indicated that it was our cabin for the journey. I climbed onboard while he and Mr. Hudson flagged down a porter to load the luggage.

My first feeling, after entering the passenger carriage, was relief – I was finally separated from the bustling crowd outside. A light and soothing sense of calmness started to return as the relative quietness of the carriage washed over me. My second feeling, upon entering our enclosed cabin, was happy surprise. I was not exactly sure what to expect of the train carriage or our accommodations, but where I found myself was beyond anything I had dreamed of. The cabin we would share was finely appointed with cushioned benches, ornate wood, and gold-patterned burgundy carpet. The two benches faced each other and allowed for at least six, we only had four, people to sit and have a conversation. I was not very knowledgeable about trains, but I was certain that most cabins were not as luxurious as that one.

I sat down next to the window, facing the front of the train – I guess I always prefer facing the way the vehicle was moving, for that is the direction I always sat when in Mr. Stafford's carriage. Edward sat opposite me. I probably would have been nervous in that moment, sitting alone with him, but I was too excited about being on the train and looking out the window – which, admittedly, was not a particularly interesting view while in the station and not moving. I simply was too distracted to pay much attention to Edward.

Within a minute or so, Mr. Stafford and Mr. Hudson joined us. I asked where our luggage was and was informed that there was a space for it at the front of the car.

From outside the train, yells of, "All aboard!" could be heard. My excitement grew. Before long, a whistle sounded, and the train began to tremble as it slowly moved forward. I peered out the window eagerly, watching as the station walls crawled by. Then, we were outside, moving through the buildings of North London. The sights in themselves were not new, but somehow felt completely foreign from that new position.

Before too long, we were moving faster than I ever had in my life. Buildings, people, trees all moved past us rapidly. Only a few minutes more and we were outside of the busy city and into sparsely populated territory. Soon we were in the country, surrounded by light green fields and blossoming forests. The good weather followed the train out of London and shone brightly on our path. It was completely remarkable and utterly wonderful.

I have been on several train rides since that day, but there is something special about the first one. I can still feel the warm echoes of excitement that it produced. Of course, the thought of that first journey leads me to the other emotions that the assignment created, and they are not all nearly as pleasant.

Twenty-Nine

BR

Watching the scenery outside of the train windows was mesmerizing. Any lingering discomfort from the crowds at the station was now far behind me. I practically had to force my eyes away from all the sights in order to pay attention to the conversation that was going on inside – particularly because I was being addressed.

Mr. Hudson had said, "So, Miss Gladwyn, I understand that we have you to thank for this journey."

I looked at him and wondered if he was feeling upset or inconvenienced. Fortunately, his face didn't look annoyed at all, but I was not exactly sure how to respond. Yes, I made some connections in the articles, but ultimately it was Mr. Stafford that had made the decision. I said, "I only saw some interesting possibilities in the various newspapers. I don't believe I'm in a position to cause any of us to go on a journey."

"Of course, of course," said Mr. Hudson. "What I meant is that you were the first to bring up any reason for this Liverpool business to possibly be connected to a Dark Book."

"It was quite brilliant," exclaimed Edward. "Father and I had also been paying attention to the attacks but could not find the thread that pulled them all together."

Although it should have been obvious, I only realized then that other Book Reapers were also reading the newspapers and looking for Dark Books. Was I really the first to make any kind of connection? Although I felt a little pride, that revelation mostly made me feel uncomfortable and even responsible for the outcome of the assignment. For fairness' sake, I had to share my doubt. "I believe that the possibility of a Dark Book exists, but I'm far from certain. My conclusions leave many unanswered questions."

"That is true," said Mr. Stafford. "However, there is no harm in investigating. And there is something about all of this that just…just feels like a Dark Book."

"Will there be anyone else joining us?" asked Edward.

"I sent several wires informing the Order of our intentions. In response, they have assigned Claude Northam to accompany us; which only makes sense as he lives in Liverpool."

I was not familiar with the name, but the Book Reapers had many members that I didn't know.

"He will meet us at the hotel tomorrow morning," continued Mr. Stafford. "Beyond that, I'm not sure. If we find any more proof that a Dark Book is behind the attacks, then I imagine that many will be sent rather quickly. I guess you could say that our assignment is exploratory at this point."

"What do we propose," asked Mr. Hudson to all of us, "that our first order of business is so as to make any headway?"

"I think," said Edward, "that we need to talk to Mr. Robert Havill, the man who survived the last attack. Surely the newspapers did not record everything that he had witnessed. Perhaps there are more clues to be revealed through him."

"Excellent idea, Edward," said Mr. Stafford encouragingly. "Does anyone disagree with this being our first task?"

I shook my head while Mr. Hudson looked very pleased with his son.

"What else?" asked Mr. Stafford.

I spoke up, "I think we should try and determine which ships are heading to, or returning from, India. That may lead us to the next target."

"Capital idea," said Mr. Hudson. "You know, Thomas, I think the future of our order is bright with such as these two up and coming."

Mr. Stafford looked at me and Edward and then said, "I could not agree more."

The rest of our planning conversation didn't go much further. Until we knew what Mr. Havill could tell us and how many ships we were dealing with, it was hard to formulate anything very solid. Eventually, Mr. Hudson and Mr. Stafford turned to talk of other things – business and politics, while I got lost once more in the passing scenery.

Occasionally I would glance at Edward, and he seemed to be similarly lost out the window, or perhaps in thought, it was hard to tell.

After about two hours, the train made a stop in Northampton and let on more passengers. Three people climbed aboard our car, filling one of the two sets of empty seats. Before long we were moving again. To my surprise, I felt a keen sense of tiredness coming over me. I guess all the excitement and stress of the morning wore me down. The rhythmic sounds of the train did nothing to help me fight the fatigue and without intending to do so, I fell asleep with my head leaning against the cabin wall. It was only when the train whistle blew – as we approached another station in Staffordshire – that I awoke and realized that I had fallen asleep.

I was a bit disoriented as it felt like I had only just closed my eyes and yet, there we were, approaching another city. As I rubbed my eyes awake, I asked, "What time is it?"

After taking out his watch and looking at it, Edward answered, "It's a few minutes past one o'clock."

We had left Northampton around ten, so that meant I had just slept for close to two hours. Not only was I little surprised at the passing of the time, but also the passing of distance – for in that time we had gone close to one hundred miles. Train travel was amazing!

When the locomotive came to a stop, I followed the lead of Mr. Stafford and Mr. Hudson and exited the cabin. I was confused for a moment, wondering if we were departing at the wrong location, but they led the way to the dining carriage. Although obviously narrow, it looked just like a restaurant, with many linen covered tables and silver place settings. A waiter served us a chicken dish that was absolutely delicious – especially since it felt like a long time since breakfast.

Looking out the window, I could see many passengers scurrying about to a small establishment serving some kind of soup. The train was scheduled to be stopped for only twenty minutes, so everyone needed to hurry or risk having the train leave without them.

When we were back underway, and back in our cabin, I felt refreshed. The nap had given me renewed energy and the food had further bolstered my alertness. With that fresh enthusiasm, I thought it was time to try and talk with Edward again. Any comfortableness that we had managed to create at the dinner seemed to be gone, as neither of us had been very forthcoming with conversation. I asked, "Is this your first assignment or has your father taken you on any others?"

"Once, before I was an apprentice," he said, "father took me on an assignment. However, I was only twelve at the time and I never participated more than sitting in a carriage while he went on to investigate something. I guess that doesn't really count."

I laughed at his comment; it was a little humorous, but mostly because I was relieved that he gave me more than a one-word answer. Maybe some of our built-up comfort around each other lingered after all. "No," I said, "that doesn't count. This is my first assignment too. Once it was decided that we would be going, everything happened so quickly. I haven't had a lot of time to think about all the things involved – including dangers – in locating a Dark Book. I'm not sure that I'm entirely ready."

"Well, I *know* that I'm not ready," Edward said with a smile. "But that is alright. That is why we are only apprentices and are traveling with others. We are in good hands. In fact, truth be told, my father was quite excited to be working with Mr. Stafford. He is well respected and it's not every day that you get to go on an assignment with a member of The Council."

I often times forgot that Mr. Stafford held such a high position and that people might revere him a little for it. I certainly revered him, but not because of his role on The Council, but because of who he was and how he treated me. Titles are fine, but character is supreme.

"I agree," I said, "that we are in very good hands."

For the remainder of the journey, Edward and I talked about his life at school and my life in the orphanage. There were a few similarities, but mostly we had very different upbringings. Although there was much in his situation that I was envious about, I could tell he had a lonely childhood. He didn't talk much about friends, mostly about his studies. I absently wondered if there was such a thing as a perfect life in this world.

Around four in the afternoon, we arrived at Lime Street Station in Liverpool. As much as I enjoyed the train ride, I had to admit that I was happy at the thought of departing. The many hours of sitting had left me restless and stiff. To my surprise, however, once the train stopped, none of my travelling companions showed any signs of getting out of their seats. Whereas I was eager to stand, they seemed quite happy to stay.

"Is this not our stop?" I asked.

"It is, my dear," answered Mr. Stafford. "But, if we wait a few minutes, the initial rush of the other passengers will have died down and we can avoid much hassle."

The thought of being back in a crowd lessened my desire to leave the train and I was very satisfied to wait for those few minutes if that meant lessening the masses. While waiting, I looked out the windows at the surging crowd of people leaving the station and going off to their final destinations. It was not quite as crowded as Euston, but the familiar twinge of anxiety that I had had was making its presence known.

After a few minutes, ten or so, we finally stood to depart. Mr. Stafford and Mr. Hudson arranged with one of the porters for our luggage to be delivered to our hotel. It felt good to stand and walk about a little. As foretold, many of the people that had been here were already gone and I was able to focus on the exciting fact that we were in a new city.

With the luggage arrangements set, we headed outside of the station. As we stepped into the early evening light, the first thing that hit me was the smell. There was something in it that was quite different than London or Bromley.

"Ah!" exclaimed Mr. Hudson taking in a deep breath. "I will never tire of the sea air."

Although I could see nothing but busy streets and various buildings around us, I knew that Liverpool was near the ocean; something I had never seen – nor smelled – before. I tried to imagine an expanse of water as far as the eye could see but struggled with such a massive concept. My heart quickened, however, at the thought of it.

"The North Western Hotel is right here," said Mr. Stafford pointing at a large gothic-castle looking building. However, after a quick glance up and down the pavement, Mr. Stafford said, "Jonathan, please wait here with Edward for a minute. Naomi, come with me. I would like to try something."

All of us looked at him with confusion. "What do you have in mind?" asked Mr. Hudson.

"I'll tell you in a minute," he answered and then indicated that I should follow him as he headed down the pavement away from the hotel. Walking closely behind him, I looked ahead to see what his destination might be; what had grabbed his attention so unexpectedly. There were a few men and women walking along, some children playing against the side of a wall, and some larger buildings in the not too far distance. Nothing stood out as anyplace or anyone that would be of particular interest.

Of all the possibilities, the least likely is where he actually stopped. In front of the group of children, all dressed in worn and patched clothing, only some having shoes, Mr. Stafford addressed them, saying, "Which one of you is in charge?"

The children, of varying ages – five years old to maybe thirteen or fourteen – looked up with faces of skepticism or annoyance. Mr. Stafford stood before them expectantly and when no one spoke up, he said, "Come on, now. Who of you is in charge?"

The largest of the boys – naturally – stepped forward and said, "Who are you, guv? We weren't doing anything wrong here." The boy then turned towards me, puffed out his chest and said, "Well now, perhaps you would like to join me for a drink, love?"

The other boys snickered at the comment. My face turned a little red, partly from embarrassment and partly from anger. I was about to step forward and tell that young street urchin just what I thought of his offer, but Mr. Stafford stepped in front of me quickly and said to the boy, "You misunderstand me. I want to hire you for a job."

At hearing that, I looked at Mr. Stafford with surprise. Hire those children? For what?

"What kind of a job?" asked the larger boy, still looking quite skeptical.

"You, no doubt, have heard of the murders and attacks recently on sailors?"

The boy nodded slowly, clearly wondering where it was all headed.

Mr. Stafford continued, "The last attack was on a Mr. Robert Havill. He survived. I would very much like to talk with him, but I don't know where he currently is. If you and your friends can find out where I can locate him, I would pay for such information. To show my sincerity," Mr. Stafford reached into his pocket and pulled out some coins. "Here is three shillings. If you can get the information I am after, I will give you a sovereign."

The presentation of the coins and the promise of more made all the children's eyes wide. That was an enormous sum for such like them. The large boy reached out his hand and accepted the coins. He then said, "Sir, you have a deal."

"Excellent! May I ask your name?"

"Anthony Flynn, at your service."

"I'm pleased to meet you, Mr. Flynn. When you have found the agreed upon information, you may leave a message for me, Mr. Stafford, at the front desk of the North Western. The money will be waiting."

"Begging your pardon, sir," said Anthony. "Me and my mates will not be welcomed too kindly in such a place. Besides, none of us can write very well."

Mr. Stafford narrowed his eyes in thought for a moment and then said, "I could meet you here, tomorrow, after breakfast. Would that give you enough time?"

"Oh yes, sir," the boy said happily. Then, like commanding troops, Anthony said to his companions, "Alright, lads, we have work to do. Get to it!" Without wasting an instant, the boys scattered off in search of the profitable information.

When I looked at Mr. Stafford, I saw enthusiasm and, perhaps, a look of longing in his eyes, almost as if he wished he could join that group of children. His attention to – and even appreciation for – those rough young ones surprised me. I was a little ashamed when I realized that I was, very recently, not much different than those children and, yet, I was already feeling a sense of superiority. I vowed to try and never forget my background and to always use those memories to have empathy for others.

As we walked back towards Mr. Hudson and his son, I asked, "Do you really think that was wise?"

Mr. Stafford smiled at me and said, "I honestly do. I will be greatly surprised if we don't have the information I asked for in the morning."

I was not so sure.

When we reached our companions, Mr. Hudson asked, "What was that all about?"

With a small laugh, Mr. Stafford said, "I was just creating a branch of the Liverpool Irregulars."

After a second of contemplation, both Mr. Hudson and Edward started laughing. There was clearly something that I wasn't understanding.

Mr. Hudson said, smiling, "Taking a page from Sherlock Holmes? How very enterprising."

I was aware of Sherlock Holmes – the stories were becoming quite a phenomenon – although I had not read them yet. I asked, "The Liverpool Irregulars? Sherlock Holmes?"

"I'm sorry, my dear," said Mr. Stafford. "Arthur Conan Doyle's character, Sherlock Holmes, is a private consulting detective and he occasionally will hire young street urchins to find out information. He calls the group his Baker Street Irregulars. The premise behind it is that these children know the streets and the goings on of the city better than most anyone else. When I saw such a group over there, I was struck with the idea that perhaps we could try the same thing. If it fails, then I'm only out three shillings."

The explanation made some sense, but I still couldn't decide if that was clever or if he was just having a bit of fun. "I guess," I said, "but I will reserve judgment until tomorrow morning."

As we headed back towards the hotel, my attention was grabbed by a magnificent structure across the road. "What is that?" I asked, indicating the massive, many columned, Greek styled building.

"That," answered Mr. Hudson, "is St. George's Hall. Impressive, is it not?"

"Very much so!" I responded in reverence.

No less impressive was our hotel. Standing at the entrance, I looked up the face of it – seven stories of tan brick, with countless windows, ornate ledges, with spires towering into the sky. My initial though of a castle was only enhanced. I found it both beautiful and intimidating.

Inside, the lobby of the hotel was vast and opulent. From the carpet, the furniture, the tapestries, everything, was exquisite. Off to the right, through a pair of open doors, was a dining room with several people already enjoying their dinner. To our left was another room, all dark wood and leather, with an elaborate sign above the door that said, 'Smoking Room'.

As we approached the hotel desk, a nicely dressed man behind it rose and asked, "How may I help you?"

"There should be three reservations," said Mr. Stafford. "One for Stafford, one for Gladwyn, and one for Hudson."

After a quick glance through a large logbook that lay on the desk, the man looked up and said, "Very good. We have room 502, 504, and 506 at your disposal." He then turned and fetched three keys from a bureau of cubbyholes. After handing them over, he asked if we had any luggage.

"It will be along shortly. Please have it sent to our rooms."

"Very well, sir. Zachary!" the clerk called out. A moment later, a bellhop stepped forward.

"Yes, Mr. Harney?"

"Please show these guests to their rooms."

"Of course. Please follow me."

We fell in behind the bellhop as he led us up several flights of stairs – I was glad that we wouldn't have to carry our luggage up all those steps. Our rooms were all in a row and I was excited that I actually had one for my own.

I unlocked the door, 502, and found myself in a beautiful space. The walls were dark wood panels, with intricate designs throughout. Brass wall sconces spaced all around would give plenty of light. There was a couch and two high-backed chairs to relax in. The bed was large and looked incredibly inviting. It was at that moment that I realized how tired I was. It was amazing that, although I had basically sat all day, I was exhausted from the travel. On the wall opposite the door were two windows. I walked to one of them, pulled the curtain aside, and gazed out at the city. As my eyes roved around the unfamiliar streets and foreign buildings, I found it sobering and exhilarating to know that I was farther from home than I had ever been.

"Everything satisfactory?" asked Mr. Stafford from the doorway.

I turned from the window and exclaimed, "Oh yes! It's quite luxurious."

"Excellent. Now, it's time for a little dinner and then an early bedtime. How does that sound?"

Despite my fatigue, the mention of food made my stomach grumble. "That sounds very good."

I joined Mr. Stafford and the Hudsons as we made our way to the lobby and the dining room. The food was good, but the conversation was limited – I was not the only one who was tired.

When dinner was completed, we returned to our rooms and found our luggage waiting for us. After saying goodnight to everyone, I got dressed for bed and was asleep before I could even revel in the exciting thoughts of the train trip, a new city, and my first time in a hotel.

Thirty

BR

Even though I had been quite tired, my sleep was not as good as home. The bed was fine but was not the one I was familiar with. Still, when Mr. Stafford knocked on my door and announced that we would be leaving for breakfast soon, I felt much far more refreshed compared to the previous night.

In the dining room, the four of us sat at a table near the windows – a sunny morning making for a pleasant view. Like the rest of the hotel, the dining room was luxuriously decorated – fine tablecloths, vases with fresh flowers, and well-dressed servers. As I looked around us, I found the room to be active and alive with conversations from the other guests, waiters constantly moving about, and, of course, the wonderful smell of food. I would never tell Melba, but the eggs, meats, breads, and preserves rivaled what she could prepare for us.

During the meal, Edward leaned over and asked, "How did you sleep?"

"I slept alright. The bed was quite comfortable, but, since it was different than my own, I found that I tossed and turned a bit throughout the night."

Edward nodded and said, "That is always the way. My father doesn't seem to notice, but I can never be completely at rest when not in my own bed."

When nearing the end of our meal, I was surprised to find a man suddenly standing before our table. He looked only a few years older than twenty, had curly dark hair, a strong jaw, and striking blue eyes. I will admit that I found the stranger to be quite handsome.

When Mr. Stafford caught sight of him, he rose from his chair and said, "Ah, you must be Mr. Northam."

"Yes, sir," he answered politely while shaking hands. "I am pleased to meet you, Mr. Stafford."

It didn't seem like the two of them knew each other, so I wondered how Mr. Northam located our table. After a moment, I realized that, although they may not have ever met, Mr. Stafford – as a council member – would likely be recognized by most in the Order.

"It is a pleasure to meet you," said Mr. Stafford. "Please allow me to introduce my companions. This is Mr. Jonathan Hudson and his son, Edward. And this is Miss Gladwyn, my daughter."

It still felt strange being called his daughter. It had been a few months, but it continued to sound foreign to my ears.

Mr. Northam gave a polite greeting to all of us, but I could not help but notice a lingering gaze in my direction. I blushed a little and, to try and hide it, attempted to look occupied with a piece of bread.

Although the table was ideally suited for four people, another chair was provided, and Mr. Northam sat at the corner between Mr. Stafford and me. Our knees accidently touched, and I nearly fell off of my seat when I jerked my leg away. His nearness made me flustered and I could not believe the effect that the man was having on me. I felt nervous and excited at the same time. A keen desire grew in me to not say anything that could possibly humiliate myself. More than not wanting to feel like a fool, I wanted any comment that I *did* make to be of some articulated brilliance – so much so that I'm not sure I would ever speak in his company.

I glanced at Edward and he looked completely crestfallen. He must have noticed my reaction and... *was he jealous?* That thought served to take that uncomfortable situation and add a measure of awkwardness to it.

"So," asked Mr. Stafford, "have you made any headway into these attacks?"

Mr. Northam shook his head and said, "No, I'm afraid not. Mrs. Dockery has been in communication with me and passed along all the information that you had gathered, but I have not been able to make any progress."

"Do you know," asked Mr. Hudson, "where we can find this Robert Havill?"

Again, he shook his head. "I only know that he was initially taken to Liverpool Infirmary on Brownlow Street, but that he is no longer there.

Other than that, I have not had success in finding his current location – for he has not been to his apartment since the attack."

"Well," said Mr. Stafford, "I hold out a little hope on that front. Although, if my resource fails, we may have a tedious morning of trying to find out where to locate Mr. Havill."

"Your *resource*, sir?" questioned Mr. Northam.

Instead of telling him about his *Liverpool Irregulars*, Mr. Stafford gave a small laugh and said, "You will see soon enough."

We finished up breakfast and made our way out of the hotel. The morning was bright and cheery, though there was still a slight chill in the air. The street was full of carriages while the pavement was crowded with people – it may not have been London, but it appeared just as active and chaotic. I could not help looking up and down the street, marveling at the unfamiliar buildings, and just feeling all of the excitement of being in a new city. The briny smell of the nearby sea was still in the air and added to my anticipation of the day ahead – for, among other things, I was eager to see the ocean for the first time.

Across the street from us, on the corner, I caught sight of a young boy – it was Anthony – waving and trying to get our attention. He calmed the flailing of his arms when Mr. Stafford put up his hand to acknowledge his presence.

"Well," commented Mr. Stafford enthusiastically, "it seems that our young friend may have something for us after all." There was no hiding the satisfaction in his face.

The five of us crossed over to the opposite corner while Mr. Stafford continued on to the children. I watched as the boy and Mr. Stafford talked for a moment and I realized that, all along, I didn't really anticipate any good outcome to the entire plan. However, I could see Mr. Stafford extract a one-pound note and hand it to the young man. Impossible as I thought it to be, there must have been some information found.

They talked for another minute and some more money was given – it looked like a few coins. The boy gave a salute to Mr. Stafford and he and his companions ran off. As Mr. Stafford walked towards us, he seemed so happy that he was practically laughing.

Astonished, Mr. Hudson asked, "Did the child *actually* provide something of use?"

"I believe he did," answered Mr. Stafford. "I have an address that will take us right to Mr. Havill."

I looked at Edward, mouth agape, and saw that he, too, was quite surprised. Mr. Northam, said, "Surely you're jesting. This is some joke to make me look foolish. You didn't actually hire those children to find Mr. Havill."

"There is no joke," answered Mr. Stafford with a smile. "I did just as you said, and, what is more, I have further hired them to provide any information they could gather on the attacks. I'm a little less optimistic on that front, but for the price of two shillings a day, we have ourselves a regular network of informants."

"Did you consider," asked Mr. Hudson, "that those boys might have given you false information? That we may find no one at the address provided?"

"It did occur to me," said Mr. Stafford. "However, it would be to their benefit to tell the truth, as I will not pay them a single penny more if they lie to me – and they know this as well as I do. No, I believe we have good information."

"Well," said Mr. Hudson, "we shall see. Being that we have no better lead, what address are we off to?"

"Number 28 Kensington. Mr. Northam, are you familiar with it?"

"Yes, very much so. Kensington is only a short distance from here."

"Excellent!" exclaimed Mr. Stafford, looking like a dog that had found a scent. He hailed down a four-wheeler and, although tight, we all fit inside. Mr. Stafford and I took one seat while the three men sat shoulder to shoulder – with hardly room to take in a deep breath – on the other seat. Along the way, Mr. Stafford explained to us that the boy, Anthony, had told him that Mr. Havill was moved from the infirmary because of security concerns. It seems that there was fear that the unknown assailant would make a second attempt. His wounds, being as severe as they were, necessitated that Mr. Havill be relocated to a place where he could still receive care. So, evidently, his doctor took him into his own home.

"All that from those children?" asked Mr. Northam.

"They were more thorough than I would have dared hoped," answered Mr. Stafford.

It was a mercifully short ride – for the three men sharing a seat were not at all comfortable. I too felt some discomfort, as I would occasionally glance at Mr. Northam and find that he would occasionally glance back. However, the same could be said for Edward.

Once at Kensington, we stood in front of a row of brick buildings. It took only a few moments to locate number 28 – it was especially easy as there was a plaque next to the entrance that read: Doctor Albert Palmer. Mr. Stafford knocked firmly on the door.

In retrospect, we probably should have handled the situation a little differently. I think we were all so excited at chasing down our first clue – plus the circumstances that led to the clue – that we didn't stop and think what it would look like for five people to be knocking at the door.

When a woman answered – middle age, long dark hair with wisps of silver, and a sharp nose – she took on an immediate expression of confusion and nervousness. "May I help you?" she asked kindly but hesitantly.

"We were hoping," said Mr. Stafford, "to see Doctor Palmer and, more importantly, his patient, Mr. Havill."

The woman's eyes roved over our group, clearly uncertain as to why a gathering of people would be at her doorstep, and then said, "My husband is currently out and I'm afraid that I could not allow anyone in to see his patient without him."

It seemed that we were doomed to wait. Even Mr. Stafford struggled to think of a way to overcome that argument. In a moment of ingenuity and, frankly, desperation, I blurted out, "But Mr. Havill and I are to be married!"

The woman, Mrs. Palmer evidently, looked at me with surprise. I met her gaze while feeling the shock that my companions had at my sudden announcement. I continued, "As soon as I found out that he was hurt, I made my way here with my father, my uncle, and my two brothers – for they would not let me be alone during this tragedy. May I please see my precious Robert?"

As the woman considered my words, I felt a little bad at having lied to her. I justified it with the thought that we were ultimately trying to save lives – I still felt bad, but a little less so.

Mrs. Palmer's face softened and said, "Of course you may see him, dear. However, he is in our small guest room and it might not be good for all of you to come in. He is still very weak."

"I can wait outside," volunteered Mr. Northam.

Not to be outdone, Edward quickly said, "I can as well."

"I think," said Mr. Hudson, "that Naomi and her father should visit the lad. The three of us will be waiting out here when you are done."

"Would that be amenable, Mrs. Palmer?" asked Mr. Stafford.

"That will be just fine. Please, follow me."

We followed the doctor's wife as she led us to a small room. Inside, lying in bed, was Mr. Havill. His unshaven face was tired and pale; clearly, he was still far from good health. In keeping up my ruse, I rushed over to him saying, "Oh Robert! I was so worried. Are you alright?"

Mr. Havill turned his head to me and opened his eyes slightly. He took a moment to focus on my face and then said with a raspy voice, "I have been better. Who are you?"

I turned my head towards Mr. Stafford and Mrs. Palmer and gave a horrified look. I could not be sure that they heard what he had said, but I took no chances. I exclaimed, "He is having a hard time recognizing me! Oh father, what should I do?"

Mr. Stafford turned to Mrs. Palmer and asked, "Exactly what is the extent of his injuries?"

With great sympathy, the doctor's wife said, "I know he has a severe stab wound and that he lost a lot of blood. Beyond that, I'm sorry, but you will have to ask my husband. Please allow me to give you some privacy."

"Thank you," said Mr. Stafford. "You are very kind."

When she left the room, Mr. Stafford stepped closer to the bed and said, "Mr. Havill, my name is Thomas Stafford and this is my daughter, Naomi. We are here to ask you some questions about your attack. That is, if you are feeling up to it."

The man groaned a little and said, "More questions? Are you police?"

"Actually, no. We are not with the authorities."

Mr. Havill closed his eyes and let out a sigh. I thought for sure that he would tell us to go away, but instead he said, "Let's make this brief. I'm quite tired."

"Of course. Thank you, Mr. Havill. First, can you tell us anything about your attacker?"

He gave a small shake of his head and said, "Not very much. He surprised me while I was heading home from the tavern. He had his collar raised and his hat pulled low, so I really saw very little. I doubt I would recognize him if he was standing right in front of me."

"And you are sure he was European?"

"Aye. White skin to be sure."

"And," asked Mr. Stafford, "he made a statement as he attacked you?"

"That was the strangest part of it all. After he stabbed me, he stood over me and said that the atrocities of the Siege of Delhi would be avenged. Obviously, I had other concerns, but I still don't know what he was going on about."

I asked, "What happened then?"

"I saw him look up – as if hearing a noise – and then run away. Next thing I remember, I was in a hospital."

"A harrowing experience," commented Mr. Stafford. "You are fortunate to be alive. Could you tell me the name of the tavern you were at?"

"The Friendly Frigate, down near the docks."

"One more question, Mr. Havill. Is there anything else that stands out to you about this entire ordeal? Any oddities, no matter how seemingly insignificant, that you can recall?"

Mr. Havill thought for a several seconds and finally said, "No. Nothing else about the attack. The only oddity, if you will forgive my saying, is the questions I have received from strangers who are not with the police."

I looked up at Mr. Stafford and saw a little concern cross his face. "You mean that others, besides us, have asked you similar questions?"

Mr. Havill nodded and said, "Two days ago I was visited by a man who claimed to be my brother. But I have no brother – nor am I courting a woman at present."

I blushed as he continued, "Still, outside of a few questions, he was no real bother."

"And you are certain that he was not with the authorities?" asked Mr. Stafford.

"Quite certain. Believe me, I have talked to many authorities as well." After a pause, while we were considering the information, Mr. Havill said, "If you don't mind my asking, if you are not with the police, then why are you here asking me these things?"

Mr. Stafford smiled kindly, putting the concern out of his face, and answered, "The police are trying to capture the man who did this to you.

We are trying to figure out *why* he did it and to make sure no one else follows his path."

"Well," said Mr. Havill weakly, "I wish you all success. For myself, I think I need to rest some more."

"Of course," said Mr. Stafford. "Thank you for your time and we hope you continue to get better."

We left the room and met Mrs. Palmer by the front door. I gave her a weak smile and said, "He started to come around a little, but became very tired." I then stepped forward and hugged her saying, "Thank you for letting me see him. I feel so much relief now that I know how he is."

"You are very welcome, dear. Please, come around whenever you like. I would never want to keep two lovers apart."

I felt bad, again, as I thought about the likelihood that we would not return. "Thank you," I said with sincerity towards her kindness.

Outside of the home, we met our three companions. "And," said Mr. Northam eagerly, "how did it go?"

"Well," said Mr. Stafford slowly, evidently still weighing the information, "his account of the attack did not shed much light beyond what we already knew. However," he paused a moment and looked at Mr. Hudson, "he said that someone else had visited him – on false pretenses of being a family member – and asked him about the attack."

I wondered what that meant why it seemed to alarm Mr. Stafford. At the statement, I noticed that Mr. Hudson also showed immediate concern. He asked, "You don't think that *they* are already pursuing this, do you?"

"I'm not sure," answered Mr. Stafford, "but my instinct is telling me that they are here."

Edward asked the question before I could, "Who are 'they'?"

Mr. Stafford looked up and down the street, as if worried that we might be being watched, and said, "Let us get into a cab first. This necessitates a new layer of caution."

At the growing concern, I became scared. Who could possibly frighten Mr. Stafford and Mr. Hudson like that? The pleasant morning suddenly felt a bit darker as a shiver of uncertainty crawled down my spine.

Thirty-One

BR

Revisiting that day in my mind, it's incredible to think that the revelation that was about to be given would be the *lesser* one. Still, it holds great significance, so let me explain.

From Kensington, we hailed a passing carriage and climbed aboard. The seating arrangement was the same as before. As soon as we started moving, Mr. Stafford said, "The concern that Mr. Hudson and I share is that a rival group, the Book Keepers – the similarity in name is purposeful, as they are largely made up of onetime Book Reapers – are evidently on the same pursuit that we are."

"The Book Keepers?" I asked. "Who are they?"

"They are," answered Mr. Stafford, "opposed to the destruction of these Dark Books and are on a mission to collect and preserve as many as they can."

The thought of someone purposely saving those abominable books was hard for me to comprehend. Knowing that Dark Books existed was alarming but knowing that there were people who wanted them to persist, was very frightening. I asked the only question I could contemplate, "Why?"

"That is a good question," answered Mr. Stafford, shaking his head. "One that has plagued me, and one that I don't think I could ever understand."

As we pulled up to our hotel, I exited the carriage with an oppressive feeling. Not only had we not received much new information from Mr. Havill, but we also could be dealing with a group of people who were working directly against our purpose. The day had started with such promise but had already become quite disappointing.

We took to the couches in the lobby and began to discuss our next steps. My eyes roved about the room looking for anyone who might be paying us too much attention – the alarm that had been shown was contagious.

"I don't think," said Mr. Hudson, "that we depart from our general plan from the train. If Mr. Havill didn't provide us with any particularly useful information, then we were to identify ships departing for, or coming from, India. I believe that that is our next course of action."

After a moment's thought, Mr. Stafford nodded and said, "I agree." He then turned to Mr. Northam and asked, "I think, Mr. Northam, that you would be best suited to find out this information. Would you be able to undertake this task?"

"Absolutely," he responded. "Between the newspaper and some contacts of mine near the waterfront, I should have the details needed within a few hours."

"Very good," said Mr. Stafford.

"If I may ask," commented Mr. Hudson, "that Edward accompany you, Mr. Northam. I think that the gathering of information is an invaluable skill and I would like for Edward to learn from your process."

"Of course," answered Mr. Northam. "I would be delighted to have him along."

I looked at Edward and saw that he was anything but delighted.

"With that settled," said Mr. Stafford. "I suggest we meet back here for an early dinner and plan our next actions."

As Mr. Northam and Edward stood, Mr. Stafford added, "Please be careful. The Book Keepers are not known to be violent, but I'm uncomfortable at their rapid arrival here."

"I will look after the lad," said Mr. Northam while Edward rolled his eyes at the perceived insult of being considered a 'lad'. I gave him a sympathetic smile.

When the two of them left, I actually felt a little relief. Despite all that was going on, I could not help but feel some stress at the attraction I had to Mr. Northam, and the worry of hurting Edward. In retrospect, it was all quite silly; for at that time, I knew nothing of Mr. Northam, and Edward was, at the very least, my friend. Comparing them was impetuous. Those finicky emotions were untimely and *mostly* unwelcomed.

"Our part," announced Mr. Stafford, "is the hardest, for we must wait. There are few things as excruciating as not acting when there is work to do.

However, I do not think this time will be completely wasted. We can lunch and then do a little shopping."

Shopping? Could he be serious? With the importance of our assignment, it seemed out of place, even disrespectful, to spend time in such a mundane and seemingly frivolous activity. Not wanting to be too rude, I asked, "Could the shopping not wait until after the assignment is finished?"

"I'm afraid not," he said with a smile. "However, rest your mind at ease. The shopping I'm referring to is far from what you are likely thinking about."

I was confused, but Mr. Stafford went on to explain his meaning. "If we are to watch, perhaps follow, sailors from an Indian ship, we will need to blend in. The docks and the surrounding areas are filled with hardworking men who don't dress like visitors to the North Western Hotel. For my part, I have an old pea coat that will allow me to seem like any other dock worker. Mr. Hudson, I'm sure, has similar clothes."

"I do."

"You, my dear," continued Mr. Stafford, "are in a unique position. Not only do you not own proper clothes for what we will likely be doing, but that area of the city is not exactly...hmm...*right* for a woman."

I understood what Mr. Stafford was saying. After all, while in the orphanage, my life prospects were to be the kind of woman that *would* fit into such a rough environment – and that was a terrifying thought. I asked, "So how will shopping possibly solve this problem? Am I just to occupy myself in some shop while the rest of you investigate?"

"Oh no, nothing like that at all," said Mr. Stafford. "You see, we are going to buy you some men's clothes."

Although that might have been the obvious direction of the conversation, my mind had not remotely considered the possibility. My mouth agape, I looked at Mr. Stafford with no words to utter. A small part of me figured he must have been kidding, but most of me was certain he was not.

For his part, Mr. Hudson sat silently, enjoying the theatre of my reaction. Mr. Stafford said, "You don't have to agree to this, but I cannot let you go to the docks at night without this precaution – even with me at your side. If for no other reason, a proper young woman would stand out and draw unwanted attention."

As all the doubts as to the seriousness of his words faded, I started to give practical thought to what he was saying. We would procure men's clothes and I would pretend to be a boy. It sounded completely outlandish, but perfectly exciting. With confidence welling up in me from an unknown spring, I said, "I'll do it!"

Mr. Hudson gave a laugh and exclaimed, "Wonderful! I think Mr. Stafford was quite right to put his faith in you."

I smiled at the compliment and felt very good that I could do something that made people proud of Mr. Stafford."

"Where are we to get the clothes?" I asked.

Standing from the couch, Mr. Stafford said, "Follow me and I will show you."

From behind us, Mr. Hudson stood said, "I don't think you will need me on this errand. I will have a small lunch and then be in my room until the two young men return. Don't hesitate to contact me if needed."

We parted ways and walked out of the hotel and right back to Anthony's corner – as we began calling it. The young leader of the street urchins was there and came directly up to Mr. Stafford, saying, "I'm afraid that we don't have any new information yet, sir."

"That is quite alright," said Mr. Stafford. "However, I have another assignment for you. I need to purchase some used clothes, boy's clothes, which would fit my daughter."

Anthony's face took on a comical look, like he wanted to laugh but was afraid to upset the man that had been giving him money. "Did I...hear you right? You want boy's cloth for your daughter?"

"That is correct," he answered simply. "Can you manage that?"

Anthony looked at me, a long gaze, up and down. I'm sure he was thinking of which one of his friends might be near my size, but his look felt more than a bit uncomfortable. He said, "Aye, we can manage. My mate Marcus is about the right size."

"Excellent!" exclaimed Mr. Stafford. "Now, here is another pound to help compensate for the clothing." He handed over the note to the wide-eyed boy. "Make sure there is a cap and shoes. If you can get the job done, I will have a fiver for you. Can you get them here by around dinner time?"

"Yes, sir!" he said, his face overjoyed by the small fortune he was being offered. After putting the money deep in his pocket, he added, "You can count on me!" and then hurried off down the street.

As we walked back to the hotel, I was amused by how much my impression of the children had changed. At first, I thought that Mr. Stafford was wasting his time and money on them. But now I wondered where we would be without their help.

Back in the lobby, I considered what we would do next. Mr. Stafford answered my unuttered question, "I think a little lunch would be good. After that, since it will be a couple of hours before we hear any news from our two scouts, I think it would be best to return to our rooms. Who knows what the night will bring, so a little rest may be a good idea."

I nodded in agreement. We enjoyed a simple, but delicious lunch, and then each went to our room. I was not sure I would be able to sleep, so I lay in bed with the intention of doing some reading, but within a few minutes I found that I had to keep rereading the pages of my book for the drowsiness that was overtaking me. I finally gave up, put the book down, and closed my eyes.

I awoke to knocking. I had no idea had long I had been asleep – it seemed like only a few minutes, but one can never judge with unconsciousness. When I answered the door, I found Mr. Stafford standing there. "Good afternoon, Naomi, did you manage any rest?"

"Yes, sir. What time is it?"

"Half past three. Mr. Northam and Edward have returned, and Mr. Hudson is already downstairs."

"Did they find out anything?"

"I believe so. Let's join them and find out."

In the lobby, we found our three companions sitting and talking. As we took seats near them, I noticed Mr. Stafford glancing about the room, examining anyone nearby. It reminded me that we were not completely alone in our assignment.

When satisfied that no one was eavesdropping on our conversation, Mr. Stafford asked, "So, Mr. Northam, Edward, what were you two able to find out?"

Mr. Northam started, "We have arrived at a particularly fortunate time. As of today, there is only one ship in the docks with any immediate ties to India: The *Merganser*. Led by Captain Powell, it's scheduled to depart for Bombay in three days' time. It's several days before any ships are due to return from India, and even longer before the next one is scheduled to depart."

"Excellent work!" beamed Mr. Hudson, giving adoration to both Mr. Northam and Edward.

"That's not all," said Mr. Northam. "Edward, with some nice ingenuity, was able to find out a little more."

All eyes turned to Edward and, although proud to be of interest, I could tell he was nervous. "I...I was able to find out the name of the first mate. In addition, I know their schedule for work. Captain Powell is a very particular man and stops his work on the ship at six o'clock sharp. His first mate, a Mr. Goddard, is by his side until that time."

"Well," said Mr. Stafford, "that *is* good work. I congratulate both of you! Not only do we have a ship, we have our two primary targets, and we have the time we need to get to the docks in order to start observing them."

"If we leave here by half past five," said Mr. Hudson, "I think that will give us plenty of time to reach the area of the ship before the captain and his first mate depart."

"How will we watch both men?" I asked.

"We will need to split into two groups. Edward, since you discovered the name of the first mate, why don't you and your father take him as your aim. Don't forget, of the three attacks, two have been on the first mate. Mr. Northam, please join me and Naomi as we will watch Captain Powell. Does that work for everyone?"

No one disagreed to the arrangement, although I was a little flustered at the thought of spending more time with Mr. Northam – and without Edward around.

"It's settled then," said Mr. Stafford. "Let us have an early dinner, and then prepare ourselves for tonight's activities." He stood up and suddenly paused, "Hello, what's this?"

I looked to see what had grabbed his attention, and there at the entrance to the lobby was Anthony, the leader of the street urchins, with a sack in his hand. He could not have stood out more if he had tried. Mr. Stafford walked quickly to him, I followed right behind, and we got there at the same time as the concierge.

"Leave this instant," said the concierge in barely contained anger to Anthony.

"My apologies," said Mr. Stafford to the hotel employee. "This young man is here to see me. I had asked him to run an errand and he is delivering the results. We will not be long."

A small look of relief passed over the concierge's face. "Very well, sir," he said, giving a narrowed eye look at the boy, and then walked back to his post.

Addressing Anthony, Mr. Stafford said, "I would have met you on the corner. You didn't have to come in here."

"I know, sir," answered the boy, "but, beggin' your pardon, for a fiver, there are few places I wouldn't go to assure that kind of reward." He held up the sack, a coarse burlap bag.

"Ah, you got the clothes," said Mr. Stafford with a smile.

"Yes, sir. I cannot guarantee a perfect fit, but they should be close enough. Poor Marcus will be without his coat tonight, but he'll live."

"Well done, my boy!" Smiled Mr. Stafford and took out the five-pound note, handed it to Anthony, and took the sack from him.

"Thank you, sir! Is there anything else we can do for you?"

"Nothing more right now, other than to keep your eyes and ears working towards finding out anything about the recent attacks."

Anthony squared his shoulders and saluted Mr. Stafford. "We will do our best," he said seriously and then turned and left the hotel.

"I believe," said Mr. Stafford handing the bag to me, "that these belong to you."

After our dinner, we went to our rooms to prepare for the night's activities. I opened the old sack that Anthony had provided and found slacks, a shirt, a coat, a cap, and a pair of very worn boots. Besides looking the part of a dock worker, they smelled the part too – not particularly pleasant, but I had little choice.

As I put on the boy's clothes, my mind wandered to the character Jo March, from *Little Women*. How could I not think of her and the times she dressed up as a boy for the plays she and her sisters put on. Our assignment was serious, I knew, but the frivolity of dressing in a costume was still present.

Hiding my hair in the cap, I examined myself in the long mirror. In some ways, I didn't recognize the ragged looking person looking back – which was exactly the point. In other ways, however, the person looking back was the person I had been for most of my life, the person I was supposed to be – a poor orphan doomed to a poorer way of life. It was an unexpected and stark reminder of where I came from and a reminder of the kindness of Mr. Stafford for taking me in.

When I stepped into the hallway – my feet sliding in shoes that were too big – I found the others already there waiting. It was quite a sight: Mr. Stafford, Mr. Hudson, and Edward, all had on large well-worn coats with coarse scarves. Their hair was a touch messy which completed the disguise. Mr. Northam was dressed as he had been earlier.

As if reading my mind, he said, "I will pick up my old clothes along the way."

Of course, of the five of us, mine was the most audacious. Everyone looked me over and I asked, "Well, do I pass for a man?"

"Oh, yes!" said Edward enthusiastically, then, "Umm…I meant that as a compliment. I think your disguise is brilliant."

"I would say," commented Mr. Stafford, "that as long as nobody looks too close, you will blend in nicely."

"What should we call you?" asked Mr. Northam.

It was a good question. Obviously, when out in public, they could not call me Naomi. I thought for a moment and then said, "Patrick. It's a name that will grab my attention, even if I don't realize that it's directed towards me."

Mr. Stafford laughed and said, "Well chosen! Now, come along *Patrick*. It's time to go."

It was five o'clock when we left, which gave us plenty of time to stop at Mr. Northam's home – he had a flat on the first floor of a multistory stone building – and for him to change.

I will never forget that last stretch of road as we neared the waterfront. The sun was low on the horizon, making for an orange sky and long shadows. Over the tops of the buildings I could see the upper masts of the ships that were docked ahead of us, their hulls still being hidden from view. My excitement grew as the water – there it was the River Mersey – could be seen. It was many times wider than any part of the Thames that I had seen; the far shore was small and barely visible in the gathering fog. Large docks jutted into the dark water all along the near shore, with countless ships rocking gently in their berths. It was a powerful sight. For all the massive boats, coming and going to all parts of the world, represented the ingenuity and advancement of man in a way that I had never seen previously. For as large as it was, the world was connected – and we were in one of its focal points.

When the carriage stopped, Mr. Northam pointed to a large three-masted vessel and announced it as the *Merganser*. We could see people onboard moving about, tying things down, and carrying cargo from the docks. It was easy to conclude who the captain was as one man was involved with everything, giving orders and pointing to locations. Another man was always near him and had to be the first mate.

It was twenty minutes until six o'clock, so we were to wait until the crew dispersed before we moved any closer. With permission from Mr. Stafford, I stepped out of the carriage and walked to the water's edge. As I looked towards the north, the direction that the river eventually met the ocean, I could see nothing but water as it disappeared into the evening fog. As I stared at the distance, I felt small and alone – even among the hustle and bustle of the docks. My world has grown much in the last day.

Per usual, though, my thoughts turned to bitter memories. Seeing those ships and thinking about the vastness of their domain, reminded me of the *Mary Celeste*. To be lost at sea seemed like the loneliest ending imaginable. *If only they had made it safely to their destination*, I thought sadly for a countless time in my life.

I don't know when Edward arrived, but I was startled when I turned and found him right next to me. Quickly regaining my composure, I commented, "This is more overwhelming than I thought it would be."

"Our assignment?" he asked.

The assignment was more than I imagined, but that was not what I meant. "No. Well, yes, but I was talking about all of this." I waved my hand at the docks and the water. "Everything is so much larger than I had ever thought. And to think of all the places that these ships will go. I feel like we are at the hub of a wheel that has spokes that reach around the globe. It's hard to comprehend."

Edward smiled and said, "I look at all this and I see schedules, cargo, inventory to document, and prices to establish. My father's business has narrowed my focus to the mundane particulars, but it's nice to be reminded of the bigger picture. It *is* remarkable when you think about it."

He seemed sincere in his words, although a little sad in talking about his father's business. I asked, "Have you made any progress with your writing career?"

"I have written quite a bit over the last couple of months; some of my best work, I think. But with regards to winning my father over, then no, no progress yet."

"I hope you don't give up," I said earnestly. "Most things in life have confused me, but I do know this: You will never regret fighting for the future you want."

Edward stared into the distant fog. I couldn't tell if he wanted to laugh or cry, but my words seemed to have penetrated his emotions. It was bold to say what I did – his life was not one for me to impose opinions onto – but I couldn't help myself. "I'm sorry," I said. "Forgive me if I overstepped my bounds."

He shook his head and gave a wry smile. "No, you're fine. I also believe you're right, but it's far easier said than done."

As the sun dipped a little lower and the fog grew in its thickness, I felt the first chill of the evening. I wrapped my arms around my shoulders, feeling the unfamiliar fabric of my old coat, and gave one last long stare at the waterfront. I did not want to forget that moment.

Without any more conversation, we headed back to the warmth of the carriage. It was welcoming inside, but it didn't last. Within a couple of minutes, Mr. Hudson, closing his watch, announced, "It's now six o'clock."

We all departed the cab and separated into our two groups. Mr. Hudson and his son went on first, walking and talking like any two men having just finished their workday. Beyond the *Merganser*, we watched as they stopped and leaned against a wooden railing. Mr. Stafford, Mr. Northam, and I were a little way behind them, walking together, but quietly. We stopped prior to the ship, trying to look like we were waiting for someone to join us.

The workers of the *Merganser* began to depart, and we watched closely for the captain. After all the men left, the first mate took his leave. We could see the Hudsons following at a distance. Finally, the captain left his ship. The daylight was fading, further hindered by the fog, but I remember the captain's eyes – sharp and decisive – which made me think that he was a good choice for a leader. As he walked from the docks, his pace was steady, and we had to hurry to keep him in sight.

He continued through an alley and turned down the next street. We carried on in our clandestine pursuit, hopefully not looking too peculiar in our hunt. Captain Powell turned into a tavern and my heart skipped a beat when I read the sign: it was the Friendly Frigate – the same place that Mr. Havill had left when he was attacked.

I looked at my companions and saw the same realization on their faces. "Let me go in first," said Mr. Stafford. "I will see where he is sitting and then procure us an out-of-the-way table to continue our observations. Give me two minutes before following me."

Mr. Northam and I nodded our agreement and watched as he crossed the road and entered the establishment.

"So, *Patrick*, are you nervous?"

It took a second to realize that the question was directed at me. "Oh, uh," not a very graceful response. "I mean, yes, a little. It's quite sobering to think that we could be very near a heartless murderer."

"Heartless?" asked Mr. Northam, as if a little surprised at my answer. "If a Dark Book is involved, how heartless, or even culpable, is this murderer?"

His comment surprised me at first, however it was a fair but difficult question. It queried the very heart, the very power, of the Dark Books. If under their influence, how responsible was the reader? I thought to my own experience, and, although I stopped myself from trying to carry out something horrendous, I had knowledge of what I was reading and guidance from Mr. Stafford. Without being armed with such knowledge, I'm certain I would have failed.

Answering his question honestly, I said, "I don't know."

"If we find our man – the reader of the Dark Book – remember that. His life may not be his own."

It was a train of thought I had not previously considered very deeply. If I came face to face with the murderer, how *would* I feel about him?

"Come on, Patrick" said Mr. Northam, "it's time."

I followed him across the street and into the Friendly Frigate Tavern. I had pictured a raucous environment, but found, instead, a subdued mood. In front of us, along the right wall of the room, was a long bar which had several patrons sitting quietly, enjoying their drinks. The rest of the room was reserved for tables and chairs – most of which were filled. The sound of conversations could be heard all around us, but none of the yelling or shouting that I somehow imagined in such a place.

We located Mr. Stafford at a table in the far-left corner and walked across the room to join him. After taking a seat on either side, he said, "Three spots over is the captain."

I followed his gaze and saw Captain Powell sitting alone at one of the tables.

"Now," said Mr. Stafford, "we wait. Nothing is going to happen while he is here. I suggest we order a little food and drink – to not raise suspicion – and be ready to leave as soon as the captain departs."

We each ordered a bowl of fish stew, although we were not very hungry, and a mug of ale. When the drinks were placed on the table, I looked at them with trepidation. My dislike of alcohol was strong, but, I knew, it was based on what is an uncommon occurrence. Uncommon or not, it's very real when it affects you.

Mr. Northam took a deep drink from his mug. Mr. Stafford only sipped his. In an effort to stay in character, I decided to have a drink of mine – one sip couldn't hurt, I thought. As the liquid touched my tongue, I had to fight to swallow the nasty tasting liquid. I put the mug down as if it might try to make me take another drink. The look I made must have been quite comical as both Mr. Stafford and Mr. Northam could not stop themselves from laughing.

I felt like a fool – no, worse, a child in front of Mr. Northam. Maybe I was. In the end, I shared a small laugh with them and could not fathom how ale was a beverage that people would ever willingly choose to drink.

For the next half hour, we sat at our table, talked a little, and always kept an eye on the captain. When he finally stood up to leave, my pulse started to race. If there was to be an attack on him, it would be soon.

We didn't stand up when the captain did, as that might have looked suspicious. Instead, we kept our heads down, and watched him leave. After a couple more seconds, just as we were about to rise from our chairs, a man at the end of the bar got off his stool and walked towards the exit. Before leaving, he raised his coat collar and pulled his hat low. It was the very description that Mr. Havill had given. The three of us shared knowing glances. *Could he be the attacker?*

As soon as the man at the bar went out the door, we got up to follow. Outside of the tavern, we could see him walking down the street to our right. Farther down the road, we could make out the steady pace of Captain

Powell. At the very least, they were headed in the same direction. Perhaps it was only a coincidence.

We followed the two men at about thirty paces behind the man with the raised collar. When we saw Powell turn down an alley, I wondered if the second man would continue forward – eliminating him as a suspect. However, when he reached the alley, he stopped, looked around for a second – he saw us, but should have had no real reason to think we were following him, or so I hoped – and then went down it. With both men out of sight, we picked up our pace and hurried to the alley. I half expected to see Captain Powell on the ground and that man standing over him with a knife. My heart beat rapidly. However, what we saw was the captain turning left at the end of the alley and the man also make the same left.

It was now clear that the second man was following Captain Powell. I tried to stay calm, tried to think of an alternative, but it was getting beyond the point of coincidence. We hurried to the end of the alley and stopped at the corner to see where the two men were. To our surprise, the street beyond was empty. There was no sign of the captain or of the second man.

I was about to ask where they went when a voice came from a dark shadow – a nearby doorway – said, "Why are you following me?"

Mr. Stafford stepped bravely out of the alley and onto the pavement. He said, "Show yourself, and then I will answer your question."

"Fair enough," was the answer from the shadows. A man, who looked to be around forty – not the captain – stepped forward into the light of the streetlamp. I caught a glimpse of his face and, strangely, saw something familiar.

"Well," said the high collared man, "this is quite a surprise. Hello, father."

Thirty-Two

BR

Our strange errand had taken a very unexpected turn. The man we were following, the man we thought might be a murderer – who still *could* be the murderer – was Mr. Stafford's son, Christopher.

The reason he looked familiar became clear as I picked out the family resemblance. More than anything else, his eyes were nearly the same as his father's, kind looking and active.

"Christopher…" said Mr. Stafford, clearly shocked at the unexpected meeting. "What…What are you doing here?"

"I imagine," he answered, "the same thing as you. I am trying to find the book."

Mr. Northam, not privy to any of the history between the two, asked, "How do we know that you are not the one with the Dark Book, that you are not the murderer?"

"Because," Christopher said with a little exasperation, "that building over there is where Captain Powell is staying while he is in port. I know this because I have been following him for three nights now. Besides, I'm not armed. Check if you like."

"That will not be necessary," said Mr. Stafford. Then, after a pause, he said, "I think, Mr. Northam, that our assignment has come to a conclusion for the night. Can you make your own way home? I believe there are some family matters to be discussed."

I was not sure if Mr. Northam believed that Christopher was harmless, but eventually gave in to the recommendation. "I can make my way from here. What is our plan for tomorrow?"

"I'm not entirely sure, but please meet us at the hotel for breakfast."

"Until then," said Mr. Northam, "goodnight Mr. Stafford. Goodnight Miss Gladwyn." Without addressing Christopher, Mr. Northam turned and walked away.

Christopher gave a small laugh and said, "I don't think he likes me very much. Also, *Miss* Gladwyn?"

I realized that I was still in my disguise and looked like, to Christopher's view, a young man. Taking my cap off, I let my hair fall out.

"Good heavens!" he said, a touch of his father's enthusiasm in his eyes. "I'm impressed."

"This is," said Mr. Stafford, "only the beginning of the surprise." With that, he stepped to the side, so that I could be fully seen by Christopher, and announced, "Naomi, this is my son, Christopher. Christopher, this is Miss Naomi Gladwyn, your sister."

Up to that point, Christopher had been completely calm, but he could not hide his utter shock at that last statement. "My *sister*?" he exclaimed. "How is that possible?"

"Naomi has agreed to be adopted by me."

Christopher looked at me for a moment and then turned his eyes to the street. Even in the lamplight, I could see the many thoughts and emotions cross his face. How would he feel about me? Would he care? Did I care?

"Well," said Christopher, regaining some composure, "I guess you're right. We do have some family matters to discuss. Shall we get out of this damp air and head back to the tavern?"

Mr. Stafford turned to me and asked quietly, "I know that this is a surprise – it certainly is for me – are you alright with having this conversation tonight?"

I appreciated his consideration, but there was too much to learn to not take the opportunity. In answer, I bunched my hair on top of my head and replaced my cap.

"Very well," said Mr. Stafford, "please lead the way, son."

We walked in silence, retracing our steps to the bar. Along our path, I made a connection that somewhat lowered my opinion of Christopher: he had to be a Book Keeper. He was trying to find the Dark Book in order to preserve it – no doubt the *brother* that visited Mr. Havill. The rift between father and son became clearer.

Back in the Friendly Frigate, we took the same corner table that we had sat at earlier. Christopher started our conversation by asking me, "So, Miss Gladwyn, I take it that you are a fellow Book Reaper?"

"Yes, sir. Well, sort of, I'm an apprentice."

"And is this how you met my father?"

"No, sir,"

Mr. Stafford spoke up, explaining, "Miss Gladwyn was an orphan, living in Bromley. She took it upon herself to run away from a particularly awful life and snuck into our home. She lived there for at least three weeks before I discovered her. Once found out, we talked about books, and discovered a kind of kinship in the written word. From there, she became my apprentice, and soon after, my daughter."

Resting his chin on his hand, Christopher gave me a long inquisitive look. His gaze made me uncomfortable, but I was not going to back down.

I met his stare and waited for his conclusion. After several seconds, he smiled and simply said, "Very interesting."

My place at the table, with father and son, was an odd one, but I decided to ask the question I had to know the answer to. Looking at Christopher, I asked, "So, Mr. Stafford, I take it that you are a Book Keeper?"

My question had no effect on him other than to make him smile. He answered, "I am."

I gave a moment to see if he would expound on his answer, but he did not. Seeing that nothing more was upcoming, I asked the heart of my query, "Why?"

Christopher looked at his father and then back to me. He asked, "Tell me, Miss Gladwyn, what do you know of the Book Keepers?"

"Very little," I admitted. "You seek out Dark Books in order to collect and preserve them."

"Anything else?"

I shook my head.

"Well, Father, I'm disappointed in you. You could have at least given some of our philosophy."

"I will not," said Mr. Stafford, "promote your twisted logic."

"Twisted logic?" Christopher asked to himself. "I don't think that is fair. Why don't we let Miss Gladwyn decide for herself."

As much as I wanted to know – had to know – how a person could reason for the preservation of a Dark Book, I was still a little frightened at where the conversation would take us. It was almost as if I feared being influenced by the spoken words of Mr. Stafford's son – much like I feared the written words of a Dark Book.

"First, what do you know of Dark Books, Miss Gladwyn?"

I answered, "They are books that are created under extreme emotional distress and carry that emotion in the words written for others to partake in. A person that reads such a book will be influenced to feel those emotions and could carry out atrocious acts."

"I agree with most of what you said," commented Christopher. "Have you ever read one?"

"Yes, sir, I have." I said, a little pleased at being able to answer so.

A look of surprise passed Christopher's face. He asked, "I imagine that the experience was not a pleasant one?"

I shook my head.

"Would you admit," he continued, "that the emotions expressed in that book were somewhat different than those you have felt before?"

It was an interesting question as the answer was both yes and no. The book had given me the emotions of the good man, his struggle to correct the wrong around him, but they also melded with my own feelings of inferiority and worthlessness. "To some degree, I would have to say that there were new emotions presented."

As if I had just made his argument, Christopher announced, "And that is why they are to be preserved."

"I don't understand," I said in complete confusion.

"Don't you see? These Dark Books contain the very rawest of human emotions. They help us to understand what the depth of man's feelings can be. They are the greatest masterpieces of written word that the world will know."

"Masterpieces?" I asked in complete shock. "How can you say that? They harm people!"

"I don't disagree that caution is needed with such powerful works, but under the right conditions, they are beautiful. Think of fire – a destructive and dangerous force. However, if used properly, it warms us and serves our purposes. These books, when used properly, advance our knowledge of the human condition, and should be viewed as something precious, not as something that should be destroyed."

I'm reluctant to admit that the argument was more logical than I had ever believed it could be. I daresay that a weakness was created in my hatred of Dark Books. Could there actually be a *benefit* from those tomes? It was a foreign thought, but one that I could not shake completely.

Mr. Stafford asked, "But is the suffering that follows these books worth the insight that *might* be gained? I vote no."

Even Mr. Stafford allowed for some potential benefit from those books, although he was clearly not agreeable to the cost of such benefits.

"And," continued Christopher, "there is the Gellar Theorem."

"There is no hard evidence for that!" said Mr. Stafford resolutely.

"The Gellar Theorem?" I asked.

"Nicholas Gellar," Christopher explained, "was a very wealthy man in Germany. He was also viewed as a tyrant. He was notoriously hard on his employees and miserly with his money. However, one summer, things changed drastically. That hard, and universally disliked, man became a great philanthropist. He went from hoarding his money to being one of the most kind, generous, and charitable men in his country."

"What changed him?"

"He claims," interrupted Mr. Stafford, "that he read a book that altered his perspective."

"Imagine," said Christopher excitedly, "a book that caused bad people to do good. It could change the world!"

"If such a book, or books, existed," Mr. Stafford argued, "one would have been found by now."

"Perhaps," admitted Christopher, "or perhaps they are so rare, not to mention harder to find – for good deeds don't make the newspapers quite like the bad ones do – that we simply have not retrieved one yet."

"Even if that is true," said Mr. Stafford, "it still leaves the moral question of free will. If such a book exists, and a person does good because of it, is the person good or is he nothing more than an automaton? A mindless machine of action that has lost control over its very being?"

"So, you are telling me," asked Christopher, "that if such a book came into your possession, you would not use it to influence others?"

"I would not," Mr. Stafford answered sternly.

Christopher turned to me and asked, "And you, Miss Gladwyn? What would you do with such a book?"

I thought about the implications of such a book existing. It could help right the many wrongs that we saw in the world. But was the cost, the taking away of one's own motives, a price I was willing to pay? I didn't know. I finally said, "I'm not sure. I believe that such a question would require much more than a few moments of thought."

"An honest and fair answer," said Christopher approvingly. "Father, I think she may be a good influence on you. Perhaps she can help allow your mind leeway for new ideas."

I felt like I had sided against Mr. Stafford. It was not true, but I felt Christopher using me against him. Mr. Stafford shook his head at his son's comments.

After a long silence, Christopher asked softly, "What is the number up to now?"

"Two-seventy-eight," answered Mr. Stafford, his eyes distant.

Christopher looked at me and said, "Do you know what the number is that we are talking about?"

I nodded, "The number of Mr. Stafford's books collected out of the three-hundred he had published."

Christopher nodded and added, "Of course it will never be an exact number, for there are some assumptions made – probably accurate, but still assumptions."

"What do you mean?" I asked.

"A few of those two hundred and seventy-eight books are only assumed to be gone. Be it in a fire, a flood, or lost at sea."

"Lost at sea?" I asked in surprise.
"Oh, yes. For one of my father's books was on the *Mary Celeste*."
I looked at Mr. Stafford, waiting, hoping – *begging* – for some kind of a denial. Instead, all I saw was a very sad face that didn't meet my gaze.

After a sigh, Mr. Stafford, still not looking at me, spoke, "It's true. I believe it was one of my books that doomed that ship; doomed your uncle and, eventually, ruined your family."

Thirty-Three

BR

$\mathbf{F}$alling. I felt like I was falling and out of control. It was like the solid floor had suddenly disappeared from beneath me. I grasped at excuses, tried to cling to justification, but the momentum of the revealed realities plunged me downward.

Mr. Stafford's son, Christopher, narrowed his eyes and asked me, "What do you mean, 'ruined your family'?"

I could not answer. My mind was consuming itself with horror. My heart was imploding with sadness. I had once asked if there was any end to Mr. Stafford's kindness, now I wondered if there was any end to his secrets.

In a quiet, ragged voice, Mr. Stafford said, "Naomi's uncle was on the *Mary Celeste*. When he went missing, his brother, Naomi's father, took it very hard and escaped to alcohol. As a drunk, he didn't provide well for his family and eventually died. Naomi and her mother moved to poor lodgings along the Thames, and, soon after, her mother died from illness. The cascading effects of the *Mary Celeste* ruined her family."

Christopher leaned back in his chair as all the implications sank in. We were silent for many seconds, until Christopher concluded, "So that is why you adopted her. You felt responsible." It was the very thought I was being smothered with.

"That's not true!" responded Mr. Stafford immediately and strongly. "Everything about the adoption of Naomi is because of who she is and my love for her."

Despite his vehemence, I could not believe him. I had made strides, I realized, towards improving the view of myself – to battling the worthless thoughts that plagued me for so long. I realized those strides had been made because that new revelation removed them all, leaving a cold, dark, vacuum. The absence of confidence felt bitter and familiar.

How could I not feel that my relationship with Mr. Stafford was only based on guilt? Over the past several months, we had shared much, but the foundation of it all was not as it seemed. I wanted it to be love, or, at least, respect. But now I knew that it was based on nothing more than a basic feeling of responsibility. Was Mr. Stafford anything more than one of the caretakers at the orphanage who looked after me as a job and not as family?

The fragility of our relationship was breathtaking. What seemed to be getting stronger, day by day, shattered completely at that new revelation and I was crushed beneath its ruins.

As I fell further into the mire of shocked and confused sadness, the tavern became stifling. The lights, the people, the sounds, the smells – everything – assaulted me and all I wanted was to leave. Breathing felt difficult and my stomach threatened to void its contents. I stood up without a word and rushed outside. I could hear Mr. Stafford call from behind me, but I needed to breathe more than anything else and didn't turn around.

The outside air was cool and slightly calming. The oppressiveness of the tavern faded but allowed me to focus on the hurt of yet another secret revealed. I paced in front of the building, wishing I was home in my room. I wanted to collapse; to give in to the emotions and disappear within myself but standing outside of a bar on the streets of Liverpool prevented that option.

Mr. Stafford was soon outside, his son behind him.

"Naomi," Mr. Stafford said quietly.

I interrupted whatever he was going to say and requested, "Can we leave?" My voice was whispered and cracked.

"What was that?" asked Mr. Stafford.

A little louder, but still halting, I said, "Can we go back to the hotel?"

"Yes, of course."

Christopher spoke up, "I had no intention of revealing secrets or creating any rifts."

"It's alright, Christopher," said Mr. Stafford. "This is not your doing in any way." Then, with a weary smile to his son, "I'm glad to have seen you again and that you are in good health. We are staying at the North Western. I do hope we can meet again before we leave."

With a noncommittal nod, Christopher said, "I'm glad that you are well, father. Miss Gladwyn, despite the circumstances, it was a pleasure to meet you."

I gave the hint of a smile – it was all I could muster. As Christopher walked away, Mr. Stafford hired one of the carriages that were along the street.

We climbed into the cabin in silence. As we started moving, a question came into my head that gave a glimmer of hope to the situation. I asked, clinging to that spark, "Mr. Stafford, no one has ever been found of the missing *Mary Celeste* crew. How do you know that one of your books is the cause of it?"

"The truth is," he answered, "I cannot be absolutely sure, but I must assume that my book is the reason for the tragedy."

"Why?" I asked, pleading for it not to be true.

"The facts of the matter are this: I had tracked one of my books to the United States. A series of sad events led to that definite conclusion. Instead of pursuing it myself – due to the great distance – I wired to a fellow Book Reaper in New York City to track down the volume. His last message was that a sailor had it and that it was proving difficult to get at. The associate was going to become a crewmate of this man in order to continue the pursuit."

"What else?" I asked, not nearly convinced.

"All that remains is simple deductive logic. We know what a Dark Book is capable of. We know that there is no rational explanation for the disappearance of the crew. Even though many belongings were left on the ship, the book was not among them. It's impossible not to deduce that my book played a significant part."

The logic was sound. It was not conclusive, but it was, admittedly, a likely scenario. I thought about harping on the bits of unknown, but I knew that it would not make a difference. Mr. Stafford was convinced of his culpability and, without more evidence – which would likely never surface – he would always feel that way. That led me back to my fear that I was taken in by him for one reason – guilt.

After another long silence, I asked, "Were you ever going to tell me?"

Mr. Stafford sat quietly for several seconds and then said, "Yes, I believe so. The truth is that I wanted to tell you the moment that you mentioned its meaning in your life. Every day since then I have struggled with this secret. I have struggled with not knowing how to tell someone that they have lost everything because of me."

Despite all of my own emotions, the sincerity of Mr. Stafford's words was clear. It had been a constant battle for him.

The carriage stopped in front of our hotel and we departed. In the lobby – very few people were about – Mr. Stafford stopped and said, "I must wait here until the Hudsons arrive. I need to check on their progress and safety. Am I mistaken to assume that you would rather be alone right now?"

I nodded, wishing there were words – his or mine – that could make me feel better.

"I will not keep you," he said. "But I have to ask: can you forgive me?"

Yes, of course, my mind thought. My heart, however, was not nearly so generous. I was hurt and utterly confused as to our relationship. Why did he take me in? Instead of answering him, I decided to clearly ask the one important question that my life currently revolved around. With a quiet and shaking voice, I asked, "Why did you adopt me?"

The question hurt Mr. Stafford. His face fell and I saw his eyes begin to tear. "I adopted you because I *love* you. I love our conversations, your humor, your enthusiasm, your kindness, your bravery. Your *qualities* are why we are together, not your past. Do you believe me? Please tell me you believe me…"

Never had someone looked at me with such pain, but I could not say the words he wanted, as I was not sure that I believed them. Through my own gathering tears, I said, "I want to believe you. I want us to be together because of love, not because of guilt. But I'm not sure that I do."

Mr. Stafford stepped towards me and I turned away. I walked quickly from the lobby, not looking back, and didn't stop until I was in my room, on my bed, and weeping bitterly. I wished for Melba. I wished for Helen. I wished for Daphne. I wished for my mother.

Thirty-Four

BR

Refusing comforting thoughts is a wicked skill, and I was a master. When I could not cry anymore, I lay in my bed, exhausted and utterly miserable. A gas streetlamp from the pavement below gave a hint of light to my room, creating shadows that befriended my thoughts.

Mr. Stafford had once said that I had saved him. But did I save him or assuage his *guilt*? Was there a difference? I felt like a balm for his conscience; a means to an end. Part of me was glad for any ease that I could give to his troubled life, as I still couldn't help but think of him as a good person.

What if he had told me, right from the beginning, about his role in my family's misfortunes – where would I be? Perhaps I would have been a case for his charity, given a life of simple ease – outside of his home and on my own. I likely would have been happy with such a circumstance. But that path can't be revisited, for, instead, we became a family. We provided care for each other, friendship, and, most notably, love. The thought that all of it might have just been a façade, that none of it was real or true, is what crushed me. It meant I was not worth the attention I had received without the tragedy of my family; that, on my own merits, I was not good enough; I was nothing.

Occasionally, my mind would allow a reminder of a way that Mr. Stafford had shown true love for me, but such thoughts were ripped apart mercilessly before they could even scratch at my depression. Happy memories were mere cannon fodder for my wounded heart.

At some point, a new and terrifying line of reasoning crossed my consciousness. Mr. Stafford was clearly guilty over his past and having me in his life could serve as a constant reminder of his pain. Far from being a way to appease his guilt, could I be serving the role of his punishment; a daily flail to his conscience? I immediately stopped that path of thinking as it was too terrible to consider and, even in my downtrodden state, I didn't truly believe it.

I'm not sure why, but my thoughts turned to the book, *Little Women*. I imagined Mrs. March and of the loving, but direct, advice she would always have for her girls. What would she say to me? Probably something along the lines of being careful to not think too much of ones' self; that pride is before a fall. My initial defense to those imaginary words was that I thought so little of myself. However, my focus, since the previous night, had been solely on me and my pain. I hadn't given much consideration – not fairly, anyway – to Mr. Stafford or anyone else.

That change in thought led my mind down a different path; one that brought added confusion. I thought about the surprising statements that Christopher had made about the Dark Books and his reason for wanting them to be preserved. He called them beautiful; the greatest masterpieces of written word. I don't know if it was because he was so passionate, or because his view was so utterly shocking, that I found it hard to dismiss. Perhaps I considered his ideas because I was angry at Mr. Stafford. It worried me that something that I thought I was so confident in – my hatred of Dark Books – could be shaken so quickly.

And then there was the potential of a book that could make people do good. If such a thing existed, how did I feel about it? Could the taking away of free will be justified?

Those thoughts were swimming around my head when I heard a solid knock at my door. It was very late – or early, depending how you looked at it – and it quite startled me. The knock was followed by Mr. Stafford saying, "Naomi, please wake."

"I...I'm awake," I said, a small amount of panic growing in my chest at what it was all about.

"Get dressed," his words were rapid and shaky. "And meet us in the lobby as soon as you can. It's urgent."

"Yes, sir," I said with a quivering voice and heard his steps disappear quickly down the hallway. *What was happening?*

My melancholy was countered by concern. I dressed quickly and hurried down the dim corridor – only a quarter of the wall sconces lit – and rushed down the stairs, breathing heavily and becoming more and more worried. Perhaps the Hudsons had found something. Maybe the entire assignment was over.

I entered the vast lobby and found that a few extra lights had been lit. It was easy to spot Mr. Stafford as he stood with the only people in the entire area. I walked with hurried step, concerned at what I would find out when I reached him. Before I was very close, I could see that there was a hotel employee standing next to Mr. Stafford and that they were both focused on a person that was sitting on a couch.

Another couple of steps and I recognized Edward as the seated person. He didn't look well. I scanned the area for his father, but he was missing from the scene.

When I finally got close, I saw that Edward had his head hanging down and was holding a damp rag to the side of his face. The rag could not completely hide the ugly purple wound behind it. "Edward," I said with concern, "what happened? Are you alright?"

He didn't move. He just sat there, seemingly oblivious to anything I had said. Mr. Stafford put a hand on my shoulder and said quietly, "He and his father were attacked. Mr. Hudson was killed."

I put my hand over my mouth and felt the heat of my escaping gasp weave through my fingers. I searched Mr. Stafford's face for any reprieve from the terrible news, but there was none to be found.

I turned to Edward and kneeled on the floor before him. My heart was breaking for the pain that he was feeling. No suitable words came to my mind – even now, I still have not found words that would have been acceptable – so I gently leaned my forehead into the top of his prostrated head.

We didn't move for a long time. I could hear his staggered breathing, the only sign that he was even alive.

Eventually, he slowly lifted his head and I could see his ragged eyes. One was red from tears; the other was growing dark from his injury.

"Could we get a fresh cold cloth, please?" said Mr. Stafford to the hotel employee. I heard the man scuttle off to comply.

"Edward," I said softly and waited for his distant eyes to focus on me. "Edward, I'm so sorry that this has happened."

He tightened his jaw as he looked to the ceiling in a valiant effort not to shed more tears. After several seconds, he said, "I…" the word choked. He swallowed and then said quickly, "I couldn't stop it." His face continued to battle against crying, but it was not victorious as a few tears leaked down his cheek.

I had no idea exactly what had happened, but I said what I thought he needed to hear. "It was not your fault. You could not have done anything."

He closed his eyes, tight, and finally lost the struggle with his emotions. He hid his face in his hands and began to weep. I got off the floor, sat next to him on the couch, and stroked his back.

When the tears subsided, Mr. Stafford handed Edward the new rag that the employee had brought. With a whispered thank you, he exchanged it for the one he had. Mr. Stafford took one of the high-backed chairs near the couch and we all sat in silence for a very long time.

As some point, I took Edward's hand. It was not romantic – I doubt he even noticed – but I was desperate for him to know that he was not alone. Loss through death isolates us like nothing else and I needed him to not give in. He was too good to be lost to misery and depression.

Time passed and I was surprised when I realized that the illumination around us was less from lamps and more from the morning sunlight. We had been there for hours. I felt destroyed – physically, mentally, and emotionally. Edward had hardly moved, outside of occasionally changing his cloth with fresh ones. I glanced at Mr. Stafford and saw that he, too, appeared quite dreadful. We were a wretched bunch.

My look at Mr. Stafford, under those awful circumstances, did make me see him differently than I had throughout the night. I started to wonder how I would feel if he had died instead of Mr. Hudson. I had been so angry with him, so scared of being anything less than a person he loved, and yet, under those new, terrible, circumstances, I felt ashamed. Despite all of my doubts, deep down, I knew that he loved me.

I cursed myself as I thought of Jo March and the time that she was furious with Amy, her youngest sister. Amy had burned a book of stories that Jo had worked on for years and Jo would not forgive her. She even refused to warn her little sister of the thin place in the ice which led to Amy falling through into the freezing water. Amy survived, but it took the near death of her precious sister for Jo to realize what she meant to her. In the light of the death of Mr. Hudson, I saw very clearly all the love that Mr. Stafford had for me, and I for him. There were mistakes made, but I could then realize that they were aberrations.

A few people started to move through the lobby as the day was starting. No one seemed to pay our little group of quiet mourners much mind. After a little while longer, Mr. Northam arrived. He approached us and said, "Well, you are all quite a sight. Good heavens! Edward, what happened to you?"

Mr. Stafford addressed Mr. Northam, "Edward and his father were attacked last night. Mr. Hudson was killed."

Mr. Northam staggered a step and put his hand on Mr. Stafford's chair in order to steady himself. He said to all of us, "Please forgive my flippant remark as I arrived. I had no idea. Edward, I'm so sorry for your loss." Mr. Northam then took one of the other high-backed chairs near us and joined our circle of sadness.

I didn't notice the hotel employee come up to us until he announced, "I have a message for Mr. Stafford."

"That would be me," said Mr. Stafford taking the note.

I watched as he opened the paper and wondered what it was about; perhaps from one of the Book Reapers, or perhaps an update from Anthony. However, when I looked at Mr. Stafford's face, I saw a very serious expression – definitely different than the sadness that we were feeling. Although I couldn't make out the words, I could see that the message was not very long and knew that Mr. Stafford must have read it several times before he looked up. "Mr. Northam," he said while standing from his chair, "please keep young Mr. Hudson company." Then, looking at me with that same serious expression, said, "Naomi, could you come with me please?"

I gave an unbelieving look at Mr. Stafford, for I didn't want to leave Edward's side.

"Please," Mr. Stafford said, a sense of urgency burning behind his eyes.

I stood up, full of curiosity, and wondered what could be more important than assisting Edward. I followed Mr. Stafford and, when well out of earshot of our group, I asked, "Is everything alright?"

With eyes straight ahead and not a hint of jest, he said, "No. That message just told me that we are in grave danger."

Thirty-Five

Entirely unprepared for what Mr. Stafford had just told me, I asked weakly, "Danger? How? Who?"

Mr. Stafford shook his head and said, "I don't know. But we were instructed to go outside."

As we crossed the lobby and headed towards the exit doors, I looked around trying to spot anyone who could be against us. I half expected to see a man dressed in black ready to pounce but found only a few guests that paid us no attention.

When we exited the building, the air chilly, but not uncomfortably so, I looked at Mr. Stafford to see which way we should head. I could tell that he didn't know, as he stood on the pavement and searched the street, hand over his eyes, with concern and confusion.

"Hello," he said after a few seconds, evidently spotting something, or someone, of interest. I followed his gaze and was surprised to see Christopher, Mr. Stafford's son, a little ways down the street.

As we approached, I noticed that there was a man standing with Christopher. The stranger looked to be close to sixty years of age, had blonde hair, a great mustache that ran from one sideburn, down his jaw, over his lip, and back up to the other sideburn.

When near, Mr. Stafford asked sharply, "Did you send that note? What is the meaning of all of this?" If it was some sort of joke, it was certainly not amusing to Mr. Stafford – nor to me.

"I sent the note," answered Christopher. "And the meaning is exactly as I said. You and your companions are in great danger."

"I already know we are in danger," hissed Mr. Stafford. "One of my friends was murdered last night!"

Christopher put his hand on his head and said, more to himself than to us, "I acted as quickly as I could. It was not fast enough." Then, with a look of sympathy, he asked, "What happened?"

Surprisingly, even though I had spent hours with Edward and Mr. Stafford, I didn't know myself what exactly had occurred. Edward was in no condition to talk and it didn't seem appropriate to discuss it in front of him.

Mr. Stafford explained, "Two of our companions, a father and son, were watching the first mate of the *Merganser* last night – just like we were watching the captain. As they followed him after dinner, someone came out of the shadows and struck the son hard in the head, knocking him senseless, and the father was stabbed."

"I'm so sorry," Christopher said sincerely.

"What do you know of it?" asked Mr. Stafford. "What reason do *you* have to say we are in danger?"

"Where are the son and Mr. Northam?" asked Christopher urgently.

"They are sitting in the lobby. We just left them."

Christopher thought for a moment and then said, "Alright, they should be safe there. This gentleman," Christopher indicated the mustached man, "is Eric Moore. He is the author of the Dark Book that we have been pursuing."

The author! I took a small step back, afraid, but a few of things occurred to me. First, the authors of the books are immune to their effects. Second, if Christopher had found the author, did that mean that he already had the book? Lastly, if the book was in his hands, why was there any danger for us? *Was Christopher the attacker after all?*

Mr. Moore stepped forward and said in a deep, gravelly voice, "I need you all to understand that I had no intention of creating anything harmful. When I was told about the attacks and how my writings may have inspired them, it made me ill. I'm truly sorry about your friend."

Mr. Stafford, who knew the guilt that such a book can cause, said, "Mr. Moore, I hold no culpability and no resentment towards you. Something you created is being misused."

With a look of relief, Mr. Moore said, "It's a great solace to hear you say that. I have done more than enough wrong in my life to add more to that burden. You see, I was a soldier as a young man, doing my duty for

Queen and Country. I will admit that I dreamt of battles and glory as I started out, but the reality of it all was horrible."

It struck me that we were about to hear a woeful tale, for if he did not have an extremely difficult experience, he could not have written such an emotional book.

Mr. Moore continued, "I was sent to India as the Great Rebellion was just underway. I was nervous, but excited – for I had never gone more than fifty miles from my home. All the excitement, however, faded within a day of my arrival. At first, we heard frightful stories of the fighting and death going on throughout the country. Soon after, I saw it firsthand. As the horrific sights compounded – death and ruin for both sides of the conflict – I started to question why it was happening. This is not a soldierly thing to do, but I had never been one to run blindly about. No answers satiated my conscience.

"In late August of 1857, my regiment was sent to reinforce the soldiers that were surrounding Delhi. The British wanted the city back and were amassing forces for a battle. In the early morning of September seventeenth, the battle begun. For five days it raged with death and destruction on a level I could have never imagined. I'm still haunted by nightmares of those horrific experiences."

I could see the pain in the man's face as he talked. Although I started to understand the basis for his Dark Book, I was still unclear how it meant that we were in any immediate danger.

Continuing his account – for it didn't seem likely that we would get any other information until he had told it all – Mr. Moore said, "Thousands died in those few days. Mostly soldiers, but innocents – women and children – were among the casualties. My questioning nature stabbed at my conscience as I continued to ask 'why'. In the end, I concluded that it was simply due to the native people of India tiring of the occupation of the foreign British East India Company. And, as much as I hated the death of my fellow countrymen, I could not blame the Indians for their stand. If the situation was reversed, would British men have done anything less?"

Warfare and politics were two things that I knew little about and, as I learned more, abhorred. It feels as if man overcomplicates things and then chooses to bring death as a resolution. I doubt I will ever understand the way of governments.

"When I returned home," continued Mr. Moore, "despite my disenchantment, I was somehow able to find some suitable employment and even married. But I was a ruined man. My experiences had left me angry and bitter. Even with the dissolution of the East India Company, I still felt poorly for the British involvement in India and those thoughts festered inside of me.

"After a few years of marriage, my wife could hardly stand to be around me. I was a miserable wretch, taking to drink as often as not. More than once did I think of doing something desperate. That is when a friend of the family suggested that I write out my thoughts, as a form of therapy. That changed my life and saved my marriage. When I took to writing, I did not stop for many hours. When completed, I was exhausted, but felt as if a burden had been lifted from my soul. It's hard to explain, but I started to become a better man after writing my journal."

I could see Mr. Stafford growing impatient. However, he did manage to wait until the story was told – no doubt from a shared commiseration – before asking the question, "What did you do with your writings, Mr. Moore?"

"I sold it."

"To whom?"

"The gentleman said his name was Mr. Nettles. We met a month or two ago and had several conversations. He seemed very interested in my journal and paid me twenty pounds for it."

Mr. Stafford, looking like he was regretting coming outside at all, turned to Christopher and asked, "Is there anything else? Should I know this Mr. Nettles? I would like to go back to comforting the son of my dead friend."

"Mr. Nettles," said Christopher, "is not actually the man's name. The buyer evidently knew about Dark Books, and therefore spent the large sum to procure it. Something struck me last night and I brought Mr. Moore down here this morning to verify a hunch."

"And what hunch is that?"

"That the so-called Mr. Nettles is here at the hotel."

"I'm not in the mood for guessing games," said Mr. Stafford. "Please speak plainly."

Christopher said to Mr. Moore, "Tell them what you saw this morning."

"Well, sir, to my surprise, I saw the man that called himself Mr. Nettles enter that hotel."

"You know him," said Christopher, "as Mr. Northam."

Thirty-Six

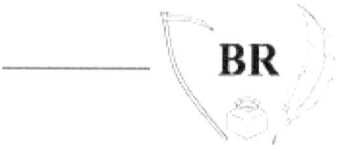

BR

All the sensation of the world around me stopped. The noises from passing carriages, the chill in the air, footsteps of passersby, none of it registered. Christopher had just told us that Mr. Northam had the Dark Book that we were after which meant that he undoubtedly was the murderer.

"Wait a moment," said Mr. Stafford, not having given in fully to the accusation yet. "Mr. Northam was with us last night – you saw him – how could he be behind this?"

Christopher thought for a second and then answered, "Our night was not a very late one before you sent Mr. Northam away. Was the attack on your friends much later than that?"

Mr. Stafford nodded gravely. "Yes, it was. The first mate spent hours at a tavern before heading home."

"So then," said Christopher, continuing the thread, "he would have had time to find them and do his foul deed."

Turning to Mr. Moore, Mr. Stafford asked, "How *sure* are you that the man you saw walking into the hotel this morning is the same man that you sold the book to?"

"Quite sure. In fact, I would dare say that there is no mistake about it."

"What do we do now?" I asked, nervous that we had been in the presence of a killer.

"We have to be certain," answered Mr. Stafford resolutely. "What we are accusing Mr. Northam of is severe. Even if he was the one to buy the book – and I do not doubt what Mr. Moore says – he might have given it to someone, or had it taken from him."

"Do you really think that's likely?" asked Christopher.

Mr. Stafford paused in thought for a moment and then admitted, "No. I don't think it's likely. However, we need to be sure."

"What do you propose?" Christopher asked.

After a few more moments of thought, Mr. Stafford said to Mr. Moore, "I think it would be best for you to go now. Thank you for your time and frankness."

"I hope I have helped; have made some atonement for what I have done," the man answered and then, after a nod to Christopher, started walking away.

I asked, "Do you have a plan in mind?"

"Yes," answered Mr. Stafford. "It's simple but should give us the information we need. We are going to box Mr. Northam in and see how he responds to the news that we have found the author. His reaction should tell us what we need to know. Christopher, would you mind joining us for a little while this morning? If Mr. Northam is all that we fear he is, it would be nice to have another person on our side."

"Of course," he answered.

"Alright," said Mr. Stafford grimly. "I don't think that I need to tell you that we need to be extra vigilant. Naomi, I'm fairly certain that Edward will come along with us and I need you to inform him, quietly, of this information. It's imperative, however, that he not act until we are sure of Mr. Northam's involvement. Can you do this?"

"Yes, sir," I said, immediately starting to think about how to break the news to Edward.

With a reassuring look at me, and then Christopher, Mr. Stafford said, "Very well," and then turned to head back into the hotel.

Christopher and I followed behind him, but as we neared the entrance, Christopher put his hand on my arm and indicated that we should slow down a little to give a bit of distance between us and Mr. Stafford.

"Miss Gladwyn," he said, "I wanted to apologize once more for my statements last night. Obviously, my father and I have a strained relationship, but I have no quarrel with you. If anything I did was hurtful, please forgive me."

I was surprised by that, for I had not blamed him for anything that was said. With all that was going on – the death of Mr. Hudson – my issues seemed rather small. "You did nothing wrong," I answered and started to walk in the hotel. However, Christopher stopped me again.

"One more thing," he said. "I was serious about the importance of Dark Books. I know that they have harmful potential, but they can also teach us so much. Please consider both sides of the matter before making any final decisions for yourself."

The earnestness of his face struck me. I had seen it before, several times, in the face of his father. They were so much alike. After a moment, I nodded and said, "I can agree to consider, but cannot promise anything."

"That is all I ask."

We entered the hotel and caught up with our group. I looked at Mr. Northam and had trouble seeing him as a murderer – for he didn't look any different.

Mr. Stafford announced, "Edward, I know that this is a difficult time, but I have some news. This is my son, Christopher, and he has information that can help us to track down the man who murdered your father."

I watched Mr. Northam at that announcement and saw surprise – but what else would he have shown?

Edward had not reacted to much of anything for hours, but that statement made him look up and stare hard at Christopher. With a hoarse voice, he asked, "What do you know?"

Mr. Stafford answered, "We can explain on the way, but we should hurry." Then, "You don't have to come. If you would like to retire to your room, that would be perfectly understandable and acceptable."

With emotion that bordered on anger, Edward said, "I'm going with you. If there is a possibility that I can avenge my father, then I must at least try."

"Very well," said Mr. Stafford, "come along then, all of you."

As we walked across the lobby, I stayed next to Edward and paced us to be at the rear of the procession. Besides wanting to give him my support, I needed to clue him in on what was going on. "Edward," I whispered, making sure that no one – especially Mr. Northam – could hear us. "I must inform you of something urgent."

He looked at me with a little confusion as we continued our slow pace. "What is it?" he asked.

"You cannot react to what I'm about to tell you, for we are not sure, and it might spoil everything. Promise me you will not react."

His confusion grew and he hesitantly said, "I promise."

I took in a breath and said, "There is a possibility that Mr. Northam has the book."

His eyes grew wide and then he looked ahead at Mr. Northam, anger in his face. I grabbed his arm forcefully and hissed, "Don't do anything!"

I could see his jaw clench and feel his muscles pulse. I continued, "We are not certain yet, but Mr. Stafford has a plan to find out. Please wait for the plan."

The anger of his face turned to agony. He desperately wanted to act – for who would not want to go after the killer of a loved one – and had to fight to remain in step with me. I continued to try and reason with him, saying, "We need to be certain. Agreed?"

After a few more moments of intense staring at Mr. Northam, Edward turned his head to me and nodded, too overwhelmed with containing his fury to speak.

As we walked outside, I kept my hand on his arm hoping that it had a calming effect. Mr. Stafford flagged down a carriage and we all climbed aboard. Like the previous day, it was a tight fit. Mr. Stafford and I sat on one side, while Edward, Christopher, and Mr. Northam sat on the other.

As we started moving, Mr. Northam asked, "What information do you have that can help us?"

"Christopher," said Mr. Stafford, "has located the man that wrote the book."

I watched Mr. Northam closely and saw that a bit of nervousness pass over his face. Not a good sign, but not enough to be proof.

Mr. Stafford continued, "We are heading there now to interview him; a man by the name of Eric Moore. He must know who he gave the book to."

"That is excellent news," said Mr. Northam, looking as if it was anything but excellent news. He then said, "Perhaps we could divide and conquer, as they say. I would like to talk with the police about last night's attack. You know, see what details I can glean. Why don't you four carry on, and I will go see the authorities."

His face started to look desperate. For my part, I had grown nearly certain of his guilt. And that suggestion of his – which would conveniently keep him out of sight from Mr. Moore – was almost as good as a confession.

"That will not do at all," said Mr. Stafford. "I think having you with us will be *most* helpful."

Sometime in the next few seconds, Mr. Northam figured out that we knew that he had the book. I stared at him and watched as the realization crossed his face, and then desperation. Without another word or any warning, he threw opened the door of the moving carriage and was going to make a run for it.

With hardly a thought, I kicked my foot out and caught his leg as he was leaping outside. He fell to the ground and, in an instant, Christopher and Edward were out of the cabin after him.

Mr. Stafford commanded that the carriage stop and then he and I hurriedly climbed out. We saw that Mr. Northam was completely subdued by the combined force of Edward and Christopher. Mr. Stafford gave the driver some money and told him to fetch the police. We then hurried over to where the struggling Mr. Northam was being held down. He had blood coming out of his nose and I noticed that Edward had some blood on his knuckles. Although frightened by the sight, in retrospect, I think Edward was quite reserved in his actions.

I had imagined, on occasion, what it would feel like to find out who was behind the attacks. The word 'triumphant' had often come to my mind. But, standing there on the street, with a grieving Edward fighting back tears as he held his father's killer, I felt only sadness. It was made worse by the fact that I had liked Mr. Northam. True, I had not known him well, but he seemed very amiable. I wondered if the working out of my various trials would ever give me what I expected.

Yanking him off the ground, a firm grip on either arm, Edward and Christopher dragged Mr. Northam out of the street and to a curb where they all sat. Mr. Stafford stood in front, looking the part of a warden, and then searched inside of Mr. Northam's coat. Before long, a wicked looking dagger was found and held safely in Mr. Stafford's hands. I watched from a little distance as I could not bring myself to get very close.

"This is," said Mr. Stafford, "a tremendous disappointment. It also presents us with a difficult decision."

What decision? I wondered.

"As you know," Mr. Stafford continued, alternating looks between me, Christopher, and Edward. "The influence of a Dark Book is powerful.

In some ways, it could be argued that Mr. Northam is not at fault for what he has done."

The shock of the statement was countered by the correctness of it. Mr. Northam had come across a Dark Book and succumbed to its power. I could not help but think of Mr. Northam's own words on the subject. Perhaps he was preparing for this very occasion.

However, three people were dead and that cannot be ignored. I thought about my own experience with such a book and, although very difficult, I didn't succumb to terrible action – but I was incredibly close. I glanced at Edward and saw him looking down, struggling with emotions.

"I must admit, though," continued Mr. Stafford, "that Mr. Northam was not an unwary victim. As a Book Reaper, he knew of the dangers that those books hold and yet, he still gave in. In fact, he may have even sought it out."

Did knowing make him more responsible?

"What do you have to say for yourself, Mr. Northam?" asked Mr. Stafford.

The captured man said, "The three lives I took are a small price for the thousands that died at Delhi. All the book did was open my eyes to a great wrong and I could not stand idly by while the British Empire continued down its path of exploitation."

His mind was clearly still heavily under the influence of the book.

"Edward," said Mr. Stafford, "the police will be here soon. We have an important decision to make. I think, under the circumstances, that it's only right that you make it. There are two choices. Choice one: turn Mr. Northam over to the police as a murderer. Choice two: we give time for Mr. Northam to overcome the influence of the book – which could take many weeks – and simply tell the police, when they arrive, that there is nothing going on here. What would you like to do?"

It was a terrible decision to make. Condemn the man that killed your father, or somehow find forgiveness and allow him a chance to be free. It was not my choice, but I'm fairly certain that I knew what I would have decided.

Before answering the question, Edward looked at Mr. Northam and demanded, "Why did you kill my father?"

With a voice clogged from his bloodied nose, Mr. Northam said, "Because he is an importer and profits from the trade with India. Also, I wanted the hunt for me to be stymied."

"Why did you not kill me?" Edward asked, tears in his eyes.

"Because a mourning son would be even more of an impediment than a dead one."

The answers were cold. Whether the book had taken all actual sympathy from Mr. Northam, I didn't know, but he came across in that moment as a heartless monster.

Edward stared at him for several long seconds, a death grip on his arm, and then turned his eyes to the distance. I could see the struggle on his face. Finally, he looked at Mr. Stafford and said flatly, "We are giving him to the police."

With that announcement, Mr. Northam renewed his struggles for a moment with his captors, but their grips would not relent.

Mr. Stafford asked Edward, "Are you certain?"

He nodded and said with a coldness that equaled Mr. Northam's, "I am certain."

Thirty-Seven

BR

Departing the police station, having answered many questions as to the guilt of Mr. Northam, I was utterly exhausted. It was only early afternoon, but I had not slept for well over twenty-four hours. Adding to the lack of sleep was the emotional cost of the last day and a half. Never had my person, inside and out, been in a more fatigued state.

Of all the evidence against Mr. Northam, the dagger was most incriminating. It evidently matched what the police had expected from their examination of the wounds of the victims. Of course, there was also the four of us – Edward, Christopher, Mr. Stafford, and me – who heard Mr. Northam confess. He would not be escaping the crimes committed.

As much as I hated what was done, especially seeing the familiar pain that Edward felt at the loss of a parent, I still could not help feeling a little sad for Mr. Northam. Any infatuation I had towards him was completely gone, so I was not feeling sad in a longing sort of way, but I felt sad for him because he would likely hang for his crimes and yet, I still could not completely condemn him. The book held a great responsibility but would probably not be seriously considered at all in Mr. Northam's trial. Although I think I would have made the same decision as Edward, as time has passed, I'm less sure of what was right. I wondered if Edward felt any doubts – or ever would – about his choice for Mr. Northam.

As we stood on the pavement, waiting for a carriage, Mr. Stafford asked, "Son, how did you find the author of the book? Usually that can't be done until after the book itself is discovered."

"Quite a bit of good fortune that was," Christopher answered. "In some respects, he found me. You see, after the second murder, I suspected a Dark Book. I have a friend in the police who gave me some details that were not made public."

"Like what?" I asked.

"On the alley walls, near the first victims, was found scrawled 'The Siege of Delhi'. It was a strange note and gave the impression of something outside the ordinary. I started visiting the taverns in the area and talking up the Great Rebellion and the siege, to see what reactions could be found. During one such attempt, I was approached by Mr. Moore and, in the course of our conversation, he talked about his journal."

"That is very clever work," said Mr. Stafford with something that was close to pride.

A silence fell over our group for a few awkward moments and then Christopher said, "I imagine that you are heading to Mr. Northam's residence to collect the book."

"Yes, we are," answered Mr. Stafford. "It has done quite enough damage, don't you think?"

Christopher nodded and said, "Yes it has. I assume that you would rather that I not come along with you."

"That depends," said Mr. Stafford, "After all that has happened, the pain and death that the book has caused, are you still interested in preserving it?"

Christopher set his jaw and said, "As much as ever. I have never denied that, when handled carelessly, these books are dangerous. But I still hold to the belief that, if handled correctly, there is much we can learn."

Shaking his head in absolute disbelief, Mr. Stafford said, "There is nothing *useful* to be learned. I think your initial assumption – of me not wanting you to join us – is correct."

"Very well," Christopher said with a sigh. "Father, I'm glad to have seen you and to find that you are well." The two men then shook hands as if nothing more than business partners.

With some softening of his features, Mr. Stafford said, "I too am glad that you are well."

I watched that frigid display of familial affection and wanted to scold them. Did they not realize how fortunate they were to have each other? Also, they were in the presence of two individuals that didn't have parents, and yet, they callously took it for granted. If I was not so exhausted, so unable to take on another emotional battle, I would have said something. As it was, even though I kept silent, I hoped for a future time to revisit the situation.

"Edward," said Christopher softly, "please accept my sincere condolences for your loss." He then shook Edward's hand and gave his shoulder a pat.

Turning to me, Christopher said, "Miss Gladwyn, *sister*, I must admit that you were quite an unexpected addition to this strange little family we have. However, I dare say, a very welcomed one. I hope that we can see each other again." With that, he stepped forward and hugged me.

His affection was surprising and touching. I had no more defenses for my emotions and could not stop the few tears that escaped while we embraced. I said, "I'm happy to have met you. Please arrange for a visit."

Christopher released the hug but held both my hands with his. There was something in one of his hands, a slip of paper, and, as I realized it, he gave me a very subtle smile. "I would like that very much."

With nothing left to say, he walked away down the pavement. I watched him until he turned a corner and was out of sight. When no one was paying me any attention, I glanced at the slip of paper and found that it had an address on it. Was that his way of saying I should visit him without needing Mr. Stafford's blessing?

After hailing a carriage, we headed towards Mr. Northam's home. Edward was alone on the seat across from us and looked about as wretched as a person could. I wanted to comfort him, but could think of nothing to say; so, I sat in miserable, but empathetic, silence.

As we neared Mr. Northam's building, I asked, "How are we going to get entry into his home?"

"Ah," answered Mr. Stafford with a small smile, "do you remember when I removed the weapon from Mr. Northam?"

I nodded and said, "Yes."

"Well, I also happened upon his key. I made no show of it, but I gathered it all the same. Of course, if it happens to be the wrong key, there are other ways to gain entrance."

I wondered what those *other ways* were but was quite impressed with Mr. Stafford's cleverness and foresight. Even Edward cocked his head, in what I will call a hint of amusement, at Mr. Stafford's confession.

We stopped in front of the simple stone building that held Mr. Northam's apartment. The three of us got out and approached the front door, which Mr. Stafford opened without bothering to knock. We walked down the first-floor corridor, past a stairway, and stopped at an interior door. He tried the handle and found it to be locked. Producing the key from his pocket, he slowly inserted it and turned. We heard a click and I could not help but whisper, "Well done, sir!"

The door opened and we were in the sitting room of Mr. Northam's home. "Spread out and search for the journal. It's handwritten, so we can safely ignore any published volumes."

It was good and helpful advice as there were many books to be found throughout the apartment – as a Book Reaper, I guess that made sense. Edward and I searched the shelves in the sitting room, but only found familiar volumes. Mr. Stafford disappeared into the bedroom.

We had not been there long when we heard Mr. Stafford announced, "I found it." Joining us, he said, "It was on the bedside table. Evidently a regular read of his."

I looked at the brown covered journal in Mr. Stafford's hands and wondered how that innocent looking volume could be the key to so much violence and sadness. I remembered the words that Edward had applied to the snake that he had once found: *It's amazing that something so small can be so deadly!*

Those thoughts and words, however, were balanced by the comparison that Christopher made to fire. That book was a great flame and had burned much. But could it also be used for good? My conflicted feelings battled inside of me and I had little strength to stop them.

I asked, "Are we sure that that is the book? Do we need to…to read it to be certain?"

"We do," Mr. Stafford said grimly. "However, our little group is not ideally situated for this. For you see, if I read it, I would be dependent on the both of you to make sure that I didn't go too far. That is a huge responsibility and I'm not sure either of you are ready for it – especially after the night we have had."

"Could not one of us read it?" I asked, terrified of the answer.

"That is the other option, but, again, you are both stretching the limits of your fortitude. It might not be a good idea. However, we must do something. We cannot leave this apartment until we are sure that we have what we came for."

"So, what do we do?" asked Edward.

"As painful as it is for me to suggest," said Mr. Stafford, "I think the safest option is for one of you to read some of this journal and allow me to supervise."

I looked at Edward but didn't see what I expected. He didn't look fearful, but rather, determined. For my part, I would have read the book if that was everyone's wish, but I was terribly frightened at the prospect.

"I'll read it," said Edward, his tone steady and his face serious.

Mr. Stafford looked at him for several long seconds and finally asked, "Are you absolutely certain? You have been through more than any of us."

Edward didn't answer immediately. I could see him searching himself for any doubt. When none was found, evidently, he said, "I'm certain."

"Alright," said Mr. Stafford, examining the room. "Why don't you take this chair here, and Naomi and I will sit quietly over there. Every fifteen minutes I will interrupt you, and this will stop at no later than one hour. That should be enough time to know if this book is our goal."

Edward nodded and took the suggested seat. Mr. Stafford handed him the book and sat on the couch near him, while I took the other space on the couch. The reading began and Mr. Stafford took out his watch to check the time.

Observing someone read must sound like a tedious activity, and, under normal circumstances, I would agree. However, under the situation we were in, I paid rapt attention. My senses were straining to pick up any signs that the exercise should stop.

For the first fifteen minutes, Edward looked calm, if not serious, but nothing more. At the set interval, Mr. Stafford interrupted him and asked, "What do you think?"

"There is," said Edward, "a lot about military service in India. Nothing I have read makes me think that this is not the book we are after. Still, I feel no particular effects or influence."

"Very well," said Mr. Stafford, "please continue for another fifteen minutes."

The next fifteen minutes passed similarly to the first – attentive and nervous. I noticed that Edward's face took on some different expressions at times and wondered what he was reading in those moments.

When the next milestone passed, Mr. Stafford announced, "It has been a total of thirty minutes. Have you formed a definite opinion yet?"

Edward shook his head and said, "No, sir. It has started to talk of some of the atrocities that Mr. Moore had experienced, and I do feel poorly for those involved. Still, I think another fifteen minutes is warranted."

Mr. Stafford stared at Edward for several seconds before finally agreeing. *How much more did we need?* I wondered. It *had* to be the right book. Could we be harming Edward by continuing? Despite my doubts, I trusted Mr. Stafford – I knew that there was no one who wanted people to be safe from those books more than him.

Edward did not make it through the next fifteen minutes. After reading awhile longer, his eyes began to tear, and his emotions grew more overt. He didn't stop reading, only pausing to wipe his cheeks on occasion.

"Edward," I said kindly, hoping that my intrusion would be acceptable to Mr. Stafford. "Edward, why are you upset? What is the book telling you?"

With a little effort, he looked up at me and then said, "It's just that…that, there was so much death. Why did all those people have to die? Because of money? That can't be an acceptable answer."

I looked at Mr. Stafford and he gave me a small nod. "I thank you, Edward. You have just proven what we needed to know. Please hand me the book now."

Edward looked down at the open volume, not reading, just staring. I was afraid that he would not let it go, that he would fight to keep reading. Fortunately, he simply closed the book and gave it over.

I rushed over to his side and asked, "Are you alright?"

"I don't know what I am," he answered and then buried his face in hands and began to sob.

"You did well," I whispered into his ear, hoping that some form of encouragement would break through his despair.

When Edward was able to compose himself, Mr. Stafford said, "Come along now. Let us return to the hotel and get some rest. None of us are in any condition for much else."

Edward and I stood and followed wordlessly. In the cab, I chose to sit next to Edward, hoping that the simple act of nearness might help convey my support for him. Mr. Stafford gave no objection.

We rode in silence, lost in thought, or simply too tired to think, and were thankful when we finally reached the North Western. As we walked through the lobby and up the stairs to our rooms, I stole glances at the journal that Mr. Stafford carried. *Could it be used for any good, after all the bad that it had done – as Christopher believed?* There was a kind of redemption in that thought.

Outside of our rooms, Mr. Stafford said to Edward, "Please try and rest. You have some difficult days ahead of you and will need your strength. But know that you are not alone. If there is anything that I can do, please don't hesitate to ask."

"Yes, sir. Thank you," was Edward's response and he entered his room.

Mr. Stafford turned to me, and, with a tired smile, said, "I think we have a few difficult days ahead of us as well. Don't think that I'm unaware of the pain I have caused with my secrets. But let us rest well before we take on that challenge. Agreed?"

Much of the difficulties that Mr. Stafford was alluding to had already been overcome in my mind. It, unfortunately, took the horrible loss of Mr. Hudson for that battle to be concluded. Still, we needed to discuss those things openly. "I agree," I said and then gave Mr. Stafford a hug – although we would have a conversation about it in the future, I wanted him to know that he didn't need to be afraid.

When I climbed into my bed, I reveled in the comfort of not having to physically support myself anymore. With muscles relaxed, my mind and heart followed suit and I was swiftly asleep.

Thirty-Eight

BR

I awoke to a room with a little light. It was impossible to tell if it was morning or evening. Even though I was still very tired, I felt immensely better. The unfamiliarity of the bed was such an insignificant trifle that it no longer seemed to bother me.

During my rest, I dreamt of absolution and redemption; of pain and healing; of suffering and forgiveness. Although the visions of my sleep faded, the remaining feelings were clear. I thought of Edward and how not a person on earth could blame him for his choice to turn Mr. Northam over to the police – well, not a person outside of, perhaps, Edward himself.

Regarding my forgiveness of Mr. Stafford, it was complete. I was relieved, with a clearer head and some returning emotional fortitude, that I still didn't condemn my adopted father. I believed that his past good, and the future good, that no doubt awaited, far exceeded any mistakes he had made toward me. If I was his savior, he was no doubt mine.

There was only one unresolved item that I battled with: the Dark Book that rested in Mr. Stafford's room. I struggled with the thoughts and ideas that Christopher had provided. *What if he was right?* was the question I could not answer satisfactorily. What if that book could serve a good purpose?

I almost viewed the book as an entity, that it had feelings. In that way, I imagined that it felt bad for the suffering it caused and longed to make up for such actions. I laughed as I reminded myself that it was just an inanimate object – paper and ink. But was it? The power of the written word had proven it to be, if not living, then at least active. Did it deserve destruction?

In a different way, I saw the book as an analogy for myself. For I was in a wretched situation heading towards a life of ruin, but then I was saved by unexpected kindness. I saw future goodness where there was none previously. If I could be saved, could the book also be?

As I struggled with those thoughts, I took out the little piece of paper that Christopher had given me. In the low light, I stared at the address and, like that fateful night in the orphanage, settled on a bold decision. I would get the book and send it to him. I would try to bring something good out of all of the tragedy.

If you have stuck with me, dear reader, through these many pages, then I wonder what you think of me. That is not an entirely fair question, as I often don't know what to think of myself. But that decision is one of the most controversial of my life and my own judgment flips and flops. If you choose to judge me, I plead that you do so with empathy.

With my sudden determination, I got out of bed, lit a lamp, dressed and brushed my hair. When I looked in the mirror, I still looked tired and my hair was barely passable, but it would suffice. My stomach growled – for I had not eaten in a long time – and that gave me my idea.

I entered the hallway and knocked lightly on Mr. Stafford's door. After only a moment, I heard footsteps – he must have been awake. I said, still quiet, "Mr. Stafford?"

The door opened and he asked, "Is everything alright."

"Yes, sir. I was just feeling hungry and wondered if you would join me for a meal."

With a kind smile he said, "Of course I would. Give me a moment to get ready." With that, he closed the door and I waited.

I wondered if we should disturb Edward. I did not know if our company, or food, would be welcomed or a bother. I decided to knock very lightly and say, "Edward, we are going downstairs for a meal. If you would like to join us, you are more than welcome."

I listened for a few seconds but heard nothing. Either he was asleep, or he was not interested. Mr. Stafford exited his room and I watched as he locked his door and put the key in his jacket pocket.

We walked downstairs, through the lobby and into the dining room. It turned out that it was evening, and dinner was being served. We were shown to a small table and, before I was seated, I rubbed my arms as if I was cold, even though the room was very comfortable.

We sat down and ordered our meal. We talked a little about how we slept and how nice it would be to arrive home. I kept rubbing my shoulders until Mr. Stafford finally asked, "Are you warm enough?"

"Not really. Aren't you cold?"

"No," answered Mr. Stafford, "I cannot say that I am. Are you feeling alright?"

"It's hard to tell. I think I could sleep for a few days." I smiled and gave a little shiver.

"Here," said Mr. Stafford, standing up and taking off his jacket. "Take this. I fear that you might be coming down with something. In fact, I would be a little surprised if we all didn't come down with something after what we have been through."

I thanked him for the kindness that I knew he would provide and felt a little bad at taking advantage of him in that way. While waiting for our food, I slipped my hand into the jacket pocket and removed his key.

When the food came, I ate a few bites – which were heavenly – and reluctantly put my knife and fork down to declare that I could not eat anymore. After saying that I was starting to feel a bit worse, I stood, gave the jacket back to Mr. Stafford, and left him at the table under the pretense of returning to my room for more rest.

I climbed the stairs quickly and felt anything but cold when I reached our floor. I walked directly to Mr. Stafford's room, glanced quickly up and down the hallway to make sure no one was watching, and then unlocked his door. I stepped inside and was struck by the thought that it was the second time I had snuck into a space that belonged to Mr. Stafford.

Being that the sun had set, the room was dark so that I had to light the lamp. A quick search of the room from the doorway didn't reveal the book. I opened Mr. Stafford's trunk – which somehow felt even worse than being in his room – and found the journal. In my hands, it once again seemed so innocent, and yet, the death of at least three men could be attributed to it. A great doubt at my intentions slowed me down. *Was this the right thing to do?* It was not too late to change my mind.

I stood there, staring at the book for several seconds while my conscience battled within me. In the end, I simply didn't know what was right or wrong. I could make many arguments for destroying the book – as was Mr. Stafford's intentions. But the arguments that Christopher made would not be silenced. And, even though I barely knew him, his thoughts of me were already becoming important. I wanted to somehow please both of them – even though that was impossible with my decision.

Pushing my doubts aside, I settled on my original plan. With book in hand, I closed the trunk, extinguished the lamp, and the exited the room. I locked the door and placed the key on the floor of the hallway – hoping that Mr. Stafford would assume he dropped it.

Next, I went to my room and waited. I knew that, when Mr. Stafford finished his meal, he would check up on me. A few minutes later, he did just that.

After a light knock, I heard him ask through the door, "Naomi, are you alright?"

Sitting on the bed, book cradled in my arms, I answered, "I am. I feel better now that I'm lying down. I imagine that I will be right as rain after a good night's sleep."

"I hope so. Goodnight."

"Goodnight."

I listened as he walked away, paused at his door – I imagined him searching his pockets and eventually finding the key on the floor – and then entered his room. As soon as I heard his door close, I jumped off the bed and, as quietly as possible, opened my door. I crept down the empty hallway past Mr. Stafford's and Edward's rooms. The thought of sneaking out of the orphanage that dark night all those months ago went through my mind. How did I end up here *again*?

When a little ways down the corridor, I hurried my steps and again descended the stairs. At the bottom, I continued through the lobby and right outside into the cold night air. As I neared the street, I prayed that I would see one of the street urchins on Anthony's corner. Under the light of a lamp, I saw a couple of children right where I hoped they would be. The last part of my plan was coming to fruition.

Doubts still nagged at me, but I pushed them aside as I quickly crossed the street. *There is no going back now*, I told myself. As I neared the boys, I asked loudly, "Is Anthony here?"

One of the boys stepped forward into the lamplight and I saw the familiar dirty face of our assistant. "Hello, love," he said with a mischievous grin. "No Mr. Stafford tonight?"

"No, just me. I have an assignment for you."

"Is that so? And what does it pay?"

I could have wrung the greedy urchin's neck. Mr. Stafford had given him more money in the last couple of days than he would normally see for several months. "I'm afraid that this task will have to be on credit," I said coldly.

"Credit? That's rich!" the boy laughed, and his mates joined in.

"I have no money to give you," I said. "But Mr. Stafford would be quite upset if you refused me this simple favor."

At the mention of displeasing Mr. Stafford, Anthony lost a little of his arrogance. "No need to be hasty," he said. "Tell me, what is the favor?"

"I need you to deliver a book to this address," I handed him the piece of paper that Christopher had given me. "Can you do that?"

Anthony took the scrap of paper and studied the address. "A little far, but we can manage."

"So, you will do it then?" I asked with optimism.

Anthony didn't answer immediately and brought back his grin. He said, "Yes, I will." Before I got too excited, he continued, "However, there still needs to be a payment made."

I glared crossly at him and repeated, "I told you that I don't have any money."

"I know, I heard you," he said smugly. "Your price is a small one – in fact, I think there are many women who would *pay* for the pleasure – a kiss, right here," he pointed at his dirty left cheek.

"Hah!" I said indignantly. "I think I would rather kiss a rat."

"Suit yourself," said the boy. "No kiss, no favor. Unless, of course, you can provide some coins."

That street urchin had me in a difficult situation and he knew it. My mind raced for any other options but came up empty. I let out a breath and said through gritted teeth, "Alright. I agree to your terms."

Without hesitation, the boy walked right up to me and stuck out his left cheek. I stared at the grimy surface and repressed a gag. I leaned down and, at the last moment, he turned his face and our lips met.

I pushed him away so hard that he fell on his backside. "You wicked little creature!" I shouted at him with anger and embarrassment.

"Calm down, love," the boy said, laughing – his friends roaring from glee. "You have just paid for your favor and included a tip!"

I glared at him some more, which only seemed to make him, and his companions laugh harder. Finally, since there was nothing I could do about any of it, I shook my head and gave him the book. I said sternly, "You make sure that this gets delivered. If I find out that it didn't make it – and I will find out – there is no place that you will be able to hide from me. Understood?"

Still smiling, he gave me a quick mock salute and said, "Yes, sir, love."

As he turned and ran off, I headed back to the hotel, wiping my mouth on my sleeve. I may not have actually been sick before, but I felt sick now.

Back in my room, I fretted over the discovery of the missing book, as it was merely a question of time before that happened. I lay on the bed, while my mind battled the justification and condemnation over what I had done.

Eventually, fatigue overcame even my self-doubting nature, and I drifted into a deep sleep.

Thirty-Nine

BR

Not a week goes by that I don't think about the lies that I told to Mr. Stafford and Edward about what happened to the book. I'm still bitter at that initial cowardice. However, that's getting a little ahead of my account. I shall resume on the morning following giving the book to Anthony and his sickening kiss.

I awoke to a loud knocking at my door. As I opened my eyes, I could see that it was morning, for the room was very bright. The knock came again, rapid and forceful – this time followed by Mr. Stafford saying, "Naomi, please answer the door. It's very important."

Although not quite awake, I measured the sound of Mr. Stafford's voice and determined that he had discovered the missing book. "One moment," I called out nervously.

I got out of bed, put on my robe, and smoothed my hair. I didn't look at my reflection for it would not help my appearance – nor did I think I could quite face the person looking back. I opened my door slowly, head slightly bowed, but eyes up to see Mr. Stafford's face.

The man I saw outside the door, although it was Mr. Stafford, looked frightening. His dress was not in the usual well-arranged manner. His hair was mussed and face unshaven. If it was not for the sober – and intense – look in his eyes, I would have feared that he was drunk again.

"Naomi," he said sternly, not even waiting for me to ask what was happening. "The book is missing. It pains me to say this, but I have every reason to believe that you are the one that took it. For your performance last night – being cold and feeling ill – must have been how you retrieved the key and entered my room."

I had determined not to deny my role in taking the book. Not only would it be a lie that I thought would fail miserably, it was the best way for the lie I *would* tell to be believed. "Yes, sir. I was the one who took it." I said softly.

"Did you read it?" he asked with concern.

That surprised me a little, for reading it never crossed my mind – not for an instant. "Oh, no, sir! Absolutely not!"

"Then where is it?"

"I don't have it. I destroyed it." That was my lie. That was my way to try and make everyone happy. Christopher would receive the book while Mr. Stafford would believe it to be destroyed.

"You destroyed it?" he asked. "How?"

"In the smoking room, there is a small stove for heat. I threw it into the embers and removed that wretched thing."

I watched Mr. Stafford's face closely looking for signs of disbelief. I saw only confusion and disappointment.

"Why?" he asked. "Why did you do it in such an underhanded way? Did you not trust me to get rid of it?"

The term 'underhanded' stung a little, but was entirely accurate and, in my opinion, not nearly painful enough for what I deserved. In a pleading voice, continuing my dishonesty, I said, "I hated that book. I hated what it did to Edward. I trusted you to destroy it eventually, but I wanted it gone. I could not wait, nor did I think I could explain myself."

"So you lied about feeling ill, stole my key, snuck into my room, and then burned it."

I nodded at the mostly accurate chain of events that was laid out. Although the destruction of the book would be what Mr. Stafford wanted, my methods were, no doubt, very upsetting to him. I added, wondering how true it actually was, "I guess I was not quite myself yesterday."

Mr. Stafford looked at me, reading my face. I did not break his gaze and wondered how much of my account he believed. Regardless, I knew he was disappointed in me and that hurt. Although I felt justified in having my own secret – after the secrets he had kept – part of me knew that there was no excuse for lying. Hadn't secrets caused nothing but great pain?

My attempt to make everyone happy seemed to be failing; for Mr. Stafford was not happy and neither was I.

"I must admit," said Mr. Stafford, his face looking more tired now than alarmed, "that this is quite disturbing. It was completely unnecessary for you to deceive me like you did."

"Yes, sir," I said with a small voice.

"Yesterday was an awfully trying day," he said, a hint of kindness returning to his eyes. "But I must ask that such deceit, even with good intentions, never be repeated."

"Yes, sir. I'm truly sorry," I said sincerely, tears starting to well. I don't know if I had ever felt so guilty in my life.

"My own actions," he continued, "have not been the most exemplary, I'm afraid. I will do better. Let us agree to both do better. How does that sound?"

"That sounds very good," I answered and then hugged Mr. Stafford, starting to cry. Through the sobs, I repeated that I was sorry.

"There, there," he said kindly, "it's not all that bad. We seem to have our obstacles, but we also seem adept at overcoming them."

His kind words of hope and forgiveness made me feel worse. I vowed in my heart to have no more lies between us.

When the embrace ended, Mr. Stafford said, "Why don't you get dressed. We will have breakfast – I think I can get Edward to join us, for he should not be alone for long stretches – and then we will decide what to do with the remainder of the day."

"We aren't going back to London?" I asked, surprised.

"No, I will book us tickets for tomorrow morning. Frankly, I could not bear all that travel after what we have been through. I have opted for a day of rest for us. Do you approve?"

I smiled, while wiping my face, and nodded. Even though I felt better after a full night's sleep, the thought of the train station and the hours of travel did sound like a lot to deal with.

"Very well. Get ready and head down to the dining room."

Mr. Stafford walked away, and I closed the door. My hands were shaking, and I felt unbelievably cold. I wasn't at all pleased or proud with what I had just done.

As I entered the dining room, I spotted Mr. Stafford and Edward. I took the seat between them and glanced at Edward; not surprisingly, he looked completely sullen.

We ate our breakfast mostly in silence. To talk about the death of Mr. Hudson seemed wrong, and to talk about anything else felt inappropriate.

As we concluded our meal, Mr. Stafford asked, "Is there anything particular that either of you would like to do today?"

I waited for Edward to say something, as I would agree with anything that he suggested. However, outside of a very small shake of his head, he remained silent and still.

With nothing coming from him, I suggested, "I think I would enjoy seeing the ocean, if that is not asking too much."

Mr. Stafford considered my suggestion for a moment, smiled, and said, "I think that is an excellent idea. There is a contemplative effect when one is near the sea, and I think that that's exactly what we all can use. Edward, do you have any objections to this idea?"

For a just a moment, it looked like he was going to say something, perhaps protest leaving his room of mourning, but he swallowed the words and shook his head.

We hired a carriage that would take us north, to the town of Waterloo. From there, the concierge informed us, we would be beyond the River Mersey and see the ocean proper. The weather was a mixture of clouds and sun, with the scale being a little heavier on the side of the clouds.

As we progressed towards our destination, the buildings of Liverpool gave way to fields and sandy dunes – the latter of which largely blocked any view of the water I was so eager to experience. Although there was not a lot to see along our roadway, I found myself happily occupied by watching the variety of birds flying around and over the nearby shoreline.

Unlike breakfast, Mr. Stafford kept a conversation going throughout our journey. Mostly it was humorous stories of his youth – including his first visit to the ocean and a particularly unfriendly crab. Even Edward, despite his justified sadness, could not help but give a half smile on occasion at one of the funny anecdotes. As little as it was, I was glad to see any break in his gloom.

When we reached Waterloo, the driver stopped along one of the sand dunes. We exited to a stiff wind that blew my hair around and whipped the wispy lengths of shore grass. I took in a deep breath and found the air to be thick, briny, and exhilarating. I walked hurriedly up the dune, knowing that the ocean would be in view on the other side. My eagerness put me many paces ahead of both Mr. Stafford and Edward.

When I reached the top, I was not prepared for what I saw: the vast enormity of the ocean disappearing from sight into the distance. There was no fog to impede my view, just an endless ocean that fell off into the far horizon. I stared until my mind became dizzy with distances and possibilities that it could not fully comprehend.

"Beautiful," whispered Mr. Stafford, who was at my side, although I didn't notice him until he spoke.

I simply nodded my head, unable to take my eyes off of the water.

After a few minutes of staring in amazement, Mr. Stafford suggested that we should find a place to sit. At the bottom of the dune, there was a large piece of driftwood that served well as a bench.

For several minutes, we sat in silent contemplation at the view before us. Silent, that is, except for the raucous bird cries and the rumbling of small waves against the shore. The scene left me in awe. Never had I experienced such a mixture of beauty, power, and mystery. I had a new respect for the brave men who traveled those seas as employment.

"I think I would like to stretch my legs a little," commented Mr. Stafford, standing up. "Would either of you like to join me?"

"No, thank you," said Edward quietly – an audible reply being progress.

Not wanting to leave Edward alone, I said, "I think I would like to stay, if that is alright with you?"

"Of course," said Mr. Stafford. "I shouldn't be gone too long." With a smile, he turned and started to walk down the beach.

I looked at Edward, who was gazing intently at the horizon, and asked, "Is it alright that I stayed?"

After a moment more of staring, he turned to me and said, "I'm glad you did, thank you. And thank you for the comfort you gave me yesterday. I am…I feel lost."

I took his hand and said, "I know the pain and disorientation that losing one's parents can have. I wish I could make it go away with some wise advice, but the truth is that it is going to be difficult for quite a while."

"I know," he said in a voice that was just above a whisper.

"But," I continued, "it does get easier with time. It's also easier with friends. Please know that neither Mr. Stafford nor myself will ever abandon you."

"I do know that, although it's still good to hear – for my faith is shaken. If something as certain as my father can be taken away, I almost feel that nothing can be certain anymore." Then, with imploring eyes, Edward said, "Tell me again that you will not forsake me."

I squeezed his hand and said, "I will not forsake you."

We sat in silence for a long time, sharing the emotions of missing our parents; a few quiet tears fell, leaving a smattering of dark spots on the sand.

Eventually, Edward broke the silence. "This morning, Mr. Stafford told me that you destroyed the book. Is that true?"

No, it was not. But I couldn't tell him the truth. I nodded my head, hoping that there would be no need for further explanation. I may have felt justified in having a secret from Mr. Stafford, but I had no justification for deceiving Edward.

"I wish," Edward said, "that I was there. That book killed my father. I think I would have liked to see it burn."

I had not fully considered Edward's feelings in the matter. Is it possible that I took away an opportunity for healing? I felt bad for that and for lying to my grieving friend. If he ever found out, could he possibly forgive me?

I finally managed to say, "I'm sorry."

"It's alright. As long as that book is gone forever."

When I saw Mr. Stafford returning, I released Edward's hand, and wiped my face. I didn't know what would become of our relationship – Edward and I – but we had developed a bond of shared pain that could not easily be severed.

"Well," commented Mr. Stafford as he was near, "now that you have seen the ocean, what do you think?"

I gave a warm smile and said, "It's even better than I imagined. Thank you for bringing me here."

"You are very welcome, my dear. Now, how about we find some lunch in town?"

The rest of the day went by quickly. We ate, walked around town, spent a bit more time viewing the ocean, and then made the ride back to our hotel. Edward's mood seemed to improve, and he was a little more active in the conversations – although sadness was never far.

We ate dinner at the North Western and retired to our rooms right after as we needed to rise early for the day of travel ahead of us.

As poorly as the morning had started – the discovery of the missing book and my lies – the day as a whole was quite satisfactory. Above all, I was encouraged by the spark of hope in Edward's eyes. He had tough days ahead, but I felt that he would be alright. I also knew that I would keep my promise and never forsake him.

Forty

Going home. I climbed out of the hotel bed with that one, glorious thought. *Going home!*

Although we found the book we were after, the trip to Liverpool felt like anything but successful. I desperately wanted it to end and to get back to normalcy. I missed Helen, Melba, and Patrick. I longed for my routine and hoped it could return a sense of stability that had been lost over the last few tumultuous days.

We ate an early, hurried, breakfast and then, with help from hotel staff, loaded our trunks onto a carriage. As we pulled away from the North Western, Mr. Stafford told the driver to stop at the corner. Here we found Anthony and his mates, and Mr. Stafford told them that there was one last assignment: to help with our trunks at the train station. I watched as the children ran off ahead of us, arriving even before we did.

The station, and the surrounding area, was quite busy, and, although a bit uncomfortable, I handled it better than I did the crowds at Euston. Anthony, along with five of his friends, carried our trunks – oblivious to the crowds and making a rude path for us – to the loading platform.

"Anthony," said Mr. Stafford to the boy, "it has been my great pleasure to meet you on this trip. Your assistance has been indispensable. As a token of my appreciation, here is your last payment." Mr. Stafford removed a ten-pound note and handed it to the stunned child.

"Thank you, sir!" he exclaimed, looking like he couldn't believe what he had just received.

"You more than earned it," said Mr. Stafford, clapping the boy on the shoulder.

When Anthony recovered from his shock, he turned to me, smiled his wicked grin, and asked, "Is there any way that *you* would like to reward me, love?"

My cheeks reddened from anger and embarrassment – for I could not help but remember the nauseating kiss. I thought of slapping him – I desperately wanted to – but I restrained myself and, instead, said, "I believe that my generosity has been more than sufficient."

Mr. Stafford gave me a quizzical look and Anthony silently mocked me – causing no end of amusement to his companions. I turned my head indignantly and was happy when the band of urchins had finally left us.

The train came along soon, and we boarded. It was the same – or at least a very similar – car to the one that we had come to Liverpool in. We took our seats and sat silently in anticipation, for thoughts of home made any conversation nothing more than an unwelcomed distraction. My mind, as I had mentioned, focused on the happiness of seeing my friends. Edward's mind, however, was no doubt focused on lonely and hurtful things as he faced an empty home at the end of his journey. My happiness was tempered by his pain.

A little way outside of the city, Mr. Stafford took to reading, while Edward and I were content with the passing views. The train stopped briefly at Staffordshire, and then we were back on our route.

The next stop, Northampton, is where we parted ways with Edward. He would not be going to London but would travel by a different train directly to Cambridge.

"Edward," said Mr. Stafford, "You will be contacted tomorrow by one of my lawyers. He will help you through any obstacles of your father's business that need to be overcome. Also, he will be able to assist with any funeral arrangements that are to be made."

"Thank you, sir," he said quietly.

"And," continued Mr. Stafford, in his kind way, "I insist that we join company again soon."

"I would like that."

"Edward," I asked, "are you certain that you cannot come to London? I hate the thought of you being alone."

He shook his head and said, "There are many arrangements to be made that I must take care of. I will be alright. Knowing that I have the two of you thinking of me, is quite strengthening and is enough for now."

I hugged him and demanded, "Promise me that you will write."

"I promise."

We arrived home that evening to the happy greetings of Patrick, Melba, and Helen. Even Dantés seemed pleased to see us as he rubbed himself around our ankles. Melba looked me over as if searching for some defect. Patrick gave me a stiff embrace – which was quite an outpouring of emotion for him. Helen grabbed my hands and demanded that I tell her everything that had happened.

We ate a welcoming dinner and, being fatigued from the traveling, went to our rooms soon after. Regardless of how tired I was, however, Helen would not let me sleep until I told her of our entire adventure. I left nothing out – save my secret of what I actually did with the book – and watched in amusement as her face took on all the proper emotions at the proper parts.

"Scoundrel," she muttered viciously, at the revealing of Mr. Northam's actions.

Although I didn't tell her about sending the book to Christopher, I, instead, told her that I sent him a letter – so that I could explain about my sickening kiss with Anthony. That event caused her to laugh so hard that I was afraid that she might suffocate. It felt like ages since I had been in the presence of someone joyful and it made me even happier to be home.

When Helen finally left me to sleep, it came quickly in the comfort of my familiar bed.

The next morning, when I came down to breakfast, I was surprised to find Mrs. Dockery at the table, talking with Mr. Stafford.

"My dear," she said standing up to greet me, "I'm so sorry for all of the dreadfulness that this assignment has caused." She crossed the room and gave me a small, but warm, hug. "How are you doing?" she asked tenderly.

Her concern was evident and very touching. "I believe that I'm doing alright. I'm hoping that a few uneventful days will be all the medicine that I need. However, I cannot tell you how poorly I feel for Edward."

Mrs. Dockery smiled sadly and said, "That poor boy. He took the worst of this, I'm afraid. But he is fortunate to have you to support him, for there is an undeniable strength in you. And, more than ever, I know that Mr. Stafford was right about you from the start."

The words were so kind and felt completely unwarranted with my lie hanging over my head.

Melba brought out breakfast – with a conspicuously large quantity of preserves that I loved – and Mrs. Dockery joined us. During the meal, she explained that Mr. Northam had been in contact with her several weeks back about a potential Dark Book. Although he eventually wrote that it turned out to be a dead-end, we now know that he had found it and, sadly, had succumbed to its power.

"I don't know what else I could have done," lamented Mrs. Dockery, clearly feeling a sense of responsibility in the matter.

"I believe," said Mr. Stafford, "that there was nothing that could have been done. As difficult as it is to accept, there will be battles that we lose."

In the evening, Mrs. Dockery having left after lunch, I found myself in the library with Mr. Stafford. I had spent much of the day reading – reveling in that most comforting and joyous pastime. I had started to read the Sherlock Holmes story of *A Study in Scarlet*. I wanted to understand better that popular character and the so-called *Baker Street Irregulars*.

However, I put my book down as I felt the time had come to speak to Mr. Stafford on two very important outstanding questions.

"Sir," I started, "I need to address a few items with you."

Mr. Stafford, sensing my earnestness, closed his book, smiled warmly, and gave me his full attention.

I continued, "You had asked me, at the hotel, if I could forgive you for not telling me about your connection with the *Mary Celeste*. I didn't answer the question at the time, for, honestly, I didn't know the answer. Now, however, I'm certain. I forgive you. And I'm sorry that I could not come to this conclusion sooner."

"When I first met you," said Mr. Stafford, "my greatest fear would be your hatred of me for what I had done. As we grew closer, my fear increased drastically. I'm relieved, to an enormous extent, to know that I have not driven you away. As I hope you know, you are precious to me."

"That," I said, "is another question I wish to bring to a close. That same night, you had asked if I believed in your love for me; that I knew that it was love that motivated my adoption and not guilt. Now, with a calmer mind, I know that you do care for me and that our relationship is based, not on a sense of duty or responsibility, but on actual love."

Mr. Stafford closed his eyes for several seconds on hearing that, and, when he opened them again, they sparkled with moisture. "I will," he said, "never stop proving that to you."

The next few weeks were quite busy. First, sadly, was the funeral for Mr. Hudson in Cambridge. Seeing Edward was nice, but he looked so worn down. He was clearly happy to see us, but part of him would not allow for much revelry – for how could it with the nearness of such great loss.

The next time that I saw Edward was at the summer Book Reaper meeting in London. The gathering was far less taxing for me than the previous one, although I was chosen to give the account of our experiences in Liverpool – including lying to all in attendance about my destruction of the book.

The Ring Presentation Ceremony was less stressful, and I spent the entire evening in the company of Edward. It was enjoyable – we even shared two dances – but Edward was notably different. His father's death had changed him in many ways. His thoughts were consumed by the business he was taking over and talk of his writing hardly escaped his lips. I hoped he was happy but could not be sure. Time would tell who would emerge from his tragedy.

The next significant event of the summer was the death of Mr. Northam. He had been found guilty of the Liverpool murders and executed. Mention of the book never came up in any of the newspaper articles about the case. I am still conflicted with the thought of exactly how guilty Mr. Northam was.

Now, months later, as I sit at the desk in my room, staring out the window at the barren trees of November, I cannot help but think of one year ago when I made the fateful decision to run away from the orphanage. Never would I have dreamed the outcome that that night would bring. As I think back over the year, I can still hardly believe it.

My mother, in her letter, hoped for a better life for me and I believe that her hope was granted. Although I will never stop wishing that she was still here. *If only...*

Despite my losses, I do not overlook what I possess. I have a family in Mr. Stafford, Melba, Patrick, and Helen. I have a warm home, things that I enjoy to occupy me, and a purpose that can help others. I also have a dear friend in Edward, whom I see not often enough for my liking, but am encouraged at having experienced continuing signs of his recovery.

Admittedly, I also have an imperfect conscience. My lie about the Liverpool book torments me daily. I have thought of confessing what I had done a hundred times, but I remain quiet. My silence is not due to the consequences – mostly – but because I'm still undecided if what I did was right or wrong. There is no question that Dark Books are dangerous, for I have witnessed and experienced the effects of their power, but if used carefully, could there be important knowledge to gain? Struggle as I might, I don't know.

As I look forward, my future is brighter than my worth, and my happiness beyond what I deserve. And, like those distant ocean horizons, I see vast possibilities. This is all marred, however, by the cloud of my own deception and the storm of my uncertainty. My life had always had darkness hang over it, but this is the first time that the darkness had been created by me. I cannot help but wonder, am I *destined* for hardships or am I *addicted* to them?

At the time of this writing, I am still very much an awkward girl, who is uncomfortable in crowds, has more self-doubt than confidence, and would rather sit quietly reading than attend the most lavish of celebrations. But I also love my family, care about others, and, despite worthless feelings, have not given up on improving myself. For now, I choose to focus on the good of the moment; the inviting fire in the library, the kindest of men sitting in the chair next to mine, and the prospect of wonderful books waiting to carry me blissfully away on wings of eloquent pages.

I sincerely hope you enjoyed this story! It would be greatly appreciated (and super helpful for an unknown author like myself) if you would consider leaving me a review on Amazon or on Goodreads with your thoughts.
Thank you! - Mark

Book Counter

Apprentice:	3rd Class	0
	2nd Class	150
	1st Class	300
Messor:	3rd Class	300
	2nd Class	500
	1st Class	750
Bibliophile:	3rd Class	1000
	2nd Class	1500
	1st Class	2000
Bibliophagist:	3rd Class	2500
	2nd Class	3000
	1st Class	3500
Deditus Libris:	3rd Class	4000
	2nd Class	4500
	1st Class	5500
Bibliognost:	3rd Class	6500
	2nd Class	7500
	1st Class	8500

Bibliodominus 10,000

BR

Acknowledgments:

I have received more help and encouragement on this story than anything else I have written. I am truly in awe of the generosity of all involved.

First, is **Anne Bollmann** (Blog: The Book Adventures of Annelise Lestrange), the purple unicorn of ideas and grammar. Her ability to parse through paragraphs and find ways to make them even better is amazing. I am incredibly thankful to have someone so talented and generous to help me – not to mention hilarious! In addition to her literary talent, her encouraging words have been greatly appreciated all throughout the journey.

Excellent and frank insight was given by **Jade Geoffroy-Jacob** (Instagram: @wingsandpages). She helped to keep the story from bogging down and become dull for the reader.

Michelle O'Brien has given me huge amounts of encouragement (always appreciated) but also keeps me honest. She has a knack at finding things that are out of place or inconsistent and raising awareness.

Next is **Helen Giles** (Instagram: @nerdishmum Blog: lifeofanerdishmum.blogspot.com). Yep, you saw her name in the story. Her encouragement over this book and my previous ones has helped me to push onward with my writing. I cannot overstate how helpful it is to have such a positive person in my corner

The next person who deserves recognition is **Lamontica Crippen**. Her tireless efforts to read through my work and find ways to improve it is very appreciated.

Next is **Jenaca Voth** (instagram: @Jenacidebybibliophile) who has the uncanny talent at finding the heart of the matter. Her thoughts and opinions have helped to fine-tune some of the ideas and concepts of the story to really bring them into focus!

Colleen Morin – not only has she been so kind and encouraging of my work, she even helped with the final beta read to refine every last rough edge.

Most importantly, is my wife, **Naomi**. How she tolerates this writing dream of mine, I do not know. More than that, she is an excellent proofreader and shines up the final product to make it as professional as it can be.

I am also thankful to **Rebekkah Stringer** (Instagram: @ardentreader), **Kayleigh McCall** (Instagram: @littlehouseonthebookshelf), **Sophie McCall** (Instagram: @lostinabookishcollectoin), and **Rima Rashid** (Instagram: @pardonmywritings) for their contributions and encouragement along the way!

I am grateful to all of you for your kindness and assistance. It means the world to me!

About the Author:

Mark King is an easy-going writer with a talent for finding enjoyment in most any situation. He's a lifelong reader whose literary interests include science fiction, adventure, thriller, and mysteries. He grew up in California, but now lives in upstate New York with his wife. When not working or writing, he can be found watching movies, kayaking, associating with friends, and of course reading.

Feel free to follow Mark on Instagram or Facebook!